COYOTE

Praise for Ana Manwaring's JadeAnne Stone Mexico Adventures

Nothing Comes After Z
Recipient of the Literary Titan Silver Award for Fiction 2022

Literary Titan Review
Nothing Comes After Z is a riveting crime thriller with a strong female protagonist. I appreciated the grounded nature of the crime and how it relates to some headlines we see in the news today. Before she can safely leave Mexico and return to her life, she has to uncover some hard truths and catch the perpetrators. I enjoyed how well the emotion is weaved into this action novel because it ensure we're invested in the protagonist and we're biting our nails when the action intensifies. Author Ana Manwaring knows how to create a storyline that easily sets up the hard-hitting action.

M.M. Chouinard, USA Today bestseller of the Jo Fournier Mystery series
"A well-written, engaging story with a bad-ass protagonist I loved spending time with. Bring on more JadeAnne!"

The Hydra Effect

Lisa Towles, Bestselling and multi-award-winning author of Hot House, Ninety-Five, The Unseen and Choke
"*The Hydra Effect* sizzles with action, tension, and peril. Great writing combined with regional flare and international intrigue make this sequel a delightful ride!"

Jan M Flynn, award winning author

"JadeAnne heads to Mexico City for a break from her partner and now ex-boyfriend. But her sharp intelligence, curiosity and inability to stay in her own lane land her in a snarl of trouble. In short order she's evading cartel thugs, uncovering a human trafficking network and confronting high-level Mexican politicos with questionable connections, all in a lushly realized setting one can just about smell. And taste—JadeAnne might be in the middle of a gunfight, but she's never immune to the temptation of a good plate of tacos al pastor. She and her loyal dog Pepper are a team you can't but cheer for."

Set Up

Heather Haven, multi-award-winning author of the Alvarez Family Murder Mysteries
"This is a blowout of a story. It starts on the backroads of Mexico in the middle of the night—just a woman, a dog, and Mexican Banditos—and escalates from there. If you are looking for a fast-paced, action-filled thriller about the adventures of a young PI and her lethal but well-trained dog, this will be your cup of tea. Or should I say Margarita? Jack Reacher step aside. You have met your match in JadeAnne Stone.

Judy Penz Sheluk, Amazon international bestselling author
In her debut mystery novel, Author Ana Manwaring offers up more twists and turns than a Mexican rattlesnake. Fast paced, with well-crafted characters and a strong female lead, there's plenty to like about this world of power, politics, and Mexican money laundering. I especially enjoyed the strong sense of place, which Manwaring uses to great effect. Well worth adding to you TBR pile.

Kirkus Reviews
"With a likeable duo and a vivid, appealing setting, this adventure series is off to a promising start"

Second Edition November 2022
by Indies United Publishing House, LLC

Cover design by Vila Design

ISBN: 978-1-64456-557-5 [Paperback]
ISBN: 978-1-64456-558-2 [Mobi]
ISBN: 978-1-64456-559-9 [ePub]
ISBN: 978-1-64456-560-5 [Audiobook]

Library of Congress Control Number: 2022948097

INDIES UNITED PUBLISHING HOUSE, LLC
P.O. BOX 3071
QUINCY, IL 62305-3071
indiesunited.net

Other Books in the JadeAnne Stone Mexico
Adventures

Set Up (2018)

The Hydra Effect (2019)

Nothing Comes After Z (2022)

Coming 2023
Saints and Skeletons
A Memoir of Living in Mexico

To
Pattie Hogan

Thanks for the good times in Mexico City and down in
Tepoztlán

Acknowledgements

My deep gratitude for the special folks whose support, consideration, care and hard work went into developing this series, especially to Lisa Towles for taking me in hand and showing me the writer's "ropes."

More thanks to J.C. Miller and Mark Pavlichek. You've worked with me for over a decade lifting JadeAnne from idea through her fourth book, and I owe you big time! Also much gratitude to Jan M. Flynn, Heather Chavez and Crissi Langwell for getting this book going. All your feedback has been invaluable.

Finally, a special shout out to my editor, Cindy Davis, The Fiction Doctor. You're curing me of all my bad writing habits. I can't imagine doing this without you.

As always, my deepest love and gratitude go to my husband David Prothero and our family for their love and encouragement.

COYOTE

Pursuit and Terror Across the Border

A JadeAnne Stone
Mexico Adventure

ANA MANWARING

INDIES UNITED PUBLISHING HOUSE, LLC

Chapter 1

Two Funerals, No Wedding

Saturday, September 8, 2007

Dylan and I beelined to La Iglesia de San Juan Bautista for another funeral. This time, Senator Aguirre and his mother, Lidia Sotomayor Buendía, had been murdered—and the killer was after me, too. I kept my hand on my gun and a sharp eye on the weekenders milling about the plaza.

I pulled my stylish bulletproof jacket tighter around my torso as we rushed through the carved doors. Dark-suited men with bulges under their jackets, wires curling into their collars, watched the mourners from positions around the church. Security detail to protect me and the fifteen-year-old girl I'd rescued from sex traffickers. I prayed they could keep us safe.

The senator's assistant Susana, met us as she scurried along the main aisle. "Hi JadeAnne. Dylan. I'm so glad you're here." She taped a spray of fresh black roses mixed with purple and white calla lilies over the end of the front pew. She carried half a dozen more silk ribboned bouquets for the pews reserved for family and close friends. Thank God for Susana Arias de Barrera. Everything looked lovely, organized, and well protected. If ever there were a fairy godmother to wave a wand to get things done, she was it.

"I'm ready to help. What shall I do?" I shouted over the organist's rehearsal.

"Take the stack of programs and put them in the pews."

I nodded and picked up the half-fold stack with a picture of the senator and his mother on the front and their dates of birth and death inscribed in gold. Susana hadn't spared any expense. But why would she, I wondered, neatly placing ten per row then zigging around to the next row and zagging to the following. Still raw memories from the last funeral dogged me. I gulped a lung full of sanctified air and counted out another ten programs then zigged into the next pew deep in thought and careened into a mourner.

"Whoa, there, girl! Let me help with that."

Dylan! My heart fluttered as he gave me a quick kiss. I gladly handed over half the pile. He started down the left side of the church, winding between pews and kissing me in the aisle as our paths crossed.

Yep, a totally different experience than my last Coyoacán funeral. I was pretty sure the luncheon afterwards would be a lot more fun, too. I only had one concern—my would-be kidnapper and boyfriend mistake—Anibal. Hence the bullet-proof couture.

So far he had not turned up or been apprehended, although half of Mexican law enforcement was looking for him. According to my dad, Quint, the cartels were paying the other half of Mexican law enforcement to protect him. Until he was safely extradited back to the U.S. I wouldn't let down my guard. Anibal Aguirre was not selling me to Los Zetas.

I stooped for a fallen program and surreptitiously

scanned the mourners trickling in for suspicious bulges and ugly tattoos. If they were there, I didn't see them. Susanna had hired a platoon of security, which she'd posted around the plaza and church; hopefully, the bad guys would be kept out or nabbed by one of the men inside.

I'd learned exactly how the cartels worked this past week. With the aid and abet of politicians, bureaucrats, and law enforcement—they were getting wealthy off organized crime. It went all the way into the presidential palace, Los Pinos. At least that's what Polo's bodyguard, Horacio, said. I caught his eye and gave a little wave before sliding another ten programs along a gleaming pew.

Horacio predicted a major war over territory between the different crime groups, especially in the states along the border, the *plazas*. He advised me to watch which cartels were taken out. His prediction: Mexico's president would pave the road with Sinaloa's gold and welcome in El Chapo.

The idea fuddled my brain. I shook my head, dropped the last program, and headed toward the front of the church, keeping watch on the people coming in. I didn't want any surprises. The organist had run through her repertoire and was talking with Susana. I recognized Loli Buendía hustling two giant urns of flowers at either side of the steps to the altar. The caskets, not open, thank God, shrank with all the stars, horseshoes, and crosses of flowers surrounding them. Arrangements crowded the floor in front the coffins, and sprays had been draped across Lidia's stark white lid and Polo's shiny black lacquer cover. The cloying scent of hothouse flowers was irritating my sinuses. I sneezed. Dylan handed me his handkerchief.

"You keep popping up from nowhere. Did you finish?" He held up his palms. Finished or ran out of programs. I went on, "Meet Loli, Lidia's great-niece. Loli!" I called and waggled fingers.

She beamed and came over.

"It's so nice to see you again, Loli." I took her hand and held it for a beat. "I'm sorry for your loss, and to be meeting under such sad circumstances—again."

The twinkle in her eyes faded. "Oh, JadeAnne, it's hard to believe. Three of my family gone in a month. Aunt Lidia and I didn't see eye-to-eye on many things, but I'm sorry she's passed. It's Polo—" A little sob caught in her throat. "Polo and I were always friends. I don't know how I'll make it through his service. Do you know what happened?"

I knew. The last funeral flashed through my mind—my client's husband shooting her to protect his cartel money laundering. Now this poor family would lay to rest Aunt Lidia, shot protecting her son from the Zeta trafficker I'd been sold to. My stomach churned, a fan of blades whirling.

Loli didn't wait for my answer. "Have you seen Anibal?"

I grimaced, my gut clenching, and raised my eyebrows at Dylan. Ignoring the question, I said, "Loli, let me introduce you to my friend, Dr. Dylan Porras. Dylan, Loli Buendía."

He poured on the Dylan charm, taking her hand and looking into her eyes. "Please accept my deepest sympathy. If there's anything I can do to help you through this rough time, please call. JadeAnne knows how to reach me." Was Loli batting her eyelashes at him?

"Thank you so much, Doctor. I'll see you later at the meal?" She *was* batting her eyelashes at him.

From behind us I heard someone calling, "Loli, *ay*, Loli. *¡Hola!*" We turned to see the fat whore Consuelo García, madam of Lidia's "gentlemen's clubs." barreling up the aisle. Wasn't she in jail? As usual she looked like a brass fireplug teetering on stilettos.

Loli groaned, "Oh, no!" under her breath, gave us a shaky smile and turned tail. Quint intercepted Consuelo as she tried to squeeze into the front pew with Senator Aguirre's relatives. He steered her away from the flower marked rows, depositing her about a third of the way back with some suspicious looking men.

The ushers, Loli's boys, Polo's butler Chucho, and a couple of young cousins I found out later, escorted mourners to the appropriate rows. Chucho smiled at me as he guided two of Lidia's little crows to the front left pew, like a falconer—one on each arm. I hoped I wouldn't be putting up with them again at the meal.

Oh, yeah, I hadn't eaten the meal at the last funeral. Anibal had dragged me out of the party to avoid one of the traffickers he'd swindled. If Ani showed up, I might shoot him.

Chucho seated me in the third row on the right. The family was bigger than I thought. Some of these folks must be Aguirres from Polo's dad's side. They weren't as well dressed as the rest of the bunch, but Lidia had to be *tía* to most of the people in the second row.

The organist glided in, black robes swirling, and began a hushed version of *O God Our Help In Ages Past.* I craned around again, looking for my men. Dylan thumped down next to me. Our housekeeper Señora Pérez on his arm, was decked out in a black dress, hat, and veil straight from 1950. She dragged a reluctant teen behind her. Poor Lily, trafficked from L.A. to Mexico City, unable to return home for bureaucratic idiocy, and now our housekeeper had her dressed in a dowdy, ill-fitting, black polyester sheath and patent flats. Insult after injury. I gave her a sympathetic smile.

Mrs. P nodded to me with watery, red-rimmed eyes. She actually cared for Lidia.

"Where's Quint?" I whispered to Dylan. He shrugged. I shifted forward and twisted toward the back again, scanning the crowd for my father. "Holy sh—" Dylan dug me in the ribs with his elbow. "Spirit," I finished, lowering my voice. "Turn around, Dyl. It's Lobo." I jerked my head.

"I've never seen him."

"I can't believe that scum showed up. He was the one who actually drugged and transported Lily across the border. He knew we'd be here," I whispered.

Dylan shrugged. Mourners still streamed to seats. I stiffened as I recognized a couple of Lidia's associates. Cartel people. I bumped shoulders with Dylan and jerked my head toward the cluster of arrivals with a *why did the guards let them in?* look.

Ignore them, he mouthed.

The music shifted to *It is Well with My Soul.* I was becoming an expert in funeral hymns. The church hushed, the ushers came forward and took their places as a cellist and a singer joined the organist. The singer's rich tenor filled the church. I'd always loved this hymn.

Finally Quint scooched in next to me from the arcade. I leaned against him and breathed, "Lobo." He nodded and put his finger to his lips. I burned to know how it could be.

The service dragged on as I'd learned was the culture here, and the really good music was a pleasant surprise. Something outside of tradition I guessed. My stomach growled, but as I'd seen before—long lines of mourners, some I recognized, most I didn't, filed past the coffins to leave mementos and flowers with lots of crying. I wasn't going anywhere soon.

Everyone got up for communion, including Dylan. I spaced out with the music, keeping an eye on the faces passing. I nudged Quint and jerked my chin toward Senator Bendicias. Now why would he come to the funeral of a cartel woman he claimed he wanted to arrest—or the colleague he had betrayed?

Dad squeezed my hand. I realized he was as alert to the goings-on as I. Perhaps more so. He knew the players.

The stream of dirges and mourners finally ended; the family cried and hugged, cracked a joke or two, and invited everyone from the front rows back to Lidia's for lunch. I greeted Polo's brother and sister-in-law. Beto looked pretty broken up. This family's ties ran deep, and he'd buried his oldest daughter Lura, the woman I'd come to Mexico to find, thirty days earlier. I was glad wife Molly and daughter Alex fluttered around with kisses and kindness. Molly dealt with all the condolences; Alex held them both together with hugs. I started toward Dylan and Quint, waiting for me at the pew. That's when I saw Consuelo, charging toward the immediate family. Lidia's whorehouse employees had their own pew—in the back. Shouldn't she sit with them? She was the madam, after all.

I headed her off. "Well, well, look who's here. Consuelo, I heard you were in jail." Too bad they let you out, I wanted to say.

"It's you again. I should have known you'd push your way into this poor family's grief." She shot me one of her mincing looks.

I minced right back. "Funny, I was going to say the same of you. I think it's better if you don't bother the Aguirres, Consuelo. What are you up to now that your houses are closed?"

"That's for me to know," she said, twirled on her toes and teetered off in her too-tight skirt and too-high heels, her rear jiggling like an uncoupled caboose. I imagined her hiding behind a pillar to find out where we were all going.

The family started its procession up the aisle toward the door, and yep, sure enough, Consuelo popped out from behind a pillar. Luckily Alex's husband cut her off, and the Aguirre and Buendía clans escaped to their waiting cars. I watched Consuelo latch onto Guillermo Lobo's arm. I grabbed Lily and Mrs. P, and hustled our group out the door.

"Where'd you park, Dad? Follow us. Dyl got directions from Loli. The cemetery is kind of hard to find."

He pointed across the plaza in the direction of Xicoténcatl. I pronounced it for him. "Yep, that's the one. Where are you?"

I pointed towards Calle Felipe Carillo. "Over there on the left."

"I'll pull around. Wait for me."

Dylan nodded and clapped Quint on the back. My, weren't they getting chummy. I felt little warmth spread through me and surveyed the pretty park full of Sunday strollers and our security. I saw the balloon clown and Archangel Gabriel was still doing his statue thing, and hopefully not blowing his horn. I didn't want any of the recently deceased climbing out of their graves—or not getting in.

I surveilled the plaza as Quint herded Lily toward the street, Horacio following, head swiveling side to side. Mrs. P dabbed at her eyes and scurried after them. Was she aware of the danger? I guessed neither of us wanted to run into Anibal, but I didn't see any of the cartel people. The legions of security must be keeping them at bay. Anibal had threatened to kidnap me to sell to Los Zetas—after he tortured my dog while I watched. My gut clenched but I willed myself to relax.

"Dyl, let's cruise the plaza. Maybe the fortune teller is here. Last time she stopped the reading, packed up, and left when she flipped up the body stuck with ten swords in its back." I tugged on his sleeve.

"Sure, why not. It's going to take Quint at least fifteen minutes to get around to us."

"Probably twenty. Look at the traffic." I pointed across the plaza to a snarl of cars.

"Jade, you don't really believe that tarot mumbo-jumbo do you?"

I giggled. "You obviously aren't from California."

We strolled arm-in-arm, trailed by two security guards. I

8

noticed the white-clad ice cream man and headed over for coconut ice cream, the guards a step behind me. As I carried the paper cups to the bench, I heard the throaty-voiced gypsy calling her trade. *"Vengan ustedes, tengo sus futuros."*

"It's her. Come on, let's do it," I insisted, pulling him off the bench, and handing over the ice cream.

"Buenas tardes, señora. Queremos nuestros futuras, por favor." I slapped a twenty note onto her table and we made ourselves comfortable in her folding chairs.

She barely looked up from the cards as she shuffled, pulled the King of Hearts, placed it onto the table, and nodded. With a smile, she laid the Queen of Hearts next to him. *"Ustedes, anamoratos."* She crossed the card with the Page of Swords and nodded again. "A young person, a girl, with a problem to solve. It will be delayed by—" she dealt the next card, the 5 of Wands. "Conflict. You will have to overcome this—" she said, and pulled the King of Pentacles. "He is a powerful and greedy man with many tentacles."

"Could it be a group rather than a person?" I asked in Spanish, flashing on the Zetas.

She pulled the Knight of Swords. "Possibly, and its leader is ruthless, impetuous. Gets what he wants. It will be a very destructive group that acts fast. Your success will depend on your planning. You must be ready. If not, this could be your outcome. " She pulled the ten of Swords again and looked up at me. "You!" she spat out, scooped up the cards and shuffled her deck, turning her back on us. But not before whisking the twenty *peso* bill into her pocket.

Dylan laughed. "What a load of crap." He took my hand as we walked off, but I felt chills run up and down my spine.

"Dyl, I'm not so sure. I got the King of Hearts and the Ten of Swords last time too. How do you explain that?"

"You're proving your Californian citizenship—the land of fruits and nuts. Coincidence." He pulled me in close and gave my ribs a poke. I squealed. "My little nut job is ticklish!" He poked me again. I spun away from him laughing, and dropped my ice cream. I had come face-to-face with Anibal. And he didn't look happy.

"Run, Dyl!" I shouted and took off, Dylan on my heels, aiming for the traffic cop stopping cars for the pedestrians.

We dashed to the street, our security guards pounding after us, and jaywalked through the stopped cars to the yellow Beemer Dylan's friend, Dafne Olabarrietta, loaned him. Nothing noticeable about *this* car in a city of black cars. Horacio pulled the limo up behind us and beeped. We squealed out and headed toward the *panteon*.

Anibal shot me a middle finger salute as we rolled by.

Chapter 2

Everyone Wants to Pay Their Respects

The Aguirre and Buendía plots lay next to each other. Signs and ribbons pointed the way. We hustled through the crowded landscape of crosses, slabs, stones, monuments, and mausoleums, decorated in flowers, mostly plastic, to a tree lined section on a slight rise. My heart raced and my gut clenched. Anibal, or any of the cartel thugs, could shoot or grab us in the congested *cemetario*.

The funeral party assembled beside the newly dug graves. Alex stood between them and sobbed, Jason trying his best to console her. The little flock of Lidia cronies clucked next to her coffin, already loaded into the contraption that would lower it into the grave, while Senator Bendicias, Mexico City's lecherous mayor Fallas, as usual giving me the once-over. Santiago and several more bureaucratic types milled around Polo's coffin. Displays of flowers barely left room for the mourners.

The black robed priest, obviously flummoxed over a double interment, shook his hands and flapped back and forth between graves—a matter of feet. Susana was trying to talk him down. We joined Loli and Molly. They greeted Horacio warmly, but tearfully. It smelled like rain.

I kept my eye on the stream of mourners pouring in. Anibal was sure to show up. Would he try anything? My muscles tensed even as Quint and Horacio flanked us, shielding Lily and me. The numbers of tearful people who gathered over the next half hour astonished me. Mexicans, it appeared, liked to show emotion and love. I stifled a laugh picturing a somber Episcopal funeral. At two, Susana signaled to the Father, and he performed the burial smoothly, standing equal distant at the head of the graves and only repeating the key lines over each coffin. The service was short and no one tried to throw themselves into the graves with the lowering caskets.

As we filed back to our cars, I noticed the armed guards. I let out the breath I'd been holding. Anibal hadn't tried to breech the security. But would he at the Celebration of Life?

"Anibal's going to show up at the celebration," I said, flatly. "He can't possibly think he can kidnap me or Lily from the party, can he?"

Dylan drove in silence watching his mirrors. I drummed my fingers , willing him to drive faster. We could be hijacked. I kept my hand on the gun in my purse. "Hurry up. Maybe he contacted the others and they're waiting for us. He had plenty of time while we went graveside."

"Jade, you watch too many cop shows. He saw Quint and Horacio behind us."

"And Lily in the church."

"He wasn't in the church."

"You sure?" I looked into my side mirror. All I could see was the limo. "Can you see behind the limo?"

"You're being paranoid. No one is following us. Anibal wouldn't dare come. The place will be full of politicians and law enforcement. Just like the church and cemetery. You think Quit would just let him waltz in and carry you girls off? Get real."

When he put it like that, I wanted to agree, but what did Dylan really know about the cartels? I looked ahead and saw the trees of a little park. Our turn was coming up fast. "Turn, turn!" Dylan twirled the steering wheel and the Beemer hugged tight to the road.

"Beautiful car, Dyl, You should get one. Or steal Dafne's. Nice of her to loan it to you." The limo caught up to us.

"At the moment, a house is top priority. But I'd consider a BMW or a Mercedes."

"You don't like living at your parent's house? They're so darling."

"Yeah, and I'm a thirty six-year-old surgeon. It's time I moved out and made my own family." He gave me a penetrating look. Electricity ran through my body. I let the pictures of me and Dylan and our adorable children in our adorable house run— "Slow down! That's the *callejon*. See the *caseta*?"

"Yes ma'am." He turned and stepped on the brake, skidding on the wet pavement at the guard booth. He grinned out the lowered window, "Sorry *compa,* it's the car. Mind of its own."

The guard stepped out of the *caseta* with a clipboard and grinned back. "Celebration of Life?" When I nodded he said, "Name?"

"JadeAnne Stone and Dylan Porras." The limo rolled up behind us. I added, "And Jackman Quint, Mrs. Pérez—"

"Oh, I know the Senator's limo and driver. I'm sorry for your loss." He waved us through. I heard a friendly "*Hola* Señora Pérez, Horacio" before we pulled away.

"Okay, wait for it...isn't it beautiful?" We pulled right in front. A bunch of empty cars lined the circular drive ahead of ours and I noticed a couple had governmental plates, including a car from the embassy. "Dylan, do you suppose Tony Garza is here?"

"Who?"

"The American ambassador, dummy." I flipped the seatbelt latch then poked Dylan in the ribs. He jumped and twitched. I slid out of the car. "Gotcha! You're ticklish too I see." I winked. "Later, dude. You're in for it."

The limo had pulled in behind us and I opened the door and helped Mrs. P out then gave a hand to Lily.

"Mrs. P, I'm pleased you've come. I know you and Lidia went way back."

"Thank you *señorita*. *Señor* Castello y Iglesias is going to read the wills. He asked me to come."

Quint joined us. "A reading at the celebration? Never heard of that."

"The California family can't stay. They will all inherit from *la señora*," Mrs. P said as we approached the door. The saucy little maid swung it wide and greeted Horacio and Mrs. P. She humphed to see me, but looked Dylan up, down, and up again. With a huge smile aimed at Dylan, she said, "*Bienvenidos a la casa*," and stepped aside. I gave him a little poke and tossed my bag onto the pile already topping the spindly table in the hall. This time I carried something worthy—maybe not a Ferragamo, but handmade and made a bold, "one of a kind" statement. So there, snooty Lidia.

Our crowd moved toward the living room, passing the glass doors into the central garden. Lidia's dogs started a yapping racket, jumping up against the glass and scratching like mad.

"Can I play with them, Jade?" Lily asked, hand on the door handle.

"Of course not, Lily. Act like a lady," Mrs. P scolded her.

"The little one is Mimi and that's her boyfriend Pico. They'd love to play with you. I don't think anyone pays them any mind except to yell at them to shut up," I said.

"Thank you!" Lily gave me a hug.

"And next time, pull something out of my closet. I don't know where that dress came from, but it probably should have stayed there. Luckily you're so pretty, anything looks good on you, Lil."

"Mrs. P insisted."

"I'm sure she did. No go! Your new friends are waiting for you." She slid open the door and fell to her knees for the chorus of happy barks and sloppy doggy kisses. "Quint or Horacio? One of you keep an eye? Anibal was in the plaza."

"I saw him, Jade," Quint replied in a low voice. "I'll stay with her."

"She doesn't want to be here, you know. Why should she? Lidia and her crowd caused her nightmare. Quint, the girl needs counselling and her family. Oh, and a decent dress. Maybe I can take care of that." I patted his cheek and towed Dylan into the living room toward Alex.

She opened her arms and folded me in an embrace. "I'm so sorry we keep meeting at funerals, JadeAnne, but I'm happy to see you. Polo—and Susana—can't, couldn't, say enough about you. I'll miss Polo. We talked every week." A new stream of tears spilled over her red-rimmed eyes. Dylan handed her a tissue and she offered him a quivering smile. "Wh-who's this kind soul, Jade?"

"Dyl, meet Alex Radcliff, Polo's cousin. That's her husband Jason over there talking to Chucho." I waved to them in the traditional "men's area" filling up with suits and cigars. They joined our circle, Jason wrapping his arm around his wife. I introduced Dylan again. "Dyl is a surgeon. He prepared at UCLA and has recently returned from residency at Cedars-Sinai in L.A."

Jason shook his hand, and said, "Impressive. It's a great hospital. They pretty much saved my dad with their enzyme protocol. Clots." Dylan nodded gravely and Jason asked, Where are you now?"

A liveried server passed a silver tray of tiny epazote quesadillas, my favorites. I took the proffered napkin and helped myself to three and wondered who was cooking. Lily streaked across the picture window with the two little dogs at her heels. I munched the last quesadilla and looked for somewhere to deposit my greasy napkin. Everyone was looking at me. "What? Sorry? Lost in space..." I said.

Dylan asked the question again, "Everyone wants to know when you plan of going back to Sausalito, Jade."

"I, oh, well, I'm not sure. We're waiting for Lily's travel permission." I didn't want to say too much. I probably already had.

Susana joined the group. "She looks pretty happy with Pico and Mimi. Poor little girl."

"She loves dogs, that's for sure. Maya and the pups have been a blessing—even if they drove Polo crazy. Can you see him living with eight dogs?" Everyone laughed.

"My cousin was a clean freak. How he managed to grow up on a farm, I don't know. He was the exact opposite of Lura. She loved to get her hands dirty," Alex said, and started to cry again.

"So, who is Lily, anyway? I thought she was one of the servers or kitchen help. She should come join us," Loli said.

"Actually, Loli, she's mortified over the dress. Mrs. Pérez dug it up from somewhere. Not only is it ugly, but it's too big."

Alex blew her nose. "It's a maid's uniform, I think. No wonder she won't join us. What size does she wear?"

Perfect! "I'm guessing 4 or 6. Why?"

"Introduce us. I'll let her pick something of mine. We need to welcome her and make sure she gets lunch when it's served. Come on." She took my arm and walked me to the courtyard door.

"Lily, this is Alex. She's got a dress that will fit you."

Lily admired Alex's grey silk fit and flare and smiled. I

would too—Alex's clothes, what I'd seen of them, were stylish and exquisite. I couldn't remember what Jason did for a living. "You two go find something suitable. I'm going in to talk to our ambassador."

"Tony was a great friend of Polo. Do you know him?" I shook my head. "I'll introduce you. Maybe he can help with your problem, Lily."

Lily's eyes widened in alarm. I shook my head and she breathed a sigh. She didn't want to advertise her situation. I'd instructed her to say she'd used a fake ID to cross the border then had lost it.

"I'll see you inside when you're ready," I said.

Lily would handle it just fine without me. I scooped Mimi from the grass and gave her a kiss. She wiggled and grinned. Someone had tied little black bows into her fur. Too cute.

I put Mimi down and patted Pico as Quint stepped out. "Hey, where are they going?"

"To Alex's suitcase for something decent to wear. Poor Lily is wearing a maid's uniform. Everyone thought she was kitchen help."

The dogs bounded toward Quint, yapping and jumping at his legs. Another door opened and a young man called, *"¡Pico! ¡Mimi! ¡Ven, ven aca!"* He grabbed each dog and backed out of the courtyard. *"Lo siento señoritas y señores,"* he said and closed the door.

"I should keep an eye on her, don't you think?"

"The dogs?"

"Lily. It isn't a joking matter Jade."

Didn't I just say that to him? "Quint, I super doubt Anibal's going to come in, threaten his closest cousin, and steal Lily from her care. Do you?"

"No, but the BLO or Cárdenas might make a play. The house is surrounded by guards, but we've learned how easily people are bought off,"

"*Plata o Plomo*, silver or lead." We were strolling in the direction of the door. Dylan stepped out to meet us. I looked at him and said, "Quint, if it meant saving my loved ones, I'd take the silver too."

"Ah, discussing how things get done in Mexico these days. Speaking of organized crime…" Dylan looked back into the living room. Quint and I followed his gaze.

"Holy crap! Who let the hyenas in? That's the woman who came to dinner at Polo's." I exclaimed. Guillermo Lobo, Daisi Beltrán and Consuelo García clustered by the bar. My cheeks felt hot. I was still naïve to how thing worked here. "I guess we misjudged the audacity of the BLO. And the efficacy of the guards. Who's the dude with Daisi?"

Quint replied, "Her husband, Hector. He's Lobo's partner in the talent business. He fancies himself a social powerhouse, but he's really one of the heads of BLO."

"They've come to stick pins into the cadaver to make sure she's dead," Dylan joked.

"Nah, They just wanted to come drink Lidia's booze and eat her food," Quint replied.

We stepped out of direct view and watched the group get drinks and work the room. Lobo and Beltrán seemed to know every official, including Tony Garza. Damn. I wanted to bend Garza's ear. He was my shot at getting Lily out of Mexico. He could slip her in a diplomatic pouch, if push came to shove. And on cue, little miss size 4 appeared through the far door, the sartorial transformation remarkable. Lily wasn't a scared teen anymore; she'd blossomed into an elegant young woman. Alex had done her up in a navy silk sheath and pearls, added a touch of makeup and swept her hair up in a loose up-do. All in ten minutes. The woman had talent. Lily even fit a pair of her pumps.

"Lily, I didn't recognize you! You look beautiful and grown up. Turn around." She twirled. "Alex, you're a wizard! What a transformation. Thanks so much! I'll get it cleaned and returned before you fly home."

"It was my pleasure. Lily is the perfect model. She fits that dress better than I do. I see more have arrived. I better get back to my hostess duties," she said and gave Lily a little hug and two air kisses before rejoining the gathering. In a moment, one of the servers pulled the sheers across the window.

"Alex is really nice. She's pretty broken up about her aunt and Senator Aguirre. I don't think she knows her aunt was involved in my—our...our— "

Quint was around her in a flash. "Don't cry, Lil. We're here for you. Stick with Jade and Dylan."

She snuggled under his arm with a pouty look. "Can I have a margarita?"

"No, I don't think so, kid. I'll have them make you a virgin margarita, if you want," Quint said.

"Just kidding. Anyway, a little late for that," she mumbled. The eyebrows on both men shot up.

"And since you're an experienced woman, I need your help with two things. Now don't freak out, but Consuelo and Lobo have shown up. You are no longer Lily, but Dylan's med school pal's sister visiting from—where have you been besides L.A.?"

"Denver. I've visited my aunt a couple of times. I could be a college student. I know the University of Denver campus really well. We always went over to the library."

"Good. Dyl, name a school friend."

"Jack. He's a plastic surgeon now, giving rich ladies new faces."

"And my name is Tiffany. Tiffany Flynn. You're showing me around. It's my eighteenth birthday gift. I start school later in the month. Jack is meeting us here and we're going to Puerto Vallarta for the weekend."

"Wow, you're a great liar, Lil...uh, Tif. What are you going to study?"

"Creative writing and theatrical costume design."

"They'll remember that for sure," I said.

"But they won't remember Lily. Or Evie." She sucked in a sharp breath and I could see her will herself not to cry. Good girl.

"Okay then, we're mingling. Let's chat, eat lunch, and at some point get in front of the American ambassador and convince him to send you home."

"But Jade, how do you know he isn't affiliated with the Beltrán-Leyva people?" Dylan asked.

"This is a celebration of life for both Lidia and Polo. Tony Garza was his contact. Polo introduced me to him at the Summit on Organized Crime. It's where I met the Mexico City mayor, Marcelo Fallas. Absolutely do not go near him. He's a total lech," I said to Lily.

Quint laughed. "Consuelo is more his speed."

"But what if they do recognize me? What do I do?"

Fear seared through my chest and I shuddered. Could Lily handle it? She had to. Meeting Garza here was our only hope. "Lie. Say something clever like 'Golly, I didn't know I had a twin in Mexico.' You can manage it. Just no pouting, crying, or shaking. You can be shy. And don't leave my side. You either, Dylan."

"Jade, this is getting elaborate. Why don't we leave? What's the point of this theater?"

"You've called the Feds about Anibal, right?"

"A marshal will be here before lunch is served. But Anibal isn't here."

"He will be. He will be," I growled through a ragged breath. Lily blanched.

I inhaled a calming breath. "Anyway Quint, I need to talk to Garza, and having Lil, I mean, Tiffany, with me to tell her story is going to get her a ticket on a US flight." The girl brightened and gestured *thumbs up*. "Getting her safely out of Mexico and to her family is our number one priority.

Beating the bad guys? Well, they're all right here. Go get 'em cowboy. C'mon Tif, let's get that margarita."

Chapter 3

Clowns to the left; jokers to the right

Lily strode into the living room on Dylan's arm, head held high. She walked in the heels as though she'd been born in them. I immediately understood her desire to design theatrical costumes and said a silent prayer she would realize her dream. Every head turned to admire or assess the new couple joining the gathering. I watched Consuelo. She wasn't looking at Lily. I saw the hungry leer. Poor Dylan. And poor Lily, the mayor was closing in. I stepped in front of Lily, effectively blocking Fallas's trajectory.

"Thanks, JadeAnne, a beer for me and Tiffany would like a margarita. Meet you at the hors d'oeuvres," Dylan replied, a little too loudly.

I spun around to come face to face with Mayor Fallas. "Good afternoon, sir. How nice to see you again. I'm JadeAnne Stone, the journalist from California. Senator Aguirre introduced us at the Summit last month. Such a tragic loss. You must be so sad, losing your friend like that." A wolfish grin spread across his jowls. Yuck.

Fallas watched Dylan and Lily move away, but the predatorial gleam in his eyes remained. He held out his hand and said, "Of course, Miss—"

"Stone, JadeAnne Stone," I repeated and shook his hand, withdrawing quickly. Eww, the old lech caressed it with his thumb as he relinquished his hold. He asked what I was writing and I reminded him of the Summit and Aguirre's request.

"Human trafficking? Not in my city. We have one of the safest cities in Latin America. But I'd be happy to talk to you about the measures we've taken to keep Mexico free of these negative elements." He held out his card and I snatched it away before he could fondle me again, a sticky sweet smile on my face.

"Thank you so much, Mayor Fallas. I'm sure you'll have a lot to add to the piece."

"Please call my assistant to set up a date. Perhaps we could talk over dinner," he replied, running his tongue across his lips.

I thanked him, the fake smile plastered to my face, and hurried toward the drinks table. I asked the white jacketed bartender for a Victoria and two margaritas, one without alcohol. He looked at me like *why bother?* but I shrugged and carried the drinks to Dylan and Lily, side-stepping the press of thirsty mourners encircling the bar.

"Margarita as ordered, Tiffany," I said as I handed over the drinks "Hey, you two, let's step out of the traffic and let others try these marvelous shrimp." I jerked my head toward the back wall.

"Any good gossip?"

"Matter of fact, the room is starting to buzz with stories of what happened Friday night."

"What did you hear?"

"Car accident going over the mountain. Both killed instantly. Aguirre hated his mother and shot her himself.

Lidia had terminal cancer and killed herself, and Aguirre, in grief, killed himself."

"Christ Almighty. Good! Here comes Quint. Let's find out what he's heard." I waved him over. He pushed through the crowd at the drinks table, grabbed a beer and joined us. "Quint, rumors of the deaths are circulating. Have you heard anything?"

"Oh, yeah. Some wild stories. Some woman is going on about *chupacabras* eating their hearts out. I thought this was a sophisticated crowd. *Chupacabras*!" he started to roar.

Lily wrinkled her brow. "A chuchu-what?"

"How's your drink?" I asked. We were practically shouting now with the din in the room. A hundred people must be crammed in and more coming. Too many looked like cartel people. What were the guards doing?

"It's good. What's in it?"

"Mostly lime juice, a little orange juice and some soda. A *chu-pa-ca-bra* is a mythical animal that sucks the blood out of farm animals and eats their hearts."

"Ick. They're not real, are they?"

Quint laughed again. "Not at all, and that is not what happened."

"And what did happen? Consuelo asked as she bulldozed into our group and sidled to Dylan with a coquettish moue. "Who is this?" I turned to block Lily.

"Hello, Consuelo. I'm surprised you'd dare to show your face here," Quint said.

"But of course I would come to honor my business partner and dearest friend. Why wouldn't I?"

"For one, the room is crawling with law enforcement and anticrime politicians. You're a known trafficker," he said convivially, his smile warm as he took her elbow and escorted her away from our group. She balked and he whispered something in her ear. I don't know how he got close, her cheap perfume clung to her like sewer mist.

Dylan stood, jaw hanging open. "What was that?"

"The madam of the whorehouse where my sister and I were kept. She's a drunk. Was she really the senator's mother's friend? What kind of people were they?"

"Consuelo is a loud mouthed, greedy, liar and you said it —drunk. She worked for Lidia, but the rumor I heard is she'd become a liability and Lidia had her picked up by the authorities. I'm guessing Lobo bailed her out."

The people kept coming. I didn't see anything resembling a celebration of life, no testimonial, no *Kumbaya* and holding hands. We were being squeezed further into the corner and people were spilling into the courtyard where another drink station and hors d'oeuvre table had been set up.

It was time to work the room. I scanned for the Beltráns —not hard to find with the copper fireplug inserted in their group. Now she was making eyes at Hector, and Daisi's tight-lipped expression said she wasn't pleased. Lobo held an unlit cigar, which he shook in some skinny bureaucrat's face as he laughed too loudly. I elbowed Quint. "Check the dude with Lobo. He looks like a trapped weasel."

"I think he's the marshal. Come on."

"Wait. I want to deposit Dylan and Tiffany with friendly faces." He nodded.

The crowd separated into three camps: Polo's people, Lidia's people, and close friends and family. Polo's people, mostly suited men with *puros* and old-fashioneds, had migrated outside. The courtyard looked a bit smoggy from the cigars and cigarettes.

In the seating area of the living room, family greeted guests, and Lidia's close friends chatted. Most of the canapés and cocktail servers were going there. Loli acted as hostess with Alex, but I could see how hard this was on both of them. I was going to have to make condolences to the senator's brother Beto and wife Molly.

At the back of the room, by the double dining room doors, Lidia's associates mingled. The men wore slacks and sports coats or leather jackets over open collars displaying gold chains. A few wore pointy snakeskin cowboy boots and pressed designer jeans. What a difference in style between the Aguirre worlds.

Daisi Beltrán was holding court, welcoming newcomers, making introductions, signaling the waiters. Really? Just because she and Lidia were on a committee together? Most of the women, although many stunningly lovely—beauty queens like Daisi —wore too bright and too tight dresses with ridiculously high heels and gaudy jewelry. But no one looked as tawdry as Consuelo. I considered Loli Buendía, probably the richest woman in the room with her charcoal silk dress and grey Tahitian pearls. What a contrast.

I leaned in to Lily. "It's all in taste and breeding, Tif."

"My mother is more like them." She spat out the word like a bite of wormy apple.

"You did great with Consuelo. She didn't have a clue," I said. "Hey, I need a new drink. Let's cruise." I patted Dylan's arm. He turned from his conversation with Quint and Horacio. "Let's wander around." He grunted.

"Jade, I felt scared. What if...?"

"You passed the test. No one else has seen you. Oh, and speaking of Consuelo, remind me I must compliment her lovely taste in home decor!" We broke into giggles.

New drinks in hand, I steered my trio to the seating area and started introductions. Mrs. P, on the fringes, wrinkled her forehead when I introduced Lily as Tiffany, but she kept still. Lily could have won an Academy Award for her performance: a marvel of the polite ingénue, idolizing her older brother, and excited about going to college later in the month. She even pulled a deb ball out of her bag of tricks. With each conversation, I noted she not only remembered every lie she'd told, but she embellished with more information and managed to keep it all straight. Meanwhile, Dylan impressed everyone. He didn't need to lie, except about *Tiffany.*

I greeted everyone I already knew and hugged and cried, held hands, and gave condolences. The hardest was Beto. Lidia was his mother, after all.

As I got up to move on, Alex stopped me and gave me a huge hug. "Thank you, JadeAnne. I know you've made Dad feel better. He and Aunt Lidia had argued. He'll never forgive himself."

"Over what?"

"The old stories. Auntie loved Polo more than him. She wasn't acting like an upstanding matron of high society. She needed to accept Anibal—typical family stuff," she said. "He and Polo never fully reconciled their differences over Anibal either. Say, where is he? I thought I saw him on the Plaza."

Chucho, Aguirre's serving man, circled by with a tray of empty plates and glasses. I set mine on it, my hand shaking, and greeted him. He said the men had gone outside and he'd join us in a moment. I hugged Alex again, and said, "I think that was a summons from my father—super long story, which I promise to tell over dinner. Anibal had best keep his distance. He's in big trouble."

"Not surprising. He always was a handful. I'm holding you to the story." Her perfect red lips twitched into a wry smile. I blew her a kiss and pulled Lily away from the murder of Lidia crows.

"Those old biddies were driving me crazy!" Lily said.

"Let's go out and chase down the ambassador."

It was time to make our move and get out of the lion's den.

Chapter 4

A Helping Hand

Dylan had ditched us at the couches and I caught sight of him with Chucho and Horacio deep in conversation near a planting of banana trees. I looked for Garza as we stepped into the garden. Quint stood in the corner by the fish pond talking to Santiago and a woman. He beckoned and we changed course. The woman turned out to be Rosi Orozco, the expert in human trafficking I'd heard at the Summit. I told her how much I'd learned at her talk.

Her handsome face lit up in delight. "Ah, Miss Stone, if only the authorities felt the same way. It's a losing battle." She waved her hand, gesturing at the assembled guests. "Here are the power brokers who could clamp down on human trafficking. But they don't."

Quint and Santiago moved off. I drew Lily close. In a low voice, I said, "Rosi—may I call you that?" She nodded, leaning in to hear over the party. "Rosi, this is Lily Flynn. It's a long story I would like to tell you, but the punchline is, Lily and her eleven-year-old sister were trafficked from L.A.

to Mexico City by Eddy Santos and Guillermo Lobo, and subsequently sold to Antonio Cárdenas, a high-ranking Zeta. I was also sold to the Zetas. My father, Senator Aguirre's crew, and I are working to shut these trafficking rings down. It's why Polo and his mother are dead. And we can't get Lily on a plane back to her family in Colorado."

As I spoke her eyes widened with a shadow of surprise then horror then determination. "And your sister? Where is she?"

Lily slumped and hung her head. "They killed her, the Zetas. I-I couldn't protect her. I made her go with me b-because He was going to hurt her. "

My heart ached at the anguish I saw.

"Rosi lifted Lily's chin and looked her in the eye. "*Cariña*, stand up straight and hold your head high. You have nothing to be ashamed of. JadeAnne, thank you for sharing this. Let's talk more. Tomorrow?" She hugged each of us in turn and slipped a card to me before gliding off to greet an acquaintance.

"Tif, I think we've found help." She shrugged, but straightened up to let me dab her face with my napkin. "Let's go. Garza is over there with Rosi. It's our chance."

By mid-afternoon the day turned warm. As Rosi introduced me, Dylan joined the group and offered to get drinks. I waggled my margarita glass.

"Tif, help me," Dylan said, and the two pushed through the crowd toward the bar. How did Dylan know I didn't want to introduce Lily, just yet?

"Mr. Ambassador, it's a privilege to make your acquaintance. I attended your talk at the Summit last month," I said in a voice as sweet as syrup. I practically curtseyed. I wanted something from this man, and I was going to get it. Quint stifled a laugh and Rosi covered a little cough with an unmanicured hand that didn't cover her dimples.

"Please Miss Stone, call me Tony."

"Only if you'll call me JadeAnne," I replied, and extended my hand. He took it and I gave it a seal-the-deal shake.

Quint circled my shoulders with his arm. "My daughter is a journalist, Tony. Stanford grad. The senator took her under his wing and got her working on an exposé on the cartel activity in human trafficking."

"Stanford. That's impressive. What year were you?'

"Masters in Journalism 2002. But actually, I'm on leave from my position as managing partner of Waterstreet Investigations and Marine Salvage—WIMS, as it were. We're out of Sausalito."

"What brought you to Mexico?" A good people person, I thought. He looked genuinely interested.

"I needed to get away and rethink my career path. My best friend lives in Zihua and when a banker asked me to find his wife who had disappeared in Ixtapa, I grabbed the chance."

"Worthington the banker? Wasn't he murdered?"

"As was his wife, the woman I was hired to find. But he wasn't murdered, exactly. I think he wanted to stiff me on the bill," I joked. "He was trying to shoot me and the wife's cousin shot him."

He grimaced, shocked. "Are you kidding? Coincidence?"

Quint stepped in. "Not at all, Tony. Jade was set up by Worthington to flush the wife, a Secret Service investigator in money laundering. She was this close to exposing his operation." He demonstrated an inch with his fingers.

"And the man is the senator's cousin?"

"Exactly, Anibal Aguirre."

"JadeAnne, does this have a tie-in to your exposé?"

"Yes, it does. I'd like to tell you about it, but I don't think it's appropriate here. The story is long, complicated, and shocking. Frankly, it's the story of why we are here today."

Dylan and Lily returned with the drinks.

Garza took a sip of water., "I don't understand."

"You will, Tony," Rosi said. "I've asked to meet with them as soon as possible, but as they are U.S. citizens, perhaps we can schedule that meeting in your office? I'd like *Señor* Santiago to be with us, as well. Would tomorrow afternoon be too soon?" Rosi asked.

"Mr. Quint, is this information accurate?" the ambassador asked.

"Yes, sir—"

I interrupted. "And maybe you can help arrange a flight back home for our Lily. Senator Aguirre was not successful with the embassy, although he met with you on several occasions." I pulled Lily next to me, putting her in his face. This guy wasn't going to say *not our problem* again. "She's suffered enough at the hands of Mexicans. Let's get her home, don't you think?"

Lily was winning her second Oscar for her supporting role. She wilted like a flower in the mid-day sun—slumped, hair hiding her face, but unlike that flower, her tears sprinkled the well-tended lawn we stood on as she quaked— in fear? In grief? Only Lily knew what she held inside. Dylan and Quint surrounded her, shielding her from the endless horror she and Evie had unwittingly entered.

Rosi positioned herself directly in Garza's personal space. He flinched and took a step back. "Tony, do I understand you denied sending this kid home?"

She sounded like an attorney. Or a very angry mother. Maybe she was both. Whatever, Rosi Orozco proved to be a force of nature. The ambassador had the grace to look abashed and agreed to meet us in his office at two p.m. the next day. He would have sandwiches ordered in. Rosi beamed, thanked him and gave a kiss on each cheek before excusing herself.

Sotto voce, I said, "What do you suppose Polo was doing during all those visits?"

Quint winked. "Let's get her on the team."

Chapter 5

Party Crasher

"I'm hungry. I thought they were serving lunch," Lily complained. "It's already five."

"That's early for a Mexican party," Dylan said. "Let's hit the appetizers."

I said, "Quint, you want anything?"

"No, but I'll come."

We threaded our way through the thinning crowd. Many of the politicians and bureaucrats had gone, but I noticed, other than the little old ladies who'd flocked out an hour earlier, most of the Lidia crowd was still presided over by Daisi Beltrán, who had commandeered the seating area. I watched through the window as I inhaled a plate of *huitlacoche* stuffed mushrooms and cheese *croquetas*. The servers scurried back and forth continuously replacing trays of food and drinks for the voracious narcos. The garbage tub behind the bar table brimmed in bottles, and the crowd acted like boorish drunks.

Currently the cartel idiots were trying to dance to

cumbias blasting from a CD player. Right in the middle of the floor gyrated Consuelo. She reminded me of a pig in a wallow. Lobo was out there too, flailing to a beat only he could hear. I watched the other dancers move away, leaving them grinding and jerking. The on-lookers clapped and hooted. Consuelo ate it up, but Lobo was too drunk to have a clue.

"Dyl, I'm getting a piece of cake." I pointed to the food table.

"I'm not going in there," Lily said.

"Want a piece?"

"No. I ate too much already." She held her middle and pooched out her cheeks.

"Never stopped me."

The CD changed to some sophisticated Latin jazz and the floor cleared. I skipped over to the cake before the vultures cleared the plate. *Tres leches*, my favorite. I carved myself two healthy pieces.

Intent on moist cake, I didn't notice the conversations around me at first, but something caught my attention.

"Carolina told me Consuelo was at the Tepoztlán house when it happened."

I wanted to shout, *That liar! Consuelo was in jail for running a house of prostitution,* but I shoved in another mouthful of cake, muffling my outrage.

"But why did she do it?" asked an overly made-up woman rolling out of her spandex tube dress. All the narco women had large, firm breasts. Probably enhanced. A gangster thing?

Another woman joined them, and said, "No, it was Lobo, not Consuelo." She explained Polo had come to murder his mother because she was going to report his illegal business. What illegal business? "Oh," the woman gleefully said, "he's a *puto.*" They'd gotten a laugh out of that. I stoppered myself with the last bite of cake.

Someone yelled to change the music and the jazz was replaced with the macarena. The crowd went wild. Everyone got up to pat their butts. I heard a crash—a short cowboy-looking dude in pointy boots and a ten gallon hat swallowing his little head lay on the floor in a shower of glass, laughing and bleeding. Where was Alex? The family had disappeared. Probably in the dining room having a nice lunch. Who was watching out for Anibal? I signaled Dylan, who came in, helped the man up, and cleaned his cuts with vodka. How could Lidia stand these people?

I was busy managing the clean up when a roar of angry voices overshadowed the music. Two men broke from the crowd, pummeling each other. I realized it was Anibal and Lobo, and Anibal was crazed with anger. He was going to beat that flabby promoter to death.

"You set me up, Lobo. I'm not going down for you and your girlfriend Farcía. You're going to pay for what you did, you traitorous fuck. I'll kill you. I'll kill you!" Anibal howled in English, landing punches in Lobo's face and gut with each utterance. The crowd stood paralyzed and puzzled.

I ran to the brawling men and screamed, "Anibal Aguirre. Stop this moment!"

I grabbed the collar of his shirt and jerked him away from Lobo with strength I didn't know I possessed. My heart raced; my blood boiled. Lobo scuttled away, a puny crustacean side-stepping a killer shark.

Anibal spun onto me fists ready, yelling, "You! It's all your fault! Your meddling and your tricks. Your luck is running out, JadeAnne. They'll get you and the brat, one way or the other."

Frozen, I watched as his fist barreled toward my nose in slow motion, like a cartoon. Then in a dream, I heard the sickening dull crack of a bone snapped in two.

Anibal screamed in pain and dropped to the floor.

"JadeAnne! Look at me! Are you crazy?"

I was being crushed by something warm. A bear? No, Dylan—shaking me. Slowly my eyes focused. Strangers circled around, stunned expressions on their faces. I looked down. Anibal writhed, moaning on the priceless rug. Quint aimed a big gun at him. I wanted to shout, "Don't shoot him, it will ruin the rug," but I didn't have enough breath to get it out.

"Jade, can you hear me? Are you hurt?"

Dylan. I pulled away from his bearhug and smiled. "Only a scratch. What happened?"

"*Gracias a Dios*. What the hell were you thinking?"

Uh-oh. Dylan was mad. "He was going to beat Lobo to death. Somebody needed to do stop him."

I glared at the assembled guests, frowning. *What's the matter with you BLO assholes?* I wanted to shout. *Why didn't one of you stop him? You!* I mentally pointed at Hector Beltrán. *We all know you manage this cartel. Why didn't you stop him?* I imagined wrenching away from Dylan and stalking up to the astounded kingpin and his simpering wife, to say, *Honey, your husband is a murderer, drug seller, and human trafficker. Now get out of this house.*

Dylan gave me a shake. "And it didn't need to be you."

"But we've got him," I said, watching the marshal handcuff Anibal and haul him off the ground. I noticed Quint kept his gun cocked and ready. The "mourners" stood silently, mouths agape, until Anibal was taken from the room. Then they erupted in conversation. Daisi Beltrán and Consuelo had Lobo on the couch, comforting him with napkin-wrapped ice cubes for his bruised face. Beltrán conferred with his men. Tension vibrated through the room.

Beto Aguirre stepped through the dining room door, haggard with grief. "Friends, my wife and I are grateful for your outpouring of love for my mother Lidia Buendía de Aguirre, and for my brother Leopoldo Aguirre. Thank you so much for joining us in this remembrance of two leaders of our society, lost in such a tragic way."

"How did it happen? Did your brother kill her?" someone shouted.

"I realize rumors have flown like *colibris* and I want to set you straight. My brother lost control of the car going over the mountain into Morelos. He and Mother were on their way to our family weekend home. A tragic accident, nothing more. My wife and I wish to bid you good afternoon and thank you again for your friendship. Please let our staff help you find your things, and forgive my poor stepbrother. Now I must attend my family." With that, Beto disappeared into the dining room, and guests began to depart.

I flopped onto a couch, exhausted from three drinks and the intense emotion of the day. Security guards had materialized in the courtyard and hallway as Beto spoke. I wondered if one of those sleazy molls ripped off my purse. I'd send a bill to Beltrán. Quint sat down with me.

"Before you start, I know, I was stupid. But I couldn't let him kill Lobo in front of us all, could I?

"Security was on its way. He might have killed you," he said, brushing my hair off my cheek. It was no longer in that sleek chignon I'd worked so hard to achieve. "You're bleeding. And you're going to have a doozy of a bruise."

"What do you mean?" I reached up and touched blood. Suddenly my head pounded and I felt searing along my temple.

He laughed. "Didn't you tell us 'just a scratch'? You'll live, but let's get your doctor to look at it." He turned away and called, "Dylan? Take a look at this. Probably got her with his ring."

"He doesn't wear a ring," I said.

"Brass knuckles then. Something gouged your skin."

"Get me a wet napkin and bring a bottle of vodka," Dylan said.

Quint pulled a bottle from the table being wheeled back

37

to the kitchen and snatched a napkin off the food table. He handed them to Dylan.

"I'm going to talk to some people," Quint said.

I looked out the window. The courtyard still had people milling around and clustering in groups, but the servers had begun to clear.

"This is going to sting." Dylan doused the napkin with vodka and dabbed my temple. The alcohol might have killed any germs, but it felt like my head had been cauterized with a hot poker. "Is this what married life with you is going to be like? You pretend to be Wonder Woman and I patch you up? I don't know if I can live that way, Jade."

Butterflies flitted through my chest. "So, why didn't someone try to stop him?"

"Why did you?" Lily said. "The world would be a better place without that monster. He's the one who took us. It was that man Anibal wanted to kill."

"Not Eddy?"

"No. That man. He promised me an audition where Evie could watch and maybe be an extra. When I saw him, I remembered it all."

"Where'd Lobo crawl off to?" I asked.

"I don't know. I hid when I saw him. He might have recognized me."

"Good girl."

Alex came in and surveyed the room. I followed her gaze: wine stains on the carpet, broken glass, cigarette burns on the seat cushions, food ground into the floor. She clenched her fists as her face sculpted in disgust. "Pigs!"

"How did all those people get here, Alex?"

"I didn't know who any of them were, besides the old ladies. That awful Consuelo followed us. I saw her in the den using the phone."

"Figures. She's a piece of work," I said.

"How's your head?" Alex asked.

"Fine. It's nothing. I'd apologize, but I couldn't stand there and let a man be killed."

"Lura would have done the same thing. I don't know what's happened to Ani. He used to be so sweet. Lura's death changed him."

"You know he was involved in the trafficking? It's why the marshal was here to take him. He'll be put on trial back in the states."

"Nothing surprises me anymore. Polo filled us in. Danny wanted to kill Lura over money?" Alex shook her head. "Such a waste."

"Anibal killed Lura's husband to save me. Worthington thought I was Lura," I said.

"Danny always was greedy. I worried when you left the wake with Ani. He hadn't been acting very stable. I chalked it up to Lura's death."

"So did I. What a mistake. I should have gone home."

"But you've met Dylan. He seems like a solid guy."

"Yeah, well, pass me my crown, I'm the Queen of Picking Mr. Right."

"*Señora* Pérez says he comes from a nice family and is a good catch."

"You know Mrs. P?"

"Of course. She's family. She told us what happened to you and that poor girl—losing her sister right in front of her. *Señora* Pérez is really fond of her. It's too bad she never had more kids of her own. She saved Aunt Lidia in the earthquake when she lost her whole family. My aunt would have done anything for her." At the thought of Lidia, Alex teared up again. "Look at me, I'm a mess. Actually I came to get your father for the reading of the wills then we'll eat. You're welcome to come." She stood up, her lithe figure a bit unsteady. It had been a long, emotion-packed day.

"Alex invited us all to the reading," I announced. The population of the living room had dwindled. The bureaucrats shook hands with Quint and bade us good night.

Lily pet the dogs in her lap, hopefully not ruining Loli's dress, and declined the reading. Dylan said he'd keep her company since he didn't know the man, anyway. The rest of us tromped into the dining room for what I assumed would be a long, boring litany of bequests.

The room had been partitioned between the tables, set in elegant china and crystal on one side, and a lectern with a microphone had been placed in front of several short rows of the dining chairs on the other. Wrapped parcels and boxes lined the wall behind the lectern. Mr. Castillo y Iglesias, a diminutive, white-haired man in his late sixties, pushed his round, wire-rimmed glasses up his Spanish nose and cleared his throat as he shuffled his papers.

The heirs quieted down and straightened up in their seats. The lawyer cleared his throat again, tapped the mic and asked if we could hear him. Although clear, his voice was quiet. Several people said "yes" "loud and clear" and "*sígale*."

Chapter 6

Bequests

At the beginning of the presentation, it was all I could do to stay awake. The Spanish went well beyond my capabilities and I drifted in and out of a semi-fugue state. But when Castillo y Iglesias started in on Lidia's actual bequests, I focused my attention on who was getting what. Of course, the bulk of Lidia's real estate holdings and their contents, including the house we sat in, a prime slice of Mexico City's *bienes raices*, was split equally between Lidia's sons, Alberto, "Beto" and Leopoldo "Polo." Castillo y Iglesias, paused, the rustle of shuffled notes filling the silent room. No one breathed.

Then he read, "I deed my dear friend Catalina Pérez Cruz my house at 1066 Amores." I guessed saving Lidia's life really meant a lot to her.

Once the personal assets had been taken care of, Castillo y Iglesias droned on about Lidia's legitimate businesses, of which Polo was named Chairman of the Board and got the salary. Did Lidia want to set him up for the presidency? Too late now.

Finally, the lawyer got to the "stuff": jewelry, art, etc. She gave everyone something special to remember her by. To a string of loyal staff, she bequeathed varying amounts of cash and a special gift of a possession, valued according to years of service, along with an envelope containing her personal thank you, a severance check, and a glowing letter of reference.

One house worker received a fur coat. Lidia's long-time driver was gifted her classic Mercedes. The gifts were given in a pecking order —family, loyal staff, lesser staff and Consuelo. She was handed a moderate sized, wrapped frame, which she ripped open to reveal an atrocious piece of modern art. I watched as her triumphant face soured to shame and anger. The piece in bold strokes and splatters resembled something a chimpanzee might have painted. I learned it was a reproduction given Lidia in a white-elephant exchange. Consuelo sat down and kept her mouth shut, but I had the feeling we'd be treated to a real scene.

Sr. Castillo y Iglesias finished the bequests and gave a few closing remarks before announcing a fifteen minute break before the reading of Polo's will. The family drifted into clusters, stretching or refreshing drinks. Most of the staff took their gifts and cleared out, now unemployed, but the chatter sounded cheerful and many eyes glistened with tears.

Consuelo marched up to the lawyer and, sure enough, began a diatribe against him, Lidia, the ineptitude of the help. Lidia had promised her the Pedrigal house and contents as well as a huge sum of money, *and* the Amores house, which she had decorated and never received compensation. She banged her fist, shouted, cajoled, but the little attorney stood firm.

He proceeded to read the bequest, "To Consuelo García I leave my copy of Soroya de Santiago's oil on paper,

"Passion," as a testament to Sra. Consuelo's passion for interior decorating and assistance over the years."

"I can't sell it; it's not even an original," she whined.

"It is what the *Señora* chose for you. She also left you this envelope." He handed her a sealed white envelope printed with Lidia's name and address. I inched closer as Consuelo ripped it open. She pulled out a letter and a check drawn off the umbrella corporation. I could see it was made out to Consuelo in an amount more or less equal to eight thousand dollars. The notation line read *la indemnización por despido*, severance pay. Consuelo was cut off.

A foul string of *groceries* poured from her lips. I'd stepped back, but darted in to snag the letter she threw on the floor before wheeling around and marching out with her check and ugly print. I skimmed Lidia's words before Sr. Castillo y Iglesias put out his hand with a disapproving look and I slapped it into his palm with a sneer. Lidia had given her *what-for* for her mismanagement, sloppy drunken excesses, familiarity with Lidia and Lidia's family, and for the unforgiveable act of going behind Lidia's back with Anibal and making side deals. So Lidia had known what they were up to.

Polo's staff trickled into the room. Of course Susana, Horacio, Omar, and a third Shrek-like man showed up. Polo's chef nodded at me as he escorted the Polanco housekeeper to a chair. Even the old grandfather from Polo's Michoacán farm showed up, looking frightened and uncomfortable, led by the little maid who had warned me about the Aguirre family what now felt like eons past. I stepped forward to welcome them.

The girl, Anibal's half-sister, said, "We are thankful you are well, *señorita*."

"I thank you for your kindness when I was a guest in the senator's home." I shook each of their hands and went to fill their drink orders.

"So will Polo give things the way Lidia did?" I asked Quint. "His house staff is here, but the thugs aren't, thank God."

"I don't know what the senator planned, although I know he changed his will after Lura died."

"So Beto inherits?"

Quint shrugged. "I think the village has been deeded to the residents. The senator and I talked about it a couple of times."

"That's cool! Good for Polo."

"Attention, may I have your attention, please?" Beto called through the microphone. "Please take your seats and welcome *Señor* Castillo Y Iglesias who is going to read Senator Aguirre's will and bequests."

The audience clapped and quieted. The lawyer began.

"As we mourn the loss of an important leader of our great country, let us remember his generosity to not only his loved ones, his staff and his friends, but to his country. Senator Leopoldo Aguirre Buendía may have exited his office before his job was done, but he has left behind a legacy, an endowment, if you will, to assure his work will continue. After the death of Senator Aguirre's beloved cousin, he reevaluated his wishes and bequests. Let us proceed to the reading of his will."

Who was cut out? Who was benefitting? Not Anibal, I'd reckon.

"Pay attention, Jade," my father whispered.

"—and to that end I shall now begin the reading."

It took a few minutes for Castillo y Iglesias to get to the actual bequests. Polo left Beto the Polanco apartment and its contents. Lura, Alex, Loli and Anibal had originally been twenty-five percent beneficiaries of Polo's liquid wealth. On Lura's death and his discovery of Anibal's complicity in the human trafficking ring in Mexico City, he had transferred their shares to endow a new foundation created to combat the trafficking of human beings, establishing Rosi Orozco as the Executive Director and deeded over one of his buildings to house the offices.

I'd wondered why Rosi had attended. Obviously this was organized long before Polo died, but it was a nice touch including his philanthropy in the actual will. Everyone clapped and the family relaxed. So far no one had been cut out—except Anibal, and where he was headed, he wouldn't need his millions. Although the amounts of the bequest were not stated, by the looks on his heirs faces, they were generous. He gave Susana a sizeable nest egg as well as a job in the new organization. Chucho received a trust for his education and the deed to an apartment. Polo provided Horacio with a trust for his children's education and enough cash to pay off his house. As Lidia had for her driver, Polo also gave Horacio the limo. His Polanco staff received large severance packages and offers of jobs in the organization. Everyone received personal letters of recommendation.

The atmosphere turned joyous, but Castillo y Iglesias shushed the crowd. "We are not done, ladies and gentlemen. Let us learn the determination of the estate in Michoacán."

His little group of Tarascans watched with interest, the granddaughter translating for the old man. It was true, Polo was giving the village to his workers and establishing a rehabilitation center for victims of trafficking and slavery in the house. The pot field would be replanted in hemp and vegetables. I was impressed. Best, the last parcel and a trust were deeded to the little granddaughter—Anibal's stepsister. I'd once demanded to know what Polo was doing for the little girl. He was offering her a life. Polo was making good on his promise to end human trafficking—he was freeing his surfs.

"And to my friend, Jackman Quint, I bequeath my holdings on Calle Tabasco in Colonia Roma and have established an endowment in hopes that he will continue the work we have shared over the past years."

"Oh my God! Quint!" I blurted then clapped my hand over my mouth. The people around us laughed. It sounded like everyone was happy. The family, already wealthy, became richer. Polo's staff were given means to better their lives, and Quint's and my work was to be legitimized and funded. *Quint's and my work.* I'd never considered this my work, and certainly hadn't seriously entertained the notion of staying in Mexico. We were standing now as the meeting broke up. Quint gave me a huge hug and twirled me off my feet before setting me down and planting a huge kiss on my forehead.

Lily and Dylan joined us from the living room. He grinned at me and suddenly I knew my destiny was here in Mexico City.

"Mr. Quint," the lawyer said, joining our circle, "as the Amores house has now changed ownership, you and your family must vacate the premise at your earliest convenience." The envelope he handed over included our eviction notice. So Mrs. P was throwing us out.

Chapter 7

The Crew

The meeting wound down and most of the laid-off staff drifted away. Delicious smells of chilis and tortillas, cooked meats, and tomatoes had been drifting through the large room for the last half hour. My stomach was complaining in a loud, angry growl.

Loli clapped, drawing our attention, and announced, "Bring your chairs everyone and help yourselves. Supper is ready."

Chucho hopped up from his conversation with Horacio and his brother Omar, and rushed to help a server move the room dividers. My mouth watered as a buffet of bowls, platters, and chafing dishes was revealed. I grabbed my chair. "Come on, you guys, let's eat over there with Susana." I went back and got another chair and rounded up Quint, Horacio, Chucho and Shrek 3—Horacio's brother Sami—, herding them toward our table. Omar joined us and, surprisingly, Mrs. P. Perfect. Just enough place settings.

We positioned our chairs, left our drink glasses, and got

into the noisy mess line. Everything smelled so good I had trouble deciding on what to eat. I settled on my favorite chilies en nogadas.

Conversations started up as our dinner companions returned to the table, plates laden, but none having to do with that happened in Tepoztlán the week before. I was amazed they were able to keep a lid on it, whoever "they" were. Obviously Horacio, and I assumed Quint, didn't want anyone to know Lidia stood up to take the bullets for Polo. But why? It was an act of love.

A waitress carried a coffeepot and a water pitcher. I held up my glass. *"Gracias."* Interesting no alcohol had been put out. Maybe there was nothing left after the cartel passed through.

The fast eaters were already returning to the buffet. I savored another mouthful of the chilis stuffed with meat and smothered in walnut sauce. This particular version was stupendous, perhaps because the pomegranate arils tasted perfectly sweet tart.

Horacio and his brothers rose as one and scooted between the tables with that rare grace some big men have, returning with plates laden higher than the first time. Dylan and Chucho were next. Susana and Mrs. P rolled their eyes. I realized all these people were well acquainted. Even Tonalli, who pecked across his plate not so much daintily, but like a chicken, peck, scratch, peck, scratch. And except for Tonalli, all demonstrated good table manners. I'd better pay attention to my eating etiquette. But at least this crowd applauded eating a lot. I went back for more, showing enough restraint to be able to sample the dessert cart in process of being set up.

When the waitress came around again, I accepted a coffee and realized how tired I was. It had been a very long day and I wanted to curl up in front of a video. Lily couldn't quite keep her eyes open. "Lil, have a coffee. Quint, get her a cup with cream. She's falling asleep."

"I am not! I just ate too much."

"No dessert then?" She craned around to see the cart loaded with sweets and licked her lips.

"I'll take that as 'what kind of fool are you?'" Everyone laughed. Sami suggested we get dessert started. "I think we have to wait for them to take our dinner plates and come around with the carts. See? There are three of them. I'm going to go visit the family table. Come with me, Dylan."

I dragged him over to the head table and introduced him to the Aguirres. The Aguirres introduced us to the Buendía side of the family. I was too full and exhausted to keep track of all the names and relationships, but I learned Loli's husband was on a business trip in Spain. Lucky him. He'd been somewhere during Lura's funeral and wake. Loli didn't seem perturbed so I wouldn't worry about it. Jason and Dylan connected over job talk. It turned out Jason was climbing the ladder at some medical equipment manufacturing company. Alex and I hugged and I told her how sorry I was again. She said it would take a long time to get over this year, but hoped Dyl and I got together and to bring him for a visit when I came to LA. Jason seconded the invitation and Dylan promised to hook him up with his hospitals and the clinic.

I next hugged Beto and Molly. We cried and each told a little Lura story. Beto admitted his shock and guilt over his mother's and brother's deaths. Quint had told them what had happened.

"Beto," I said, "I watched your mother stand up to protect Polo. She made the ultimate sacrifice."

"But if my mother hadn't been affiliated with people and activities where something like this could happen..." He hung his head and added, "We all knew Eddy was a rotten apple. He brought Lobo in and opened the door to people like the Beltráns. We warned her. We pleaded with her." His tears sparkled under the candlelight. Molly hugged him and thanked me for working to stop the terrible things going on in Mexico.

She took my hand. "JadeAnne, you've got a good team. Your father is top notch and has some backing—not just Polo's but in the US. It's too late for my brother-in-law, but not for Mexico. Please continue Polo's," she paused, "and Lura's work. Investigate. Write your articles. Open the world's eyes to the horrors going on here." She nodded toward Dylan, and added, "He's a good man and he's interested. Stay here. He might be Mr. Right."

I felt myself blush. "I've got to get Lily back to her family before I make a decision, but I'll take your advice— I'll give Dylan a chance."

The magic dessert carts circulated the room, refilling as soon as something was selected off them. I had a coconut flan with a side of coconut ice cream, coconut being my ultimate comfort food. Dylan ate a slice of traditional apple pie and two helpings of *arroz con leche* swirled with *cajeta*. I wasn't sure I'd be able to stay upright, and hoped I wouldn't humiliate myself with a nosedive into the dregs of dessert on my plate. I held up my cup as the coffee waitress passed. God, I'd be on a diet for the next month after this dinner.

Alex stood up and clinked her champagne flute.

"Oh, no! More?" I whispered to Dylan. The room fell silent except for the clinking of forks and spoons on dessert plates.

"Thank you all for being a part of our lives. We, the Aguirre and Buendía clans, have suffered hard losses this year, but we shall endure and come out the other side stronger than before. We've survived worse. Our clans have always lived side by side, finally unified through Lidia and Tito's marriage. Together our family is a force. And our family would never be as much as it is today without our friends." She tipped her glass toward the tables of friends, associates and staff. "I want to thank you all for your love, friendship, and service. And I especially want to thank Susana Arias de Barrera for handling the arrangements for today's gatherings, and my cousin Loli who has held me up in this terrible time. I love you guys."

The crowd clapped as the servers finished pouring champagne for all.

Loli stood up with Alex, and said, "Let's lift our glasses in a toast to the grand dame of our clans, Lidia Buendía. May she sit at the feet of God and tell him what to do!"

Everyone laughed and clinked glasses.

"And to my dear cousin, Senator Polo Aguirre, a man with a vision of the future and a plan for righting the wrongs of his country. May he stand behind God and whisper in his ear."

More toasts followed. The testimonials had begun and everyone seemed to have something endearing or funny to say.

"Quint," I called across the table. He looked up. I pointed to my watch and jerked my head toward the door. Lily was slumped against Mrs. P, possibly asleep. Dylan was being a sport, but I could see he had faded. Only the Shreks were lively and participating in the activities.

"Dyl, I'm exhausted. Lily is asleep. You look like a soggy newspaper. Let's go."

A new beverage station had appeared, and now a small combo was setting up in the corner. Dancing. This was going to go on all night. I checked my watch: 10:45. It was the wake Lura had wanted.

Quint put up some resistance, but I pointed out the Aguirres had turned in and the party was down to the young people. Okay, so I'm barely thirty, but tonight I felt about a hundred and six. Dylan agreed. I collected my crew.

"Quint, sir, I've got an early call tomorrow and I've

never been much for a Mexican Hat Dance."

"What's that?" Lily asked.

"You know, that dance you learned in sixth grade." She wrinkled her brow. Dylan and I hummed a few bars, jumping foot to foot with the beat.

"Oh, that one. It's Mexican?"

"You must have cut class that day. Everyone learns the Mexican Hat Dance."

"Enough. If we're going, let's go." Quint sounded irritated.

"You have a car, stay if you want. We'll just leave."

"Not without protection. I won't have you girls walk into that house without it being checked first." Shivers ran down my spine. "The security was sent by Bendicias. I don't trust him."

"You left one of them in charge of the dogs!" I said.

"My puppies! Quint..." Lily wailed.

"Ah, come on Jade, look what you've started."

Dylan said, "We could all go to Seeg's for the night, he's got room." I glared at him. "If it would help," he added, lamely.

"Not without the dogs," Lily and I chimed.

Dylan turned to Quint. "What's happened to women?" The *boys* got a good laugh out of that. "But really, man, I have a six a.m. surgery."

"All right," Quint snapped. He beckoned with a wave. "Horacio!"

The Shreks trotted over to us. "*¿Que pasa, jefe?*"

"The girls want to leave. I need you in the car with them. Omar, Sami, you come with me. We'll go now, check out the house, and let them in when it's clear."

"Yes, sir," they chorused.

"We'll meet you at the cars," I said, as the music cranked up. Yep, Mexican Hat Dance. "Let's say goodbye and thank you to Alex and Loli."

I herded Lily before me and dragged Dylan behind me and made our goodbyes. Thankfully my handbag still awaited me on the table by the door—with the gun in it.

Chapter 8

Safe Haven

Sunday, September 9, 2007

Lily snored in the backseat while we waited at the curb for Quint and company to secure the house. I noticed Dylan parked us under a dense tree between street lamps. Horacio got out to join Quint and his brothers. Dylan pulled me into a deep kiss. I'd forgotten how acrobatic making out in a car could be. The gearshift dug into my side and the reach across the console engaged my core muscles to nearly cramping. How did kids do it, I was wondering when a large shadow thumped against the window and about stopped my heart. I wrenched away from Dylan, pulse pounding, fishing for my gun in my purse and yelling, "Lily, get down, get down!"

The shadow jumped against the window again and barked. His madly swinging tail beat a tattoo against the side of the car. Dylan blew out a breath and started to laugh a little hysterically. He opened the door and Pepper lunged toward me. "Whoa, big boy. Hold on. She's getting out." He grabbed Pepper's collar and kept him half out of the car."

"Sit!" I yelled. Pepper pulled off Dylan's lap and sat down on the curb. "Stay! I'm so sorry, Dylan. He didn't hurt you did he?"

"No, I'm sure everything is fine. Would you get out and greet him?" Annoyed.

I hopped out and Pepper ran around the car to greet me. "Down. Down! Pepper. Yes, Peppi, I'm happy to see you too, but why are you outside?"

Maya galloped up and Lily sprang out of the backseat, flinging herself around the golden. "Lily!" I screeched, "Careful of that dress."

Lily was up and skipping toward the house, Maya loping beside her, my admonishment lost to the quiet street.

I cuddled up to Dylan after giving Pepper a pat, hoping to pick up where we left off. He tasted delicious of burnt sugar and brandy.

"Do you have everything? Let's get you inside. Let's go." He didn't sound very cuddly, or wasn't happy about the gate. Or the dogs? Would Quint let the dogs loose like that?

"What's the matter? Would you like to come in for a night cap?"

"No, I have a six-thirty surgery and I've had enough to drink today. I need to go, Jade," he said as we passed through the vehicle gate standing wide open. The limo filled most of the short driveway, all the doors open. "I'm concerned the gate was left open."

I shrugged. I could barely keep my head up and had no capacity to actually think. "I wasn't in on the security plan today," I said, leaving out that the open gate had alarmed me too.

"Lily, stop!" Dylan bellowed. She was about to open the front door and turned back as a gun blast sounded from the back garden. I had the Semmerling in my hand in a flash.

Now I was wide awake. "Jade, Lily, back to the car. Come Pepper. Come Maya!"

I kicked off my heels and ran for the gate, dogs happily bounding at my side. Dylan's and Lily's leather soled shoes rang out against the cobbled driveway. More shots. Shouts. Lily screamed. I shoved the gate closed as they passed through to slow down whoever was inside. "Get in the car and lie on the floor."

"Are you out of your mind, Jade? *You* get in and *we're* leaving," he said, breathless from the mad dash.

"He's right, get in," Lily panted, as she wrenched open the door for the dogs and dove onto the floor after them.

Dylan turned the key and the Beemer roared to life. "Get in, *now!*"

"But I can shoot them as they come out the ga—" I said as another blast cut through the hedging and angry bees, and plant debris buzzed by my head. I dove in as the car jumped away from the curb. We peeled down Amores, tires squealing around the corner on two wheels.

"Is everybody all right?" Dylan asked. "Dogs?"

"I'm scared, Dylan. What about the puppies?" Lily's voice shook. "What do they want, Jade?"

"We know what they want. Dyl, we have to go back, I can't leave Quint. Oh, God, what if was an ambush? The BLO people knew we weren't there and these guards came through Senator Bendicias, the one who screwed us in Tepoztlán. I know Quint didn't trust him or his guards."

Lily wailed, "What if Mrs. P goes back to the house? And my puppies!"

"I wouldn't worry about that, Lily. Why would she?"

No one had a good answer.

Dyl drove fast, too fast. Only drunks would be out on the streets at this hour, a status which could include us—well not Lily. We caromed around another corner and nearly creamed a VW Beetle taxi letting its passenger out in front of a well-lit house. Dylan spun the wheel and stepped on the gas as we swerved. The Beemer miraculously hugged the road and we sped on, spinning around corners and circling blocks the closer we got to Seeger's house.

"Are we being followed?" I asked in a low voice.

"Not sure, but I wasn't taking chances. I'll loop again the other way and approach the house from the west. Dafne keeps the car in the garage so it will be out of sight."

I hung onto the armrest as we cut another turn too fast and tight. Headlights turned onto our street and came at us fast, the vehicle taking up most of the narrow car-choked pavement. "Look out! Stop!"

Dylan hooted and spun the wheel. "Not in my neighborhood," he yelled as we cut between two properties on a narrow pedestrian path. He turned down an intersecting alley and curved around a structure jutting into the cobbled roadbed and jerked to a stop.

Lily popped up from the back where she'd crouched. "Where are we?"

"Home. I'll get the door, Jade. You pull the car in. Wait in the car. I'll come get you." His tone did not invite questions or argument. I clambered over that pesky console and shifted into first.

In seconds, he'd opened the lock, loosened the chain, and swung one of the large doors wide. I aimed into the narrow space, cut the lights and the engine, and the door closed, plunging us into darkness. We held our breath. I held the gun ready.

"Lily, if something happens, I'll hold them off and you run. I've got my gun and Pepper."

A tiny voice replied, "Run where, Jade?"

"Anywhere. Away. Hide. *If* we're compromised. Come on, I saw the door. Let's get ready to bolt. Leave your door open."

I batted the overhead switch when the dome light

tripped. The bright flash was enough to find the outside door, and we tiptoed, holding the dog's collars, to wait for it to open. If it wasn't Dylan, I'd release Pepper and shoot the first in. Pepper would get the second. The third? I'd shoot again. We held our breath. The dogs kept still, sensing something was wrong.

Why didn't Dylan come? The seconds stretched into moments. The moments grew long, until Lily whispered, "What's keeping him? I'm scared."

"I am too, Lil. Shhh. He'll come."

In the darkness I heard a clock ticking away. Imagination? My arms tired from holding the gun. The garage creaked and popped as the night grew colder. City noise sounded like wind, punctuated by distant sirens. Wait! Did I hear footsteps? Yes. Two sets. I tensed and whispered, barely audible, "Keep still." I resumed shooting stance.

The door latch rattled, and rattled again. Someone grunted something too low to hear. Pepper growled. I heard Lily's breathing turn ragged. Please don't hyperventilate, Lil, I silently prayed.

Metal scraped against the lock. Why doesn't he turn on a light? The mean girl on my shoulder said, "Because its *them,* not Dylan." I shivered and mentally told her to shut up. The key scraped into the lock, it turned, the door whined on its hinge, someone stepped over the jamb. Pepper's growl deepened. The overhead light flashed on. I let Pepper go and aimed...

"Pepper! Good boy, good boy," Dylan's voice said, from behind the swinging door.

Lily shrieked, "What took you so long Dylan?" and pushed past me, barely able to contain Maya.

"Hey, hey, I had to get the key and everyone was asleep. It's one in the morning."

Seeger stepped into the garage, yawning. "Lily, Daf has your bed ready. Go on. Hurry. Hi Jade. Welcome."

"I'm so sorry, Seeger."

"Forget about it. Just come."

Dylan took my hand as Seeger flipped off the light and locked up. They led me back to the house where Dafne closed and bolted the doors behind us in the dark."

"Now, you guys, tell us what's up. The same black car has gone by twice. I thought you went to a funeral, Dylan," she said.

"Yeah, I'll leave Jade to tell the story. I have to get some sleep." He pulled me in and gave me a lingering kiss. I held on as he gently pulled away. "I've got to sleep, *moñeca.* I'll see you tomorrow night." With that he disappeared through a door and I heard water running.

"Come on, Jade, I've got a couch set up for you upstairs. You can tell me all about everything." She shined a little beam from a flashlight ahead of us to the stairs and we went up.

The room was a study with a cushy couch, now made up as a bed. Dafne poured us each a glass of *vino tinto* from a carafe and we settled down on top of the light comforter to chat, our guns in reach.

"Well, it isn't exactly how I'd have set up a date with you, but I had planned on inviting you to lunch to ask for your expertise. Dylan doesn't approve and won't ask for me. I guess I should start at the beginning so you understand." I looked at my watch. "It's a long story, are you sure you're up for it now?"

Her laugh tinkled like crystal bells. "Hell, yes! I'm off tomorrow. Go on." She clinked our glasses and I began.

The clock downstairs chimed three.

"Daf, what am I going to do if Tony Garza won't get Lily home?"

"*Oye, amiga,* it wouldn't be legal, but I have a few connections. You can never tell Dylan."

"Dylan isn't as straight-laced as you think. He told me you've got connections."

"He did, did he? I'm forced to have a word about blabbering then."

"Maybe I should have prefaced that—you can never tell Dylan I said anything..."

We giggled and clinked our glasses to sisterhood and secrets. We'd be sisters-in-law. I rolled the sound of that around my mind, producing *escalofríos* up my arms. Jumping the gun again, Jade, I warned myself.

"You could arrange to get Lily home?"

"It might be with a *coyote*, and I certainly can get a birth certificate, passport and parental permission papers forged. The passport would cost, though. I can make a call if you like."

"Would you? if the meeting doesn't go well, I have some money. I feel responsible for the girl. If I'd left them with the group they'd be home."

"It's called denial, Jade. Those girls would be Arabian concubines, addicts on the street, or the little one sold to a rich family to work until she dropped."

"But he called for a helicopter."

"And the Zetas flew in, picked up the kids, and they've never been heard from again."

"No one could be so cold." But I knew it was true. Why couldn't I accept it? "Yeah, you're right. Anibal stole the BLO cargo of kids and sold them to the Zetas. Somehow, he planned to add me to the cargo. Pulling the American girls out of the lot saved me and one of them."

"And never think you're safe. Not even when you go home. Not until you've stopped the trafficking cells. I'm here if you need me. Now go to bed or you'll be a total mess tomorrow. I'll find out what's going on at the Amores house. Night-night." She stood up, collected the bottle and our glasses, and flipped off the light.

I crawled under the comforter and conked out before my head hit the pillow. But sleep failed to refresh me. Scary dream after scarier dream plagued me. When Dafne pushed the curtains aside, flooding the room with light, I startled out of a cellar or cavern in utter darkness, where I cowered, hiding, covering someone—Lily, or was it Dylan? Protecting them from what was coming on the buzzing whine of an engine.

I shook my head to dispel the frightening sense of betrayal and abandonment clouding my vision. Where was I? I patted for my dog. Gone.

"Bad dream?" Dafne asked.

"What time is it? Where's Pepper?"

"*Medio día.* He's in the kitchen. Lily and Maya are anxious for the pups. I'll make breakfast for you while you shower in my bathroom. I can take you home to change."

"Thanks, Daf." I headed down the hall to the door she pointed out. She must be living here.

Twenty minutes later I joined Dafne and Lily in the kitchen. Coffee steamed from a full carafe, filling the air with the scent of hope. The shower had helped, too, dispelling the paralyzing yet undefined fear I'd felt after the dream.

"Good morning, Jade. I slept like a log. How about you?"

"Ah, to be young again. Lily, you look as fresh as...well, as a fresh-cut lily. Cute top." I turned to Dafne at the counter, slicing papaya. "Yours?"

"Yeah. I keep some casual clothes here for my days off."

"I've noticed the capital is pretty dressy. I took a job right out of school in the financial district of San Francisco. Between the boring office work, traffic, and crowds, and having to wear hose and heels every day, I gave it up to go back to grad school. We are super-casual at the investigations office." I snorted. "Try to get a bunch of tough investigator types to dress up. I'm lucky to keep a couple of them out of board shorts and beer tees."

"What's the matter with board shorts?" Lily wanted to know.

"What are board shorts?" Dafne asked.

Lily described the skateboard culture and Dafne recognized the garment in question. They were just "short pants" here. The kitchen clock read 12:47. "Lil, we have a two-thirty date at the embassy, eat up and Dafne will take us home to get ready."

"If we have a home," she said into her eggs, putting the kibosh on our good feelings.

"I sent one of my people by. A limo is in the yard and the gate is locked. He rang, but no one answered. It *was* seven a.m., though."

"You have people? What do you do?" Lily asked.

"I'm working at the family *bienes raices* company and apprenticing under our property management division chief. *Mami* has insisted I get a real estate license too, so I'm studying for that. I'll probably go back for an advanced degree in something—business admin or accountancy, or whatever I need to take over when *Mami* retires. I'll eventually be Chairman of the Board. Maybe a degree in brain numbing boredom? I have a little sideline, too. I've got a bit of a knack as a negotiator. I sometimes negotiate the release of hostages. Kidnapping is a big thing here. Possibly we could negotiate your freedom from the two cartels."

"No way I'd pay those scumbags a *centavo!* They don't own me. Nobody does," I said.

"Go ahead. Convince a Zeta of that. Let me know how it turns out." Dafne's tongue rolled through the sarcasm. She reminded me of my sister.

"What are you talking about?" Lily's Spanish had improved over her three weeks with us, but Daf and I spoke rapidly. I didn't really want Lily to know what we were talking about.

"I suggested we negotiate your release from the contracts that guy made. What's his name?"

"Anibal Aguirre. He's in custody. Going back to the US with a marshal to be tried for kidnapping, trafficking, and I wish, treason. It's a hangin' offence," I drawled, causing Lily to giggle and try out her own version of A*mer*cun.

"Let's go, girls, finish up." Dafne wasn't interested in our American jokes, or she didn't understand them and didn't want to.

"Lil, get Alex's dress. I need to have it dry-cleaned today. Dafne, is there somewhere nearby I can drop it for one-day service?"

"Sure, we'll stop. I'll meet you at the garage."

In daylight, nothing looked mysterious about the garage or the approach to it. The cut-through turned out to be across Seeger's lawn, but we didn't use it to leave. A narrow cobbled alley ran along the property line right to the garage. If a car had been following us, it would have been pretty easy to see us drive in. I guessed that's why we had to wait in the dark. I checked out the parked cars as we left Seeger's neighborhood. No surveillance; I relaxed a little.

"This is really nice of you, Dafne. Any more news about what's happened at our house?"

"Nope."

The guard's shift would have changed by now. Quint should have called. Horacio should have gone home—but she'd said the limo was in the drive. I looked at the passing neighborhood, fidgeting, drumming my fingers. I worried the fringe on my bag. Dafne cranked up a song on the radio and sang along.

We turned into a block of commercial establishments and Daf nosed the Beemer into a parking space. "The *tintorero,*" she said, pointing to the third storefront on the right.

Lily tossed the dress, landing it on my head. "Oops. Sorry."

I took it in and was promised the garment at four. Plenty of time to finish the meeting, get back here, pick it up and return it to Alex before their evening flight tomorrow. Making the meeting on time was the problem. "How long will it take us to get to the embassy?"

"Twenty minutes, maybe fifteen if traffic isn't bad. Who's driving?"

"Horacio, I assume." Worry nagged at me again. And became vicious as we turned onto Amores.

"Don't worry. You'll have just enough time to change and get there," she said and pulled across the driveway in front of the gate. Yes, gate closed. Yes, limo in drive. Maya sat up and barked. She'd been away from her babies too long and, although they were eating small amounts of solid food, they still nursed. Maya was full and uncomfortable.

"Do you mind waiting until we get in?"

"Not at all. But why don't you call?" She handed me her cell phone and I dialed.

Quint answered on the first ring.

"We're outside. Is everything okay?"

"Where the hell have you been? I didn't know how to reach Dylan and you didn't take your phone."

"Sorry, it was the phone or the gun in my evening bag. I had the gun."

"Then why didn't you just shoot Anibal and be done with him?"

"Right. And why did you let the dogs out last night? Hey, will you open the gate, please?"

The buzzer sounded and the latch clicked, letting us in. I waved thank you to Dafne and she sped away. We rode up to the first floor in silence and joined Quint in the kitchen.

"Where did you go?" Quint's voice sounded strained.

"Dafne's house. Were you worried? It's so cool, Quint! I've got my own room, sort of." Lily said.

"Lil. We don't have much time. Please wear a dress and look as innocent and bland as you can. We need this guy's help."

She whined, "I want to wear what I have on."

"Don't start. Just change. I'll race you up."

She tore off with me losing ground behind her. I shouted over my shoulder, "Feed the dogs, please."

We had forty-two minutes to make it to Tony Garza's office.

Chapter 9

Embassy: to assist American citizens who travel to or live in the host country

We joined the men in the kitchen five minutes later. Lily had on a pastel plaid dress that qualified as dorky. I wore a patriotic navy and white sundress with a sailor collar and a red tie with white flats. I also qualified as dorky. Lily carried a patent pastel-pink envelope clutch, and I wore a white shoulder bag with a silver chain. Ugly. Perfect. Inside I had my passport and tourist papers. Lily had nothing.

"Let's go," Horacio said. "We'll fill you in on the way."

He'd turned the car around and opened the gate. At the driveway, we found two guards with big guns on duty. Horacio helped us into the backseat while Quint settled in front. The guards saluted as we drove off.

"So? What was up with the open gate and no guards?" I asked.

"I thought it might be a trap when Beltrán left with young Aguirre. I told Dylan to take you somewhere if the gate and limo doors stood open. Thank him for me."

"So you weren't actually worried."

"We had more on our hands. BLO operatives picked us up outside the wake and followed us home. They didn't realize you were behind us. When we pulled into the drive, two tried to rush us. I didn't recognize the men, but they've gone to meet their makers. You didn't see guards because we were hauling the bodies out of sight until I could make arrangements. I heard their car peel out."

"What kind of car?" I asked.

"Non-descript color. Sedan."

"It followed us. We ditched it. Dylan's smart."

"Yeah. He's one of the good ones," Quint agreed.

"You keep saying that."

"What did the men want?" Lily asked.

"They didn't have time to say."

"Have you made arrangements?"

"Yeah. And I've arranged a safe place to live, too."

"We're moving?" Lily sounded alarmed. "With the dogs?"

"With the dogs. I'm fairly confident we'll be left alone tonight. They'll know we have their men and extra guards. I doubt they'll risk anything so soon. But they'll be back. It ain't over 'til it's over."

"We could go back with Dafne and Seeger," Lily suggested.

"Honey, you don't want to jeopardize them. There's an apartment above the offices the senator deeded to me. We'll go home after the meeting, pack up our stuff—and the dogs—and move," he said.

Horacio circled through the Insurgentes *glorieta* onto westbound Reforma. In a couple of long blocks we turned right into Colonia Cuautémoc and zigzagged a few narrow streets before arriving at the embassy's back door. I'd walked around in the neighborhood before and recognized where we were—America. The property may have been surrounded by fading jacarandas, but no mistaking the marines' uniforms and the massive American flag. Horacio held the door while we climbed out, and a handsome marine whisked us into the building.

Another marine led us through the maze of halls to reach Garza's well-appointed office in the southwest corner on an upper floor. I wasn't sure how many flights we'd climbed, but the view up Reforma into the *Angél de la Independencia* monument, gold gleaming in the bright sun over Garza's shoulder made me shiver. The Greek God of Victory gave me hope we hadn't come on *Mission Impossible*—your mission if you choose to accept it, Jade...

The ambassador cradled the receiver of his phone and stood up, gesturing to a row of seats placed in a semicircle around the desk. "Welcome Mr. Quint. Miss Quint. Miss Flynn. Our other guests are on their way. Please be seated."

"Thank you for seeing us on Sunday, Ambassador." I reached across the desk. He took my hand in his and gave it a warm shake. "Your view is impressive, sir. Inspiring," I concluded and sat down.

He smiled. "People are often too intimidated to comment. It's magnificent, isn't it?" We all gazed at the statue.

The door opened and Rosi Orozco and Sami Rafiq joined us. I introduced Sami. Rosi and Garza had known each other for years, we learned in the brief round of small talk.

"Shall we get started?" Garza asked.

"Yes, thank you. As you know we have a problem of an American citizen unable to return home due to a lack of papers. The problem is complicated by additional factors I would like to detail for you."

Garza nodded and he said, "Go on."

I recapped the conversation with Rosi the day before and

concluded by saying, "Lily needs a stable, loving home and proper medical support. Living here, we have had our house attacked twice. Once by the Zetas and just last night by the BLO, trying to kidnap us. We fear for our freedom and our very lives. Please help us. Fly Lily home."

I sat down. The only sound was the water pouring into my glass as I filled it.

Rosi spoke first. "This could be a story with a happy ending, Tony. Hasn't this little girl lost enough? She's the American citizen you've sworn to protect. It's why you're here, isn't it?"

Garza rubbed his chin, a quizzical look on his face. "This is a wild story. Unfortunately, as I've told Senator Aguirre, I'm not sure what I can do. I can't issue a passport without identification. Did you look at the throngs lined up outside? They all want passports or green cards or permission to enter the U.S. I can't let everyone in, regardless of their stories."

"But I'm an American. Ask me who's president. Ask me who won the Super Bowl. Ask me where I go to school. You can check that. I want to go home!" Lily shouted, bursting into sobs that wracked her thin frame.

Rosi was up and holding her in a flash, patting and crooning until the girl quieted. Garza's face burned red. I practically could feel the heat.

"And what about you, Miss Quint? Why are you staying in Mexico if you are in danger?"

"I made a promise to this girl I'd see her home and stop the human trafficking ring plaguing this city."

"That's a large undertaking better left to law enforcement, I'd say," Garza rejoined.

"Tony, don't patronize her. JadeAnne is doing what any compassionate and concerned citizen would do. You have the capacity to arrange Lily's transport back to her aunt. Don't I recall you have family in that part of the world? Your grandmother? Go visit her and take Lily home."

"Rosi, I don't know. It's the same problem. I fly commercial. I'm not sure how I would get her through customs without a passport or birth certificate and a letter from her parent or guardian."

"For God's sake, I'll write a letter assigning you as guardian and—" I looked at Lily, grinning— "I bet you are pretty good forging your mother's signature. You can sign her name."

Lily put on a sheepish grin. "I did it all the time. I signed her checks to buy food when she was too drunk to go shopping. I can write the letter in her handwriting. I wrote all my excuses for missing school. Evie's too."

"Look, Ambassador, why doesn't she write a letter requesting a new birth certificate right now and you expedite it through channels? Have them fax it to you. We can't wait much longer. We're being forced to move again because the cartels know where we live. We can't go on living with this fear—literally."

"My job is to uphold laws, not break them, Miss Quint."

Rosi interrupted, her voice harsh. "Your job is to assist American citizens who travel to or live in the host country. These citizens need help. What if it had been your daughters trafficked to Mexico? This girl *is* your daughter. And that poor family hasn't been able to bury their child because she's held here in the morgue until she has authorization to be shipped back. Miss Flynn will accompany her little sister's coffin, with your say-so. Tony, it's your responsibility to get these girls out of danger. It's too late for ten-year-old Evie."

Garza's face fell. Rosi sure had the knack for guilt tripping the ambassador. No one in the room maintained a dry eye, especially Tony Garza. I wondered if they had something going on; she knew all his triggers.

He picked up the phone and punched a button. "Mrs. Tomsky, please bring me a ballpoint and a legal pad." He clapped the receiver into its cradle and sat back in his leather chair.

The secretary appeared with several pens and pads, placed them on a writing table near the door, and left. She was a real throwback to the sixties in a pencil skirt, tight cashmere sweater, and French twist. I pegged her at about retirement age. She'd probably been a secretary since she went to work and never changed her style, I thought as Garza typed at his keyboard. Government work was one of my mother's suggestions. "They pay well, you always have a job and the retirement package is good." And you can wear the same outfit every day for forty-five years.

"Lily, there is a pad and a pen. Please copy this, sign and date it, then put it in the envelope with my name on it. Give it to Rosi who will slip it in the mail." He printed the letter and handed it over to Quint who passed it to Lily. Lily went to the table and started copying. My heart beat a little happy dance. We were going to get Lily back to the U.S.

"You'll need to hang on for a couple more weeks. I have to get the birth certificate then issue the passport. Once that is done, I'll be in touch with you, Mr. Quint, and we'll make arrangements to get her on a military flight to Denver. Please leave your contact information with my secretary."

"Thanks so much, Ambassador. Now all we need to do is stay vigilant and safe for the next two weeks and maybe we can all go home." I stood up and reached out to shake his hand once again, thinking I should feel elated. Why did I feel like the other shoe was about to drop?

Chapter 10

Moving Up In the World

"I'm going home!" Lily sang as she skipped through the maze of halls and stairs to the back door of the embassy. I wanted to caution her. Garza was under pressure from us and especially Rosi Orozco, but a million things could happen between now and whenever the birth certificate arrived. If it arrived. Yet I couldn't smother her joy. Lily acted happier than I'd ever seen her. I couldn't help but say a little prayer that the Universe would, just this once, move to send this girl, her dead sister and six dogs home.

The marine escort held the door open into the yard where the limo waited. "Congratulations, Miss. Happy trails to you. Have a safe journey home," he said, with a friendly salute.

Quint, Lily, and I returned it and climbed into the car.

"We've got a quick stop to make on our way home," Quint said, and read an address from the back of an envelope to Horacio.

I knew Colonia Roma was an older district located on

the east side of Insurgentes more or less opposite Condesa and Zona Rosa. I'd read it was built up during the late 19th century to about 1939. Much of it was Beaux Arts, or *Bellas Artes* in Spanish.

Horacio turned the corner in front of a small park and found a parking space. We were on a narrow treelined block of Calle Tabasco before it ran into Jardín Pushkin. Named for a Russian author, I liked it already.

We piled out and followed Quint down the block of mostly two-story apartment buildings with offices and small businesses on the ground floor. Each was a different faded color, and I guessed were built in the twenties and thirties, Ours sat at the end of the block, a charming, if somewhat decrepit, pink art deco edifice with several businesses on the ground floor. The corner space looked empty and Quint directed us to the door, jangling an old-fashioned ring of keys, sifting through until he found the one that let us into what might easily become a reception area for a suite of offices. Everything was rather organic. No sharp angles, instead rounded corners and squat, hobbit-y doors. Marble floors. I'd give those up in a heartbeat. Too cold.

The suite contained moderate-sized office spaces with built-in cabinets overlooking a walled garden, an interior work room off the reception hall, a lovely tiled bathroom, an interior room with the familiar wiring for technology and a storage/receiving area jutting off the back abutting the alley.

Off the reception area double hobbit doors opened to a wide staircase leading up to the flat. Hardwood floors, wool carpeting, stylish brightly colored furniture that proved to be super comfortable, four bedrooms, two of which overlooked the walled garden. All the windows had wrought iron grills and little window boxes with flowers blooming. Each bedroom had a full bath with deep claw footed tubs, pedestal sinks, and bidets. And the tiles!

"I call dibs on this corner room," I yelled, and flung

myself on the cushy bed, inhaling the flowery scent of Polo's laundry detergent. Susanna had washed everything.

From down the hall, I heard Lily squeal in delight. "This one's mine!"

I trotted over. Lily twirled in the middle of a bright, soft lavender and cream room with a narrow view of the park and the trees along the street. Like mine, it had lovely moldings and deco style ironwork. Her bath was green and silver, where mine was blue and gold. Everything gleamed clean and tasteful.

"Who do you suppose lived here?" Lily asked.

"Dunno. Ask Horacio. I bet it was the senator's girlfriend or his mistress," I said.

"That's a good one. Who'd be interested in that old guy?"

"Girls! You pick your rooms? I found mine."

We followed Quint's voice to a deep room divided into a bedroom and a porch or office overlooking the interior garden. Again, it was situated to catch the daylight and felt open and airy. It had the feel of my grandmother's bedroom and porch. It would be perfect. Quint's bath was brown and gold.

"We really get to live here?"

"We really do, at least until your papers are ready."

"Quint, where do I park the combi?"

"We'll look at the garden next. We have to go through the kitchen to get there like in our current house. I think there's laundry downstairs."

"You know what I like about this place?" Lily said.

"What," Quint responded.

"There's no red."

I laughed. "I so agree! Let's check out the kitchen and the yard. It's fenced, right?"

"Yes, with electronic gates."

"Do the other tenants get to use it? Do you get the

rents?"

"I don't really know what the deal is. I have a meeting with Castillo y Iglesias tomorrow then I'll help Chucho dismantle my office and move it. He's at Amores now working on it."

"Chucho! Is he coming here?" Lily's face lit up.

"Too old for you, kid. He's a college man." Quint said.

"Oh, he's that old? Well, he's cute anyway."

The kitchen wasn't anything like the Amores kitchen. It had a high end espresso maker and a range oven combo to die for. I might consider cooking. I'd have to. Mrs. P wouldn't be coming as far as I knew. How would we pay her? "Take a look at this kitchen."

"Look, someone's even put flowers on the table for us," Lily said.

I frowned at Quint and he beamed. "Susana. And check it out." He opened the refrigerator to display an interior packed with fresh food, condiments, beer and sodas.

I recognized a couple of containers of leftovers from Amores. "When did she do this?"

"While we met with Garza. We can grab our things and the dogs and sleep here tonight. I saw a pizza joint as we drove in. Sound good, ladies?"

"Yes! Pizza!" Lily flew over the moon at the mention of pepperoni.

"Shouldn't we check out the garden before we commit to moving in? What if we can't let the dogs out?"

"We can do whatever we want, Jade, but let's go." He stepped to the stairs door and held it open. This set of stairs had been carpeted in indoor/outdoor carpeting. We wouldn't be listening to the pack thunder up and down. Nor would we hear intruders. I shivered. This place was darling, quaint, and beautifully appointed. But it didn't come with the same security as Amores. I trudged down behind Quint and Lily, pondering the issues we'd need to address to safely live here.

Lots of windows facing the street and back alley. Climbable trees planted next to the building. A service area accessible through several other tenants' businesses, although our space actually had a small walled-off section that might be secure if we took precautions.

The garden beckoned to me. Everything had been recently painted. The decorative moldings, tiles and furniture combined the brown with stark white, turquoise and cobalt. In the center of a tiled starburst, a fountain splashed into its bowl. Urns and many-sized Talavera pots brimming with plants and several well-pruned lime trees, a pomegranate, and a row of grapes hung with fruit.

Plantings of geraniums, chrysanthemums, roses and plenty of flowering shrubs and succulents, lined the ivy-covered walls topped by glass, pikes, and razor wire, most of which entwined with the vines, making it hard to see. It was also capped with an overhang of razor wire and barbed wire on the outside.

"It's the Garden of Eden," I said. "Except for the razor wire." Whoever built this was as security conscious as we needed to be.

"Ain't it though. I thought you'd like this. I think there's enough room for the dogs," Quint said, tipping his head toward the rectangle of grass running from the garden door the length of the house. "And you've got the park across the street. Maybe you'll think of settling in after the mission is complete."

"Stay in Mexico?"

"What do you have in California?" Quint asked, linking arms with me to promenade through our new yard.

"Well, everything, Quint. My home. The Sarasvati. My orchids. My business. And my parents, I suppose." I looked up at him and caught a cloud of sadness pass across his face. I couldn't see his eyes through his aviator glasses, but I realized what I'd find if I could. Quint truly cared for me. He didn't want to lose me. My heart swelled. "You know, Dad, it's not a bad idea. Let's see how things go with our mission and...Dylan."

"He's a good man, Jade."

"He is. But once my Worthington money is gone, how are we going to live? Didn't you lose your income with Polo's death? Like the rest of the crowd?"

"I have contacts and Aguirre's endowment. There's a lot going on here. My services may be of use to paying clients. Aguirre and I had talked about it. Why do you think he set me up?"

"I'd wondered—at least fleetingly. I haven't had a whole lot of time to sort out what's happened."

"Nah, me neither. It's coming down fast. My intuition says something's going to blow. We need to be ready."

"Funny you'd say that. I had a tarot reading in the plaza and the gypsy said the same thing."

"You believe that crap?"

"Sure, why not. I'm a crazy Californian," I said, repeating what I told Dylan the other day.

"Actually, you're Vietnamese/American, but I'd bet Charlie made sure you didn't grow up with that."

"You'd win that one. Sometime I'll tell you what life at the Stone residence was like. Now, let's go back to Amores and pack up. It will be better to move during daylight, don't you think?"

Quint checked the time. "Yeah. Lily," he called, "let's go back to Amores and get your dogs."

"Sweet!" came from the other side of the walled yard.

I hoped the guards were still on duty.

Chapter 11

Leaving the Cathouse

The dogs barked and wagged and bounced, joyously greeting us as though we'd been gone for weeks, not hours. I didn't think they liked the Amores house. Bad vibes. Pepper sniffed me all over, taking in the smells of Colonia Roma. To Lily's delight, the puppies knocked down their barrier and joined the fray.

"You know, Lil, they're about old enough to give away. A couple more weeks. What do you plan on doing with them?" I asked.

Her shoulders slumped and she pursed her lips, but declared, "Mrs. P wants Cider," and pointed to a light blonde female. "Dafne said she'd like a puppy too. Seeg isn't so sure, but couldn't we take them over tomorrow and he'll want one as soon as he meets them. I just know it."

"It doesn't matter. Dafne gets what she wants. It would make a great wedding gift. We'll get all their shots and finish weaning them. Everyone can come and choose theirs. Are you sure Mrs. P wants a dog—a big dog?"

"Oh, yes. She fell in love with Cider ages ago. Haven't you seen her cuddling her? She's always feeding her treats. It's why she's so fat."

We'd pulled a prepared snack out of the fridge. I silently blessed Susana as we sat around the table eating the sandwiches, talking and enjoying the antics of the goldens. I didn't really know their names, but Lily could tell them apart and they were learning to come when she called.

Cider was not the runt, but lightest in color and a chubby compact size. Her feet weren't huge like Jack's. He was the largest and most aggressive of the litter, often shoving the others, especially little Cookie, the real runt, away from the teats. Sadie's coat was reddish and her body lean and lanky. She had an adorable "come hither" expression I found a little too irresistible. Sexy Sadie. Wouldn't Pepper like a playmate? And then the twins—Roli and Poli. Absolutely identical males, perfect show dog heads, silky curly-haired ears, rich golden yellow coats, sweet, rough and tumble dispositions. Lily could tell them apart. They needed to go as a pair.

With and evil grin, Lily asked, "Which one do you want, Quint? If you want Roli you'll have to take Poli too. I wanted to give the twins to Polo, so I named one after him."

"How do you tell them apart?"

"Poli acts more like a senator," she said, squelching a giggle.

"Boring?" I joked.

"Don't speak ill of the dead, Jade."

I snorted. "So Quint, which pup do you want?"

"I'd hoped to change the subject."

"You don't want one? What about you, Horacio? Wouldn't your kids like a dog?" Lily asked.

Kids? I realized I knew almost nothing about Shrek 1. He popped another Dos Equis and chugged half of it. "*Sí*. My Gloria has been after me to get her a dog. I think Cookie will be the right size for our family—see, she's not going to get so big." He's bent down and scooped her up, waving her little paw at us. She squirmed in his hand to reach his face and started madly licking him.

"Ah, she loves you Horacio." I said. "What about your brothers, would one of them like the twins?"

"Sami is allergic to dander. Omar has cats."

Lily, voice serious, said, "Quint. You have to take Jack."

"Why Jack?"

"Because I'm keeping Roli and Poli." The pair tussled under her chair and she pulled them by the scruff into her lap and gave them big kisses. I realized the two she always had under her arms were these. If she could get three dogs back to the states, I'd be flabbergasted. Garza wasn't hot on transporting Lily and the coffin. Rosi Orozco was going to have a bit of cajoling to do for the dogs.

"Okay gang, it's time to go upstairs and pack your things. Susana left some boxes and duffels in the hall. Grab what you need and start packing. Horacio, can I get you to pack up the dog food, bedding, and what not?" Quint asked.

"Okay *jefe*. Shall I put the dogs in the car?"

"Not yet. Lily, once your things are down in the entry, take the dogs out. We don't want any accidents in the sen—I mean Horacio's limo. Jade, can you check the laundry and see if any of our stuff is still there? You'll need to move your bus, but I think it will be better to let one of the Rafiq brothers or Chucho bring it over. In fact, I think we should move it to a garage for servicing and safe keeping. What do you think, H?" Quint asked.

"Yes, it needs to disappear," Horacio said.

My gut clenched. "You really think we could have problems? Anibal was arrested. Anyway, every time he came near us he got into trouble." I sniggered. "You'd think he'd have learned."

"You would. But your buddy was taken out of a funeral

party by a member of a powerful organized crime family, not arrested," Quint said.

Lily shrieked, fear clouding her face. "What? I thought —"

"I didn't want to alarm the gathering, but the marshal was killed."

Tremors gripped me. My nemesis at large? In a shaky voice, I said, "Well, he's in deeper shit with them than he ever would be with us, Quint." I laid my hand on his arm, my eyes boring into his. "Anibal stole a cargo of kids from the BLO and transferred them to Los Zetas. There can only be one of two outcomes: the BLO had sold the lot and didn't deliver or the group was for sale and they didn't receive anything. How much do you think twenty kids would net? Anyway, from what I've heard, the kind of people who traffic in humans, drugs, arms, or whatever, don't turn the other cheek. Anibal has more trouble with the cartels than us —or the U.S."

"*Él sería desperado.* Desperate men do desperate things. We are not safe from him or either organization, *señorita* Jade," Horacio pointed out.

"I see your argument, Horacio. But won't you just call me Jade?"

"Claro, *señorita*...Jade."

"He's right. And our new digs won't be as fortified as these. However, one thing we'll have going for us is close neighbors. I want you girls to get to know people as soon as we arrive. The rest of the crew and I will be setting up an office."

"What kind of office are we doing?" Lily asked.

"I don't think you 'do' an office Lil," I said using air quotes.

"So, what, then?"

"Listen, we have more important things to *do* than argue grammar. Let's get busy packing."

I stood up to refresh my coffee, and saluted. "Yessir, sir"

"That's better," he said.

"Lil, you want anything?"

"Another Coke."

I grabbed it out of the fridge with the cream, slopped a tot in my coffee and popped the cap off the Coke, handing it to her as she got up from the table.

"See you boys soon."

Quint's head swung up from the notes he jotted. "Hmm? Yeah. Don't take too long."

The news changed everything. Were three groups after us? Who was Anibal working with? I grabbed a duffle and a shopping bag as did Lily and our wagon train scaled the mountain to our rooms. The pups could manage the stairs now, albeit slowly. Maya took the rear, nudging them along, especially Cookie. Pepper arrived on the second floor first as usual and sprinted to our room. He already had my running shoes and the leash by the door when I entered.

"Good boy," I crooned.

Pepper did a little did-I-hear-we're-going-for-a-walk dance but dropped to the floor with a disgusted sigh when he realized we were not. My dog read me like an open book.

"Sorry, boy."

I didn't have much to pack. I tipped the dresser drawers into the duffle. Lotion, brush, bag of jewelry, I placed into the shopping bag. I tossed a dirty towel on top of the stuff in the duffle and threw in my shoes then cleared my personal stuff from the bathroom into a kitbag. We'd need the towels I guessed, so I packed them and the terry robe Quint had bought. I grabbed a couple of books and magazines from the sitting room.

My datebook...where was that? I searched around finally discovering it under the slipper chair with a dried up ball point pen. Finally, I got my suitcase down from the shelf and packed my hanging clothes then made a final scan of my suite, checking under the bed, chairs, behind the shelves and doors. What a slob. I found shoelaces, underwear, my Glock, and my pajamas under the furniture. By the old fashioned phone, a pile of notes, numbers and cryptic messages I could no longer decipher scattered across the table. I stuffed everything into my tote and made one last pass around the room and closet. I stripped the bed and carried the bedding to the elevator, yelling to Lily to do the same.

"Are you done?" I asked, poking my head through her door.

Jack and the twins had a three-way tug of war going with a blanket, and Lily, bum up in the closet, dumped stuff into a box. I grabbed the rest of the bedding and lugged it to the elevator, returning for dirty towels. The clean towels I packed into another bag with some of the trinkets and stuffies she'd acquired since I rescued her. We worked in silence until I realized she was crying.

"What's the matter Lil?"

"I miss Mrs. P. I want her to come."

Ah—something we hadn't anticipated. Our untrustworthy housekeeper had cared for the girl, had been her rock in the midst of a nightmare. I had an inkling of how Lily must feel for *Señora* Pérez. The former nurse had been a comfort to me too, after we'd found the trafficked children and I'd been shot. And poor Lily ached for her mother—the mother who was never there for her. I got it. My story was different, but I was a motherless child too. I wasn't physically abused by anyone, and I didn't need to protect a younger sister, but I'd been ignored, neglected and criticized by my mother. She was too busy with her clubs, charities, and tennis, her luncheons and theater. She was too busy popping Valium and sipping martinis. Once Brittany was born, my mother was too busy molding her into a *mini-me* to actually offer me any mothering. I squatted and gently pulled the girl out of her closet, enfolding her into my arms.

"I know, I know, Lily. She's been so kind to you. Maybe we can talk to Quint to see if she can come in and help us. Would that make you feel better?" She nodded. "Meanwhile, won't I do?"

She clung to me and mumbled "Uh-huh" into my neck, sputtering and jerking with sobs like aftershocks. I held her, stroking her hair and murmuring soothing sounds. I needed this as much as she did. I'd had my ex, Dexter Truette, to hold me, protect me, for so long I'd lost my ability, won through a childhood of loneliness and selfcare, to tamp my fear and bolster my own strength. She was only fifteen. I'd have to be a rock for both of us. A smart rock. We were so not out of danger.

"Jade," she said, squirming out of my embrace and pushing Maya away, "are you already done?" I nodded. "Can you help me finish getting my stuff?"

"Of course, it's why I came in," I said and smiled into her beautiful brown eyes. "Let's go." I pushed into the closet and started pulling clothes out. Where did all this shit come from? "Lil, I'll pull things out, you fold and box. Hand me that other box and I'll put shoes and your, um, your stuff in it." I held up a gnawed barbie doll with most of her red hair chewed off. We laughed.

"Puppy toys. I found a box of dolls and stuffies in the back of the closet. The puppies like destroying them."

"Yeah, I'll bet they do. You haven't let them chew shoes, have you?" I asked as I pulled a ruined tennis shoe off the closet floor. "Not good, Lily. You have to punish them if they take shoes. If you don't, no one in the house will have a full pair in a few weeks. They're old enough for gentle training and in a couple weeks, real training."

"How will I give them away?" Her voice sounded alarmed and as sad as a Christmas tree in February.

"I know." I blew out an Eeyore sized sigh and tossed two

more shoes into the box. Both chewed. "But think of it this way, you're giving the dogs to people you love and they will grow up to offer Mrs. P, Dafne...me, the same comfort in trying times. Paying it forward as it were."

She brightened, an angelic curve spreading across her lips into her eyes. "I like that. Yes. I hadn't thought about it that way. I guess I can do it."

A shout echoed up the stairwell and manifested itself into Quint's voice. "Aren't you ladies done yet? We need to get going."

I climbed to my feet with the filled box and walked it to the elevator, depositing it with my things. At the stairs door, I leaned in and yelled, "Almost done with Lily's packing. You can bring down the elevator for all my stuff."

I heard the door clang shut and the elevator start its descent. "Okay, let's get it done before Quint has a cow."

"Mom used to always say that. Before...before..."

"Work, Lil. I tossed a duffle at her." She caught it and started dumping in the contents of her drawers. I cleared the rest of the closet and bathroom. Really, there wasn't much stuff, mostly just doggie things.

"Done?" Quint stood in the doorway.

"One more pass through to see if we missed anything," I said. "You and Lily can take those." I pointed to a box and the duffel. "I'll check and carry this last one. You've got all the pups, right?"

"Yeah. Come Maya, let's go for a ride," he said. Maya hopped off the bed grinning, tail fanning the air. After food, she loved the car. Lily followed them lugging a box.

The elevator door closed again, leaving me alone in the cathouse. I looked under and around everything and found a few more chewed toys, a sock, Lily's notebook, two paperback romances in English in the bedside table and a huge well-chewed bone under the radiator. Yuck. The irony of the cathouse filled with dogs didn't escape me. I grabbed the last box, bone and all, and actually skipped to the elevator. This house held no nostalgia for me. Good riddance. We were off to brighter digs and happier days. I hoped.

Chapter 12

No Cook, but the Kitchen is a Dream

The atmosphere in the limo popped with excitement. Quint and Horacio cracked jokes and Lily giggled, our apprehension over Anibal forgotten for the moment. The big dogs wagged and the pups jumped around excitedly as we backed out of the driveway. Lily leaned over the front seat and dialed the radio to a top 40 station, Mexican style. I shoved Pepper from the door saying, "Move Peppi!" then signaled him to *stay* as I hopped out to close the gate for the last time. From habit, I looked up and down Amores. Shit! A black SUV idled along the curb several doors down. I couldn't see who was in it, but Quint and Horacio were right to worry. I jumped back into the limo, slamming the door.

"Watch the doors, Jade. Ya don't want to wreck H's new car."

"No, but I don't want to get caught by our stalkers, either."

"*¿Qué pasó?*" Horacio asked.

"They're here, watching us, three doors down," I

responded in Spanish.

"What's here?" Lily asked.

Quint's Spanish had improved since I'd met him. If I spoke slowly, he often got the gist. He craned around to look behind us. "We're always in danger, Lily. Never forget that. Until we get you safely home, you need to be looking over your shoulder," he said.

She spun around and peered out the rear window. "I don't see anything. Oh, wait. A black car just pulled out. It's them, isn't it?" she stated, bottom lip trembling, the exuberant air of moments before expelled.

"Don't cry. It could be anyone," I said with more conviction than I felt, irritated Quint had worried her. "Hey, you guys, anyone else ready for pizza?" That should change the tone of things. Maya woofed. Everyone laughed, but I could see Horacio and Quint watching through the side mirrors. Interesting watching them communicate silently. I held myself back from turning around. We cruised sedately to the light. It turned yellow and Horacio floored it, swerving through a left turn. Left? Why not right to Insurgentes? I snuck a glance as we rounded the corner. The SUV was stopped at the light. That's why.

A tune Lily liked came on the radio and she leaned over the seat again to crank it up. She belted out the lyrics in perfect, accent-less Spanish. When had she learned pop tunes? We cruised for several blocks and made another left. Horacio knew his *colonia* and circled, turned, cruised a couple of *callejones* and the next thing I knew, we were passing Parque de Mexico in Condesa. We'd ditched the SUV. But I knew better than to relax. If they knew where we were going, they'd be there ahead of us.

"*¿Horacio, tú piensas ellos saben donde vamos?*" I asked him.

Quint answered in English. "Not if they're watching the Amores house."

Lily's face tightened and dropped, hair masking her expression. "You're scaring me."

"Yeah, Quint. Stop with the non-answers. We were having so much fun before. Whoever *they* are, we lost them and they don't know where we're going. Hey, turn that one up for me! I love Thalia." I sang along. "*Da da da-den te, tengo sudor en la frente!*"

Lily joined me as we shouted out the words and backseat danced, rocking the tail end of the car. The puppies loved it. By the end of *Sudor, Sweat*, an oldie from the 90s, we'd blown through the *glorieta* circling Metro stop Insurgentes, and spun out the other side into the east section of Zona Rosa. I remembered it from another trip. The American library, Bilioteca Benjamin Franklin—an oasis in a foreign land.

"Look, Lily! There's the library. It's all English. We can go get books. Hey, I brought your romances. You like that genre?"

"I like sci-fi better, you know, like Star Wars."

"But you like reading?"

"Uh-huh. I can get away from all the bad stuff in my life in a good book. Can we go there tomorrow?"

"Maybe. Let's see how the move goes," I said, thinking, *let's see if we've ditched the cartels.*

Horacio turned again into a neighborhood I'd never seen. We twisted around blocks and plazas, and I was sure I caught a glimpse of the *glorieta* again, but he turned along a park and swooped to a stop in front of our new home. How did he do that?

"We're home, girls," Quint sang out. "Quick now, get the dogs in Lily. Jade, help us unload." He handed Lily the keys. "H, before we get out, check the street, would you?"

"*Claro, jefe.*" he replied and got out. He crossed the street, disappeared around the corner and trotted back, scanning in the other direction. Leaning back into the car, he said, "I don't see anything, boss."

Quint and I jumped out and hurried around the limo, grabbing as much as we could carry from the trunk. Lily struggled at the entry to unlock the door balancing squirming pups. I ran up, turned the key in the lock; the door swung open. Pepper and Maya rushed in, sniffing the new surroundings. Lily put the pups down in the entry and jogged back to the car for the rest while Quint and Horacio lugged duffels and boxes to the door. I collected the load, moving our worldly goods to the stairs. Sadie ran along with me, biting at my pants hem. Jack left a puddle in the middle of the floor.

"I'm going to find the mop," I yelled to anyone in range and started opening doors. In the storage room I found a cleaning closet with all the usual supplies and wheeled the mop bucket and mop over to a utility sink I hadn't noticed earlier. I was beginning to appreciate the marble floors—easy cleanup.

Quint loaded up and took off through the stairs doors. The stairs were dark. I found the light switches, flipping them on. The empty building echoed as the dogs' nails scrabbled over the tile and our shoes clacked and clopped. I put the mop and bucket back in the closet and hustled to help with the hauling. Quint returned from the limo with another load, this time food. I grabbed half and we trudged up to the apartment. One benefit of all the stairs I'd lived with lately, my thighs and rear had become powerhouses of energy. However, I noticed my appetite had also increased. I hoped I hadn't gained weight, and promised myself I'd stop eating the daily *pan dulces* I unloaded into the cupboard.

"That's it, Jade," Quint said as he lowered two final bags to the table. "I'll leave you to it and get us a pizza. H is parking the limo in back. He'll have a slice and go home. He says he'll leave the limo visible near his house for a while in case anyone is looking."

"Good thinking. Do you think we're okay here? Will we have any guards?"

"I dunno. I don't trust Bendicias and it'll take some doing to get the embassy to loan out the marines."

"Shucks, Dad, that guy who escorted us was pretty cute."

"Already throwing over the good doctor?"

"Not on a bet. I was thinking of Lily. He looked about sixteen. Anyway, our girl will be happily back in Colorado at school with all those cute skiers by first snowfall. She told me she liked to ski."

"Jade, don't count on the marines. What we're asking is way outside the scope of Garza's job. Transporting the coffin to Colorado has its challenges, but is probably easier than sending the girl back. Forget the dogs. Actually, the dogs only need a certificate of vaccinations. Rabies, mainly."

"Don't even go there, Quint. We can't let this girl down. Meanwhile, Rosi wants her to see a counselor. She's been through major trauma."

"I am aware. I've spent many nights sitting with her when she's awakened from nightmares screaming. She doesn't really remember them, or won't say, but I'm guessing they violated her every way to Sunday. It's part of the breaking in they do to destroy their self-esteem and will to fight back. Lily was lucky she wasn't started on heroin by the time we found her. I don't recall bruises or black eyes. Had she been beaten?"

"Slapped, shoved. I got them before the real training started. Her bruises are where we can't see. I remember noticing some bruising on both their thighs when I found them."

"That little one?"

"Lily said she tried to protect her," I said, voice low. A bolt of pure hatred zinged through me. Wolves. Sharks. Hyenas. And they were still after us. Would we ever be safe?

"Rosi is right. Can I leave it to you?"

"You know, Dad, Lily really misses Mrs. P. Maybe we should keep her on."

"Are you kidding me, Jade? Yesterday you wanted her behind bars."

"Lily is attached to her. Maybe she can take the fourth bedroom and stay in the apartment until Lily is on the plane. Cut her a deal. No outside communication until Lily is gone. Offer her 20 or 30% more than she's getting now. Or offer to help get the Amores house readied for whatever she wants to do with it. She's grateful for the protection you've provided to her family."

"We can't protect them forever, Jade. But maybe you're right. Let me consider it."

"If it helps sway your thinking, Mrs. P is a *waaay* better cook than I am." I grinned, although I was advocating to bring a potential enemy into our camp. "Now let me put this stuff away and set the table. The beer is going to get warm," I said pulling two six-packs from the bottom of the box I'd been unloading.

I mulled over the conundrum of Mrs. P as I stowed the groceries. She no longer would be reporting to Lidia Buendía, but her connection to the BLO worried me. Yes, we'd proved she'd been threatened with the death of her only living relatives, but what was her loyalty to Lidia? A job? No one was *that* loyal to an employer. And after all, she, *Señora* Pérez, was the one who had rescued Lidia from the rubble after the earthquake. It was Lidia who owed loyalty—and paid it through the bequest.

That Lidia and Mrs. P had bonded was no secret. Someone must know the entire story. Probably Polo. And now he was gone too. A tsunami of grief crashed over me and I had to sit down for a moment or three before continuing on with the kitchen. Maybe I'd have a Cuba Libre when I finished—with ice. I needed it.

Sounds of Mexican radio filtered into the room from the hallway. I hoped the neighbors didn't mind. I tore a section of paper towel off the roll, honked a few times and wiped my eyes then installed the roll onto the holder.

I pictured Mrs. P in Anibal's Condesa kitchen and in the Amores kitchen, considering where she'd kept things. Efficiency and organization—the key to good cooking. A glass-fronted cabinet next to the stove seemed the logical place for herbs and spices, coffee, tea, and chocolate. The fancy espresso maker sat on the counter next to the cooktop. It would work. The kitchen and pantry came fully equipped, so all I had to do was set the space up to my liking. The Sarasvati had a deep cabinet-style pantry I loved and used. If we stayed here, I'd be set to become a domestic goddess, preparing amazing gourmet meals for Dylan and our friends —yikes! where did that come from?

I had a job to complete; I couldn't fantasize about Dylan. I didn't even know if I'd live through what had to be done. Anyway, it was the rushing into relationships that had messed me up. Take Anibal, for example. Sure he was cute and sexy, but what a disaster! Even Dex and I'd gotten together in a torrid whirlwind, moving in and setting up shop before we'd really gotten to know one another. Sure, sure we'd been together longer than many marriages. Although we enjoyed each other's company, we didn't really want the same things. My stomach lurched with shame at the truth. I made him look good; he made me a good daddy. And we made a good business team. Well, I didn't need a daddy anymore, and I'd been gone so long I'd probably lost my interest in the business.

"What's there to eat? I want a Coke."

I looked at the clock. Almost dinnertime and Quint would be back with pizza any minute. "Sure, Coke, but we'll be eating really soon."

"Where are the glasses?"

I shrugged. "Let's go through the cabinets and find out what we have."

"Can I bring my radio in?"

"Okay. Good idea." I looked around, wondering where to start, and spied a radio on the little built-in desk in the far corner. "Hold on, Lily. There's one over here."

She followed my gaze, turned it on, finding her station, and the kitchen filled with the cheerful mix of pop and rock in both Spanish and English, cumbias and the occasional heart breaking mariachi tune. Lily sang along with all of them. I chimed in on the English oldies. Lots of Pink Floyd and Beatles. We were dancing around the prep island with spatulas and eggbeaters, belting out, "We don't need no education, we don't need no thought control..." when Quint, Horacio, and, to Lily's delight, Chucho, came in with pizza, salad, a bottle of rum, a container of ice cream and another bag of *pan dulces*. I turned down the radio and Chucho handed me a large bouquet of flowers.

"From Susana," he said.

I pulled a blue vase from the pantry that coordinated with the dishes and placed the arrangement on the counter while Lily set another place for Chucho and found trivets for under the pizza boxes. I tossed the salad.

"Where are the dogs?" Quint asked.

Lily answered, "In my room."

"For once a quiet dinner," he said as the chorus of barking and howls echoed throughout the apartment.

"I'll get them," I said. "That's a cry for pizza."

"How did they know we had pizza?" Chucho asked.

Lily and I tapped our noses in unison.

Chapter 13

Try to Explain Lockdown to the Dogs

Four empty pizza boxes later, Chucho and I set out bowls of ice cream and a platter of *panes*. I put my scoop into my rum and Coke with a couple maraschino cherries, coining a Roma Libre. Horacio followed suit.

Quint asked, "Everybody satisfied?"

We nodded and groaned or patted our stomachs. "It's time to discuss how we will live here safely," he went on. "We don't have the same security as we did on Amores. It's only a matter of time before word gets around we're here. We don't know who followed us in the SUV today, but I expect within three days we'll receive a visit."

Lily blanched; my good mood tanked.

"So what do we do?" I asked.

"First, the Rafiq brothers will each take a shift with a rotation of the six additional men I've lined up. Chucho will move into the fourth bedroom until his apartment is ready. He and I will act as inside security."

Lily brightened up and cast mooning glances at the

young man. He turned a bit rosy, but avoided looking at her. Quint must have been clear on what the relationship was.

"Jade, I'm counting on you to keep your gun handy and to see that the apartment windows and doors are locked before dark every day. During the day I think there's enough happening on our block that we are safe from invasion," he said. His lips turned down. He added, "However, ladies, unfortunately you will not be able to wander around on the street or go to the park without an armed escort." His sad visage morphed into a firm, *I brook no nonsense*, glare.

Horacio interjected with, "I've assessed the security of the courtyard garden and you can take the dogs out there as long as you are armed. Lily, that means you can't go alone. I'm sorry. But it won't be for much longer."

Her face lit up. "Because I'm going to my aunt and uncle soon, right?"

"We hope so. But no, Horacio means we've got solid intel on who is after you, and how to stop them."

"Besides Anibal? We already know who. The Beltrán Leyva Organization and Tito Cárdenas of Los Zetas," I said, disgusted. We'd known this for ages.

"We needed proof. With your identification of the Zeta men now in custody, we have names, addresses, and planned movements. The senator's team is working on clearing out the hornet's nest as we speak. But the BLO side is trickier."

"Why? Eddy Santos and that old guy Lobo kidnapped me and Evie and carried us across an international border, and held us without our consent with the intent to traffic us in the sex trade. What more do you need? Take me to the police and I'll swear to it."

I looked at Quint who looked at Horacio. We'd all been there when Eddy was shot, but he'd disappeared. Last I'd heard, Eddy had not turned up alive or dead. I was convinced Fatso Farcía was behind a cover up. I didn't think any of us wanted to scare Lily with the truth—we didn't know where he was. At least he'd stayed away from the celebration of life.

Quint was speaking when I tuned back in. "... need more proof. With Eddy missing—"

"Missing! But you—" Lily looked at me accusingly—"you said he was dead."

"Good work, Quint. No, I said we saw him get shot. Now we don't know where he is."

She shivered, although the kitchen felt warm in the balmy evening. "Eddy will come for me. You've got to find him."

"Yes, that's what I was telling you. We have information that will corroborate your story, implicate Lobo, and convict Santos of killing your mother. You can thank your Qadir for that," Quint said.

"Yeah, he hacked Santos's phone texts and emails. The idiot admitted it to Lobo. He said he was looking for the next mark."

"It can be proven it was Eddy's phone? And Lobo he texted?" Horacio asked.

"Santos had been under investigation for human trafficking by an L.A. taskforce. They've confirmed it. His prints and DNA all over the house, the phone, and the chair Lily's mother was tied to," Quint said.

I added, "Qadir's cousin is in law enforcement in L.A. He sometimes gets called in to consult. Okay, this is good then. I'll have to phone and thank him. But how did you know?"

"I've got a connection on that taskforce too," Quint replied.

"Then why don't the police arrest them?" Lily asked.

"Eddy is missing and Lobo received a text about the crime. That doesn't make him guilty of anything more than withholding knowledge of a crime from the authorities."

Chucho said, "If you can get me Lobo's number and

email address, I can hack him." We all swiveled our heads his way. "What? It's what I do. Or, It's what I can do. When I graduate, I want to work in law enforcement. Senator Aguirre was going to get me a job. Right now I'm only apprenticing on his taskforce."

A smile spread over my face. "Is that so, Chucho? Well, let's call Qadir and get the info. I can reach him early in the morning. Will you be here tomorrow?"

"Chucho is helping me dismantle my office. He'll be here setting it back up sometime in the afternoon. After that, he'll be here working daily. Chucho, you've graduated to IT supervisor."

The young man beamed. "But Mr. Quint, I need the internship to qualify for my degree."

"No worries, you can still be an intern—our intern supervisor of IT."

"Will you sign my internship papers for my department at UNAM?

"Of course. Whatever you need."

"A workspace? I only had my room at the senator's."

"Have you seen our suite of offices?" Chucho shook his head. "In that case, people, let's go look at the offices and make some decisions."

I led the way as we tromped down the broad stairs to the double doors. I already had my keys on a lanyard and futzed around looking for the right one. When I inserted the key, I realized the doors looked like ornate wood, but were really steel. Somebody had been thinking about security.

Quint took the lead, pointing out the various spaces: the largest office with an outside window, door, and tiny enclosed patio—I envisioned it filled with succulents and a pair of cushy outdoor chairs—he claimed for himself. Next to it, a not so large office with a window and even smaller patio he said would be for Susana, his operations manager. Across the hall from Susanna's office with a window into the reception area, was the large workroom now with shelving and a copy machine, which had not been there yesterday.

Quint explained it was the common workroom that we all would use when the tables, computers and supplies arrived. "Jade, I want you to take on the job of procurement. Susana has to deal with closing down the Polanco apartment. Once she finishes, she'll manage all that, but we can't wait."

I nodded. I could do that.

The tour continued. A small storage room was behind the workroom, another decent sized office with a small patio sat next to Susana's and, finally, across the back end of the building was the command central tucked against the space backing onto the alley. "Chucho, I want you to design our communications area," Quint said.

I could see him already planning what he needed and where it would go. The space had high windows emitting natural light, and a door to the garden next to the walled-off loading area, where the limo now sat.

"So where's my VW bus going?"

Horacio said, "Garage." He pointed across the compound. "We'll bring it over next week. Tomorrow one of my cousins is picking it up on the *grua,* sorry, tow truck, and taking it for servicing at his *taller.* He'll keep it for as long as we need to hide it."

"Do I get any say in this?"

Quint winked. "None."

"Alrighty, then. But Quint, who gets the third patio office?"

"You've got the workroom," he said, sidestepping my question.

My phone rang. Dylan. "Hi! You done for the day?" he asked.

I went back to the reception area for some privacy. "We finished the pizza, but I'd eat again with you—"

"What's up?"

"Right now looking at the office spaces. Horacio and I are relegated to an interior common room. But I get to outfit it. I think it's his plan to keep me here. So are you coming over?"

I hung up feeling giddy with anticipation. Dylan would be here in half an hour.

Lily's teasing spiraled through my Dylan daydream. "So your boyfriend is coming over?"

"You don't want him to come? I thought you and he were great buds," I teased back.

"We are. What are we going to do now? There's more ice cream."

"For one thing, we're going out to the park with the dogs. Quint, Horacio? Up for a walk?"

"I am," Chucho said. Lily grinned.

"I highly advise against going to the park, especially this time of day. Did you not understand the rules?"

"Try to explain it to Pepper and Maya. They need to run. We'll go as a group today. I will not go at the same time each day, but I have to take my dog out daily. Or you do. Is that what you want? To jog with Pepper and Maya for an hour?"

"Jog? I don't think so," Quint said, grimacing.

"Okay then. That settles it. I'll manage my own responsibility."

"I run every morning. I can take the dogs," Chucho volunteered.

"There you go, Daughter, stop being so obstinate. All you have to do is ask and we'll help."

Chapter 14

Running with a Gun

The crew piled into the limo and Dylan's car. We drove to an open space near a school when Jardín Pushkin didn't have a track for running. People and dogs poured out onto the sidewalk. Pepper lifted his nose, sniffed to the cardinal points and let out a howl. I unclipped his leash and he took off at a dead run in the direction of the track. I bolted after him. It felt like days since I'd moved my body and my mushy muscles engaged slowly."

"Should've warmed up first, Jade." Dylan panted as he came up beside me, Chucho on his heels. I wrinkled my nose at Dylan. He should talk; his huffing said he hadn't been to the park lately, either. Maya and Dylan's *Xoloitzcuintle*, Roger, sprinted past us in an attempt to catch up with Pepper, clowning around Maya in his goofy, gangly way. I turned around and jogged backwards to see Lily and the little Frenchie, Noémi, trotting behind us while Quint and Horacio strolled within shooting distance. It would have to do.

We'd run from a paved walkway to a path that cut

through some trees onto a sports field. The grass still felt spongy from Hurricane Dean twelve days before. Mexico City had suffered flooding in the low areas and the storm stretched from the Gulf all the way to the Pacific coast. I felt the altitude and the pollution as I ran.

"I can't wait to get back into my routine, Dyl," I huffed as we slowed to a walk. The dogs and Chucho were turning into specks at the far end of the field. "They need it too. Shall I whistle them back yet?"

We had advanced far enough into the field we could see anyone approaching, but it was getting dark and paranoia grabbed at me. I patted for the Glock in its holster, relaxing a bit with its lethal heft.

"They're okay, but running with a gun? I don't know if I can get used to that, Jade," Dylan complained.

"Hmm. Yeah, new for me too, but ya gotta do what ya gotta do."

Chucho had circled around and jigged up to us, Roger on his heels. They were made for each other. "*Oye*, Dylan, Roger is a great dog!"

From a distance a voice called, "Wait up you guys!" Lily with Noémi under her arm. I waved and we watched her approach. She put Noémi down and the little Frenchie barreled toward Dylan and Roger, wagging.

"Man, she's heavy," Lily exclaimed.

"She loves treats. I can't stop my mother from feeding her tidbits all the time and she's beginning to look like a potbellied pig. I've got to get my own place," he said, casting a sidelong glance at me. A hint? I turned my Mona Lisa smile on him.

"Come live with us. Chucho is moving in." Lily gave him an excited smile. "It's going to be so cool here."

"Not for long, kid," Quint's voice broke through the gloaming. "Dylan, help me explain to these headstrong women the danger they are in. You can't be running around dark parks."

"Or walking on crowded sidewalks or running to the store to pick something up or having a coffee at that cute cafe we passed or...or *anything.*" Lily said, pouting.

"That's right, Lil. But you can try to beat me at Lotería. Betcha can't."

"Why Chu, because you a *college man*?" She blew out a disgusted breath. "I'm good at card games. Just teach me how to play and I'll whup your butt. You'll be yelling 'uncle' in no time."

"*¿Tío?* Why would I yell that?"

Dylan explained, "It's some weird American expression meaning *basta.*"

"It'll never happen kid." Chucho challenged. "Does anyone have a flashlight?"

Three cell phones appeared to illuminate the track as the lights of the city rose around us. I let out a piercing whistle; Pepper and Maya thudded back.

The view from the *cancha,* playing field, twinkled romantically from lights on the distant mountains to the south and west and the skyscrapers looming up from the haze of city surrounding us. The air smelled of damp earth, mown grass and, as the gibbous moon waned, I could see the river of stars flowing so close overhead I reached up and captured one in my palm. Dylan enclosed my star-filled palm in his warm hand, linking our fingers, and fates, I hoped.

We walked in silence across the spongy earth toward our new possibilities. The stars' energy filled us—I could feel it —leading us home. For the first time since Polo's thugs carjacked me off the Pan American highway, I fully relaxed and let my feelings, like the popping of champagne in a crystal flute, bubble the sheer joy of being alive up to the surface, a tickle on my skin. Dylan pulled me close, bent down and kissed my neck, and a flood of heat surged through me.

Behind us, Lily chattered on about her school and what she wanted to study when she got to college. Chucho let her babble, grunting now and then, but Noémi's weight probably had him winded. I dug my elbow into Dylan and jerked my head back toward the kids. He turned and snickered, whispering, "There's a sucker in every crowd and Noé always finds him."

Quint and Horacio brought up the rear separated by several yards, keeping eyes peeled for anyone lurking or approaching. Pepper and Roger led our group, prancing ahead and stopping to sniff the air periodically. Maya tagged along with Lily, of course.

"Stop!" Quint called out. We all stopped. Pepper stood at attention pointing his nose into the dark path through the trees. He growled. Roger's back went up although there was no hair to rise. "Get down; be quiet."

I pulled the Glock from its holster. *But it's wet and muddy*, I wanted to say as I dropped, Dylan next to me. Chucho dragged Lily to the grass and shushed her. The men advanced. I now saw their infrared glasses. Someone or someones were in the trees.

"Call Roger," I whispered.

Dylan let out a shrill whistle and Roger reversed course, settling into a crouch between us. Fernando Torrens had done *something* right. The thought buzzed by like a fly: how had he broken so bad? Pepper came too, still on guard.

The copse stood about thirty yards ahead. All I could see was black. If whoever waited had glasses too, they could pick us off, even lying on the ground. I guessed they didn't. "You okay, Lil?" I whispered. "Hang onto Maya."

"I'm scared."

"Me too. Stay still, Chucho protect her."

"*Claro, jefa*"

The night crowded down like a smothering blanket. Just

when everything was going so well. Had they found us? Had they known all along? And who? The same old question I'd vowed to answer. Quint and Horacio had split further, circling toward the line of trees. Quint was right, we needed to stay inside. How could I do that? *Please God, don't let there be shooting.*

Quint disappeared into the thicket. Horacio blended against it as he edged toward the path we needed to take. We inhaled a collective breath and held it.

Suddenly a shout and Horacio sprang into the trees, disappearing into the gloom. The shouting grew in volume and I let out my breath. One voice—Anibal—and he wasn't too happy about meeting up with Quint. "You fucking asshole! Get off me!" he shouted. Then "I'm delivering the bitches—you won't stop me." A roar of pain. "I'll kill you, Quint." And silence.

Horacio emerged, coming toward us. Pepper bounded out to meet him, Roger at his heels. I called out, "Safe to get up?"

"Yes. Come on, move," he said as he reached us, "We don't know if there are more of them or he's acting alone. ¡Apúrrate! Quint has him contained and is calling the marshal. You get into the trees and wait until I've scouted out the route home. When I call, you come. Fast."

"Okay. Thanks," I said. "Come on, people and dogs, let's jog."

Dylan took Lily's hand, helped her up and got her running then scooped up Noemi and started after her. I took off, Chucho right behind me. By her howl, Maya was relieved to be going home.

We all gasped for breath from our thirty yard dash into cover. Lily flopped onto the dirt, Chucho, bent at his waist, hands on knees, sucked in air. Dylan crouched, arms around his dogs, whose tongues lolled and dripped as they panted. Pepper danced around me, whining for permission to round up Anibal. "Quint's got him Peppi, relax."

"G-got who?" Lily squeaked.

"Anibal. I recognized his voice.

"I thought he'd been arrested," Dylan whispered, squeezing my hand.

"You missed that. They killed the marshal and Beltran's little brother impersonated him. Took Anibal out of the gathering right in front of us," Chucho said, voice low.

I hadn't realized Chucho was so familiar with the thugs in this town, but I guessed anyone connected to Polo knew the score. Maybe Chucho could do a little research and find the killers. I doubted the police would do anything. It probably was the police. I should have known he'd be right back on the street. *Plata o Plomo.*

We fell silent. Pepper's ears stood straight up, his head cocked slightly. He was on alert but still sitting against me. The sounds of evening in a megalopolis droned, white noise filling the darkness of our cover. Pepper sprang up, stiffening too high alert. Branches crackled. He started to quiver awaiting my signal. Someone was coming and not on the path. I pulled my gun.

"What's happening?" Dylan breathed into my ear.

Another crackle and a thump. Pepper whined.

"Jade," Lily started.

"Sh! Hold Maya's collar," I hissed as I gave Pepper his signal. He shot into the trees, barking.

"Jade, Jade, call your dog!" Horacio's voice. "Where are you people?"

As a unit we exhaled. I whistled.

"Where are you H?" Chucho called.

"Over here. Lost the path."

"Follow Pepper." I jumped up and directed the flashlight on my phone toward Horacio's voice.

We heard crashing in the underbrush and Horacio and Pepper lumbered onto the path, shadows separating from the black of the trees. Creepy.

"Are we safe?" Dylan asked.

"It depends on what you call safe. I'll lead you back to the cars, if that's what you mean. We didn't get the accomplices. *Señor* Quint saw two men jump into a black car and speed off."

"And Anibal?" I asked.

"*El jefe* has taken him."

"Jesus, he's a loser." I felt like I'd stumbled into the Keystone Cops. Horacio bumbling into the trees, Anibal getting caught every time he made a move on us—this would be pretty funny if it weren't so scary and plain sad. Why couldn't that asshole leave us alone? They lost. I was damned if I was going to sit around our armed camp twiddling my thumbs and eating *pan dulces*. "Guys, let's get back and start making a plan. We need some allies with authority. Aren't there any honest law enforcement in this city?"

"Not with any clout, Jade," Dylan said as he helped Lily up.

"I'll go first with Pepper, Roger and Chucho. Dyl, stick with Lily and Maya. You'll have to carry Noémi. We can't wait for a slowpoke. Horacio, you bring up the rear. Single file, and everyone keep your eyes peeled for any movement. Be ready to drop to the ground. Let's go." I ordered as I headed across the park. We'd be ducks in a row if the bad guys had goggles.

The muted night sounds of the capital amplified as we picked our way across the open space toward the street. Trucks grinding into low gears in the *glorieta*. The thump of bass from a car passing the park. A night bird squawking. I swiveled my head, monitoring the edges of the field. No moving shadows beyond traffic on the street. No! Wait! A flash.

"Down!" I roared and dropped to the grass as the sound

of a rifle pierced the air.

Like dominos, the others set down behind me. Pepper took off, an arrow, straight for the sound. Lily whimpered in Dylan's arms. I prayed the shooter didn't have a night scope, wouldn't shoot my dog. We lay still for endless moments while the city night surrounded us, deafened by our frightened breathing, in the middle of a field, getting soaked from the hurricane soggy turf— exposed.

I risked raising my head to find Pepper. He'd disappeared into the black at the edge of the park along the low wall separating turf from street. I relaxed enough to think again. I'd seen muzzle fire and heard a shot. Nothing more. Pepper had not been killed, but what of the shooter? Who? Where? Something moved in my peripheral vision. A figure silhouetted against the street lights.

I whispered, "Stay down and stay quiet. Horacio!"

"*Sí, señorita. Lo visto,*" he replied, shifting into a shooting crouch. I did the same.

"Goggles?" I whispered.

"I don't see any," Chucho replied. I craned my head to look at him.

Chucho'd pulled a pair of what looked like opera glasses from somewhere and studied the figure about halfway to the cars. He stopped, searching the area, but I couldn't see a weapon. "Chuch, does he have a gun?"

"I don't see—"

In a sudden movement the man's arm came up. I took aim—

"Stop! It's Quint," Horacio yelled.

A car engine roared to life and squealed away from the park. Pepper bounded out of the dark and danced around Quint, yipping joyfully. Dylan let Roger go and he joined the celebration dance. The bad guys were gone. For now.

Chapter 15

I told You So

Horacio herded us through the office door. No one spoke, but I heard the squish-squish of my soggy running shoes on the stairs. Good thing I had another pair for the morning run.

"Don't even think it, Daughter." Quint's voice sliced through my mental plans as he joined us at the big kitchen table from the back door.

"Think what?" Lily asked. "You guys, I'm all muddy," she whined.

Quint plunked a bottle of tequila and a handful of shot glasses onto the table, which he slid to the men. "Go take a shower then. Jade is thinking about her dry running shoes. Planning to go out in the morning. Do I need to point out—"

Dylan's eyebrows shot up. "She is not! Why would you think that?" he said, paused then added, "Sir." He held his hand up to decline the tequila bottle. Chucho poured himself a dollop.

Quint snorted, lips flattening into disgust. "I can read her thoughts." He shook his head. "JadeAnne, Chucho will run

109

the dogs. You and our Lily are on lockdown. Neither of you will leave this building without my expressed approval and a security detail until we get to the bottom of this attack."

"Yeah, where's Anibal this time? Do we have a basement?" I asked.

"A basement? Nah, do you need one?" Quint winked. Horacio laughed, but Lily's face wrinkled into confusion.

"Where is Anibal?" I demanded.

"Service room on the roof. Every building in Mexico has one. He's secured."

"Then why were we using the Amores laundry room as a holding cell?"

Dylan stood up. "Hey you guys, Jade, surgery in the morning. I've got to go." He leaned over me and kissed the top of my head. "Don't go out, Jade. Promise me. I'll come after work and take the dogs for an evening run. Why don't I pick up enchiladas for everyone?"

I looked at McDreamie Dylan and melted at the soft shine in his eyes. "I promise, Dyl. But Lil and I have a nice dinner planned for tomorrow, so hold the takeout. We'll cook for you." I scraped my chair out and stood. "I'll walk you down."

Dylan scooped his Frenchie off the floor, and said, "See you all tomorrow. Let's go, Roger."

Downstairs, Dylan grabbed me by the shoulders and gave me a light shake. "What the hell are you doing? Trying to get yourself and the rest of us killed? You can't go running around as you please. A big dog and a big gun aren't going to protect you from some narco's bigger gun, or the four men who hustle you into a van. Please Jade," he said, and pulled me into an awkward embrace nearly crushing poor Noé, who wiggled to get down.

I grabbed the dog, set her onto the floor, and turned to Dylan. "Dyl, I won't go out." I kissed him properly.

My heart beat with the rhythm of his as he held me. I

didn't want to let go.

After bolting the steel door behind me, I trudged back up to the apartment. It was getting late. All the day's excitement had worn me out. In the kitchen, Quint and Chucho talked over another shot. Horacio was gone and I could hear Lily's radio playing behind her closed door.

"Lil went to shower?" Maya thumped her tail and grinned.

"We were just discussing your reckless disregard for the danger you are in. Jade, you are not in Sausalito. You can't just go out to the park at your whim. The BLO is a giant squid with tentacles everywhere. You show yourself and someone sees you. The only thing saving you and Lily right now is—"

"—is you lot? Come on Dad, I get it. Go ahead say it! Get it over with."

"Say what?" he asked.

"You know."

Chucho laughed. "*Tu se lo dejiste*"

"What? Jade? In English please."

"He said, "'you told her so'."

Quint hooted and threw his arm around my shoulder as I got up to leave. "Yeah, but I wasn't going to say it."

Chapter 16

Under Attack

Friday, September 14, 2007

If we were watched or threatened, no one noticed between the furniture and equipment deliveries. I spent most of the week on the phone ordering supplies and services, directing delivery traffic, organizing offices and work stations, and keeping my "staff" on task. I'd come 6,000 miles to do the job I did at home, except without the lovely Mt. Tam and bay views. But I had to admit, the set-up of our headquarters was exciting and kept both Lily and me from pulling out our nails in boredom. Lily was an excellent worker, that is, when she wasn't checking on Chucho. He said she was a big help, doing what, I didn't ask, but he had the coms room set up and functioning by Friday afternoon.

Quint had spent most of his time "out." At meals he evaded my questions, and Horacio shrugged when I asked him what was up. Obviously something was afoot. Strange hardened-looking men with jacket bulges tromped up and down the back stairs to the apartment. Until Quint occupied his office, he'd laid claim to our living room to work. He'd kicked us all, puppies included, down to the office suite while he met with his contacts.

I pulled Lily aside after seeing a couple of gringo-looking CIA types climbing the stairs behind Horacio. "Hey, Quint has some more guys up there. Can you slip into your room and eavesdrop? Is this about Anibal?"

"He'd kill me, Jade."

"All you need to say is you had to get puppy pads or lunch or your book. He'd just send you back down here. Then he'd kill me."

"I have to help, Chuch. We're wiring up his bank of computers and monitors."

"Then why are you hip-hopping out here in the hall?"

"Oh. I always dance to *Party Like a Rockstar*." She grinned and held out an earbud.

I threw up my hands. "No, that's okay. Hey, gimme your pod and go up pretending you're looking for it."

"Jade!" Lily shrieked.

"Okay, never mind. Crank it up. I need a little partying." I twirled around and did a locking routine to the tinny beat. Lily cued the song up again and we locked and popped in unison, Maya and Pepper swirling around our legs.

"Hey, we should get the puppies and teach them to hip hop," Lily suggested.

The door buzzer sounded. "I don't think so right now. That's Quint's credenza. Once that's in, we'll make him meet people down here so we can find out who they are. I'll get the door. You get Chucho."

Lily giggled and tore down the hall. Was I wrong to let her spend so much time with him? She had a huge crush. Thankfully he'd only acted like a big brother, but one thing could lead to another. I made a mental note to ask Quint to have another talk with him as I peered through the door's peep hole. A man in a logo-ed delivery jumpsuit stood in front of the door clipboard in hand.

I craned my head to see the truck. We should be receiving Quint's furniture from Office Depot de Mexico. I'd confirmed the company sent its own trucks. Why did his overall have a red G on it? And where was the truck? We had blocked off a loading zone with no-parking signs for our deliveries. The curb in front of the door was empty.

"Hello, can you show me the purchase order?" I called through the door. I heard Chucho's trainers slapping toward me. I swiveled toward him. "Something's off. I can't see the truck and the guy's uniform is wrong." I looked back through the peep hole. The man grinned, holding up a blank clipboard and a handgun aimed at my eye. I jumped back. "Gun!"

Chucho had wired alarms throughout the suite. He slammed his palm against the workroom button as he passed. A claxon blared over the blast of the gun. I dropped to the floor as the building shuddered with the thunder of footsteps on the apartment stairs. Quint and two men burst through the blast door, guns drawn. Quint and one of the men cut to the back door and I heard the familiar roar of Quint's hand cannon. The other man motioned me with his gun to get out of the way.

I fled into the workroom. Chucho had the gun cabinet open and grabbed an M16. "Lily? In the com room?"

Chucho nodded. "Come on. You two need to go to the saferoom."

He herded me toward his man cave. Lily crouched behind empty computer boxes. Shouting came from the walled yard. I pulled Lily up and Chucho shoved us into a closet I hadn't noticed before.

"Lock the door and don't open it until one of us comes to get you," he said, in tempo to the echo of boots clanging up metal stairs.

Saferoom? More like an airless utility closet with barely enough room to sit down on the tatty loveseat shoved inside. The door slammed and I patted around in the dark for the locks. I found three.

"Jade?" Lily's voice quavered in the gloom. Only a small nightlight glowed low on the wall beyond the loveseat.

I squeezed her hand. "It's okay Lil, we'll be safe in here," I said, in a voice more confident than I felt. I didn't have my gun and, other than a flat of bottled water, the room appeared devoid of anything else. I checked my phone. No bars. Okay, no communication with Quint, but from the sound of boots on stairs, I had guessed the action was to do with Anibal. A rescue? Why wait all week?

"How the hell did Anibal's people get onto our stairs?" I said aloud.

"They've come for *him*? Not us?"

"I dunno, Lily. Probably both."

The silence stretched to snapping. Lily trembled and finally started to sob as I stroked her hair. What could I say? The swirling emotions overwhelmed me also. I held her closer until her crying subsided into soft hiccupping.

"I-I-*uhp*- I'm to blame. If I ha-hadn't-*uhp*- gone with those men. Oh Jade, my sister. My mother! They're gone because of me. *Uhp.*"

"No, Lily, you and Evie are victims of a ruthless criminal and a weak, addicted mother. You had no control over any of it. You did what you could. And now my dad and I are doing what we can." I shifted on the lumpy cushion. "We'll get you and Evie's casket to Denver. I promise."

She dropped her head to my shoulder and I kissed her temple as she shuddered under the weight of her guilt and grief.

We must have dozed off because the next thing I knew,

Horacio pounded on the door. "*Señorita* Jade! Open the door. *Ya se acabó,* it's over."

I gently shifted Lily and lumbered out of the low seat to pat around again for the locks.

Lily woke up at the rasp of the locks scraping. "Is it safe?"

I popped the door open to Shrek's ogre grin and gulped in fresh air then pulled Lily into Horacio's protective arms. "Did you stop them? It was about Anibal, wasn't it?"

"*Sí, Sí.* Two dead. Quint is up there now, questioning the other."

I cringed at what Quint might do. "And the man at the door?" I asked.

"Furniture delivery."

"But he had a gun."

Horacio snorted. "That peephole doesn't tell the entire story. A man behind him with the gun."

"Oh. But you got him." Lily asked, burrowing deeper into his side.

"*Sí, señorita,*" he said.

"And who were those men? CIA? How did they happen to be here during the attack?" I asked as we reached the blast door to the apartment.

"Coincidence. Your papa is putting together a network of law enforcement, security, and allies from our two governments. I can't say who those men were, but they fought well. The attackers are unfamiliar to us." Horacio unlocked the door. "Go on up.

"One more thing, H, how did they get on the roof? And why during daylight?"

"It's a continuous roof for everyone in the building, but the only access is through the neighbor's space. They couldn't sneak in during the night. The man we detained is wearing a uniform from a pest control outfit."

"Quint was right. We need to establish communications

with the tenants," I said.

"I'm hungry, Jade. Can't we go up and make some lunch? Hungry, Horacio?" Lily asked as she pulled away from him and bounded up the stairs.

I looked at Horacio. "Want lunch?" He nodded and we followed Lily.

Sinchronizadas, melted ham and cheese on flour tortillas with avocado, onion, lettuce and tomato. I pulled out some hot salsa in case anyone wanted it. "Lil, find Chucho and ask how many he wants. And you? How many?"

She looked over the ingredients, pursed her lips and shrugged. "Two? What else are we having?"

"A salad and some of the chili piquin Sabritas Susanna bought. Go get Chucho." I put a platter on the table and started slicing the vegetables and shredding some lettuce.

"Um, I-I'm scared to go down there," Lily said, hanging her head.

"Of course you are. You've had a fright. You stay here and I'll find the others." Horacio guided Lily to a chair and handed her the Coke he'd popped for himself. Without Mrs. P, we maintained a help yourself policy. He turned to me. "May I have four?"

"Sure, H. As many as you want." Susanna had purchased about two kilos of sliced ham and Chihuahua cheese. And tons of flour tortillas. "Grab me a Victoria before you go down?"

Horacio opened my beer and poured it into a glass while I started to assemble sandwiches. "Thanks, man."

Quint came in as Horacio went out.

"Dad, what happened?"

"Quint, we were locked in a tiny dark room with only bottled water" Lily whined. "I was so scared!"

"I know, honey. But the room is to protect you girls."

Lily let out a dramatic sigh. "I know. I'm going to get

the dogs." She pushed away from the table and scooted out of the kitchen.

"Lily needs to talk to a counselor. She thinks everything that happened is her fault," I said.

"Yeah. Maybe Susanna can arrange someone to come in."

"We need to get Mrs. P back."

Quint blew a derisive breath through his lips. "I never thought I'd hear you ask for 'the traitor'."

I slapped a ham and cheese packed tortilla onto the hot comal. And another, spatula at the ready to flip them. "How many, Dad?"

"Not going to respond to that? Four, thanks," he said as he opened a Corona.

"We need her. Where's my dog, by the way?"

"Chucho has him. Not a cook then?"

"Or a babysitter, house cleaner or bottle washer. Tell me about your guests. But first, where is Anibal?" I slapped another two *sinchronizadas* onto the comal after tucking the hot ones into a tortilla towel on a plate and sticking that in a 200°oven.

He regarded me for a beat. "Anibal is determined to kidnap you and Lily to complete his deal."

"Yeah. Who were the attackers?"

"Hired. They came to rescue Anibal. and so far we haven't got a name of the employer."

"Farcía Luna," I said.

"Or Lobo."

"Ani tried to kill Lobo. Why would he want to rescue him?"

"Orders from Beltrán, mebbe."

"Oh, come on, Quint. Beltrán doesn't care about Anibal. He's a thorn in everyone's side. The BLO people would be happy to see him go."

"Then why did Beltrán's little brother rescue him from

the marshal?" He frowned, eyes hard.

I shrugged, biting my lip. It didn't make sense, either way. Ani had screwed the BLO. Maybe they wanted to kill him. But why let him go? Or the little bro' is a buddy of Anibal. Maybe he was in on the deal.

"I might have the story, Dad."

I flipped another pair of sandwiches and started on the salad as I shared my theory with Quint. The kitchen filled with the divine smell of fried cheese and toasted bread on tendrils of steam rising off the *comal*. My stomach growled. Well, no wonder. It was almost three-thirty.

"That's plausible, Jade. How'd an old man get such a smart daughter?" he asked, kissing the top of my head as he passed to grab another beer. "They're about the same age and Chucho confirms Carlos pals with Eddy Santos. They're connected."

"Do you think Anibal, Carlos, and Eddy were in the scam to sell the kids together? Or what if the BLO and the Zetas are working together?"

"That's stretching it, Jade."

I shrugged again. Eddy Santos and Anibal were scumbags. They probably were screwing over their own group. "Well, we know Eddy set up the kidnapping in LA. Quint, do you think he set up other kidnappings in other places?"

"Yeah. I'm sure of it."

"Is he dead?" I asked.

"Chucho tracked his movements. He was picked up in Tepoztlán by the police and taken to Cuernavaca to a hospital. Records indicate he was treated and taken into custody by the AFI. He couldn't find anything else."

I started a new pair of sandwiches toasting. I didn't think I could stand around a hot *comal* all afternoon. "Someone high up and connected has to be behind it."

"Just what I was thinking. From what I've heard, it's

brother Hector's job to secure government protection."

"Farcía."

"My guess too—Farcía."

Maya galloped into the kitchen, Pepper on her heels. She sat down next the stove, eyes cast toward the burner, and grinned. Pepper trotted up to me wagging.

"Hello, Peppi. Good run?" He leaned into my leg and woofed. Maya thumped the floor with her tail to get my attention. "Okay, who wants a treat?"

The dogs bounced up and headed for the pantry where I'd stored the biscuits. We'd been here, what, four days? And already they knew where the treats lived. I snapped a bone and offered half to each.

"Where do you suppose Chucho is?" I asked Quint.

"Dunno. Probably checking on something in his cave."

We laughed. I wondered how Chucho was so well-trained in security while I set the table for lunch. "Get Lily and the guys, will you? We're ready to eat."

Quint nodded and said, "Make a plate for Aguirre."

"What? I thought your colleagues took him with the intruders."

A sly grin crossed Quint's face. Now what? "Dad, why do we still have Anibal?"

"He has to be extradited. I don't trust the Mexicans to hold him."

"So we wait for the next attack? Are you crazy?" I called to his back.

The kitchen flooded with energetic puppies bouncing and tumbling over to their mother. Pepper sighed. Lily followed the puppies, thudding across the floor in her Doc Martins.

She pulled out her chair and plopped onto it. "Why is Quint crazy?"

I passed her a *tamarindo* soda and a plate, the *sinchronizadas* laying open for salsa. Lily could hear that?

"You thought he was normal? Help yourself to whatever you want."

Pepper pricked up his ears then I heard the sounds of the men. I hustled the platter of sandwiches to the table and grabbed an assortment of drinks. I really should make a pitcher of *jamaica* or something. But this cooking thing was already boring.

"Okay, we're assembled. First, I don't want to be a cook. Who agrees we need a housekeeper?"

Lily's hand shot up. "Mrs. P! I know she'll come if we ask her." She turned to Quint. "Please, Quint?"

I knew how to guilt trip him. He'd have to say yes. Especially when I sicced Dylan on him, but I said, "Second, will you all please tell us exactly what happened here today? And how will we prevent it from happening again."

I glared at my father. He should have sent Anibal with the CIA guys, *if* they were CIA guys.

"These *sinchronizadas* are delicious, *señorita*," Horacio said. Chucho nodded mumbling something through a full bite.

"Shall I make more?" The men shook their heads. Thank God.

"I gotta run, I'm meeting with Santiago," Quint said, checking his watch.

Horacio nodded. "*Vamos compa.* Chucho and I have to get that furniture squared away."

Chapter 17

A Bribe

Still plenty to do in the offices before we could get to work, whatever that work was—Quint had yet to fill me in. He'd oft repeated, "If I tell you, then I'll have to kill you." A joke that now grated on my bones, and I didn't mean my funny bone. After lunch, Lily went back to her room. I double checked the locks on doors and windows so she could nap with the goldens. A nap sounded good, but I had still so much...yet, tomorrow was another day. I'd satisfy my curiosity about our roof, stop by and chat with Anibal—bribe him with lunch for information.

Once I had a packet of *sinchronizadas* steaming and a plastic container of dressed salad, I grabbed a bottle of water, loaded a bag and made my way to a window overlooking the outside stairs to inspect the landing. I wasn't brave enough to open the back door until I was certain no one lurked within our compound. I had a clear shot into the walled garden, the patios, the garage door and under the stairs leading to our backdoor. I couldn't see anybody.

What I hadn't noticed before was the small structure over the garage. Was that where Anibal was being held? Sure, the rescuers could have crossed the roof from a tenant's property, but it didn't make sense. There had to be access to the structure and vents. I was no architect, but, hello! I could see these things sticking up.

I patted Pepper goodbye, and put my gun and keys in my pocket. I'd try the garage.

After locking the door behind me, I crept down the stairs and found the key to the garage on my ring. My combi hadn't moved in yet, but otherwise it contained the usual stuff for yard and building maintenance and, sure enough, there was a door. Locked, but I, as the *ama de casa,* the homemaker, had the key. Cement stairs ran nearly straight up, ladder-like, open to the roof. No wonder I hadn't seen it. I crawled out and circled the windowless structure to the west-facing side. In the distance mountains rose into the clouds. This side had a dirty transom window ajar over the door.

"Anibal, are you hungry? I've got *sinchronizadas* for you."

Nothing.

I rattled the door knob. Still nothing. A car horn blasted on the street below. My blood pressure soared. I kicked the door, a dull thudding of rubber on solid wood. Something clanked inside.

"Anibal. Do you want food?"

The clanking of a chain got louder and a string of *grocerias* fit for a brawling sailor, shot out the little window.

I hunkered down against the door. No sense advertising my presence to the neighborhood. "So I take that as no? Okay, I'll take your food back to the kitchen. Pepper will love the ham."

"You bitch! You know I'll fucking get you one of these days. You won't be so smug then."

"You didn't answer my question." I tried to keep my voice neutral, conversational.

"You did this," he growled. "You started all of this. I lost my cousin and my brother because of you. You and your interfering father. *Pero mis cuates* are going to get him. And you and the little slut will be delivered to the life you *coños* deserve."

The pure vitriol of his speech took my breath away. My pulse thrummed in my ears. When I spoke, my voice quavered, barely audible. I couldn't let him do this to me. Sucking in a long cleansing breath, I counted to four and blew it out my mouth to the same count. Immediately I felt my mind and muscles relax. I tested my voice. "Yes or no, Anibal. Lunch? I don't think anyone plans on bringing you dinner." Something banged into the door, possibly an empty paint can. "What's it going to be?"

He remained silent for a long moment, and said, "Give me the food."

"Okay, but you need to move away from the door. If you try to get near me, I'll shoot you. And before I open the door, I want some answers."

"What the fuck, JadeAnne? Give me my food. This is illegal, you know."

I so wanted to retort, *It's legal to kidnap and sell humans into slavery.* But I bit my tongue and stood up. If I stretched, I might be able to lob the water over the transom. Maybe I could slide the tinfoil wrapped sandwiches through too.

"Anibal, it's clear you double-crossed the BLO and now are cheating the Zetas, but who put you up to it? I know Eddy and Lobo were behind nabbing the girls from L.A. Lobo is probably in the hospital from the beating you gave him. And Eddie is dead, shot by your good pal Tito Tormenta. I saw him do it. Why are you persisting with this folly? Someone must be helping you. Tell me."

"You don't know shit. Gimme my food."

"I'll be happy to give you shit and let you eat it for what you've done, but I'll give you ham and cheese, salad, and fresh water if you tell me who sent the three thugs to rescue you this afternoon."

"What the fuck? They sent people?" Anibal's entire tone had changed from aggressive to surprised and maybe a little awed.

"Yeah, *they* did," I emphasized. "Tell me who, Ani. Before these warm cheezy sandwiches cool off."

The growl was back. "Stupid bitch. Eddie isn't dead. You're full of shit."

"How would you know? You were hog-tied in the back of the house, then shoved into the trunk of Polo's limo. I saw it go down, Anibal. I saw it." My voice cracked. Black ops and murder weren't my first choice of live entertainment.

The chains clanked and he shouted, "I saw Eddie Sunday. We planned the attack at the park." He couldn't conceal the triumph in his voice.

What was he so triumphant about? He'd failed his mission. Lily and I were still here and he was a prisoner. Crazy Ani. Polo was right. "So you and Eddie Santos are partners in this trafficking venture? Neither of you are smart enough."

"Fuck you, Jade. Smarter than you. You could have gone home and saved yourself."

"And I chose to save a little girl instead. I've got humanity. What do you have? Everything your family said about you is true. You're a total loser."

"Bitch! Did you just come here to taunt me? Where's my food?"

"It's right here, Ani. And I'll give it to you as soon as you tell me who you are working with. Was that really a US Marshal who frog-marched you out of the gathering? Or Hector's little bro Carlos? Maybe you and Carlos killed the marshal outside. Whatever the truth, you're in deep shit,

Anibal."

He remained silent. I'd hit a nerve, or maybe I should have waited another day when he was really hungry.

"And just as an aside, if you doubt what a loser you are, think about how every time you come near me and my family, you end up a trussed pig in a storage room. Just answer my questions and I'll feed you and protect you from the cartels coming to kill you."

That was a stretch. I'd likely hand him over. I waited for his response. The traffic noise had increased as we'd "chatted." People must be coming home from work. I wondered when Quint would get back. I couldn't risk him catching me up here baiting Anibal.

"What's it going to be, Anibal? Truth or Dare time."

"I'm hungry. Open the door and hand me my food."

"You, Eddy, and Carlos decided to pull a scam to cheat the BLO? Imagine how pissed Arturo and Hector will be when they find out Carlos was involved. Their own brother!"

"It wasn't that. It's not what we planned. BLO was never involved. It was Eddie's and my operation. Carlos knew the buyers. That's all."

I wished I could see his face, his chin sawing back and forth. I'd know if he was lying. But I guessed this was as good as I would get. If it were true, it surprised me and I had a tidbit for Chucho to look into. Maybe I'd get Qadir on it too. I tapped the bottle of water over the window sill and listened to it bounce. He scrambled after it.

"Where's my food?" he yelled. "Open the door."

"Not a chance." I stretched up onto my tiptoes and inched the salad then the packet of ham and cheese over. It fell with a slap and the chains clanked in time to Anibal's grunts and scrabbles.

"You're welcome," I called over my shoulder as I rounded the shack toward the stairs.

Dylan proved our savior. Lily and I spent the evening, jumpy, cranky and mind-numbingly bored. I called for pizza —again—and Chucho picked it up. But pizza failed to lift our spirits.

I needed some exercise. Pepper wanted another run and Maya wanted her own piece of pizza. Maybe it was the re-hash of the day's events putting a damper on our meal, but the vibe in our kitchen basically sucked. I desultorily stirred a bowl of vanilla ice cream to soup. Quint had not shown up, adding to my worry. Chucho didn't know what was going on; Horacio'd gone home to his family. And Lily hadn't flirted with Chucho, a sure sign she was down.

"Lil, I need exercise. Want to crank up some music and dance?"

Chucho grinned and slipped a crust to Maya. "*Sí, claro.* Let's put on some cumbias." He hopped up and wiggled through a dance routine. Lily half smiled.

"Yeah. That sounds great. I'll dance with you, Chuch." I said, dropping our plates onto the counter and taking a few salsa steps. I didn't have a clue how to cumbia.

"You guys! I don't know how," Lily whined.

I grabbed her hand and hauled her onto the bare floor in the dining area. "Lily, get your speaker. Chuch, help me shove the table against the wall. There—" I pointed.

He dialed in some bouncy music with a double beat and trumpets on his phone then demonstrated. I stepped behind him and imitated his moves: right leg pivot back, left foot step in place, right step back to neutral. Left pivot back, right step in place, left return to neutral and repeat. Yeah, and all the while arms bent and held just above waist height and hands making little circles.

I could move my legs, but as soon as I added the arms, the legs stopped. Lily giggled and leaped in front of me, making sexy hand circles and moving her hips to the beat. "Watch me, Jade." She turned around to face me. "It's like this—" She took my hand and stepped and rocked and swiveled. I stepped and rocked and swiveled with her. "Okay, so now add your hands. Like this—" she added a dainty rhythmic circling to her footwork. Chucho danced around belting out the lyrics, something about a coocoo. I flailed.

But it worked; the damp clay weighing us down dried up and cracked off. The puppies tumbled between our pivoting feet and Maya wagged in time to the double beat. Pepper, not one for extravagant displays of silliness, allowed me to pull him to his hind legs and dance.

"What's going on here?" Quint yelled from the kitchen door. We turned. Grim-faced, he glowered.

"What?" Lily yelled.

"Turn it down! I could hear the music from the street."

Chucho bounded to the table and turned off his phone. "Hi, *jefe*. We saved some pizza for you."

"Why are you so late? Where were you? I've called several times."

"Yeah. Let me freshen up and eat. We'll meet after."

"All of us?" Lily asked.

"No. You and Chucho can go to your rooms."

The pall drifted down, dark and oppressive. I dragged myself back to the kitchen and pulled Quint's pizza out of the warm oven and the salad from the refrigerator, dreading the news.

I handed him a beer as he sat down in front of his food.

"Jade, I haven't been able to make any headway on our problem up in the *bodega*. I've been talking to the—"

My phone rang, cutting him off. Dylan. I held up a finger and spun out of the room. "Hi Dyl. You off work?...uh huh...okay. No we've been learning the cumbia...Chucho. He's quite a dancer." I closed my bedroom door behind me. "We had a trying day. I wish you were coming over...tomorrow? El Grito, oh I remember you telling me about that... Sure! I'd love to go, except Quint won't let us out of the house. An invasion... Three guys tried to rescue Anibal. Quint is worried and cranky...mmmm, uh-huh, okay. You can try. It might be easier if I just sneak out though... Okay, see you tomorrow." I hung up.

"Maybe I should go to bed and leave Quint to his bad tempered self," I commented to Pepper who'd sprawled across my bed. He rolled into his back and wagged, a clear *scritch my belly* invitation.

Quint knocked. "Jade. Are you done?"

I gave Pepper a quick scritch and promised I'd do a better job when I came back.

Chapter 18

Try and Stop Me

Saturday, September 15, 2007

Pepper nudged me awake when someone knocked on my door. He held the leash in his mouth and I realized Chucho was waiting to the dogs for a run. I rolled out of bed and padded to the door, angling myself behind it as I let Pepper out, and mumbled, "Thanks, man."

"Sure thing, Jade. Go back to bed," he said. I followed his advice.

Several hours later, I lurched up, downed two aspirins and got myself into the shower. It was a shot night for Quint after his *spin-your-wheels* day and I'd helped him finish the bottle. As the hot water streamed down my back, washing away the boozy skin crawlies, I reviewed our conversation. Quint was frustrated and depressed over progress to legitimize Lily and fly her to her family. Rosi had been glum and discouraging at their meeting. Garza was waffling. The

CIA guys took care of the intruders, but had made it clear they weren't interested in Quint's mission, whatever that actually was. Santiago was not forthcoming with security. And my dad was not pleased to hear I'd talked to Anibal. The only bright point in our conversation was my news that Eddie Santos and Carlos Beltrán were Ani's cohorts. It was a starting point.

I soaped my hair with the last of my Loma shampoo from home. What would I do now? I'd never planned to stay in Mexico so long. I'd never planned on a lot of things that had happened in the past six weeks. How could I?

Quint and I'd brainstormed several scenarios with our shots. The last sounding more like fantasy than possibility. Ani, Eddie, Carlos, and Lobo were operating on their own—not likely due to the costs involved with kidnapping, transporting people illegally into Mexico, taking care of them until sale. It would require a large upfront investment, but Lobo might have that kind of money. Or, the BLO financed the operation for their own interests and the three were ripping them off—very risky business. If Ani, Eddie, and Carlos got caught, they'd be killed. And a third possibility. An ugly third possibility. What if Ani, Eddie, and Carlos were tasked to negotiate an alliance with Los Zetas? I'd heard they were sworn enemies. I didn't believe it could happen, but anything was possible.

I climbed out of the shower, dried off, then started on my hair. I had to look good for Dylan so I pulled the blow dryer out of the cabinet. I'd try a loose ponytail of soft ringlets. It would keep my hair out of my way in the big crowd later, and I'd be able to see around me better—just in case Ani's pals showed up.

Speaking of pals, something about Ani turning on his pal Lobo at the funeral party really bugged me. It didn't fit with scenario #2 at all. Possibly Lobo didn't pay up his promised investment, but it's unlikely Lobo would have finked on Ani to Hector if he were involved. So what did it mean? I was still too dull to puzzle it out.

After scrambled eggs and bacon, my energy lifted and I descended to the offices to continue organizing. We were due to receive a load of book cases, two desks, and six filing cabinets from Office Depot at 11:30. I hoped it wasn't the same driver. He probably wouldn't come back. I busied myself in Quint's office arranging his desk and unpacking his computer. The clean lines of the new blond laminate credenza looked good. And he'd chosen a black leather executive chair for his desk. Everything had a Danish modern feel. I hoped his bookcases matched. Somehow I hadn't pegged my dad as the designer furniture type and wondered where his furniture had come from and how much money he had left.

The door buzzer sounded and I texted Chucho and Horacio, who was setting up his work station in the common workroom. They could answer the door today. Soon the delivery man and I were slicing off the packaging in reception and moving each piece to its new home. It looked like we'd be operational by the middle of the next week. Right about the time I estimated I'd be catching a plane to Denver with Lily, Maya, Roli and Poli. I was sure Rosi would set the ambassador onto the right track.

At my computer—I'd set up a workspace for myself on the first day—I perused the Office Depot and Staples catalogs for good deals on supplies. We'd need everything, especially paper, USB drives, and jacks and cables. Quint's first purchase had been an iPhone for everybody. Lily was beside herself with excitement. She ran around snapping photos, documenting our progress, but she was still in bed. It was only two, after all. And Dylan was picking me up at five.

We'd decided he would pull up to the garden gate, toot,

and I'd dive out the gate into his Ghia, keeping my head down until we'd cleared the *colonia*. We planned to stop by his house so he could shower and change while I visited with his parents, Eladio and Gabriella. We'd go casual—no purse, just jeans, tee, tennies and sweatshirt for the *madrigal*, the wee hours. Dylan said we'd be up most of the night, eat late in Coyoacan's Mercado de Antojitos and probably drink a lot. He'd booked a room for us and another for Seeger and Dafne, who we were to meet after our visit with Dyl's parents. Dyl said I could leave an overnight bag in Dafne's car, but my phone and cash needed to go under my clothes. The plaza would be teeming with pickpockets, especially during the fireworks. I couldn't wait. We'd dance, maybe even a cumbia now that I was an expert, and share bites of our tacos and sips of our drinks, hold hands, hug. It was going to be a real date! Well, except for the gun I'd be carrying.

"You're what? You are willingly putting yourself and your friends in harm's way to shout *Viva México* at midnight? I hadn't realized my daughter is insane. No, Jade. You cannot go out tonight. I can't protect you. No!" Quint practically shouted, his face twisting with alarm and incredulity.

"Dad, I'm thirty-two years old. I can decide for myself," I said straining to keep my voice neutral. I didn't need to bring up old hurts and accusations, but really, he'd never been a father to me. Why start now? Even if he was right, I wasn't about to admit it.

He rounded on me, wringing his hands. "Are you stupid as well as insane?"

"Maybe, but I'm going on a real double date with my boyfriend, his brother and fiancée. I'm not letting criminals destroy my chance with Dylan. Even you say he's a decent guy. Don't I deserve that?" I wanted to stamp my feet and blow a raspberry at him. Lily's music notched up a few decibels.

"The question is, do Dylan and his family deserve to be drawn into your trouble? Trouble that might get them killed."

"I don't want to argue, Dad. Everyone is aware of the danger and we've decided to go. I'll have my gun and Dafne has arranged a couple of friends to keep an eye out. We'll be fine." I pointed to my overnight bag. "And we're staying overnight in Coyoacán so we won't be on the road late. I'll check in if it makes you feel better. I already promised to send photos to Lily."

"And I suppose now Lily will think she can go."

I raised my eyebrows as the proverbial lightbulb lit up. "Why don't you take her? Chucho is going out. Call up Rosi and see what she's doing. You might have fun." I waved a flourish with my hand calling The Force into play.

Quint got a funny look on his face and a spark in his eye. Hmm. Did I call that right?

"No, I…ah, I don't think that would be appropriate. Anyway, I got the idea she and Garza had something going."

I laughed. "Yeah, partly right, Dad. They *did* have something, but it's long over and the friendship survived. I saw how you flirted with her. Call her up!" I cocked my head to the side and gave Quint my most convincing look. *These are not the droids you are looking for.*

"You think so?"

I grinned. "Go get her, Dad. See you tomorrow," I grabbed my bag and headed downstairs to the door. It was five o'clock.

Chapter 19

Tequila Like Liquid Haloes

Gabriella ushered us in with big hugs and plenty of warmth. Eladio hovered behind her grinning. She took my arm and led me toward the living room.

Dylan snorted and said, "I come home every day. Why don't I get this kind of greeting?"

"*Hijo,* you don't bring a pretty girl with you every day," Eladio said, playing the straight man.

"'Ladio! Don't embarrass your son. Come, JadeAnne, have a glass of wine with us while Dylan gets ready." She offered me a glass of *vino tinto* from a silver tray and gestured to the couch. I sat down and Eladio followed. Gabriella slipped out to the kitchen.

"Thanks. No wine for you Eladio?"

"No, I'm not much of a wine drinker. Prefer tequila, and that bottle you gave me is excellent. You know your spirits."

I laughed. "I don't really, but the man at the liquor store obviously did. I'm glad you like it. Tequila bars are becoming popular in California and I've gone for a couple of tastings, but I haven't learned the superior brands. I tend to prefer *añejos* to silver or gold, though."

"A woman with taste. So do I. The older the better. I once had the honor of sampling the finest tequila made. It was over 100 years old and poured like molten gold into the glass. One of my friends and I visited his great uncle, a very old agave grower on the coast. His family had grown the plant that makes tequila for centuries, and for a time they ran a distillery, although the old ways of making tequila are not used any longer. The family had a cellar like makers of wine keep cellars, but his was filled with tequilas produced over many years. Hunched over with age, he hobbled down the slope, my friend and I following behind. It smelled musty and appeared cavernous in the dim light. He asked, 'Do you boys like to sip fine tequila? Or do you swill that rotgut they put into margaritas these days?' My friend assured his *tío* he savored the rich flavors of the good stuff and never drank margaritas. The old man swung his cane toward a section of shelving in the deep shadows along the back wall and said, 'then go choose a bottle from the bottom row.' We had to sweep away cobwebs and dust, but selected a bottle with no label and carried it back to the old man. He wiped away a bit more grime until we read the date. 1873." He paused to let the weight of his story sink in.

"Wow. I'm impressed. I didn't really know tequila aged well. So how was it?"

Gabriella returned and placed a platter of tiny quesedillas and a rich brown salsa onto the table with some cotton cocktail napkins. I licked my lips. "Chili guajillo? Mulato?"

She beamed. "No, my own *mole* recipe. Help yourself."

I took a napkin and plate and spooned mole over several of the tiny treats. "Delicious! Thank you, Gabriella."

"Eat all you want, I have another batch coming. They are Dylan's favorite."

Eladio was busily stacking quesadillas onto his plate, which he drenched in *mole*. Gingerly he tweezed one into his fingers and popped it into his mouth, rolling his eyes and half groaning in satisfaction.

I laughed again and asked, "So Eladio, after you swallow, tell me what the tequila was like."

He chewed with his eyes half closed, obviously savoring the *botana*, but when Gabriella returned to the living room with a bottle and four tiny blue glasses, his eyes popped open and crinkled in pleasure. "Ah, my beautiful wife has brought your tequila to sample. Let me finish my story and maybe Dylan will arrive in time to help us toast our independence."

I wasn't so sure I wanted tequila with my wine, but I ate another quesadilla and turned my attention back to Eladio, who had set his hors d'oeuvres plate back onto the low table.

"Our host made a great show of cutting a lime and arranging it and small mouth blown glasses on a round wooden tray, before carefully removing the wrapping and the cork, and giving the bottle neck a long sniff, a far-away look on his face as though he were communing with heaven itself." Eladio paused as I leaned in, intrigued. "*Tío* handed around the glasses and poured a golden dollop. He held up his glass and said, 'I'm and old man now, and I can't take it with me. Drink up.' and he downed the tequila in one gulp. We followed suit and he poured another round. This round we tasted, slowly. It was the sweet taste angels' wings were they melted." He tipped his glass toward me and sipped.

We were silent for a moment before Eladio continued his story. "Old *Tío* lived only another year or two, and when he died, his family sold the property to a developer who bulldozed down the buildings and built a fancy golf club. My friend never heard if the cellar was found. Rumors say bottles sometimes come up through the ground in the golf course, but no one has ever found the entrance to the cave.

Maybe one day..." He looked off into space with that dreamy expression.

"Didn't your friend go back and ask about it? I would have," I said.

Dylan appeared freshly showered and looking totally sexy in sand-washed jeans, an indigo Weezer tee-shirt and trainers. Simple is sexy in my book. "Dyl, we're going to have a toast to *Tio* and his hundred year old bottle of tequila," I said.

"*Papi*, you didn't bore Jade with that old fable, did you? Don't believe a word of it, Jade. It's total BS. A drinking story."

Eladio shook his head in disgust, but I saw the twinkle in his eyes. He winked. Gabriella rejoined us with the platter filled with hot, oozing quesadillas.

Dylan blew her a kiss. "*Mami*, you made my favorites! *Oye, papi*, let's toast to *mami's quesadillas*."

"Good plan, *m'hijo,*" he said and poured the four glasses. The liquid did look a bit like molten halos. Eladio handed them out and we held up the amber shots.

"To my beautiful wife, Gabriella. May we eat her *quesadillas* and *mole* now and ever after." Eladio slammed back his shot.

"To Gabriella!" Dylan and I chorused and slammed ours back. Gabriella blushed and sipped.

"Another round? JadeAnne you need to taste it now."

"Please!"

Eladio refilled our glasses and we sipped between bites of the *botanas* and chit chat about Dylan's day, the Sarasvati, my houseboat, and why I hadn't brought Pepper to visit while we went out. By the fourth round, I was feeling pretty mellow and wondered if I'd overdone it. Tequila had a way of sneaking up on me. Eladio waggled the bottle my way and I covered my glass, shaking my head. "Thanks Eladio, but this celestial ambrosia is going to my head."

He nodded. "And you two need to be on your toes in that crowd. Who's driving?"

Dylan answered. "Change of plans, Jade. They're picking us up here in a half hour and Seeger will drive. Jade, no one will know his car. I think it will be safest for us. Mami, I won't be back tonight. We got rooms over at the Ágata. Free parking and breakfast. We can walk to the plaza. And tomorrow we can get massages if you want."

Gabriella lit up. "My fancy son, the doctor. It sounds lovely—"

The door banged open and Seeger barreled in to give his mother a kiss on her cheek and grab a handful of *quesadillas*, which he stuffed in his mouth. Chewing he rounded on Eladio, who had stood to greet Dafne, and gave him a bearhug. "*Viva México* you guys!" he said, through a mouthful. "*Mmmm, que rico, mami.*"

"Seeg! don't talk with your mouth full," Dafne said, giving me a *what-am-I-your-mother?* look.

"Sit, sit. Let me get more glasses," Gabriella said, over her shoulder as she bustled off to the kitchen.

"You kids ready for the big evening?" Dafne asked.

Dylan slipped his arm around me and nuzzled my neck.

"*Pues,* Dyl is ready for the after-party," Seeger quipped. Eladio winked at Gabriella as she set down two more shot glasses. Viva Mexico!

Chapter 20

El Grito

Seeger drove the "scenic" route to Coyoacán. We jigged through one neighborhood after another for an hour, avoiding main commercial streets, especially Insurgentes and the Periferico, on Dylan's orders. I appreciated his concern, but what was the likelihood of being seen driving in a car not associated with me? They'd made me go out the back with Dyl and cut between properties to the next street where Seeger pulled over and picked us up. I shook my head and sniggered, but I kept a lookout for any cars following us.

"What's so funny?" Dylan asked.

"This whole caper is like some spy movie. Or a getaway novel or something. But I'm enjoying the city tour. Where are we now?" The scenery looked familiar. We crossed a traffic-choked boulevard and I smelled trees.

"We're in Coyoacán. We'll be at the hotel in a couple of minutes," Dafne said, leaning between the seats. "Tomorrow we'll take you to the Frida Kahlo Museum. It's right in the neighborhood. I love her style, but I'd look godawful in the clothes."

"Anyone would. The woman I came to find, Lura, was some distant relative of hers. Small world."

We skirted *el centro* on narrow cobblestone streets. No cars followed us. The houses looked old, with tile rooves and painted tile decorations. Bougainvillea covered the high walls and ancient trees shaded the uneven sidewalks, torn up by layers and layers of roots overflowing the berms. Lovely. Seeger maneuvered the car through several sharp turns and we landed at the colonial-style gate of the Ágata Hotel Boutique and Spa. A quaint white stucco building with red tile, arched windows and wrought iron balconies rose behind the wall. I was charmed. Seeger pulled in, and we alighted to the sounds of birds chittering in the trees.

The hotel only wowed me more as the bellhop guided us to our rooms. Muted creams, greys, and sand in our room were offset by sleek, modern furniture on a grey and cream graphic patterned carpet. Mexican textiles and art added interest to the huge bed and walls. Even the bathroom looked inviting. Ours had a two-man round soaking tub. Dylan and I grinned at each other. A far cry from making out in the front seat of his car. This felt like a honeymoon.

We finished putting our things away while Dylan gave me the rundown of what would happen tonight. Lots of firecrackers, so stick close and steel my nerves to the sharp pops. He said the crowd drank in pace with the hour—the later it got, the drunker the revelers. But the plaza would be filled with families, kids, grandparents, pods of teens and strolling mariachis until *el grito*.

"How about my gypsy? Shall we get our cards read again?" I joked.

"Yeah, I can't wait," he replied. "Maybe she'll predict our happy life together."

"She did give a negative read, didn't she? Twice."

Seeger pounded on the door, yelling. "Hurry up, you

two. You can get a room later."

We laughed and Dylan called back, "Meet you in the lounge in a minute."

The walk to the plaza in the waning light of day took us about ten minutes of stumbling over tree roots, uneven sidewalk and cobbles, but the scents of the gardens and sounds of celebration buoyed us for the excitement to come. In Frida's quiet neighborhood, I had trouble picturing the mass of humanity we would soon join. Dafne cackled when I commented on how lovely the evening was.

"You wait, girl. If you don't need that gun to shoot baddies, you can join the whackos shooting theirs straight up at midnight. Somebody always gets killed."

My chin dropped. "Really? People are allowed to shoot inside city limits?"

"Welcome to Narcolandia. Who's going to stop them?"

I was shaking my head and slowing down. Dylan put his hand on my back to move me along. Maybe Quint was right. Maybe this was a terrible idea.

"The plaza will be filled with narcos?" I asked. I heard the quaver in my voice.

"Daf, look what you've done. You've scared her. I'm sorry for my sick humored fiancé, Jade. No, the plaza will be filled with good Mexican citizens celebrating their independence from tyrannical dictatorships."

"And drunks, idiots, and pickpockets," Dylan added.

"All loyal citizens of our good republic."

I laughed. "All right, you guys, I'm fine. But how did you know I'm carrying, Daf?"

"Because I am too."

Seeger stopped and spun on Dafne. "You what?" We almost ran them down.

"Oh cool down, Seeg. I always carry in crowds. It's a perfect night for robbery, extortion, and kidnapping. Jade and I will keep you boys safe."

The men were tongue-tied. But the sounds of music floating from a soft roaring in the distance said we'd almost arrived.

We entered the plaza from the side near the *antojito* market. Although still full of quesedillas, my traitor mouth watered and my stomach rumbled, it smelled so good. "When are we eating?"

"Probably after *el grito*," Dylan said.

After midnight? I checked my watch. It wasn't even nine. I'd look for the ice cream vendor.

The plaza was full of people. Kids ran around everywhere. Some people wore costumes and masks. That was what I should have done—masked up. Then no thugs would recognize me. I saw a face painting booth and pointed. Dylan shook his head—no way, José. Instead, he took my elbow and directed our group to the margarita cart, buying each of us a double. They were made with real limes. We stopped for churros, *esquites*, and I got my coconut ice cream. The living statue, Angel Gabriel, had taken up residence by the fountain and amazed revelers with his ability to stand stock still in the current of humanity flowing around him. His tips jar overflowed.

I jerked my head toward the jar. "I bet he can move like lightning if someone tries to steal his tips." Dylan nuzzled my ear in response.

We promenaded with the growing horde. A band had started up on the bandstand and we drifted toward the music, a rousing trumpet-filled mariachi tune. Couples two-stepped on the crowded dance floor. I dropped my half-drunk margarita into a can and slipped into Dylan's arms. Dafne and Seeger had already been swallowed by the circling dancers. We two-stepped into the current. The song ended and another started right up. Dylan leaned into my ear and exclaimed, "I thought I recognized the band. It's Mariachi

2000! They're the best."

I smiled up at him, hoping my look wouldn't betray my total ignorance of mariachi music. Anibal had once confessed mariachi was the music of drunkards. Judging by the crowd, I'd say he'd pegged that one. But the band itself was tight and professional. The next song was one I knew, *La Bamba*. The crowd roared and sang along. Even I sang along as we danced. Next we got a slow dance, a heart wrenching mariachi version of *Bésame Mucho*. Dyl held me close, so close I felt his heart beating. He bent down and kissed me and I wasn't sure if we were still dancing or if we'd floated away from the noise and activity. That is until Seeger and Dafne bumped into us with rude kissing sounds. Sheesh! But if we'd kept it up, I worried my heart might explode, it was hammering so fast. Yeah, maybe we should get a room.

"Hey, let's switch partners for the next one," Dafne suggested.

Seeger grinned, taking my hand and pulling me out of Dylan's arms. I made a little salsa move before waving goodbye, and we were off in the current of dancers stepping to *Cucurucucú*, another big crowd pleaser. Seeg confirmed the band played standards, but I'd guessed when everyone knew all the words. I would have to get their CD and start learning the songs.

A new song was playing by the time we bumped into Dylan and Dafne again. They were laughing and trying out silly footwork that was totally out of rhythm with the music. Seeger dropped my hand and made a gallant bow as he yelled *"¡Gracias!"* over the music. I curtsied, well, as best one can in jeans, and mouthed *por nada*. Dafne danced into his arms. I pulled Dylan toward the benches.

"Let's sit for a moment," I said, through my heavy breathing. "I'm not getting enough exercise."

"That will change soon. We're going to get the passport,

take Lily home and return to a normal life."

"How's that? They want me too," I said, watching the passersby. So far the faces were those of regular *ciudadanos,* Mexico City people. I hadn't noticed any prison tattoos or bulges under shirts or creeps paying any attention to me. I leaned my head on Dyl's shoulder. "I long for normal, Dyl, I really do."

The others joined us, and Dafne said, "Let's walk."

The earlier promenade of girls trailed by mothers and grandmothers going one direction, and boys circling the other, with kids darting every which way, and husbands playing checkers and nipping off bottles, had morphed into an unruly multitude.

I checked the time. Ten-thirty. That explained the disappearance of families with kids and the growing legions of staggering partiers. By midnight it would resemble a zombie apocalypse, or the drunks would be sleeping it off in the gardens. But the hour approached where the heavies would outnumber the normal people. I declined when Seeger suggested another round of margaritas.

As it turned out, people-watching was one of Dylan's favorite activities. We found a bench and watched the parade mill by, making up stories to go with the faces.

"Would you like another churro or something?" Dylan asked.

"Sure, but not a churro. Or corn. Or ice cream. Did you see any of those big sugar cookies?"

"Yeah, over on the other side of the church a vendor has *pan dulces*. I'll be right back."

"I'd rather have *panque* if they have it fresh. It's my favorite. And a bottle of water too, please."

"I'll buy a bag of stuff. I could go for a *cuerno*. Stay right here. I don't want to lose you." He bent to kiss my cheek.

I waved my fingers and shifted my gaze as Dylan was

swallowed into the tsunami rising around me. The crowd moved like a tide, individuals subsumed into a blur of streaming color, rushing through pinch points in the walkways and eddying in the wide plaza before me, but always moving. Even the shouts and laughter melded into a river of indistinguishable sound punctuated by a high trumpet note or the crack-crack-crack of a string of firecrackers. I watched a pod of teens break from the tide, a tributary of hoots and antics. They stopped by a drinking fountain, hitched up their drooping pants, and pulled matches out of pockets then lit scores of twisted together firecrackers. A uniformed officer shot toward them from the crowd as the popping started, causing the kids to run into the stream of celebrants and disappear.

Faces appeared and disappeared. It was hypnotizing, and I momentarily relaxed in the glow of an evening with Dylan and the possibilities ahead of me. A clown appeared with balloons, handing a red one to a tiny girl. A triplet staggered into the milling swirl, singing a drunken song, arms over each other's shoulders before they were swallowed from sight. A couple stood out against the muddy blur, she in a tight red dress tottering on too high platform shoes, her brassy hair catching the light; he in a tailored suit cut to unfortunately enhance his apple shape. She stumbled slightly and he turned in my direction to catch her before she went down. Lobo. With a purple and yellow shiner.

I ducked as though I were tying my shoe and surreptitiously observed them from under my hair, my heart pounding. Oblivious, as usual. I'd bet my next paycheck that bitch Consuelo was drunk. They stumbled on against the tide, and I figured they were too drunk to notice me even if I confronted them face-to-face. A rush of fear washed over me. It didn't mean I was safe. Lobo and Daisi Beltrán were buds. What if Daisi and Hector were here too? Maybe with a contingent of security. I watched the burgeoning crowd, which was beginning to lap up against my bench. Already a couple of people had tripped over my toes. Good thing I'd worn closed shoes. The thought crept up on me—I really was insane to be here where I had no protection. Dyl and I should go back to the Ágata. I could think of several things we could do while hiding in our room.

"Hey! Watch it!" I shouted at the back of another idiot who stepped on my toes. He half turned and I saw a tattoo on his neck, but couldn't decipher if it was a Z or a snake. Did it matter? I sprang up ready to bolt over the bench into the garden when someone caught me around my middle. I twisted around, reaching for my gun.

Dylan grinned at me, shaking a bakery bag and wiggling his eyebrows. "Got *panque*, *cuernos* and a bunch of other stuff to eat with the champagne when we get back to the room. Seeg and Daf will meet us in the lobby at one. We'll have time to dance again to the last band. It's Los Dynamite. Kind of punk, kind of rock, and they're from *El D.F.* but they sing in English. You know them?" He looked at me and straightened up, grabbing my arms. "Jade, what's the matter?"

I tried to temper my grimace, but wasn't successful. "Lobo and Consuelo staggered by a little while ago. Then a guy with something tattooed on his neck stepped on my foot. This was a bad idea."

"Jade, it's too crowded for anyone to notice you. Look, I got El Grito 2007 caps for us." He pulled a pink ball cap out of his knapsack and handed it to me. "Put it on. Pull the bill down. No one will recognize you in this mass of bodies. Just another 2007 hat. If there's danger, it's from the press of people. We need to be careful of that."

I slid the hat on, pulling my ponytail over the sizing tab and cocked the bill at an angle, hopefully obscuring my face. "I don't know, Dyl. I'm worried. We should go back to the hotel." The din was so loud, I had to yell.

"You want to go back? It's only a half hour more 'til El Grito." He tilted his head and frowned. I could see he understood, but wanted to stay. "I'll tell you what, we're safe on this bench. Let's stand on the bench. We'll be able to see over the heads to the stage. It's right over there," he said, lifting me onto the slats and pointing to his left. He hopped up and circled me with his arms. Another couple climbed up on the other end of the bench. She was gorgeous and dressed to kill. No one was going to give me a first look with that glamor queen standing next to me. I smiled.

I craned my neck to see over the seriously packed plaza crowding up in front of the stage. A crew was setting up chairs behind several microphones already in place. How had I missed the speaker towers? Spotlights played over the plaza and I could see what must be the Los Dynamite and roadies with instruments milling around behind banks of amps and speakers.

More people piled in. A solid wall of bodies packed in front of our bench. Although it wouldn't be impossible to shoot us, the revelers afforded us some protection, and unless the baddies also stood on something, they couldn't get me in their sights. Of course, the plan was not to shoot me, but to kidnap me. I looked behind us. Uniformed personnel guarded the fenced off swaths of garden. It was unlikely drunk Consuelo would swoop in with lardy Lobo and snatch me from Dylan's arms.

A man in a grey suit stepped onto the stage. Fancy-looking men and women trailed him to the chairs set up behind the podium. One of them looked familiar, Mayor Fallas. A younger man in a white-collared shirt with sleeves rolled up joined the luminaries, shaking hands and greeting some of the women with air kisses. He bustled to the podium and stepped behind the lectern, tapping the mic to test it. Live. He looked out into the audience and grinned. *"¡Buenos noches, Mexico!"* The crowd roared. "I'm Alonso

Maldonaldo Trejo, the head of our independence day committee here to welcome you to the *fiesta!*" The clapping sounded like thunder. Alonso patted his hands down until the audience quieted. "You all know why we're here—to celebrate almost two hundred years of independence from the tyranny of the Spanish Crown."

More cheering, whistles, shouts of, "*¡Viva!*"

"On this night 197 years ago," he continued, "Father Hidalgo rang the bell of independence and delivered the very first call—*El Grito de Dolores.* If you remember your primary school history, the war for independence lasted over a decade, but we have lived as an independent nation for almost two hundred years!"

The crowd went wild as the church bells pealed in honor of the occasion.

When the old bells stopped reverberating, Alonso continued, "Tonight to lead us in El Grito de Dolores, we have our distinguished *Alcalde* Fallas, mayor of the greatest city in our nation! Let's give him a big hand," he said and turned to lead the mayor and his wife up to the mic, clapping over his head and grinning like a fool before backing away and sitting down. I wondered who the rest of the delegation were.

Fallas gave the usual boring politician speech that went on too long and mostly said "hooray for me."

Dylan whispered his interpretation of the speech in my ear, keeping me in stitches until the smarmy egoist and his wife encircled each other's waists and waved to the crowd. It was the clichéd photo op every politician delivered. And it was 11:59. A projectile sailed across the heads of the audience and splatted onto the stage. Alonzo scuttled out and grabbed another mic. "Countdown time! Everybody. 12-11-10-..." We shouted with the emcee, "*siete...seis...cinco...*"

Fallas counted down on his fingers and we all shouted with him, "*... dos... uno. Viva Mexico! Viva Mexico! Viva*

Mexico!"

The plaza felt like it would lift off. Everywhere faces radiated joy and pride. The bells rang again, an allegro for fireworks blasting overhead and Mexico's National anthem blasting out of the banks of speakers, "Mexicans at the cry of war, make ready the steel and the bridle..."

I apparently was the only person in the audience who didn't know the words. Everybody sang.

And the fiesta got under way.

Chapter 21

The After Party

Sunday, September 16, 2007

The dignitaries left the stage and the band members I'd seen before the shout were slinging guitar straps over their shoulders. The drummer tapped out a military drumroll and the lead strummed an electric chord. Firecrackers popped crazily and where they went off the crowd parted. The plaza thinned out and again the faces of revelers shifted. The crowd looked younger. And pretty wasted. I smelled *mota*, pot, on the air.

The band kicked into their first song.

"Is this Los Dynamite?" I shouted at Dylan. He nodded and hopped off the bench now there was room on the ground.

"Let's dance," he shouted back and handed me down.

"I'll need another margarita to dance to this. Punk? Really Dyl?"

He laughed and towed me to the margarita line. I wished I had earplugs. I hadn't appreciated punk rock when it was popular, except for the Cars and the Police, which might not technically be punk, but I didn't really know. We hit the front of the line and got double shots again. I swilled mine and let the driving beat move my feet. The lyrics were in English.

Tequila imbued me with the spirit and we tossed our cups in unison. Dylan twirled me into the roistering mass gyrating to the driving beat. It was loud. The tenor of the evening shifted once again to something frenetic and sinister. Too many aggressive gang tats and tarted-up teens. I observed the people around me and began to feel like I'd fallen into a 21st century version of West Side Story. Call it South Side Story—and the relentless rhythm was firing up a rumble. I grabbed Dylan and jerked my head toward the pavement. Glass, broken booze bottles, trash being ground into paste under the people's feet. We were in the middle of the mosh pit and the frenzy was a swarming hive of angry yellowjackets. I noticed the gang mudras, hand signals to friends, chin pointing, tensions rising. We had to leave, now.

I pulled Dylan's arm and he folded me into his chest and rocked me wildly to the beat. I squirmed away. He didn't see the danger and grasped my hand, twirling me back in. From the corner of my eye I caught movement, not dancing. A pod of prison tats sharking through the crowd, pushing dancers out of their way, opening a path toward another school near the bandstand jigging, cheering, passing flasks and bottles between them and their girls.

I swung into Dylan and yelled, "Trouble ahead!"

He hooted and yelled, "You know it, baby!"

I pointed to the tats and caught sight of several Zs. Fear gripped me. These weren't teen gangbangers. "Dylan, let's go. Now!" I shouted, pulling him as hard as I could. One of the sharks turned leered as he passed and flashed a handgun. "Dylan. They're armed." I yanked out of his grasp and spun away from the band, pushing and shoving through the bodies.

Dylan must have woken up from his dance trance and realized what was about to happen. He shot ahead of me, grabbing my hand and pulling me across the plaza to the bench. I hopped up, eyes riveted to the bandstand.

"There'll be injuries. I'll have to help."

Was Dylan really saying he wanted to get involved? "No you don't. Call 9-1-1. Let the police handle it."

"Jade. I'm a doctor. I took an oath."

"Yeah, to cause no harm, not to risk harming yourself. Give me your phone."

He tossed it to me as he shoved off into the panicking throng, calling over his shoulder, "Ambulance 065. Dial!"

The band kicked it up a notch and the fighting started, punctuated by the incessant blast of M80s. Or gunshots. Dylan jumped into the fray.

The crowd's roaring, screaming, shouting, melded with the pulse of drums and guitars, drowning the vocals. I saw a woman shoved and fall, trampled as the hundreds of partiers fled. I dialed.

By the end, five were dead, three trampled in the stampede out, two of the jigging kids executed—I'd witnessed the leering shark pull the trigger—and scores injured with bruises, cuts, scrapes, and a few broken bones. By the time the riot squad showed up, the Zetas had sliced through the on-lookers and undulated away. The speed with which they disappeared stunned me. Maybe the tats acted like shark's denticles. I remembered from a science unit on fish, how shape and texture of the mineralized deposits allow sharks to move through water effectively. Maybe the tats facilitated movement through smoggy air. I snorted. The Zetas certainly were pre-humans—anything could be true.

Dylan was at work with the *paramédicos*, attending to

the more seriously injured. He and a solid-looking older woman were securing one of the jigging kids to a stretcher as he groaned. A couple of guys carted him to an awaiting ambulance. By then the plaza was clearing out, Los Dynamite had been extinguished and I dangled my legs off the stage above where Dyl worked. *Viva México*. What a disaster. At least it wasn't a personal disaster. Quint was going to give me a ration for sure. I yawned and my stomach growled. It was 1:30 a.m. We'd had snacks and alcohol hours ago.

"Hey, girlfriend," Dafne sang out, emerging into my line of sight. "What a party, no? You guys about ready to get something to eat? The *mercado* will close at two. Hey Dyl. We gotta go," she ordered.

He stood up and stretched as the paramedics took another victim to the ambulance. He assessed the remaining victims and said, "Yeah, it looks like they don't need me anymore. Let's go. I'm famished."

One of the cops and a paramedic approached him with back slaps and handshakes. The cop said, "*Oye*, doctor, join us for brews one of these times?" He handed over a card Dylan slipped into his pocket.

I hopped off the stage and approached him.

Dylan reached out for me. "I will, Alejo. Meet my *novia*, JadeAnne."

Alejo and I waved before he turned back to Dylan. "You still in the *colonia*?"

"Yeah, man, at *casa mami y papi* for now. Saving up to get my own place."

"I hear you, Dyl. I doubt I'll ever leave. *Pues*, I better get back to work. Say hi to Gabriella for me."

I took one of Dylan's arms and Dafne the other. Seeger grabbed her other hand and we trotted off to eat.

The Antojitos Mexicanos presented a scene of normalcy

and calm. Brightly lit, the warehouse sized building crammed with typical stalls of eateries. Two margaritas, half an ear of corn slathered in cream and two pastries didn't cut it. "What are we eating?" I asked.

"Whatever you desire, *mi reina*."

Ah, I had become Dylan's queen. Nice to know. "What are you guys eating?"

Seeger didn't hesitate. He pointed to the back corner. "*Pozole rojo*. Best in the city back there at Doña Rosalita's stall. Daf?"

She was eyeing a plate of something meaty smothered in *crema* with thin sliced radishes and cabbage on top. It looked and smelled delicious, oozing red and green salsa. I realized it was a tri-color dish, matching the flag. "*¡Viva Mexico!*" I said.

Dafne raised her eyebrows. "You catch on fast."

Dylan dragged me to a counter case stuffed with red tinged sandwiches. "*Pambazos*. Stuffed with chorizo, cheese, and potatoes." He stepped up to order three.

Dafne carried her plate over to an empty table about midway between us and Seeger and tipped up four chairs, waving as Seeger turned in our direction. The market wasn't crowded, being almost closing time, but still quite a few folks were eating. A man passed by with something smothered in a white sauce with pomegranate arils sprinkled on top. "*Chilis en nogadas*," I crowed. "That's what I want."

"Good choice. Traditional. Here," he said and handed me some bills, gesturing to a stall to the left of us.

Order in hand, I joined my group at the table. Someone had brought a tray of tiny blue rimmed glasses filled with green, red, and clear liquid. One of each for each of us. Dafne explained, "Green lime juice, white tequila, red *sangrita*, called *banderita* shots. But don't shoot them back. These are for sipping. You savor the flag as you savor the drinks." She cut out a glass for me, pushing the rest across the table.

I sipped the tequila chased by the lime then the spicy tomato-colored looking *sangrita* Dafne said was grenadine and chili. Tasty. I watched the few people coming in for signs of trouble while my friends chatted about the event, where Seeger and Dafne had been during the excitement (at the other stage dancing to *banda* music) and what we all would do after breakfast. The tequila, by the third round, had killed my energy and all I wanted was to be carried home. Preferably to the Sarasvati. The lapping of the bay against the hull and the gentle rocking with the tide would be balm for a tired soul that had seen too much too fast.

"...Jade, oh Jade—earth to Jade!" Dylan was saying as he poked my side.

"Uh, sorry! I was thinking about my houseboat. Dex better be watering my orchids."

"There you go, Dyl, you're such a dud, your date is thinking about her flowers," Seeger teased his brother.

I snickered, but jumped to Dylan's defense. "No, no, I'm just tired. The third shot got to me."

"The shots got to me too, but I needed a few drinks to dull the horror."

"*Ja ja*, Daf. Bad joke." Dylan glared at her.

She replied, "I don't know how you can work in the emergency room. It would gross me out."

"Good thing you're the property manager and business executive not the doctor then," Seeger said.

"Yeah, good thing. And good thing one of us can stand guts and gore," Dylan added.

"And good thing you guys are stopping with the unpleasant conversation. Let's move on to something cheerier," I said.

"Like going back to the Ágata for a soak in the whirlpool tub," Dafne suggested to Seeger.

"Like sleeping," Dylan and I chimed in unison.

Chapter 22

Independence Day

We awoke in each other's arms around mid-day. The concierge had assured us the breakfast buffet would be served until *comida* so we had time to try out the jacuzzi tub before calling Seeg and Daf to meet. One thing led to another and we finally ordered room service and opened the bag of last night's *panes*. I wondered what we were missing. Not that Dylan wasn't worth a *chorizo* or plate of *huevos rancheros*. He turned out to be a wonderful lover and just thinking about him set my heart racing. I basked in the glow of our love making.

"You ready to go?" he asked, nuzzling the back of my neck with his freshly shaved face.

I turned around and kissed him. "Yep. Where are we going?"

"First to Frida Kahlo's house for the tour. Next to lunch, and later back here for massages and cocktails. We have late checkout. Seeg wants to eat at Mesón Antigua before taking us home."

We hooked up with the others in the lobby and set out the two blocks to the Frida Kahlo Museum, lining up for entry tickets along the blue wall with tourists from around the world. I'd visited before, but this time I noticed Frida kept mirrors everywhere and many of her paintings mimicked or carried further the photographs she posed in. She developed her signature style in part to camouflage her damaged legs, but I realized that another part of her style was to emphasize her fluid sexual boundaries—the unibrow and mustache. I inspected photos where she posed as a man. Some of the photos where she posed with other women radiated distinct sexuality. Not just the victim of polio and a serious accident, married to a difficult, artistic man, Frida was unable to fully realize her talent and aspirations, perhaps for the mores and cultural expectations of the times? Only Frida could tell.

I poked along, inspecting everything. Dafne and Seeger basked in the courtyard under the late summer sun, and Dylan fidgeted trying to hurry me along. I guessed he wouldn't be my best travel companion. I could take hours in a museum and liked to visit all of them.

"Hurry up, slowpoke," Dafne called out. "Dyl went to the gift shop to buy you the book, since you didn't have enough time to see everything."

Always teasing. I'd have to remember that about Dafne. I pulled a *What? Me slow?* face and dropped into a chair across from them to wait for Dylan. He came out with a Frida headdress of flowers and braided cloth.

"You'll look fabulous in this, Jade." He handed me the actually well-designed garment. "It's a replica of one she wore in California. It's in one of the paintings."

Dafne tried to keep a straight face. "Where's she going to wear it, Dyl?"

"I can disguise myself as Frida when the traffickers

come looking for me," I joked.

"Not funny, girl. Unless you draw in the eyebrows and moustache."

"Yeah, my bro' loves kissing men."

"Okay, you guys. It was a thoughtful gift and I'm grateful. It will make a good conversation piece at home. Thank you, Dylan," I said, kissing his cheek. "Let's go. Didn't I hear something about *comida*? Where are we going?"

We were headed for the gate when Seeger answered me. "Jardín Santa Catarina. You'll love it. It's one of those typical, colorful Mexican places, Mesón Antigua. Decent food, and on Sundays they have entertainment. I've got my fingers crossed, today it's the troupe from the university that does humorous parodies of politics, people, you name it. Even newlyweds. You remember them, don't you Dyl?"

"Yeah, they made fun of everyone in a style brought from 16th century Spain. Aren't they Jewish? They play *cajones, ¿no?*"

"The wooden box drums? I learned about them in my Spanish class. Sounds fun! Is it far?" I asked.

"Far enough we'll grab a taxi ," Dylan said.

We'd reached the plaza and crossed it to the main avenue out of *el centro*. Dylan hailed a green taxi. Allegedly the green taxis were the safe ones. We wouldn't be held hostage until the driver emptied our wallets, pockets, and ATM machines. I must have had a frightened look on my face because Dafne held the door and said, "Hop in. And don't worry, I've negotiated many taxi hostage situations." Not very convincing.

I studied the scenery along the ancient tree-lined Av. Francisco Sosa as we passed grand residences to stop at a tiny park marked by a yellow adobe church at one end and the many colored restaurant at the other. We got out, less the fare but with no hostage situation and strolled across the cropped lawn to the restaurant and ascended the stairs to an open air dining room of wooden tables and brightly painted caned chairs. Colorful paper cutouts of birds, skulls, flowers and animals garlanded the ceiling. A guitarist crooned in a corner. Excitement and joy rushed through me. I loved this place. Heck, any place with orange and Mexican blue walls and dollhouse colored furniture that smelled this inviting was my kind of place.

"I knew you'd love this restaurant. We all do. It's been the Porras family Sunday outing destination for most of our lives," Dylan said.

"Sometimes we'd go to Gandhi after, or the plaza, and sometimes we'd go to a cool coffeehouse with newspapers from around the world on the tables—do you remember that, Dyl?" Seeger asked.

"I'm surprised you do. You were pretty small."

The waiter brought our menus, beautifully designed in the same bright blues, pink, orange, red and purple as the walls and chairs. "May I bring you anything to drink? We have a special tricolor margarita with grenadine, blue curaçao and coconut infused silver tequila in a pitcher."

Dafne's eyes lit up. "Let's try it, Seeg."

He nodded and held up four fingers. The waiter hurried off to get the drinks. It was four o'clock, yet we'd been up so late last night, it felt a little early to start drinking. But what the hey? A little hair of the *burro* might get my blood moving. I felt pretty heavy after too much sugar and alcohol and not enough sleep, but smiled to myself, what Dylan and I did instead of sleep had been amazing. Dex and I had never set off fireworks during our love making. It was the difference of grinding gears in an old school bus and launching a rocket. We'd fit perfectly and Dylan instinctively knew exactly what I liked. Even before I did. I sighed.

"Too many choices, Jade?" Dylan asked me.

I snickered and nodded. If he only knew.

He continued, "Any of the house dishes are remarkable. I'm having the *filete Dalí*—medallions of steak on a bed of Iberico ham with a sweet red wine sauce and an organic fig and chipotle salsa."

"JadeAnne's face didn't look like she was confused by the menu," Dafne said, and winked at me.

The smartass. "There's so much to choose from," I said. "What are you having, Daf?"

"Mmmm, traditional for me. Chicken *mole*. Their *mole* is exquisite. Seeg? You?"

"My usual. *Ancho* chilies stuffed with *manchego*, corn, and mushrooms doused in a red sauce. Check the name out." He flashed the menu at us. "*Cielito Lindo*, heavenly. Heavenly food for celebrating almost two hundred years of nationhood with the people I love best. I'd call this heaven." He tipped his newly poured purplish drink toward us and said, "*¡Viva la vida loca!*"

"*Viva! Viva!*" we echoed.

The waiter came back and asked how we liked the margaritas. Way too sweet for me, and once it poured into the glass it looked more like it should have noxious steam rising off it. But it did look great in the pitcher.

"Yummm," Dafne purred.

The waiter looked relieved. "What can I bring you?"

We ordered. I'd finally decided on the *filete de Veracruzana*, fish smothered in olives, capers, herbs, tomato sauce, and the little blond chilies I liked. I needed a lighter meal, if you could call this light. My jeans felt too snug around my middle.

I'd been telling myself for several weeks I needed to slow down on the *panes* and booze especially. It felt like everyone here drank a lot. "Dafne, how do you stay thin eating and drinking like this? I'm pooching over the top of my jeans."

"Who says I'm not? Since I met Seeger, I've put on four

kilos. I can't squeeze into my college wardrobe any more, but who wants to look like a coed in *La Capital*?"

"Well, I agree with that. But I'm feeling like a stuffed pig."

She explained, "I don't drink during the week when I have to work or study. I never miss breakfast, enjoy a decent comida and only eat soup or salad for supper. And the hot chocolate and *pan dulces*? Forget it. Once you've eaten a hundred *conchas*, you've pretty much had the experience. My advice? Skip the tortillas, rice, and beans too. Save traditional Mexican food for occasions, like Independence Day." She grinned, raised her muddied margarita and shouted "*¡Viva!*"

Diners from nearby tables raised their glasses and shouts of *"Viva!" "México!" "Por La Independencía!"* rang across the room. Dafne dipped her head in "You're welcome."

Seeger laid his hand over hers. "My shy flower."

The guitarist played a rousing song most of the diners knew and sang with him. Everyone clapped; he raised his guitar and bowed in thanks then left the room. In his place, the touted troupe of Spanish theater tumbled onto the dining porch and started singing hilarious songs about the state of Mexico, its history and famous figures. The diners erupted in laughter. While we enjoyed house flan doused in coffee liquor and dusted with ground pecans, the troupe moved table to table spoofing the diners. A new bride laughed so hard she cried. I prayed we'd get out of there before they got to us.

"¿Más cafe, señores?"

Dylan nodded. *"Sí, por favor."*

Too late. The troubadours launched into a silly song about wife swapping. Dafne laughed hysterically and announced Dyl and Seeg were brothers as she tipped them a $20 peso note. They sang another song more bawdy and fast paced than the last. The restaurant ate it up. Dylan turned a girlie pink and Seeger's expression was mortification. I couldn't understand a lot of it. Slang and *grocerias,* they told me on the ride back to the Ágata to get our overnight bags and head home. I didn't hear anything more about a late supper, thank God. I was stuffed, over tired, and ready to get quiet with my dog and my journal. Although the massage might have been nice. Dylan must have been feeling the same, because he fell asleep slumped against my shoulder in the car on the way home.

Chapter 23

Capa y Espada

I called Quint with my arrival time, the conversation short and terse with instructions to approach from the south after circling a few times.

"I repeat, do not come if you are being followed or if you pass a black Suburban, license plate 665 HSY DF MEX."

"Okay, Dad. See you soon," I said to dead air. What was that about? Phones tapped? How would they tap ours? U.S. phones on different carriers? Anyway, who were *they*?

"Seeger, something's going on at my place. Quint wants us to circle and look for a vehicle," I said, repeating the license plate. "And make sure we weren't followed. Wasn't worth arguing the baddies don't know your car, but to be safe, I think I should keep my head down."

"You can use your new disguise. Put the headdress on. That will confuse them," Dafne said straight-faced.

I couldn't tell if she was kidding. "No way! I don't want to call attention, I want to deflect it."

"She's joking. Dafne is my standup comedienne. Get down. I'll watch the mirrors and Daf can check out the vehicles parked in the neighborhood."

"He wants us to come in from the south. Do you know how to do that? I sure don't."

"*Claro.* We'll take neighborhood streets. All this *capa y espada* is kind of thrilling. Like international *espionaje, ¿no?*"

"I guess, Seeg. This sneaking around and not being safe has gotten old. I just want to get back to normal." An image of fog tumbling down the canyons of Mount Tam flashed in my head. Cold and clean, smelling of the sea and dampening the sounds of the harbor as it flowed over the bay. I so wasn't ready to deal with the traffickers after a lovely day and night. Dylan stirred. Poor man, he'd had a late night and long day before we left for Coyoacán, and we'd had little sleep. And too much imbibing. How long was he going to put up with me and my baggage?

Seeger exited Circuito Interior onto a boulevard I didn't recognize. From there we moved into a neighborhood of modest walled homes. We circled through the neighborhood until Dafne was certain we hadn't been followed. He made two more rights then left onto another street, which we followed for blocks. Again he turned left and began weaving through the next neighborhood, this time apartment buildings. He cut through several alleys and doubled back, making his circles wider. We inched east. Twice he pulled over, doused the lights, and said, "Duck," then backtracked away from Colonia Roma. Unless *they* used surveillance tag teams, the vehicles were different and both had families in them, but better safe than sorry.

I yawned. Dylan stirred. "What's going on? Aren't we back yet?"

"Go back to sleep. We're practicing dodging a tail," Dafne joked. Or, I guessed she was joking.

He bolted up and looked out the window. Twilight approached, but it was plenty light enough to see everything. "What the heck are we doing in Napoles?"

"Circling, dodging, backtracking. Jade's dad told us to approach from the south and be sure we weren't followed," Dafne stated matter-of-factly, as if all this *capa y espada, cloak and dagger,* were an everyday occurrence.

"You're enjoying it, aren't you?" he said.

"You bet, Dyl," Seeger replied.

"Yeah, but I need to get home and to bed. Five-thirty surgery. I got a call while you were bringing the car around."

"So we risk it and go straight to Jade's? That would piss her father off."

"That's not what I said, Seeg. Just get a move on. I'll keep watch too."

I repeated the vehicle description and *placa* number and we continued in silence. I was lost, turned around and so, so tired. I closed my eyes and drifted as the car jogged around blocks, opening them when I felt the car slow. Seeger and Dafne had been talking in low voices and, hearing alarm in Dafne's voice, I tuned in to listen.

"What is it?" I asked. The neighborhood seemed familiar, but in the gloaming, I wasn't exactly sure. "Are we in Roma?"

"We are. Keep your head down. I've gone past your building and there's a black Suburban with possibly two people in it. Daf couldn't see the *placa.* I'm coming up behind it."

I realized we were at my building. At the corner we turned right and drove two blocks then turned right again. Seeger pulled over and got out, Dafne slid into the driver's seat and Seeger hopped into shotgun position. "You two stay down," he said.

She shifted into gear and circled back onto Calle Obregon to pass the suspicious vehicle again. Seeger read off the plate number, "665 HSY a DF plate."

I dialed Quint.

"You're right. We can't get into the alley. *They're* watching," I said. He asked if we'd seen any other cars. I held the phone out and relayed the message.

"No, Quint. We've checked and no other cars appeared to have anyone in them. But these jokers can see the front door and the alley entrance. We can go to our house."

"Quint, can't you do something? I want to come home. How's Pepper?" He said Pepper was fine and he'd call someone and let me know when it was safe. "Okay, Daf, let's drop Dylan off and go to your house. Quint will call when it's safe."

"You know, Jade, you're not ever going to be safe in that room without blackout curtains. I noticed I could see right in from the street," she said.

"I close the curtains at night."

"Not good enough. You need that room invisible from the street. You could trade for one of the back bedrooms, I suppose, but that just would endanger someone else. I'll consider what we should do."

"*Hermano, muchas gracias por cuidar a mi novia,*" Dylan said through a yawn as the car picked up speed on a through street.

I burrowed into his arms, exhaustion and fear stealing the weekend's joy.

Chapter 24

Adding Up

In "my" room at Seeger's, I paced like a caged jaguar. Dafne had gone home to get ready for an early work appointment in the morning. Seeger snored in front of some *futbol* match on TV. Why didn't Quint call?

In my bones I feared a confrontation with 665 HSY. With my new info from Anibal, I'd added a third party to the *they're-after-us* list. I totted it up in my head: 1) BLO hoping to recover their inventory: Lily; 2) Los Zetas determined to repossess both of us and probably snag Pepper in the deal; and 3) Anibal's posse of Eddie Santos and Carlos Beltrán planning to rescue Anibal and grab Lily and me to hand over to the highest bidder. I discounted Lobo as part of that crew. He wasn't going to break with his BFF and benefactor Hector Beltrán. Too much at stake there. But the idea the BLO and Los Zetas were in a negotiation to form a joint trafficking scheme wouldn't let go its claws. Why would they do that? I heard they were mortal enemies. Of course, much of what I "heard" was hearsay, fantasy, gossip, and conjecture.

No one in my circles knew what was really going on. Or, those who knew, weren't saying. Like that scumbag Farcía Luna. How could the government put him at the head of one of the main agencies to combat organized crime when he was paving the way for the cartels to operate? Wealth and power. I'd always like economics and this was a simple economic system: bribe officials, military, and law enforcement to assist and protect in the making of a shit ton of tax-free money through illegal means. The old *paving the road with gold.* But this wasn't news. The problem was, how could I extract Lily and me from danger and stop the trafficking? I looked at the clock. 10:10. Why didn't Quint call?

The bed invited me to crawl in and relax. I plugged one of Dafne's meditation tapes into a player I found on a shelf, lay down and closed my eyes. The disembodied voice on the cassette soothed my worries as she annoyed me with her cool, buttery intonations. She instructed me to go to my safe, peaceful place. Did I even have one anymore? I used to. I practiced yoga regularly and ran every day. I meditated on the deck of the Sarasvati fog and shine. Was I calm then? Why did I stay here? What was I going to accomplish except maybe get myself killed or worse? I pictured my lovely view of Richardson's Bay and the hill of Tiburon and Belvedere, the lights on Mt. Tam at night above Mill Valley and the fog billowing over the Headlands into Tam Junction. My blood pressure dropped and I drifted on the outgoing tide. Words floated into my mind, formed sentences. Existential questions to ponder. *Why don't I go home? What am I trying to prove? Where do I really belong?* Then people floated by: *my parents, my dead sister, Dex. They didn't see me, didn't turn their heads my way. Quint floated through, turned and waved. Lily implored me to help her. Dylan radiated pure love—for me.* I floated back to consciousness. Was this my answer? Was I doing the right thing? I wondered as the Sarasvati washed out on the tide.

The clock in the entry chimed eleven. I patted around for my phone, eyes still turned inward, and sat up shaking out the cobwebs. No call. I contemplated dialing Quint, but he'd said to wait. I blew out a strangled breath. I wasn't his minion. I could jolly well dial.

My phone lit up, buzzing. Ah, the power of positive thinking. "It's about time."

"It's Horacio. Your *papi* asked me to call."

"Hi, H. So what's going on? Is everyone safe? Lily?"

"We've had some excitement, but we're all fine. Lily is still in the saferoom with Chucho and the dogs. We've eliminated the men from the Suburban and confiscated their weapons, but another team managed to get to Aguirre—"

"Did we lose him?" I interrupted.

"No, but he was injured in the shooting and has been taken to the hospital. Your father has gone to the embassy to arrange his extradition. Santiago and the two CIA operatives are meeting him there. I'm waiting for Santiago's team to claim the bodies."

"What's to say Anibal won't be rescued from the hospital?"

"He's going straight to surgery and police have been stationed outside the door to the operating room."

I felt my ire steaming from its cauldron. "Will he live to be prosecuted?"

Horacio chuckled. "You get right to the point, *¿no?*"

"I'm coming home."

"Quint wants you to stay the night where you are."

"Well, too bad."

"It may not be safe out there."

"I've got my gun and I run fast. I'll call when I arrive. Be at the door. Armed!" I hung up. I shouldn't boss Horacio around, especially against his *jefe's* orders, but tough. I needed my dog and Lily needed me.

"Seeg. Seeger! Wake up," I said, nudging his shoulder. The TV was still blaring a game, but I doubted it was the one he had been watching. I grabbed the control and punched it off. "Seeg!" My nudge morphed into a prod.

He stirred. "Wha—?" Spit foam collected along his inner lips and he smacked and swallowed a couple times before opening his eyes. "Who won?"

"I don't know. I need to go home, but I don't know your address for a taxi."

"No taxis this late. I mean, it's dangerous. Hold on, I'll drive you. Let me wake up." He rolled off the sofa and stumbled down the hall to his room.

I didn't really want him to drive his car. It had been seen in the neighborhood and Horacio had said there was another team. If anyone had gotten away...stop! I couldn't think that way. No one was watching. No one would remember or recognize his nondescript beige compact car. We'd be safe. We had to be. Dafne would kill me if anything happened to him.

"*¿Listo?*"

I gritted my teeth. "Yes, ready."

He grabbed his keys from a hook by the back door and steered me toward the garage. The car was open and we slid in. Seeg pressed the door opener and we were on our way. Traffic was light late on Independence Day and we made good time. I gave him the Cliff Notes version of the Roma activity. He asked a few questions and offered some insight into the problem of organized crime in Mexico. For a civilian, he was surprisingly knowledgeable and calm about cartel attacks and trafficking. But it wasn't like he was reading about it in the paper. This was real.

I texted Quint's phone as we approached the house and instructed Seeger to drive up onto the sidewalk as close to the door as possible. He punched off the soft jazz playing on the radio. We'd made a couple of passes through the immediate neighborhood and hadn't seen any suspicious cars or loiterers. I made a note to find out which cars belonged to which neighbors. It could help future surveillance.

"Okay, Seeg. That's my door." I pointed. He drove onto the sidewalk through the wheelchair access and slowed to a stop. I saw the office door cracking open and I opened my door. When I could see Horacio I said, "Thanks, Seeg. Now get out of here!" and sprinted the few feet toward my door. The rush of a projectile whizzed past my shoulder and I heard the thunk as it embedded into stone. I dove for the open door. Horacio stepped out and blasted a rifle over the car's roof as it peeled into the street, thumping over the curb. Someone screamed. Arms grasped me, pulling me into reception. The door slammed.

"Oh, God! What if *they* follow him?"

Quint's voice came from the workroom. "I've got a team on him. If Seeger is followed, they will intervene.

"What? How? What team, Dad? Why didn't you call me?" I sputtered, leaning into the door. Quint was on the computer.

He jerked up from the screen. "Why didn't you stay put?" Angry.

"I'm getting Lily. And Pepper. She must be scared to death."

"She's playing checkers and eating ice cream."

"Horacio said she was locked into that awful room."

"She is. Chucho is with her."

"I'm letting them out."

"No, I'm putting you in."

"No way, Quint. I'm ready to do what needs to be done here. Brief me."

"Someone shot at you as you ran from the car. Seeger hit a pedestrian, presumably the person who shot at you, or an accomplice. A special security team has arrested one man, removed two bodies, and have detained Anibal in the hospital. I think it's your man's hospital. How was the weekend, by the way?"

"How was my weekend? Focus, Dad. What's important here? Why would *they* shoot at me?" My hands trembled. I fisted them to keep Quint from seeing I was scared. Why *would* the traffickers want to shoot me? I'd be of no value wounded or dead.

"My guess is Anibal's friends want revenge. He blames you."

I eyed him, frowning. "Tell me something new." I raised my eyebrows. "So? Tell all. Oh, speaking of friends, we saw Lobo and Consuelo lurching through the crowd in Coyoacán." The computer beeped. An email had arrived.

Quint's expression turned to alarm. "I told you not to go. Did they see you?"

"No. Drunk as usual, especially Consuelo."

"How do you know someone else didn't see you? How did Aguirre's friends know when to show up?"

"You think they came because I was gone? How would that matter to them? Think, Quint. Could I prevent them from taking Anibal better than several armed, trained men? Get real."

He read his email. "Aguirre is out of surgery. He'll be fit to travel in a day or two. I've contacted the US Marshal's office and they're sending someone. They don't like it. They've lost two good men because of that asshole."

I flopped onto a wheeled secretary chair. "And the locals? Is anyone helping catch these guys?"

"I've got a team. Who do you think is guarding the civilian you've put in danger because you can't follow direct orders?" He was tight jawed and growling.

"Okay, okay. I'll call Seeger and make sure he's home. But I'm getting Lily now. It's late. She, we, need to go to bed. And I need my dog."

"Do not call Seeger. Leave the man alone. The less you have to do with any of that family, the safer they will be."

I gazed over his head and noticed a new painting. Colorful boats moored at an island of flowers. "That's a cheerful painting. Where'd it come from?"

"Something of Mrs. P's. She came by this morning to talk about coming back to work."

"When did the trouble start?"

"This afternoon."

"In broad daylight?"

"They tried to sneak in."

"Did Mrs. P know Anibal was here?"

He gave me the Quint stare. "Now don't go starting that again, Jade. Mrs. Pérez had nothing to do with the attack."

I shrugged. "I'm going to the saferoom."

He coiled. A cobra ready to strike. I backed away in my chair.

"You aren't listening to me. Someone took a potshot at you. We've been penetrated—"

I interrupted, "You mean Ani's crew showed up to spring him from the storage room. What does it have to do with me? I'm getting Pepper."

He blew out a slurred stream of invectives. Or maybe just exasperation. Okay, I was being uncooperative, but locking up a little girl and *my* dog didn't make sense to me.

"Jade, you're hardheaded. Go knock and tell Chucho they can come out. The email was my security captain telling me the problem has been taken care of. They are interrogating the men now."

I shook my head in disbelief. "Why didn't you just say that to begin with?" I spun out of the room and streaked down the hall yelling, *"Alli alli oxen free."* I could hear Pepper barking at the door, which popped open to Lily concentrating on her next move.

"Everything taken care of?" Chucho pushed through the rush of puppies bouncing into the hall. I watch two squat, leaving large puddles.

"Lily, get the mop! How long have you been in there?" I asked Chucho.

"Too long. I'm going to check in, see what I can do." He and his trail of mini goldens trotted off. Quint would love the dogs invading his work cave.

"Stop. Lily, come on. We have to get these dogs out and clean up their messes."

"It's my move. I'm winning. You said that wrong, by the way. It's 'All ye, all in free.'"

"Right. Think you've won. Pack it up."

She hopped a red tile over two black ones and punched the air with a winner's stance. "Woo hoo!" She packed up the board and tiles and tossed it on top of a pile of boxed games I hadn't noticed before. Seeing my expression, she said, "Under the couch."

Quint discussed the day's events with us over a snack of orange cake and hot chocolate at our usual meeting spot, the kitchen table. Mrs. P had whipped up a baking dish of cheese enchiladas in a tomatillo sauce, rice, and a pot of beans for dinner before she went home, but the meal sat in covered dishes on the stove. We'd be set for the next day, I thought as I made room for everything in the fridge.

"Anyone want anything else?" I asked, interrupting Horacio's report. No one answered. I sat down.

"Aguirre is under guard in the recovery room. He lost a lot of blood but will make a full recovery. Dylan removed the bullet and sewed a couple of veins back together. If the shot had been five centimeters to the left, he would have died."

"Who shot him?" I asked.

"We won't know which gun until it's gone through

ballistics. Your Dylan isn't a gun expert."

"Dylan, my Dylan? He was home sleeping. What do you mean?"

"Aguirre was removed to Dylan's emergency room where they could get him in. Being Independence Day, the hospitals and emergency centers are filled. They called Dylan to come in."

"That's awful. Poor Dyl! He was exhausted. But I bet the irony wasn't lost on him."

Lily pouted. "Why didn't he let that horrible man die?"

"Don't say things like that, girl," Quint snapped. "Only God gets to decide if we live or die."

The kettle whistled. I shoved up from the table to fix my tea. I agreed with her. Anibal was at the root of everything that had happened. Okay, I couldn't blame him for my own stupidity in accepting a date with Fernando Torrens, but everything else? I wondered if his cousin Lura, the woman I came to Mexico to find, knew what he was up to. I'd never know. That is, unless God told me. And she wasn't saying.

"I didn't know you were a believer, Dad."

He grunted and excused himself.

"H, what exactly happened here? I thought that's what we were discussing."

"Not for me to say. I'm going home now. Everything is locked and the guards are stationed around the property. Let Chucho take the dogs out."

"*Oralé*," he agreed and bussed his dishes to the sink then wandered off to collect the puppies.

"Jade, keep your blinds pulled—all the time. They'd setup from an empty apartment across the street. I could see right into your window," Horacio said.

"Are you sure we're safe right now?" I was getting scared. All this talk—maybe it's why Quint wouldn't tell us everything.

"You won't be safe until you and Lily are out of Mexico,

and even then you'll be looking over your shoulder. I don't mean to scare you, but you don't understand how these people work. Either we eliminate them, or they eliminate us." He got up and started for the door.

I followed him. "So there's no way BLO and Los Zetas could form an alliance?"

"Why are you asking that? It's hard to imagine. Now go to bed and let me get home."

"*Pues, buenos noches*, Horacio." I locked the office door behind him, my thoughts swirling.

Chapter 25

The Embassy Fails Its Mission

Monday September 17, 2007

Piercing morning light outlined the old fashioned blinds in my room. I didn't want to wake up yet, but Quint knocked insistently.

"Wake up, Jade. Get up. We're going to meet with Rosi and Garza in an hour. Coffee is ready."

"Good morning to you too." I yawned and rolled over to pet Pepper. Gone.

"Chucho took Pepper for his run."

Answered that. "I'm coming. Give me twenty minutes to shower." And get my words in order.

Mrs. P placed a platter of *huevos mexicanos* onto the table as I arrived. Lily set down a pitcher of orange juice and trilled, "Jade, she's back! Isn't it wonderful? Mrs. P is back and she said she'll stay." She hugged the housekeeper who nudged her toward her seat. I said good morning.

"Eat your breakfast, Lily. Don't let the eggs get cold," Mrs. P admonished.

I realized I'd been the one to put a bug in Quint's ear about bringing her back, but I wasn't thrilled to see her. Not since she showed up and immediately we were attacked. But I had to give her a little credit. She couldn't have divulged any information *they* didn't already have. But maybe she knew who *they* were. I'd have to bring this up as soon as Quint and I were on good terms again. I served myself some eggs and slathered the salsa over the top then tore off a piece of hot corn tortilla and shoveled in a huge bite. Yes, I'd missed the meals.

Mrs. P served a plate for Quint and one for herself and sat down in Horacio's chair.

"Where's H? Isn't he coming with us?" I asked.

"Where are we going?" Lily asked.

Quint put down his fork and swallowed a mouthful of sliced strawberries. "You aren't going anywhere. Jade and I have a meeting with Rosi and the ambassador to find out where we are in our process. I have the head of my security team joining us to report on his interrogation last night. If nothing else does, this should light a fire under Garza. We need your passport and a flight out. Horacio has other business today. Rosi is picking us up."

"Is Seeger okay?"

"Yes, he was not followed. However, I want a meeting with the Porras brothers. He should not drive that car for a while, and he should be on the lookout for strange vehicles following him or in his neighborhood."

"You mean they might have gotten his license plate."

"Yes. You put an innocent man in grave danger, Jade. You need to do what I say."

I hung my head. I had no business going to Coyoacán with them and even less having Seeger drive me home." I mumbled, "I will."

Again we were met by marines and escorted up to Tony Garza's office through a back entrance. Rosi had quizzed Quint about yesterday's attack and both of us about Anibal's attack at the park as we drove across Zona Rosa. I learned little, except Quint had hired his security team through an American company licensed in Mexico. Presumably without ties to corrupt government officials.

Rosi was livid that these attacks against us were continuing. She asked questions in different ways and spent some minutes silently mapping out her arguments. We were to volunteer information only when asked. I hadn't known she attended law school before going into nonprofit management. I'm sure Quint felt as heartened as I did to have her advocating for us.

Our audience with the ambassador was brief and disappointing.

"Please, sit down," Garza said, gesturing to the couch. An assistant brought in a coffee service on a tray. "Thank you Mrs. Smith, that's all we need. Help yourselves." He waved toward the refreshment and sat down behind his desk. "Now, how can I help you, Rosi?" He sounded tired and frustrated.

"Tony, these people have been attacked. Mr. Aguirre mounted an armed attack on the group in the park near their home. Mr. Quint apprehended him and held him in the roof *bodega* until the US Marshal's office could make arrangements. The residence has been breached twice by Aguirre's group trying to free him. Each time Aguirre has made it clear he intends to capture the American teen and Miss Stone to complete his sale of these women into the sex trade. U.S. citizens are not safe here in Mexico and the child still has no legal documents. I insist the embassy send the child home immediately."

Garza had listened, head bowed, fingers steepled as though he were praying. I guessed he was because when he made his rebuttal, it wasn't anything we wanted to hear. "Rosi, there's nothing I can do. The legal team put the kibosh on the forged signature. We've contacted Denver, and I've got an attorney working on establishing the aunt and uncle as the girl's legal guardians, but it could take months to get through the courts. I don't know what else to do. I have arranged to ship the body to the relatives, however. The Medinas will receive it next week." He raised his head from his prayer pose. I felt sorry for him. He looked sad.

"It isn't good enough, Tony. The girl needs medical attention and a stable environment. Mother Mary, she's been locked in a saferoom twice in three days. She hears gunfire and knows people have been killed. Aguirre, by the way, is in the hospital. He will recover, and should be arrested. Two marshals are dead because of him, and yesterday two more men were killed by Mr. Quint's security team when they breached the house. How many people will die before the United States fulfils its responsibility to protect its citizens?" Rosi played the patriotism card.

"Mr. Quint, don't you have contacts to call upon for help?"

"Ambassador, I've turned our home and offices into a fortress, but that's no life for these girls. I'd send my daughter home, but as an adult, she doesn't have to listen to me. She's pledged to get the girl to her family in Denver. I respect that, and I'm doing everything in my power to help her in her mission and protect them while they are in my care. The least you could do is loan me a couple of off-duty marines while we wait. And perhaps provide a psychologist. I don't have endless resources since my backer, Senator Aguirre, was murdered."

Garza sighed. "I don't want to say no, but loaning out U.S. military is highly irregular. I'll see what I can do and ask our staff psychologist to assess Miss Flynn. I'll have her call you, Mr. Quint." He checked his watch. "I'm sorry, folks, I have another meeting in ten minutes. I have to say goodbye for now. Rosi, I will speak with you soon. Please keep me updated. I can and will run interference with the marshal's office if you need it."

He held out his hand, first to me then Quint. We shook. Quint thanked him for his time, and Rosi said goodbye. I was livid and kept my mouth shut. He wasn't going to do anything.

"One last thing. I asked Mrs. Tomsky to send regular updates to you on our progress."

Rosi smiled and said, "That's really appreciated, Tony."

We fell silent except for our footsteps clattering through the long hallway and echoing off the bare floor and walls as we followed the marine to the stairwell.

"Thanks *por nada*," I mumbled. "So Rosi, what do you suggest we do?"

"*Oye*, let's get Aguirre out of the picture. Once he's gone, his direct threat goes—"

"But not the threat from Ani's crew, the BLO or Los Zetas, although I admit, we haven't heard a peep from that bunch since the funeral."

"Who exactly are his crew?" she asked. A marine held a heavy door for us. I paused and held up my hand in thanks to the young man.

"Rosi, Eddie Santos is alive and well and he's hooked up with Carlos Beltrán, one of the Beltrán brothers. Anibal pals around with them. I think something is up beyond the botched kidnapping and trafficking."

She pursed her lips and started down the stairs. At the bottom, the marine who had greeted us at the gate unlocked the door and escorted us to Rosi's car. I thanked him and we got in. No one spoke until we crossed the "border" back into Colonia Cuauhtémoc.

COYOTE

Would *they* be waiting for us?

Chapter 26

Stagnation

"Let's get lunch and figure out what to do. You guys want to eat? There's a cute restaurant nearby I enjoyed last time I was here." As usual, with all the tension, I felt hungry.

"It's only 10:45. Unless you want breakfast, nothing is open yet," Rosi replied.

Quint added, "And you shouldn't be out in public anyway. We have plenty of food at home."

I ignored him. "Maybe there's a good coffee place? We need to discuss this. The plan is stagnating."

"I agree with JadeAnne. We need a Plan B. Let's try Qūentin Cafe over on Calle Obregon. Best coffee in *La Capital* and close to your house. Very hip—you'll love it Jade," she said as we passed through the Insurgentes roundabout. Quint remained silent but radiated displeased vibes.

Heavy traffic crawled with loud honking and obnoxious exhaust pouring in through the circulation system. I sneezed. We crept past Insurgentes Sur alongside a typical black SUV blasting rap over the sonic booms of bass. Our entire car vibrated. Those kids would be deaf by thirty. Finally we edged off the *glorieta* and headed east into Roma North. Rosi turned right on a tree shrouded street and we passed through a mixed use section of the *colonia* I'd not visited before. I saw several coffee places and some lovely Bellas Artes buildings, both homes and apartment buildings. Many had been converted to businesses. Pedestrians, bicyclists, and even roller skaters appeared young and hip. I saw plenty of dreads and yoga tights and some *tres chic* designer outfits. I could like this area—if I were allowed out to enjoy it.

Rosi tucked her white Toyota 4-door into a spot on a residential street lined with compact cars. I kept an eye out for any vehicles following us, but none turned down our street.

Quint acted jumpy, and I said, "*Cálmate, Papi.* I've been watching. We're good."

"Good? But are we safe?"

Rosi laughed, a joyous sound. I pegged her to be about Quint's age or maybe his decade. She still maintained a youthful appearance and energy. I liked her. She placed her hand on Quint's arm and said, "Let's not worry for the moment, Jackman. We'll be off the street in the patio and it's better to speak away from the girl, don't you think?"

Her soft tone soothed the beast and he nodded. Jackman she called him; Rosi could charm a stampeding bull, which Quint imitated expertly. I chuckled and realized I'd be glad if he took an interest in her. What if they started dating? We rounded the corner and darted across the street into Qūentin Cafe, a blend of modern and funky with a daily menu, marble-topped pedestal tables with black iron and wood slat chairs, slate colored walls, and top of the line equipment. The sound of grinding beans and the aroma of roasted coffee steaming out of the presses sent me into heaven. And the case of delectable treats! I didn't know what to pick.

Quint told me to keep my eyes open after he took our orders and sent Rosi out to secure a table with her *cascara*, tea made from coffee cherries and what she called "the most delicious homemade croissant in the city." I decided to try Chiapas estate grown beans brewed into a double espresso with a croissant. Quint? House blend regular coffee—black.

"So it sounds like we can write off the birth certificate and passport. Is it an election year? Is Tony worried about his posting?" I asked.

"No. He's popular. But he is a stickler for procedure, and he can't be bought. The man has integrity. Too much of it for my country." Rosi pulled a face. We laughed. I wanted to ask if she'd dated him, but figured that would be presumptuous.

"How long do you think a custody trial will take when the mother is dead?" Quint asked.

"I don't really know how the U.S. does things. Isn't that jurisdiction of each state? Family law was my area of concentration, but I studied in California, not Colorado. When will Lily turn sixteen? She might be able to apply for her paperwork herself after her birthday."

"Not for a while yet," Quint said. "But I originally did some digging on the internet and we have filed a DS-64 to report her passport stolen. Unfortunately, no passport turned up in the records, so my guess is her mother never applied for one. Garza is aware of this and I'm betting it's part of why he has reneged on using the forged letter. We're stuck between the proverbial rock and hardship. She's too young to have had a photo ID issued. We've applied for her birth certificate but to receive the certified copy, we need someone to request it who qualifies and can send in the notarized form. We thought Garza would do it. Surely one of the embassy attorneys can apply. With that, we can get the passport. A custody hearing would take months to get on the docket."

I savored my coffee and inhaled the croissant, a perfect

flaky, buttery treat still warm from the oven. I should learn to make these. "Anyone want another croissant?" I asked. They shook their heads. "No? You don't know what you're missing, Dad. I'm getting another and finding the bathroom. You want anything?"

"No thanks," they said in unison.

I held my hand toward Quint. He took it and kissed my palm. "Uh, Dad. *Pesos*?"

For a beat confusion crossed his brow. He laughed. "I've reunited with my long lost daughter and have become a bank. A sure sign of parenthood." He handed me fifty pesos.

Rosi's hoots came again. "My kids are grown and have their own money now, but I remember. Now I ask them for money. The nonprofit world isn't always lucrative, but with Senator Aguirre's generous bequest, I think I'll be able to both accomplish my mission and put aside what I'll need for retirement. My kids will appreciate that."

"Being independent is the goal, I agree," I said, "but I've been either too busy or on lockdown to get to a bank. As soon as I'm released from protective custody, I'll get some cash, but thanks for the loan Dad." I winked at Rosi. She knew I'd never pay him back.

When I returned, Quint and Rosi had their heads together in deep conversation. I hoped it was personal. They stopped talking when I sat down. I felt a frisson of energy run up my spine. Quint must have been talking about me. Maybe not the right kind of personal.

"What did you brainstorm while I was away? Shall we buy a forged passport and jump on a plane?"

"Wouldn't that be the easiest plan?" Rosi said, voice dripping sarcasm.

"So what should we do? We can't wait for months living with this constant danger."

Rosi wrinkled her forehead and considered me for a moment before speaking. "You can leave whenever you want. Tony would send an escort to put you and the dog safely on a plane. What's keeping you here?"

"I hope in part it's her old man," Quint said. "I want her to stay and work with me. She's becoming a good investigator and with her writing skills, she'd make a great team member. You might talk to her, Rosi, about some of your writing needs."

I felt my cheeks flame. How did Quint know my writing was good? So good, I'd not worked at all on my trafficking article. "I'd love to interview you, Rosi. I'm researching an exposé on human trafficking I plan to publish in one of the important magazines. Maybe the Atlantic. You'd be a great resource and make an interesting interview subject. Hey, I should do an interview on you and your work, including your plans for the new agency. I bet it could spawn investments."

I checked my watch. Close to twelve. No wonder the place was getting crowded. "Have we any part of a plan?"

"No. But we should take this meeting to the house," Quint said.

Rosi stood. "Thanks so much, Jackman and JadeAnne. This has been fun. I don't get out much either. I can't stay today, but we'll speak in a day or two. I'll put more pressure on Tony and maybe we can get the embassy to request the certified birth certificate. That won't end our problems, but at least we'd be able to start making a real plan for Lily."

Quint made a 360-degree assessment of the patio and nodded. We bussed our dishes to a waiting plastic tub near the door and cut out to the sidewalk. Quint's arm shot out, holding us back. He nodded toward a kid in slouchy pants with a tattooed neck poking from his baggy t-shirt. I squinted and inspected the tattoos. Snakes, a triangle, wavy lines. I didn't see a Z or any numbers. Quint stepped in front of me as he walked passed us. I caught the teardrop tattooed at the corner of his eye, but no other gang signs. And they weren't prison tats.

"A wannabe, Quint."

Chapter 27

I'm Solving the Problem

Horacio's face held a grim expression as he opened the office door and checked the street, his hand tight around a snarling Pepper's collar.

What now? "Peppi boy. It's me!" I shouted. He started to wag, but H didn't let him go.

"*¡Apurrense!* Hurry. We've got guests," he said.

The barrel of his weapon peeked around the door. We never should have moved. I would have rented back from Mrs. P to keep us safe. I shoved my door open and streaked, for the second time in twenty-four hours, into the office, Quint on my heels. I heard Rosi's car squeal around the corner at the end of the block. Horacio slammed the door.

"Rosi? She'll be safe?" I croaked between gasps. Again my heart bongoed against my ribs, pulse wildly doing a punta, beat, beat, beat, beat-beat-beat. Pepper jerked free and jumped up to smother me with doggie kisses. I staggered under his weight and hugged him.

Quint, bent, hands on knees panting, asked, "What the

hell happened here, H? Where's the kid?"

"Saferoom. We're going to need window glass. Yours, Chucho's, and the kitchen door shot out. Revenge, *jefe*. Aguirre's gang is loyal."

Quint nodded. "Let's talk."

"Ya think? I can't imagine anyone sticking to that loser," I said as we moved down the hall. "Your office? With that window, will we be safe?"

"The offices were designed with bulletproof glass. Whatever the senator had going on here, he made sure it was well protected." He spat a breath and unlocked the door. "I'm not catching the irony. Text Chucho," he commanded. "We need him."

I whipped my phone from my pocket. "Shouldn't we get Lily?"

"Not yet. I don't want her on this operation."

Chucho pushed open the door and joined me on the couch. Sunlight filtered into the office, illuminating the dust motes twinkling in the shafts. My stomach growled.

"H, what happened? Conjecture? Or do you have evidence it was a planned revenge? Were they after the girls?" Quint asked.

Horacio gave me a quick, confused look. I swiped the dust to swirling, and said, *"Conjetura."* He nodded in understanding.

"Jefe, francotirador. Shots came from the roof of the building behind us on Calle Obregon. *Dirigido. Tres, nada mas.* But this was left on the door." He handed over a crumpled paper.

Quint handed it to me, shrugging his shoulders. "Translate?"

I smoothed the paper and thought for a moment. "H said a sniper shot out the windows. Three shots, three windows. This more or less says 'Heads up, assholes, the bitches are ours and your time is up. Turn them over with Aguirre or you die.' Not the brightest bulb doing the writing. Most of the words are misspelled."

"We don't need a proofreader, Jade."

"Just sayin'..."

He rested his forehead in his steepled hands and closed his eyes, a gesture I'd learned was his thinking stance. The small room fell silent as though it held its breath. Only the dust danced through the shafts of light.

I watched my dad as he mulled over the problems we faced. I'd noticed he looked older than when I first met him. All this worry and responsibility was wearing him down. I felt a clench of guilt twist my guts. It was my fault. If I'd only minded my own business. Gone home after Lura died. Maybe patched it up with Dex—well, as they say, if *ifs* were Porsches... but I couldn't spend my time beating myself up now. We needed solutions. I had no control over Anibal, but I did over Lily and my situation. Screw the system, I'd take matters into my own hands. I slipped my phone out of my pocket and texted Dafne.

Quint was still cogitating when her answer dinged into my phone, *Done. I got a 50% discount but the passport will cost eight hundred dollars. Can you do that?*'

I texted back, *You bet. How soon*?

She replied, *Sooner you get a passport photo, sooner he can do it.*

I thumbs-upped.

"What's going on, Jade?" Quint asked.

"I'm solving the problem. Lily and I need to get out of Mexico. We're doing it."

"You heard Garza today. It could take months. If Rosi can convince him to bend the rules, maybe we can speed up the process, but..." His voice trailed off.

"What happened in the meeting, *jefe*?" Chucho asked.

Quint re-capped our morning.

H responded with a "*Jesucristo*."

I said, "I don't think Jesus had anything to do with it, H."

Chucho shook his head glumly. "If the legal path is blocked, we need to forge our own."

"Exactly my thinking, Chucho. Dafne is arranging a forged passport. It will cost eight hundred bucks."

"Jade," Quint said, his lips stretched tight across his teeth, "she still won't be able to get across the border. It will generate a flag when it's scanned."

"So, the Americans will arrest us at the border. We'll be out of the traffickers clutches. We'll arrange to have the Medina's waiting at the port of entry. He's an attorney, for God's sake. Surely he can do something for his niece. In fact, why hasn't he done something already?"

My text dinged again.

"Dafne says it will take the guy five days to deliver from receiving the photos. She'll come pick them up, but we must have them taken to U.S. passport specifications."

Chucho lit up. "I can do that, Jade. Easy. We can have them today." He started to get up.

"Where are you going?" Quint growled, not pleased with the turn of events.

"To get Lily."

"No! We are not finished here. I don't want her involved and more frightened than she already is. This morning's attack shook her to her core."

"Is she in there alone?" I asked.

"Mrs. Pérez and all her dogs are with her."

Ah, of course. I'd forgotten we'd rehired the housekeeper. The heiress housekeeper. "Okay. Leave her, Chuch. Let's figure out how we'll get her across the border."

Horacio considered my comment and said, "We need my brother for this conversation. I suggest we adjourn, get the windows fixed, take the photos, and get Sami to meet after he gets off work.

"Are we safe to invite him for dinner?" Everyone's head swung toward Quint.

"We can't go upstairs until the windows are fixed. I want all the windows replaced with bulletproof glass. Can anyone do that?"

"With the violence in this country, I'd bet most glaziers can," I said.

"Then Jade, I'm tasking you to get on it now. I want the three blown-out windows replaced today."

Was he kidding? "I can call, but sorry, glass replacement isn't one of my superpowers." I didn't care if I sounded snarky. Jackman Quint wasn't the boss of me.

Chucho suppressed a chuckle. I winked at him.

"I'd prefer you leave my employees out of your resentment of my leadership, Miss Stone."

What? Now he was a mind reader. Sheesh. "Your expectations are not realistic, Quint, but I'll get started on the calls. H, you'll call Sami?" He cocked a finger at me. "Good. Chuch, go get Lily and Mrs. P. Tell her we'll be— how many for dinner?"

"Looks like you're having a party. How many do *you* want?"

"Now who's being snarky?" I hissed, hoping the men wouldn't understand my English. "Ya know, Dad, they've got us between the rocks here. We have to take matter into our own hands. Why don't you call Rosi and ask her to come to dinner too."

"I can't invite people over with snipers on the rooves. And what do you expect to do with a passport that won't go through the scans?"

"Dad, it's what we're going to talk about. Call her. And Dyl planned on dinner with us. I'm inviting Seeger and Dafne. You need to talk to her. She's pretty connected."

"Where will you put all these people?"

"Dining room table."

"But Mrs. P—"

"*Sí, señor. Aquí estoy.*" She joined us in the office.

"*Señora,* can you manage an informal dinner for, let's see..." I paused to count the names off on my fingers—me, Dyl, Seeg & Daf, Lily, Quint, Chuch, H and Sami, and Rosi — "ten."

"*Diez? En la comeador?*"

"*Claro. Algo sensillo. Ensalada, tal vez pollo?*" I suggested. "Lily and I will help you."

She tapped her lip considering the proposition and agreed. "We'll need four chickens. Perhaps it would be best to buy cooked chickens and concentrate on a fresh vegetable, *aroz y un postre, como mi pastel de vainilla y naranja.*"

"Orange vanilla cake sounds good to me. Will you make your Mexican rice?" I checked my watch. Two—plenty of time. "Dinner at eight?"

"*Es perfecto.*"

"*Gracias,* Mrs. P. Quint, you follow that? She'll make a nice dinner with cake for dessert. Lil and I can help get ready while the glass people take care of things. I'll go call now."

Within the hour I'd gotten a company to take measurements and promise to have the three windows fixed before dark. I'd never have that kind of service in the States. Mrs. P took an armed security man and a shopping cart through a circuitous route into the neighborhood. Others covered her from the roof. I watched her disappear? around a corner—just another *abuela* with a rolling shopping cart. She arrived home with four hot chickens, a bag of grey squash, red jalapeños, onions, and oranges. As I helped her unpack, I noticed a jar of long brown beans. Real vanilla pods. This was going to be good. She also had beer. Lots of it.

I'd left a message for Dyl on his cell, texted Dafne, who accepted for her and Seeger. Quint reached out to Rosi and H called Sami. Rosi agreed to pick Sami up on her way. Too bad it wasn't a party for fun.

Meanwhile, Quint arranged a team 24/7 to guard us and patrol our block. He'd met with police and other officials, both Mexican and American. We were now as safe as we were getting. Lily and I remained on lockdown, which meant we had a house full of restless dogs. Chucho hadn't been able to take care of the mid-day outing, more than tossing puppies onto the patch of lawn off the office. Pepper padded room to room behind me, rolling his eyes toward the door and flopping onto the floor with big sighs. Maya imitated him, although her eye rolling was mostly toward the kitchen.

Chucho barreled in with a bag brimming with lettuce from the farmer's market, dumping it into the sink and starting the water to wash it.

"Hey Chuch, let me work the kitchen. Maybe you could take the dogs out? Check on what the security team is up to. When you get back the glass will be replaced and I'll go sweep the mess. Deal?"

"I've already done most of the glass in my room and Quint's, so you'll only have to clean up after the repairs."

"Easy for me then."

"Have you seen Lily?" He asked.

"I think she's in her room listening to music. Why don't let her beat you at checkers later."

"Not going to happen," he said, eyes crinkling. He called Pepper and told him to get his leash. My dog tore through the apartment to our room and returned wagging madly, leash in mouth, meeting Chucho as he knocked on Lily's door. I heard him inquire if Maya was free to take a walk. I couldn't hear what Lily said, but Chucho replied with, "Soon, Lily. We'll form a plan tonight at the dinner." He and the dogs thundered down the stairs and the door slammed.

What a cutie, I thought as I washed the salad greens. How could he have been abandoned by his mother? Why did I get adopted by a wealthy family and have a soft, safe life, a good education and pretty much anything I wanted when others, Chucho and Lily, had such hardships? Life was so unfair.

Chapter 28

Even if I Have to Walk

The afternoon zipped by. Mrs. P and I distracted Lily with the cooking, vacuuming, and table setting. Our housekeeper was trying hard to make amends and create normalcy. Maybe I should ask her to rent back to us. The cathouse was way easier to protect. Quint would think I was insane, if he didn't already. I'd made an about face on my opinion of Mrs. P—well, sort of and she was working hard to convince me. I didn't know what had happened regarding her family in Cuernavaca, but no one seemed concerned for them anymore.

Chucho and I had long since cleaned up the mess of glass after the glaziers finished. Allegedly, we were AR15 rated on that side of the second floor. I'd arranged to have Lily's and my bedrooms done tomorrow, as well as the office windows. Maybe I could have the entire building wrapped in bullet proof siding. Did such a thing exist? I'd have to talk to Quint about looking into getting a patent and manufacturing it. I started to giggle. My thoughts were getting too weird.

Quint hadn't shown himself since two, and Mrs. P had disappeared, leaving her cake baking in the oven. I put the finishing touches to the table, straightening the silverware and lining up the glassware with the knives. Debutant training was hard to shake. It wasn't like any of my dinner crowd would notice. Except Rosi. I had the impression she hailed from a wealthy family. I'd have to share stories with her I decided, as I placed the vase of flowers Susana had brought me onto the center of the table.

I looked forward to Susana joining The Firm, as I'd started to call it. She'd take over daily management. But where did I fit in? I knew the ropes. I'd been running Waterstreet Investigation and Marine Salvage for a couple of years. Was I still a partner? I hadn't really talked to Dex since the day he'd dumped me with orders to return his VW bus in good condition. No way was I driving it back to California. I'd learned too much about the cartels since I arrived in July.

My phone rang. Seven o'clock, right on time. "Hi, Dyl. How was work?" I flipped on the overhead light then sat down on my bed in my towel, skin steaming.

"Long. Luckily I didn't have too much to do. I guess you heard what happened."

Pepper rolled over for a scratch. I stretched out and petted him with my free hand. "Yeah, I hope your hand slipped and severed something important."

"JadeAnne Stone! I can't believe you said that." I heard his car door close and the engine come to life.

"Tell me you didn't think of it. Pretty big irony, you being called in to save Anibal Aguirre."

"Hold on." He dropped the phone and I heard a blast of a car horn. "Sorry, some idiot stopping in the middle of the *glorieta*. I'm going home for a quick shower. I'll see you at eight. I'm picking up Seeg. Dafne said she'll drive herself.

She's going home tonight."

"Good. Don't dress up. This is a simple dinner. More of a dinner meeting.

"Yeah, I've heard what Daf's up to. I'm not so sure it's a great idea."

"Me either, and you can share your better idea with us over Mrs. P's vanilla and orange cake—you should smell the kitchen!"

"If I don't have a better idea, or any idea, do I still get cake?"

I felt the smile in his voice and the twinkle in his eye. "I'm pretty sure Mrs. P would say yes to anything you want." Pepper nudged me with his nose. I sat up and scratched behind his ears.

"I'm surprised you agreed to bring her back, and, now that she's a property owner, she agreed."

"My idea, actually. She's an amazing cook. Anyway, Lily needs someone. We may have to take her to Denver with us," I joked.

Dylan blasted air through his nose. "Right! Hey, I'm home. I'll see you soon. Bye." He hung up.

Now I had to decide what casual outfit to wear to look fabulous for him. Quint had made noises about the bulletproof vest. I wasn't turning to him for fashion advice any time soon.

For what it was, dinner turned into a success. The cake helped. So did the beer. Mrs. P put out some of her tiny quesedillas, *una salsita,* and the beer in a tub with ice. We gathered in the kitchen chatting and imbibing while she got the food sliced, plated, and onto the buffet with a stack of plates. She was in a fine humor, joking and laughing with us. She remembered Seeger, who, it turned out had been in school with one of her nephews. While she and Seeger poured the wine and sparkling water at the table, we finished up the *botanas*.

"Come everyone, please get your plate and have a seat," she said, dipping her head toward the dining room. "Bring your beers."

Like the refined group we were, the men stood back to allow the ladies to enter the dining area first. I waved Mrs. P to the head of the line and dragged Rosi and Quint behind her. Lily hung back, probably to get a seat next to Chucho. Quint, Rosi, Dylan and I filled one side of the huge table while Horacio capped the end. We easily could fit twelve. Maya grinned and sat down next to Horacio, filling the empty space.

"Where are the puppies?" Dafne asked. "I want to see my new babies. How soon will you wean them?"

A sore subject, Lily shifted in her seat, twirling her fork. I piped up, "I made Lil keep them in her room. They're eating solid food, but they still nurse. I'm guessing another couple of weeks. But it really depends on what we decide to do about our situation." I felt the happy social bubble deflate. The table fell silent but for the clinking of cutlery on china.

Quint broke the silence. "Since you've opened the discussion, Jade, why don't you summarize what happened at the embassy today."

I groaned and dropped my fork. "It was a total bust. Garza reneged. He's not going to use the letter to order a birth certificate." Lily slumped in her chair. "But he doesn't have to. He can order it with no permission. I checked it out. Somebody needs to tell him." I leaned around Dyl and gave Rosi a questioning look.

Rosi said, "I don't know anything about getting American birth certificates."

"But you have the ambassador's ear. I'll print out what I learned. His legal department can order the document. Then we can apply for her passport. It will take some time, but you heard what he suggested. That would take months."

"What did he suggest?" Dafne asked.

Lily sat up and directed full attention on me, eyes practically boring into my face. "You didn't tell me," she said, her tone an accusation.

"Sorry. You were in the saferoom. Gee, was that today? So much has happened, I've lost track of time. Anyway, the ambassador has chickened out of our little subterfuge and suggests the Medina's, Lily's aunt and uncle, petition for custody. He's an attorney and probably knows how to expedite the process, or knows someone who does, but with Lily's mother deceased and father's whereabouts unknown, it adds complications to the process. Garza estimated nine or ten months at the earliest for them to assume guardianship —"

"Nooo, too long! Jade I can't live like this, locked in a storage closet because people want to steal me." She threw down her fork with a clatter onto her barely touched plate. "I won't do it. I'll walk across if I have to."

The table turned as one toward Lily, pausing conversation, filling forks, taking bites. None of us had experienced the girl so adamant over anything before. Chucho grinned. Mrs. P, alarmed, said, *"Cariña, no hablas tan—"*

Quint interrupted, "Lily, that's enough."

She threw her napkin over the mush she'd made of her dinner and fled from the table in tears." Mrs. P followed her. Her door slammed.

"And that's exactly why I invited you all for dinner. We're not waiting for papers. Dafne has contacted a forger. We're getting a passport made. We should be leaving in a week or so. It's now a matter of the logistics to reach and cross the border. The Medinas can meet us in El Paso or Laredo or Eagle Pass. Whatever."

"Why don't you and Lily fly to Denver?" Dylan asked.

Quint explained the situation.

"Lily would be in the U.S. Surely the family could step in and claim her. Pay the *mordita*, and she'd be free," Seeger said.

"Seeg, it's unlikely a bribe at the airport would do the trick. It's not like here," Dafne informed him.

"I remember those immigration officials from my college years. I never tried, but they looked like they'd be happy to fleece anyone they could," he said.

"That wasn't my experience in LA at all. Why was Denver so rough for you, Seeg?" Dylan asked.

Dafne stuck her tongue out at Seeger. "Oh, he's exaggerating. It wasn't bad at all. They were always nice to me."

Rosi shared tales of airport customs and immigration and Quint followed with, "You haven't seen anything until you try to get into a communist country."

"I know, Quint," she said, "when we went to China we were quizzed for ages. We were tourists. My father wanted to see the Great Wall. The officials were certain I wasn't a twelve-year-old, but a midget pretending to be his daughter and he was a terrorist. It was a nightmare. I've always thought it was because we have different names—"

I cut in. "Could be, but as interesting as this is, we aren't getting anywhere. If Lily can't use her forged passport at airport immigration, why *don't* we walk across? Or drive across. The last time I came back from Rosarito Beach, the immigration guy asked what our nationalities were and we said U.S. and were waved through. No biggie."

"Because you were within the free zone. Mexico City is not within that zone. I think the zone is about twelve miles from the border and it has to do with vehicles, not people. By the way, has anybody done anything to get Lily a tourist card? The senator should have taken care of that, but I never heard anything about it," Quint said.

I popped up and strolled to her door and knocked. A muffled, *"¿Quien es?"* sounded from inside.

"It's me. May I come in?" I heard something that sounded like yes and opened the door, and stuck my head around. "Lil, did the senator get you a tourist card for Mexico?"

"A card? Like a credit card?"

"No, more like a long, narrow paper giving you authorization to be in Mexico for some period of time."

"I don't know. Why?"

"Well, you need it when you go out in Mexico in case an official asks you for it. But Quint wants to know."

"Maybe, I kind of remember some papers."

"Do you have it? Let me see?"

"I don't know where it is."

"Can you look? Bring it out. We're about to have cake. Come have some. We can ask Quint why it's important."

She shrugged and sat up. A good sign. I rejoined the dinner party.

"Can anyone explain how a tourist card might be helpful?" I asked.

Sami, who had spent most of the conversations filling his hollow leg, looked up, and said, "If Lily has a tourist card, it proves she showed accepted identity documents to enter Mexico." I snorted. Sami continued, "You do know proper identity papers are the ones that display a president on them, say Benito Juárez on the twenty-peso note. You say Senator Aguirre may have obtained the document for her?"

"If there is one," I said in my snarky voice and grimaced.

"Let's hope she finds it," Horacio said.

"Again, why? Will one of you explain how a Mexican tourist card will get her into the U.S.?"

"It won't, Jade," Rosi said, but it might help Tony get her a real U.S. passport.

"I've already ordered a forgery. Dafne, can I give you travelers checks?"

"Sure. I have to go to the bank tomorrow."

Quint squinted, and said, "How much did you say this little escapade is going to cost?"

"It's my money so why does it matter?"

"Why does what matter?" Lily asked, as she flopped back into her chair.

Mrs. P began to clear the table and I got up to help. So did Dylan.

"Thanks, Mrs. Pérez," he said. "It was a delicious dinner."

She smiled coyly. "There's cake still."

Dylan was a charmer, that's for sure. All the women liked him. "We'll help you get it ready," he said.

I started clearing the buffet while they cleared the table. Quint yelled, "Bring more beer." to my back as I stepped into the kitchen. Cake and beer? Ugh. I put the dregs of the chicken platter on the table. Then I pulled a bottle of Tía Maria and another of brandy from the pantry, and put them on a tray with some glasses, and carried it to the table. "Who wants coffee or tea?"

Back in the kitchen I said, "I've counted four coffee drinkers and one for tea." Mrs. P, measured coffee into the pot. I cracked open Quint's Superior. Dylan entered balancing a tray of water glasses. "Dylan, coffee?"

"Yes ma'am." He checked his watch and yawned. "I've got another early day tomorrow."

"Can you stay for the rest of the meeting?"

"This is a meeting?" He grinned that delectable grin and leaned in to kiss me.

Mrs. P shoed us out of the kitchen with the coffee and tea. Quint was telling Sami and Chucho a funny story about his tour in Vietnam. Dylan sat down with them. Rosi had moved next to Lily at the end of the table and their heads were together, deep in conversation.

"So Dafne, what did the forger say about timing?"

"A week or so, but he can't start immediately. Are you sure you want to try this?"

"We're living under guard. We've been here three days and have been attacked three times. It's no life. And Lil needs to get settled with her family. School has started. She'll be left out of everything. But..."

Dafne picked up the conversation. "But if she can't get off the plane, what good will it do?"

Rosi looked up and called across Quint's conversation, "It's what Lily and I are talking about. We're brainstorming a Plan B."

"Come eat dessert at this end of the table so we can talk."

They stood up and circled the table, sitting where Horacio and Maya had been. I moved down too. Sami, we need you in on this.

Mrs. P entered with a triple layer yellow cake, cream between the layers, and an orange glaze over the top. It smelled of tropical flowers. We broke into spontaneous clapping. She blushed through her smile and sliced the cake, sending plates around. I hopped up and handed out forks, cups and Rosi's tea fixings, and the coffee. Quint passed the liquor.

Once everyone had cake and drink, Quint held up his beer. We followed with our glasses or cups. "To our new team, as of yet unnamed, and to the successful completion of our first assignment—Lily's safe arrival in Denver," Quint said and slugged off his brew.

"To Lily's safe reunion." "To Lily's homecoming." "To us!"

"Okay, you guys, let's eat cake!" I said. "And while you're enjoying this heavenly *pastel* please consider how we're going to pull this caper off." I stuffed a bite into my mouth and turned glassy-eyed over its sweet citrus-y richness. "Mrs. P this is celestial."

Nobody spoke, but groans of pleasure circled the table. I poured Tía Maria into my coffee and doused it with cream. Cream in Mexico was one of the unexpected delights I'd miss back in the States. Dylan caught my hand when I set down my cup and gave it a squeeze, mumbling something through a mouthful. Was he tuned into my thoughts? I wasn't sure I'd be able to leave him behind. He swallowed and said "Good!" Uncanny.

Finally, the cake was reduced to sticky crumbs Lily was swiping off the platter with her fingers and letting Maya lick. I'd slipped a little bite to Pepper, too, when no one was watching. I tapped my cup with my spoon.

"We need to get a plan in place. No more fooling around. Best scenario, Lily and I get on a plane to Denver and her family meets us at the airport."

"Not going to happen, Jade," Quint said.

"Because of the passport situation."

"Yes. But if we could convince Garza to authorize a passport using the tourist card, that would work." He raised his eyebrows at Rosi.

"Jackman, I'll try, but he is well aware Lily doesn't have legal identity papers. He doesn't want to jeopardize his position. I can't really blame him. He has a lot to lose."

"I couldn't find a tourist card," Lily said.

"It doesn't matter. We're making progress. We have purchased a forged passport, which should arrive in about a week. We know we can't use it at US immigration, but we could drive across the border and say we were in the free zone shopping."

"That's a bit thin, Jade," Sami said.

"You're our attorney, what do you suggest?" I asked.

"Wait for her people to gain legal guardianship."

I tossed my napkin at him and bleated, "You're no help!

What are we paying that high retainer for?"

Sami bellowed in delight. "Since cake doesn't constitute a legal binding contract, I don't believe I *am* your attorney. And since I'm not, I suggest you get a *coyote*."

Dafne clapped. "It's what I've been saying.'"?

Lily shrieked. Quint groaned, dropping his head to his hands. It was as if the air were sucked out of the room for a beat until Chucho's chin dropped and he expelled a, *"No mames!"*

Mrs. P rounded on him, expression askance. "Language, *hijo."* and the table erupted, everyone talking at once.

I stood up, clacked my spoon against my coffee cup a second time. "Settle down, people. We're trying to make a Plan B to back up the Plan A. A stands for airplane and that, as my dad would say, *ain't happening.* Let's think."

I surveyed the assembled brains. Chucho and Seeger probably didn't have any contacts. Horacio had been a cop and Sami practiced law. Between them, they must have made allies in the underworld, if it came to that. Rosi, I was certain, had access to some sort of underground network for hiding women rescued from traffickers and moving them to safety. And Dafne was a shoo-in for surprise contacts. She probably counted *coyotes* as friends.

"Okay, you guys, here's what we've got: Lily and I, and therefore Quint, Chucho, Horacio, and the rest of you who come here to visit, are in mortal danger. The only reason we're having a dinner is because we've retained a detail of private guards to protect this property. You all know Anibal Aguirre, Eddy Santos, and Carlos Beltrán are after us. They, and Los Zetas, have tried to recover their assets—us— too many times. Folks," I shouted, "Lily and I are not going to take it anymore!" I raised my fist into the air. "We're going to Denver and to hell with bureaucracy."

Chapter 29

Plan B

"So, you highly specialized and super trained brainiacs, how are we going to successfully realize this mission?"

I looked at Quint who'd gone pale. Too much estrogen in the atmosphere? Rosi's broad smile had taken over her face.

"Rosi, your confidence is inspiring. Share your thoughts."

"We might have a chance of getting you back across the border through the smuggling routes we've used with other trafficked women. An underground railway, you might call it. But it's dangerous, unpredictable, and takes some stamina. Frankly, I think we can get you to the border without the network. But the crossing will take favors and cash."

Quint had straightened up, interested now. "What kind of money? And are you actually owed any favors?"

"I can call in a few. As for costs, an operation like this is going to cost us upward of ten thousand."

"Dollars or *pesos*?"

"Come on, Jade, nobody is doing anything for 10,000

pesos. That's not even a thousand dollars."

"Just hoping, Quint. Our resources are dwindling, what with this office we're setting up."

"Hey, we'll get that bequest soon. It will all work out," he said, obviously trying for positivity.

"My uncle will help," Lily offered.

Dafne interrupted. "Let's not think about money. I want to hear Rosi's ideas. And I have a couple of contacts myself." Smug. "But first, is there any more coffee, *Señora* Pérez? I think it's going to be a long night."

"Claro, señorita, ahorita vengo. Permiso." Our housekeeper excused herself from the room.

Dafne thanked her and called down the table. "Lil, help her, would you? Maybe clear the cake plates? And ask for more beer for Quint. Anyone else? No? *Bueno.* But could you bring a bag of chips or nuts or something to go with the beer?"

Lily flounced out, the kitchen door swinging behind her.

Horacio spoke up. "We're talking about smuggling two American citizens across the border to deliver one to family in Denver. What border crossing are we considering? Do you have a map, Jade?"

I shrugged and shook my head. "Quint?"

He rolled his eyes. "Chucho, can you download a map with Mexico and Denver on it?'

"Sí, claro, jefe. Voy." He strode toward the stairs, and, turning back to the table, said in Spanish, "I'll get the smuggling routes map."

I laughed. Seeger raised his hand. "Pass the talking stick to Seeger...shush. Let him speak."

"Thanks. I don't know anything about trafficking routes, but I do know Interstate 25 runs from El Paso to Denver via Albuquerque and Santa Fe. I've driven it many times. And the border crossing is pretty easy. I needed my student visa and my passport. We all got our student visas at the embassy.

Why don't we drive her across with a forged student visa?"

Rosi's sharp breath said it all. Now this was a plan.

"Rosi, do you think we could get Garza to have a student visa issued to her? We'll get her a forged Mexican passport. That wouldn't be connected into the digital database at the U.S. border, would it?" I asked.

"If it were a real visa in an assumed name backed up by a fake passport, it might work."

Lily reappeared with a tray of cookies and a thermos of fresh coffee. "What might work?" she asked as she set down the tray.

"How would you like to study at an American university?" Seeger asked.

She gave him a *what, are you, new?* look. "I'm fifteen. I've barely gone to high school."

"No, Lily, not for real," Dafne said. "While you're up, pass me the coffee, would you?"

Lily carried the pot around the table.

"Didn't you tell us you wanted to go to university to study creative writing and what was it—theater?" Sami asked. "Here's your first role. You'll be a Mexican eighteen-year-old on her way to attend the University of New Mexico in their theater department."

"But I want to study theatrical costume design."

"It doesn't matter what you'll study, *cariña*," Rosi said. "You played the role well at the celebration of life. All you need to do is add a Spanish accent and you'd pass right over the border with your Mexican passport and student visa, especially if your American aunt was taking you to college."

"Yeah! We could fill the car with purple dorm room sheets, towels, lamps. I remember all the stuff I took to college with me. We'll make it look authentic. But, you guys, why would I have gone to Mexico City from San Francisco to take my niece to college?"

Mrs. P had been intently watching the exchange. She

said, "You aren't coming from California, *señorita*, you and your Mexican husband are taking his niece to school."

I furrowed my brow. This made sense. "And who, exactly, is my husband, Mrs. P?"

"*Señor Dylan, por supuesto.*"

Dylan colored, but his eyes twinkled over a goofy grin and a heatwave rolled through me.

"You know, it might just work. If, of course, we can get that student visa." I leaned around Quint and pinned Rosi with a plea. "If you can convince someone to expedite the fake application through the visa department. What do you think, Quint?"

He yawned and stretched. "I think we've got a workable idea, thanks to Mrs. P, but your boyfriend is falling asleep and most of us have to work in the morning. Let's list some action items and go home."

"Good idea. I'll check in with my forger and see if he will make a Mexican passport instead. But I'm going to need a name, Lily. The best lies are the closest to the truth, and easiest to remember. How about Liliana Flores, so same initials and when we call you Lili, it makes sense?"

Lily nodded, eyes hooded. The kid was tired. And stressed out. I yawned and stretched. I felt like I'd been tied in a knot. I could go for a massage, especially if Dylan were giving it to me. Our eyes met and I gave him my half smile. Wouldn't want him to know I was fantasizing lasciviously about him. He winked and pushed back from the table.

"Thanks for dinner. I've got a six-thirty surgery so I better get home to bed. I'm assuming there's nothing I need to do yet. Jade, will you see me down?"

"Are we safe, Quint?" I asked, as I got up and slid my arm around Dylan and rested my head on his shoulder.

"Wait a bit while I check in." Quint pulled his phone from his pocket, punched a number and stepped away from us.

I felt Dylan lean toward my dad, listening, but unfortunately I couldn't hear the conversation over Dafne and Seeger getting ready to leave. She was coordinating with Rosi, who had assigned herself to call Garza the next day and plant the student visa idea.

"*Oye*, Jade, are you free to have coffee or something in the afternoon? Rosi and I will both have things to talk about. We're meeting in Condesa at La Selva at four-thirty."

I pointed to Quint and replied, "If the warden permits me a furlough."

They both laughed. "I can pick you up on the way from my office, if it would help," Rosi said. "Maybe it would be a good idea. I could stop in and chat with Miss Lily. It's important she is kept in the loop and she understands what we are planning. She needs to feel secure and have the opportunity to talk about what she's feeling. The success of the plan depends on Lily playing her part perfectly. It might be daunting for her. She's gone through so much already."

"I would appreciate that, Rosi. There's just so much we can do for her. She needs counselling."

"And you? Have you talked to a professional about what you've endured? Quint shared a bit of your story. If you want to talk, I'm available."

I gave her a hug. "Thanks, Rosi, I appreciate everything you're doing for us. I know Quint does too. He admires and respects you. We're both grateful you're on the team." I was careful not to get too sappy. I didn't want to scare her away, just hoped to put a bee in her bonnet about Quint. From what I knew so far, Rosi would make a fine stepmother.

"Yes, and I admire him, too," she said in a soft voice. "He is truly one of the good guys."

Quint joined us and waggled his phone. "Adan reports the streets are clear. His team sighted a drive by forty-five minutes ago, but all vehicles within a two block perimeter are accounted for. Two men are stationed on the street to see you all out. I'll cover you as well. Adan is on the roof. Let's go.

Most of the goodbyes and thank yous had been said, but I heard the group make a special effort to thank Mrs. P again as they clattered down the stairs. Dylan was driving her home. I prayed my friends would be safe. And speaking of safe, I had to take the dogs out. "Chucho?" I yelled. "Can you take the dogs out with me?"

"*Claro, senorita, un momentito.* I'll get my gun and notify Adan we'll be in the garden. Are we bringing the puppies?"

"Yes, they need to go out the most. I sighed, lowering my voice. I don't know how she will do when she has to let go of them. I'll meet you at the back stairs in a minute." I headed to Lily's door and knocked. "Lil, Chuch and I are taking the dogs into the garden. Want to come? The puppies need to get out before bed."

The door opened and thirty-six paws stampeded into the hall. What a racket! I whistled and thudded toward the kitchen. Pepper and Maya bounded with me, and the puppies wiggled and woofed behind us. I gave them all a treat at the door and only one piddled on the floor. We got into formation: Chucho and his gun, Lily, Maya, the puppies, Pepper, and finally me with my gun. We'd be safe in the garden since the security team had cleared out the building across the way and stationed guards, but the stairs were scary. A guard whistled and waved us down. I felt better. For the moment.

Chapter 30

It's War

Tuesday, September 18, 2007

I was in a dark cave with bars on the entrance. I saw kids, lots of kids. Many were crying. Most were nearly naked. I wanted to help them but I couldn't get their attention. I called out and tried to move toward them, but I was in a small cage with something growling. I couldn't see it and the kids couldn't see me. The growling got louder and a deep black shadow rose over the huddle of children. Several disappeared and I could hear smacking and screams, grunts, mean laughter. A girl who looked like Lily took off her shoe and banged it on the metal bars. Thap, thap, thap! Wake up, Jade, wake up. Thap, thap. I'm awake, can't you see me?

Pepper stood over me, licking the sweat off my face. "Wha—? Peppi," I groaned. I'd been dreaming. My bed was torn apart, the bedding half on the floor, and I was dripping with sweat.

Thap, thap. My breath caught and my heart raced. Thap, thap, thap. "Jade? are you awake?"

I gasped for air and croaked, "Quint?" Pepper bounded to the door.

Dad pushed the door open illuminating the room enough to see the destruction of my bed. Pepper pushed him toward me as I gasped.

"I heard a commotion. Bad dream?"

I crawled into his arms, shaking. He stiffened, but held me until my heart slowed and my breath was regular. "Sorry," I said. "Panic attack."

"No worries, what's an old dad for?" he said, trying to make light, but he didn't really cover his awkwardness.

"I guess you haven't much experience with children's nightmares."

"Ain't that the truth," he muttered. "No, Jade. I'm sorry. Are you ok now?"

"Yes. I was caged with a growling beast, but I couldn't see it. I could only see kids in trouble, being devoured by a black shadow. I couldn't help them. The shadow grew and spread and..." I took a shaky breath.

"Look, I don't want to make things worse for you, but I got a call from the hospital—"

"No! No, no. No! Don't tell me. He's escaped." I gripped my father and gazed into his face.

The lines in his forehead deepened and his hair took on a grey cast. He aged before my eyes and said, "Left two guards and a nurse dead."

I trembled. The black shadow devouring everything in its way. "What will we do?"

"Try to sleep. We will need all our energy to complete our mission. I've already notified the security team to expect trouble. You and Lily should go to the saferoom." He gave me a squeeze.

"And sit up all night scared and helpless?" I said into his

chest. "No, let her sleep. I'll make coffee and we'll stand watch." I let go of Quint, grimacing, and dropped my feet to the floor as he stood up.

"Make coffee, but you girls need to be safe."

"I flipped the light on and squared off with him, jaw set. "No way, *José*." I brushed past him, tossing my ponytail.

"I guess you told me," he muttered, following me to the kitchen.

"We need a plan, Quint. They shot out windows. What will they try next? I mean, they have Anibal, isn't that enough?"

"These kinds of players operate on violent aggression, and they never want to get even, they want to make a profit. They'll come in here, take you girls, and kill the rest of us in the most horrible ways they can devise. You've seen it on the news and the internet. You did two things Aguirre can't forgive."

"What? Free myself from a life of degradation in trafficking hell?" I slammed the filled water kettle into its heating element and flipped the switch. "And what else?"

Quint rummaged through the cabinets for something.

"What are you looking for?"

"Cookies."

"Pantry, left side fourth shelf up." I poured beans into the grinder and pressed down on the lid. The sharp grinding covered Quint's words. In a moment I tipped the grounds into the French press and asked, "What? I missed that."

Quint ripped open a package of chocolate sandwich cookies and tossed it onto the table, sat down. "You caused Aguirre to lose face in front of his associates. His deal went sour. You stole the American girls twice and yourself once after you'd been paid for. And probably worse in his mind, you left him. Never mind his interest in you was for what he could gain, you proved again what the world has said about Anibal Aguirre throughout his life. He's worthless, a loser—

a bastard."

"And he isn't?"

"As we well know, but that isn't the point."

The kettle burbled and cut off. I considered this from the emotional angle rather than the greed angle as I poured the boiling water and plunged the grounds to the bottom of the pot. Anibal wanted me to love him even as he plotted to sell me into sexual slavery? I sighed and put the coffee and mugs in front of Quint. "How twisted can ya get?"

"And the culture he has aligned himself with says one must always right the wrong. It isn't enough to recover you girls and make the best of the deal—he'll have to make good on the little one—but he needs to avenge himself and the injured business associates through a violent, gruesome public statement. I'm predicting that means killing me as horribly as he can. And probably your dog too. He'll make you watch and suffer. Cárdenas will demand nothing less. I'll die. What they would do to you is far worse. We cannot allow them to get to you or Lily."

My hands shook as I poured my coffee. I'd already slopped cream onto the table. I wasn't sure if I were angrier than scared. "No we cannot. Nor you, nor any of our group. Horacio said I was a soldier, well, I am now. And I'm no run-and-hide chickenshit. What's the plan, Stan?" My words precipitated a rush of adrenalin through my body. Or maybe the caffeine? was taking hold. Whichever, I was wide awake and ready to fight.

"You need to get dressed and put on your vest. Are your guns cleaned and ready?"

"Of course. And Lily?"

"We need to get her out of here. If she's not going into the saferoom, she needs to be hidden somewhere."

"Dafne will come get her." I picked my phone up and dialed. After apologizing for the time, it was 12:19, I gave her the lowdown. She said she'd arrive in twenty minutes.

We'd bundle Lily and the dogs into her car from the garage-side door.

We hustled into Lily's room. Quint gently woke her while I grabbed clothes and stuffed them into a bag with her phone, brush, and toothbrush. "Quick, get dressed, Lil. Dafne's on her way," I said, shoving her toward her bathroom.

"Why am I going to Dafne's?"

Quint came back, huffing from exertion. "Carrier's at the bottom of the stairs with the bowls and a bag of food. Chucho is walking the puppies."

I wiped a spot of toothpaste off her chin. "Would you rather stay in the saferoom?"

"No way. But what's happened?" She slid her gaze between us.

"Anibal has been forcibly removed from the hospital. Come on, get moving."

"My book!"

I grabbed the copy of *The Children of Húrin*, the last Tolkien book, and dropped it into the bag I carried. "Good choice, kid. One of the themes is true courage versus arrogance. We need true courage now."

Quint hurried her out of the room. I ran to my room, jumped into jeans, and joined them at the back door. I shrugged into the vest. I'd go first. Chucho was already in the empty garage opening the door for Dafne to drive in. Once she was in, he would close the door and position himself on the roof where he could watch the street and the *callejon*. Our security team was invisible, ready for action. When the text came, we were to as quietly as we could, descend the stairs and slip into the garage. Quint would signal an all clear to Dafne who would peel out and take a circuitous route back to Seeger's. Horacio was stationed in Condesa to pull any tail off the Beemer. It sounded perfect for a thriller. But it wasn't a novel. It was our lives.

My phone rang. "Yo, Dad."

"Make sure all the doors and windows are locked. Are the curtains pulled?"

"Everything is locked. Chucho took care of it before bed. Why?" I asked.

"When this comes, it's coming over the roof or through the balconies. Windows and doors, the easiest entries."

"Do I need to worry about the office windows?"

"Make sure the steel door is locked."

I held the phone away from my ear. "Chuch, steel door locked?" He shouted yes. "Quint, relax. With you and the team out there and Chucho and me inside, we'll pick them off as they come." I wished I felt as confident as my words sounded. He hung up.

"Unless they start a fire. You'll be trapped," Lily offered.

"Oh thanks, Lily, that's a cheery thought."

Chucho's phone buzzed. "That's him. Let's go." He picked up a scary-looking rifle, and pulled open the door, holding it so I could pass.

I towed Lily behind me. "Duck down, Lil." I felt her knees press into my back. In lock step, we crept down the stairs, Chucho two steps above us. Right... Left... Right. Slow moving, but I had time to observe the surroundings. I held the Glock with both hands ready to aim. Left... Right... Left.

A movement caught my eye and instinctively I swung my arms up and aimed. Nothing there. My blood pressure did not lower with the gun. Right. Left.

Below the door opened and Dafne waved up at us. I stepped down faster.

Right. Left. Only ten more steps to go. Nine. Eight. My chest felt like it would explode. Seven. A swarm of bees jetted over my head hitting the stucco, sending it flying.

Chucho cried out. "DUCK!" and sprayed the rooftop with bullets.

Lily screamed. I untangled my feet and dragged her the last six steps. Dafne darted out, grabbed the girl, and yanked her into the garage under Chucho's fire. I skidded in behind them.

Quint yelled something from the garage roof and his gun boomed. Dafne pushed Lily into the backseat with the dogs, and yelled, "Keep them down. You too, Lil. Jade, help me with the door."

I ran to help. The screech of metal on metal almost disappeared under the Brrrraaaatt! Boom! Tatatatat! Braaaatt! Boom! of the gunfight. Dafne lunged into the driver's seat and peeled right into the ally, left into the street. In a moment's lull, I heard her tires squeal around the corner at the end of the block. And silence.

I yanked the garage door closed and ran the bolts through. I'd have to wait here. I sagged against the back wall, the hammering in my chest making me gasp. God, not a heart attack. Not here. I didn't want to die in an oil reeking garage in Mexico. I sucked in as much air as I could and felt my heart rate slow. I took another breath, held it, and blew out. Okay, not a heart attack. More like a panic attack. But I felt better.

I dialed Quint. No answer. My blood pressure headed up again. Another breath. I dialed Chucho. His phone rang just outside the door. I scooted over and peeked out. Phone. No Chucho. I tapped the door open further, Glock aimed, afraid of what I'd find, heart doing a drum solo. They'd hear it outside, I was sure of it. I willed myself to calm down, reach out, grab the phone, pull back into the garage. Yanking the door closed behind me, I plunked down onto the filthy cement. Where was Chucho? Where was Quint? And what about the security team?

Boom! Boom! Boom! Quint's gun. Not from the garage roof. I tried to pinpoint the direction. Brrraaattt! Chucho's assault weapon, I realized, coming from above me. I crawled to my feet and found the stairwell to the roof. A soldier should fight, not cower in the dark.

Crouching, I listened. From the sounds of the gun, Chucho was by the *bodega*. Shooting west? But the security was on that building. Return fire sprayed the side of the *bodega*. Quint's big gun boomed again; A man cried out from across the *callejon*. I'd seen the flash from Quint's muzzle up on the roof of the house. But Quint said the security men were on the neighboring roof. Chucho's phone buzzed in my pocket. I ducked back into the stairwell and answered the text. *I got the shooter across from you. Come up here.*

I texted back. *I'll tell him, Jade.*

Thx keep your head down.

I sprang out of the stairwell and skittered around the *bodega* calling, "Chuch! Chuch!" He showed himself for a moment and shrank back into a shadow. I edged toward him, delivered the phone and message.

"Stay here. Anyone shoots at you, return fire. I think Quint got him, but he may not be dead. Just cover me while I climb up the house." He jutted his chin at a precarious-looking ladder embedded in the side of the building. I nodded and he slinked away from the *bodega* rifle slung over his shoulder, sprang onto the ladder lizard-like, and scuttled onto the roof.

Quint stepped out from behind a chimney and saluted, ducking back when a shot rang out. Chucho dove out of sight. I squatted and peered around the corner across the alley. I saw a flash of light as the shooter shifted position. He was fully exposed to me. Couldn't Quint see him? I texted his position.

Quint: *shoot him*

Me: *in cold blood?*

Quint: *it's war?*

I read the subtext: man up.

The enemy watched the *bodega* for movement, but not at roof level. I'd have to expose myself to make the shot. Who was I kidding? I was a novice markswoman. The text buzzed again, *shoot now got you covered.*

I lunged out, dropped to my knees, arms swinging up to aim, and pulled the trigger in one swift, wild, heartbreaking moment. The man sprawled facedown, his gun clattering out of reach. He hadn't made a sound and he wasn't moving. I gagged back a reflux of acid.

Quint: *good work*

Me: *now what?*

Quint: *stay put*

I'd watched the chimney while I texted. Two shadows moved out against the hazy night sky and trotted behind what I guessed was an air-conditioning unit. A rectangular outcropping anyway. I shivered. The night was cooling off, and my tense body couldn't warm up, even with all the blood it was rapidly pumping. I edged to the east for a better view of the roof. A shadow moved south, a gangly shadow with a couple too many legs. It was subsumed against the street trees and I lost it. I wanted to go in and take a bath, warm up, unwind.

I ducked back to the stairwell and ran down into the garage and to the door. I crouched, peered out. Dark shadows. The clopping of rubber shoes on pavement, fuzzy whispering, clack of metal on metal, the cocking of a gun.

The blast rocked me out the door to the ground. My ears rang and I couldn't hear anything. My phone buzzed. I slowly picked myself up and turned to lock at the garage. Chunks of cement littered the floor and the ceiling seemed to be sagging. What? I crouched and read the texts.

Quint: *you ok?*

Me: o*k. what happened?*

Quint: *bodega blown up.*

Me: *I heard them in the alley.*

Quint: *on it. hide.*

Staying under the stairs to the kitchen, I edged into the garden. I'd be invisible in the borders once I got past the roses. I had the Glock cocked and ready. A sliver of moon shine lit up the wall along the house. No baddies lurking there, but I'd be exposed if I tried to sneak along that way. I had to get to the far corner into the tree. Its canopy was thick and the corner black. The moon went dark behind a cloud. I sprinted to the garden and dove behind a bush. If I made noise, I couldn't hear it. Hopefully all anyone would have heard was the splashing of the fountain I'd forgotten to turn off. I squatted and waited, watching the yard. I felt high, like I'd toked a J. So weird not hearing anything. Nothing moved. Nothing exploded. I crept to the tree and climbed.

From the tree I had a view of the *callejon* and the garage. The *bodega* resembled bombed out rubble. And I could see why. Two figures crouched by something big on a tripod. Something they fussed with and aimed at my house. The only thing was the garden wall was too high to get a good aim. I texted.

Two guys in the alley against our garden wall with a big gun on a tripod. Trying for the house. Get out of there.

Quint: *We see them. Get down against the far back wall.*

I slid out of the tree for cover and buried my head into my balled-up body. A distant Brrrraatt! Brattaatt! Boom! And more silence hissing in my ears. I hoisted myself back into the tree and peered over the wall—and wished I hadn't.

Chapter 31

Me and Chucho—We're not Soldiers

The wail and whoop of police and rescue vehicles came later.

I could hear again, but the constant hiss like steam escaping a pressure cooker annoyed the hell out of me. A pressure cooker. Good analogy for the situation. Tempers and tension building to a boiling point. Quint was livid. One of the security guards allegedly vetted by Santiago lay in a pond of blood—his blood, leaked from an automatic rifle's perforations. The other had escaped the peppering of bullets to take one of Quint's cannon balls in the chest.

The big gun turned out to be a grenade launcher. Chinese, I thought I heard Quint saying. But why only one shot?

Chucho and I sat at the table, the bottle of tequila and a fresh pot of coffee in front of us. Quint paced up and down the living room yammering on his phone. Chucho wore that spaced-out, glassy-eyed face of shell shock. I probably did too. My stomach roiled and my body shook, I was wound so tightly. He'd never killed a person before. I'd now killed two. I shut that thought down, banished it back to the dark web of my mind.

"We can think about it on another day, Chuch. Push it all into the deep folds of your memory for now."

"But you don't understand."

I reached across the corner of the table and took his hand. "Yes, I do. Yes, I do."

Quint stomped in and whipped a chair around, lowering himself to straddle it backwards. I slid the tequila and a shot glass across the table. He poured, swilled it back, poured again, contemplating the amber liquid for some moments before chugging it. "How are you holding up?"

Chucho hung his head. "*Jefe*," he started and paused. "I don't know, I, uh..."

"Me either, Quint." I swigged off the coffee cup shaking in my hands. He reached out as if to steady it then dropped his hand back to the table. "We're not soldiers," I blurted.

He frowned. "What a mess. We've got to interview the scumbag locked in the storage closet before the police come snooping around. One of the men in the alley was Santos, Jade."

"You saw him? I-I..."

"I told you to get down. Did you look over the wall?"

"Yes. I saw." I listened as my voice changed. Accusing. "And I followed your orders and killed a man."

"Self-defense."

"And now the police are involved."

"What's more disturbing is Santiago's hand-picked security team is corrupt."

"*Jefe*, I don't think I should be here."

Quint put his head into his hands. "Don't you two fail me now. It's a shit show, but we'll find a way to complete the mission."

I stumbled out of my chair and put my arms around my

dad. "No one is failing you, Dad. But you gotta understand, we killed people. We aren't trained or prepared or even passionate about those strangers. We're just regular people who hoped to live good lives. I killed Zocer, you didn't, and I've been living with that ever since. I let you think it was you because you *are* a soldier and *you* can deal with it. We? Chucho and me, we...we can't."

"You'll have to, because this ain't over. I don't know what Aguirre's people hoped to gain. He's behind it, without a doubt. How Santos got away again before we fired, I don't know. A car waiting on the street, probably with Aguirre in it." He gazed into the distance, so lost in space he didn't register Horacio coming in.

I gestured to a chair and the bottle. He sat, but shook his head to tequila. "Coffee then?"

He nodded. I poured and got up on my wobbly legs for the sugar.

"Lily is safe with Porras. Dafne went home. I reconnoitered the area. No surveillance, no tails. What happened here?"

Quint drifted back into the conversation after a beat of silence. "They didn't try to enter the house, but the *bodega* is rubble. Victim to an old grenade launcher. I don't think they were after the girls."

"*Pues*, what did they want? Quint, you say 'they', but you mention Eddy Santos. How cannot this be about kidnapping Miss Jade and Miss Lily?" He sipped his coffee and gave me an appreciative nod.

"Eddy Santos was in our alley with two unfamiliar men. One had his face shot off—" Chucho bolted from the kitchen, his skin a sallow shade of grey. Quint's exhaustion dug into his shoulders. He continued, voice strained, "We may never know who he is. The other I didn't know, but we'll find out. This betrayal comes from high in the power structure. It was the security team that opened the door to

Santos."

"Santiago's team? They've bought off the tsar of organized crime? No, this was not about the girls, boss. Aguirre has more importance than we thought. Or it's blow-back from the senator's death. One way or the other, I'm saying revenge."

Horacio and Quint exchanged a silent conversation, coming to a deadly conclusion. I saw it radiating off their skin like an aura. A black aura. I poured a slug of tequila into the dregs of my coffee and took a gulp.

"They want to kill us. And they have the manpower and weapons. I can't protect this location. Not against grenade launchers. The windows were a calling card, or a mistake. Aguirre may be out of the hospital, but he's in no condition to run an op. We need to get on the move ASAP."

This was good news. Forget the embassy, the red tape, the push-back. Lily and I needed to get out of Mexico to safety with our dogs and...well, Dylan and Quint. The realization slammed me upside my aching head. I couldn't leave Dylan, not yet, and I wouldn't abandon my father. That little devil on my shoulder laughed at the cliché. She pointed out the irony of me playing turnabout with glee. I couldn't, I wouldn't do it. I wasn't leaving Quint to die for my mess.

I pushed the tequila away and stood up. "Quint, Dad, I won't leave you to clean up after me and probably get murdered. I love you. You're crossing the border with me and Lily and the dogs. And we're not waiting around for legal papers."

Quint's color improved, but probably because I'd embarrassed him. He gaped at me.

"She's truly your daughter, boss."

He grunted. "It's going to take time, Jade. We have to plan. We're running for our lives."

"Yeah, I tried to get a plan going tonight and you guys weren't very cooperative. Now we need to figure out where to live while we make this plan."

"Boss, can't the U.S. help us?"

Quint drank down another shot of tequila. The clock ticked in the silence. "I'm thinking, H."

"I'd say you're drinking not thinking, Dad."

He cracked a goofy smile, and replied, "It's when I do my most creative work." We laughed, the moment lightened. "I'll have something to say in the morning."

My gut wrenched. "We're sleeping here?"

"Where else would we sleep?" Quint asked.

"I mean, what if they come back? Eddy is out there somewhere."

"But not with a grenade launcher. We killed it; it's gone into police evidence."

Horacio guffawed. "Boss, it's probably gone to some gangster in exchange for a bag of cash. But nobody likes Aguirre. It won't go back to his crew."

"So you think we're safe tonight, Horacio?"

"Not what I said. But as far as Eddy Santos knows, his guys took you out."

"That's pretty farfetched, H," I said.

"What?"

"She means unlikely."

"So I can go to bed?" I asked, sliding out of my chair.

"I'll take the first watch. Get some shut-eye boss."

"Okay, goodnight then. Quint, let me help you up. Come on." I took the shot glass from his fist and guided him out of his chair. He hadn't quite finished the bottle, but I guessed his thinking would still be super creative.

Pepper gave me the onceover, twice—sniffing me, licking the scratches from the rose thorns and stucco sprayed off the shot up *bodega* walls. Finally satisfied I was fine, he scratched on the door to go out. Poor dog, he'd been locked in through the entire attack. I still had my vest on; I shrugged him into his vest and we crossed the hall into the kitchen. Horacio was no longer at the table. I crept to the back door and cracked it open. So much for stealth, Pepper nosed me aside and rumbled down the stairs into the garden. I followed with the poop bag. One thing I couldn't figure out was how our wall wasn't damaged in the shootout. Something didn't make sense. Where did Chucho shoot from? He had to be across the *callejon*. But didn't Quint say he was on the roof? Could it be there had been another shooter? One of the security men maybe?

Pepper, finished with his business, trotted back to me. I would have to investigate during the day. See where the bullets came from. Have a talk with Quint and Chucho.

Chapter 32

Message in a Box

Wednesday, September 19, 2007

Quint was gone when I woke up. Mrs. P bustled about the kitchen feeding Chucho and Horacio and getting started on the day's meals. The biting scent of roasting poblanos filled the room. Oh goodie—*chile rellenos*. I stumbled to the coffeepot trailed by Pepper and filled a cup, taking a tentative sip for temperature then a big gulp. Mrs. P's coffee would clear the cobwebs.

The vibe at the table felt lugubrious, exhausted. Maybe hopeless. I tried to smile at the men, but they kept their eyes on their breakfasts. Pepper whined at the door. I aimed my smile, more of a grimace, at Mrs. P and mumbled, "*Buenos días.*" as I passed the stove to open the door for Pepper. In full daylight, I doubted snipers would be lurking on any of the rooves.

Mrs. P shot me her disapproval before greeting me.

"What happened to the *bodega?* Where is the *señorita?*"

I ducked into the pantry for Pepper's bowl and kibble. I wasn't quite ready to detail the night's horror.

Horacio related a synopsis of the attack, while I watched Pepper from the landing door. He nosed around, checking everything out and wagging excitedly near the gate. Had he found something or was someone out there? I interrupted Horacio. "Pepper has something at the gate."

He exhaled a *not again* breath and lumbered to his feet, heading toward the door. "*Me voy.*"

I patted his arm as he passed me to thud down the stairs. Pepper paced and whined. Chucho came to the landing to watch with me. No heads showed in our *callejon,* but he could be crouching. We'd have to put up mirrors or something. As Horacio neared the gate, Pepper barked and started digging. Something was wrong. H pulled his handgun from under his shirt, and I jumped back into the entry, yanking Chucho with me. He paled and scuttled backward. I kept my eyes on Pepper. My heart clenched. I couldn't lose my dog.

H, gun drawn and cocked, inspected the ground. He turned and shrugged. Nothing. Why had Pepper been digging? Horacio punched the gate code and shoved the right half. The gate stuck, probably roots or debris from the night's events. Pepper stood statue still, pointing. H bent to pull the rod holding the left half and swung it inward as far as it would go and waited, *en guard.* I held my breath. Nothing happened. Pepper sniffed and blasted out the gate, frantically barking. Horacio pushed the left half outward and peered around gun first. Pepper's barking escalated to a frenzy and died off as H stepped into the *callejon,* reappearing immediately carrying an open box. I strained to see what was in it. The expression on Horacio's face chilled me to the bone. He reached in and pulled the grizzly surprise out by its curly hair. Perseus with Medusa's head. But who was playing Medusa?

"Call your father, Now!"

Chucho fled. Mrs. P gasped and sank into a chair, covering her mouth. I got it. I'd lost my gulp of coffee, too. I grabbed a tea towel from the drawer and covered the box. We didn't need to be looking at—it. We needed to get back to something normal. Pepper needed his food. I needed another shower and clean clothes. I'd sweated out my PJs during a night of nightmares and more than stinking, I was soaked through. I poured a large glass of water and excused myself. Quint would be home soon.

Home, now that was a loose definition of this place we'd landed, I thought as the hot water streamed over my head and down my back. I inhaled a lungful of steam and forced it out, squeezing my diaphragm to rid myself of every bit of toxicity. The oily horror of death and gore and cruelty clung to every inch of me. I scrubbed my skin, my mouth, my hair, everywhere until I felt raw. The lovely rose scent of my soap made me gag. Everything was wrong, confusing, abhorrent. I'd killed men. I had come to Mexico to restore a wife to her frantic husband and instead of solving the case, sorting out my relationship with Dex and getting a needed rest at the beach, I'd become a killer. My stomach lurched over again; the shower washed my tears and bile down the drain. I wished I knew what was going on, how all this had happened. How would I tell Medusa's grieving family he was here, on our kitchen table under a tea towel? Who was he?

Quint banged on the bathroom door. "Hurry up, Jade. We need to deal with this."

I peppered Quint with questions when I returned to our kitchen boardroom. "Is he one of the guards? Have you called the police? What about Santiago? Why is this happening to us?"

"Whoa, enough questions. I spent the morning with Santiago. I believe he was not involved with the attack. The security team incurred a fatal auto accident on the way here. All but one of the men were killed. The other is in the ICU. Santiago now admits the accident is suspicious. His department has taken over the investigation into the accident and the attack. As to who this head belongs to, I can only theorize. Where're Chucho and Mrs. P?"

"Neither will come in here while that...that—box sits on the table. Shouldn't you notify someone?" I asked.

Quint turned his Quint squint on me and continued with his agenda. "My theory: leaving the head was why Eddy Santos was in the alley." He leaned toward me across the table.

Challenging me to disagree? Why would I? It made sense except as a message, it was confusing. What team sent it? "And since he's ensconced in the BLO, is this a warning from them?"

He shook his head. "No. Doubtful. Santos is in deep with Aguirre. It has to mean something to Aguirre's crew. Hey, let's make a diagram. Grab me some paper, would you?"

I checked my exasperation. A diagram? I wanted answers and safety, not pictures. But it wasn't the moment to dissent. "Sure, I'll be right back. Maybe you could take the box outside?"

He pulled a face, but got up and headed for the back stairs.

I ripped some pages from my notebook and gathered several pencils, dropping them onto the table before I knocked at both Lily's and Chucho's doors to let the housekeeper and our IT department know the kitchen was clear. Mrs. P came out. Chucho didn't answer. He'd probably left home. He'd be safer back on the streets.

Quint had traced a coffee mug to form three overlapping

circles, a perfect Ven diagram. He busily filled in names under the label he'd given each circle: Quint's Crew/Law Enforcement, BLO, Aguirre's Crew. In the center overlap of the three groups, only one name was listed. Anibal. I read the names ascribed to each.

"Quint, what about the Zetas? Shouldn't Cárdenas be in here? You need four circles. But the Zetas don't need to connect to ours."

"And we don't know they connect to the BLO. No, at the moment this is our theory: Aguirre, Santos, the younger Beltrán brother, Lobo and Consuelo conspired to hijack a BLO shipment awaiting sale. One of these jokers—"

I interrupted. "Zocer. I'm betting Zocer brokered the deal. Add him to Ani's crew."

He flicked the page to me. "You transcribe. One of these guys, Zocer maybe, brokered the deal with Los Zetas who picked the kids up in a helicopter, but didn't get Lily or her sister. I'm guessing the payment was not transferred at that time because Aguirre couldn't go to the helicopter without you. I'm also guessing the shootout was the BLO hoping to get their merchandise back and take out the thief."

"How would they have known?"

"Think! One of these bastards—" he stabbed the oval overlapping the BLO and Ani's crew— "knew all about it and may even have delivered the cash back to Beltrán. Now who might that have been?" He was fidgety and giddy anticipating the bulb lighting up over my head.

I drummed my fingers on the wood, cranked my stiff neck side to side, and straightened my slouching spine. Let there be light. "Guillermo Lobo!" I almost shouted. "But Anibal didn't know it before he participated in his kidnapping in Tepoztlán."

Quint tooted a flourish on his air trumpet. "Now you've got it."

"But it isn't Lobo's head."

"Of course not. It's one of Aguirre's people. Eddy is playing both sides."

I looked the list over. The same old same old. The head didn't match any of them. Was a player we didn't know involved? Quint's phone jangled. He glanced at the screen, picked it up and rushed out of the room. "What was that about, Peppi" I asked my dog. "Who's the head, boy?" He pricked up his ears and looked toward the office stairs. "Who's coming? Let's see."

Pepper and I opened the door to Horacio and Señor Santiago. Quint joined us and hustled the men off to look at the head and the damage from the grenade launcher. I was not invited. I banged on Chucho's door again. Still nothing. Mrs. P emerged and said she was going home. Call her when things calmed down. I couldn't blame her. I wanted to go home too.

"I left meatballs and salsa. *Adios, señorita.*"

Chapter 33

The Marines Have Landed

Chucho ushered me in and admitted his work was making him feel much better. If only I had some work. Ordering office supplies, for an office we probably would never open now, wasn't a smart use of my time. Neither was worrying, but the hovering bodies were specters I couldn't swat away.

I didn't mince words. "Shall we talk about it? He moved the box, and Santiago and Horacio are here. I want to know what you saw last night. Who you saw. Are you up for it?"

Chucho swung his feet onto the computer table, toed over the keyboard and chewed his lip for a moment. He nodded. "Sure, I guess. What did I see? Several men with assault rifles. You shot one of them. I didn't know them. They weren't any of the security we'd arranged. I was with Quint. We met two of the men at Santiago's office."

I shoved a stack of computer programming books onto a shelf and sat down on the chair they'd occupied. The room already had that dry, buzzy feel of electronics. How many computers did he have in here? Three? Plus a laptop? "Who did you meet?"

"Chavez and Delrio. Their company has contracts with a bunch of the governmental agencies for extra security when warranted. The U.S. Embassy uses them for events outside the embassy, they said. Santiago vouched for their reliability. I looked them up. Here." He handed me a thin sheaf of documents. "Everything I could find on them. And this." He leaned over to rip a sheet off the printer and held it out.

The police report of the car accident with both men named. I snatched it away from him and skimmed the article. The woman who called the police said a black SUV going too fast ran a red light and plowed into the front driver side wheel sending the security company's van into oncoming traffic. A delivery truck hit it knocking it over a car onto its side. The two men in front were killed and the third man survived. The one in the ICU. My intuition shouted in my ear, *His head is not in ICU.*

"Chuch! Did you read this? Look for another report. Missing persons. See if a hospital has reported an ICU patient missing."

His feet thudded to the floor and his fingers clacked over the keyboard. "I found it. *Security guard injured in auto accident disappears from ICU. Jose Carrillo (26) employed at Seguridad Internacional de Mexico, S.A.de C.V. If you've seen this man, please contact..."* Chucho scrolled past the number to show a photo of the missing man.

"Print that," I demanded, and stepped to the printer. The copy slid into the tray, I snatched it and ran.

Pepper, as usual, beat me up the stairs. I was yelling, "Quint, Quint!" through my panting. Altitude. I made a face at my denial. Too many tacos, beer, *pan dulces* and too little exercise. "Quint!" I yelled again.

He stepped into the hall. "Restrain yourself Jade. What's so important?" I handed over the sheet. He inspected it and strode back to the kitchen. I followed.

"Santiago, my IT department has identified our head." He passed the copy to the tsar of organized crime. Santiago read it, studied the photo and put the page next to the now empty tequila bottle.

Horacio reached for the page, scanned and nodded his agreement. "This is him. Now I understand the bruising on his head and neck. Poor bastard."

"*Señor* Rafiq, I agree with you. This man was murdered."

"They all were, Mr. Santiago," I said. "The car accident was deliberate. Another crew, a crew hired by Anibal Aguirre or his associates, took the place of the security you recommended for us. Didn't Quint tell you the police have the bodies of three security guards killed during the attack? Go look. They won't be the ones you vetted."

After all was said, we were no closer to understanding the message our head came to tell. But we'd reached a consensus: Anibal Aguirre was out for revenge against me for causing him to lose face with Cárdenas and his associates. Against Quint for interfering. Against his family for a lifetime of perceived slights and inequities. So, nothing new. All this didn't tie the cartels together, or give us any security. And we still had no papers for Lily. I'd talked to her on the phone. Of course she was thrilled to shadow Dafne at work and sounded as though she thought she'd landed in heaven when Daf took her home to meet Dorotea. Both Dafne and Dorotea had committed to taking puppies.

Relaxing back to normal things: plans for the future, finding homes for the puppies, my next date with Dylan—dinner—started putting life into perspective. Life wasn't just the horror show I'd landed in the day Polo's thugs hijacked Pepper and me off the *PanAmericano* Highway in July. It felt like a century past, even if it was only two months. So much had happened, starting with Polo's cousin, Lura, being blown up by his rival for the Zihuatanejo *plaza*. I'd learned a *plaza* wasn't a place of community gathering, but a strategic outlet for drugs, humans, arms, cash and anything else on the illegal market to be received or shipped. Ports, airports, border cities, if you controlled the *plaza* you controlled money and power.

And the Mexico City *plaza* was lucrative. Organized crime pretty much ran the airport. If you wanted it, you could get it. And if you wanted to ship it worldwide, *no problemo*. Chucho had set me up with one of his computers, showed me some tricks with searching and ¡*ya listo!* I had information at my fingertips.

Mexico wasn't unaware of its human trafficking problems. Already this year the congress had passed a law on human trafficking and *el D.F.* and all thirty-two of the states, passed anti-trafficking measures. But Mexico was in the top five of the worst rated countries for child prostitution. And forced labor. And every kind of servitude in between. Everything I read pointed to the hopelessness of the mission I'd embarked on. I dragged myself up with a stack of anvils on my shoulders to get dinner ready. How could our beleaguered group possibly put even a tiny dent in human trafficking here?

At least Lily was safe until they figured out where she was. Then I'd put more people into danger. I poured Mrs. P's spicy salsa into a saucepan and adjusted the heat under it. I felt guilty inviting my boyfriend over for dinner because of the danger it put him in. Boyfriend. I blushed to myself. I hadn't thought of Dylan as my boyfriend before.

"Been out in the sun, daughter? You're pink." I felt the color wash into my hairline and spread to my ears. He knew full well where I'd been all afternoon. Quint chuckled that low, mellow sound I'd come to relish. "Or thinking about Dylan?"

"He's coming for dinner and I'm berating myself for inviting anyone into this deadly, what'd you call it? Shit-show."

"I hear that, Jade. But I guess you didn't get the news—we're under the protection of the military now. *Marineros* patrolling. And Garza has sent two marines. The entire neighborhood is under surveillance. Our tenants already are considering breaking their leases," he added regretfully.

"Are the marines here now?"

"Yep."

"Can you contact them?"

"Why?"

"Dad, I'm dying, stiff, crazy from no exercise, and so is Pepper. I want them to take me running."

"Are you out of your fucking mind, girl? No I will not allow it." My father took on the caricature of a guy whose head was blowing off.

"I need to go out. I can't stand it anymore. Dylan won't be here for an hour and a half. I could run for thirty minutes, shower, and have dinner on the table when he arrives."

Marine Private First Class Javier agreed. He was pulling his second shift and hadn't exercised either. But Quint was adamant—we were not to run in the park across the street. I called for a cab to ferry us to Del Valle. Javier was cute and flirted shamelessly with me, but I secretly hoped I'd run into Dylan, Roger, and Noémi before they arrived at the residence for dinner. Pepper hoped to see them too. I could tell by the way he sniffed the air and wagged as we closed in on the park. When I opened the door, it was as if the starting gun had sounded. He was off and running. I took after him. No longer hampered by wounds, slowpokes, or out of shape runners, I sprinted after him at maximum speed until my winded lungs and a stitch in my side slowed me up. I felt every taco, every *panque*, every *cacahuate japones* and Victoria. For God's sake, my thighs rubbed together.

As I slowed, Javier pranced up behind me and made a

little circle dance around me while he scoped out the territory. I picked up my pace to a gentle jog as we neared the bend, my fingers mentally crossed I'd find Dyl at "our" bench. Javier jogged backwards, watching our backs. He was carrying. So was I. Suddenly he was on alert. Pepper galloped by, turning to me as he passed, tongue lolling from a huge doggie grin. Roger was on his heels. And Javier was reaching for the gun.

"Stop!" I shouted, skidding on the damp turf as I half turned to see Dylan flying toward me. I waved and leaned my hands onto my knees while I caught my breath. Javier wore a confused expression. "My honey, Dylan."

"You have a boyfriend?" he asked, lips turning down.

"Javier, I'll still invite you to dinner tonight," I teased.

Dylan caught up and threw his arms around me, sweeping me onto my toes, then twirling me off the ground in a bearhug. When he set me down he gave me a rather inviting kiss and I wished I weren't rooming with my father and a crew of strangers. I shifted out of his embrace and drew him toward Javier, standing a few feet away, trying to appear nonchalant.

"Dyl, meet my security detail, Javier. I've invited him to join us for dinner. Finally, a bodyguard who enjoys running."

Dylan reached out to shake, pumping Javier's hand enthusiastically.

"Javier, this is Dr. Dylan Porras and that crazy boy—" I pointed to Roger bouncing around Dylan's legs— "is Roger. He's a Xoloitzcuintli, a Mexican hairless dog." I looked down the track and sure enough, Noémi rounded the bend at a trot. "And that's Noémi." I gestured at the huffing dog.

Dylan thanked Javier for his service in keeping me safe while we waited for Noémi to catch up. "No Isabela today, Noé?" I bent down to pet her. She jumped up as though she wanted to be carried. I scooped her into my arms and she gave me a sloppy kiss through her Frenchie snorting.

Dylan laughed and shook his head. "Okay, Jade, you win! I owe you...what did we bet?"

I winked at Javier. "You agreed I could keep her if I could pick her up."

"Now I remember, but the deal is you have to take Roger and their dad, too."

My heart melted. I will. I will, I thought. I blew him a kiss. "Let's get moving. I told Quint I'd be back in thirty minutes, as if he believed me, but I don't want him to worry. And Mrs. P's *albóndigas* are calling. I need to clean up and get everything ready before my dinner dates show up." I winked and eased into a slow jog behind Pepper and Roger. The men joined me, Javier jogging backwards again, keeping watch.

"Besides Javier, who else is coming?"

"The other marine sent by Garza, Chucho, Dad. You."

Javier tipped his head and asked, "Dad?"

"You didn't know Quint is my dad?"

"You don't really look like him. More like your mom, no?"

Dylan appraised him. "Observant. I feel safer with you on the team, Javier. You're a marine?"

"Call me Javie, everyone does. And yeah, Private First Class. I got this cool duty at the embassy because I speak Spanish. I'm pretty lucky. I even have grandparents here in Mexico City."

"How wonderful for you, Javie. Where are you from?" We started into the wooded turn. We'd all better keep our eyes open, but I wasn't too worried with Pepper out front.

"Denver. But after my service I'm going to UCLA. Uncle Sam's going to pay for it. I'm going to learn how to surf."

Dylan perked up. "Hey, I graduated from there. And I did some surfing. What do you plan to study?"

"I dunno, business maybe? Law? I'm not really into

computers that much. What else is there?"

"I got my degree in Journalism," I volunteered. "Hey, there's our bench. Let's take a rest and let the little girl catch up again. Then Javier and I are going to run like the devil is after us to get back in time." Pepper was already sitting in front of it waiting, and Roger danced around when I flopped down.

"You like to write, Miss?"

"Miss! Call me Jade, everyone does," I quoted Javie's words back to him with a smile. He *was* a cute kid. "Yes, I'm working on a story about human trafficking here."

"Heavy stuff, man, uh, mis—Jade. Where are you from?"

"Sausalito, just across the Golden Gate Bridge from San Francisco. I have a friend staying with us from Denver and L.A. you might meet. Do you like Denver?" I patted the spot next to me, but he shook his head.

"I'm on duty, Jade. I have to keep watch."

"In that case," Dylan said, "I'll sit next to the pretty journalist. Isn't Lily at home?"

I shook my head. "Long story. She's gone to visit the big house with your future sister-in-law."

He narrowed his eyes and lowered his voice. "Seeg called and gave me the rundown. I figured it's why you're over here with a bodyguard. Seems like a decent kid. Lily would love him."

"Yes, she would. I hope we can keep him," I breathed into Dyl's neck. "A highly trained soldier is exactly what we need. It was awful, and, as Quint says, it ain't over."

"When it is, over I mean, I want you to start seeing a therapist. What you've experienced and had to do to survive is more than any human should have to suffer alone."

I'd been thinking the same thing, but I said, "For now, let's run!" and I blasted into the track with Pepper and Roger keeping pace. Javie overtook me with his powerful and fluid strides in less than a moment. Poor Noémi was lost in our dust.

I was a new woman with a new attitude when I put Mrs. P's delicious meal on the table. The run loosened up my tight muscles and the shower washed away my negative mood. I'd put on a cute dress, left my gun in my undies drawer, and fixed my hair and makeup. After all, I'd won the bet. Now I really did have a boyfriend. I wished Lily were here. How lovely for her to have a chance to flirt with a cute, upstanding marine. The other guy was a lot older than Javie and a little standoffish. He seemed uncomfortable with the invitation, but I noticed he and Quint had a lot to discuss. As soon as we finished eating they disappeared down to Quint's office. Chucho, the odd man out tonight, went back to his computers, leaving me with Dylan and Javie.

I refilled our mugs with Mexican hot chocolate, "just like my mom makes" according to Javie. "What's going on with Quint and the corporal?"

Javie blew on his frothy drink and set it aside. "Too hot. I think they're talking about additional security detail. The corp's got a leave coming."

"What about you?"

"Nah, I don't think so. I'm only six months in. I'm thankful I wasn't assigned to Iraq. It's hell over there. Corp likes me. Maybe he'll get me assigned to the job with Mr. Quint," he said with a hint of wistfulness. "I like family dinners. I only get to visit *mis abuelos* sometimes, and I have a hard time understanding their Spanish."

"You aren't fluent?" Dylan asked.

"No man, I mean, sir. My parents speak Spanish at home and I can talk with them, but I grew up in English only schools. I can't really read in Spanish and I can't write it. None of my brothers and sisters can. I'm the middle of five. How's your Spanish, Sir?"

Dylan hooted. "Jade, I've completely fooled our new friend. Javie, I am fully fluent in Spanish. I grew up here, born just blocks from the park. And please, call me Dylan." He winked at the boy. "Everybody does."

"You're Mexican? I thought you were from California like Jade, with UCLA and your name—like Bob Dylan, and all. You went to medical school in a foreign language? You must be really smart."

"Or really dumb to attempt it," Dylan quipped. "My mother is American. We always spoke Spanish and English at home and I took loads of English classes. I'm one of four. Mom named us for American folk singers."

"Sweet. I plan on being bilingual. It will help me get a better job."

While the men talked I cleared the rest of the table and filled the dishwasher. Now I checked the time. A few more minutes of chatting while I washed the pots and Javi had to get lost. I wanted Dylan, Roger, Noémi, and Pepper to myself. I filled the rice pot to soak and scrubbed the salsa pot, clipped the lids back on the leftovers, and put together a little doggie bag for Javie. He had to stand guard all night.

"Javie, here's a little snack for you while you patrol tonight. It's ten. I think I hear your corporal on his way up to collect you."

"You can hear that?"

I jutted my chin at the trio with noses stuck out the kitchen door, ears pointing up, tails twitching. Okay, Noémi's entire rump wiggled.

"I never had a dog. But I'm getting one as soon as I move to California. Thanks for dinner, Miss Jade. It was *muy rico*. As good as *mami's*."

Quint and the corporal came in. Javie saluted his officer and thanked Quint for dinner, before turning to me and asking, "Will we run tomorrow?"

"I sure hope so, Javie. Thanks so much. Don't forget

your snacks. There's enough for both of you." I handed a big thermos and a couple of cups to the corporal. "Coffee. Be safe tonight."

Now all I had to do was get rid of Quint.

Chapter 34

What's a Plan without a Map?

Thursday September 20, 2007

My dreams flowed like honey after Dylan left. I added 'get my own place' to my mental to-do list. At least one of us had to. Dylan got up too early to be running home to sleep every night. And it felt like ripping off bandages when he left. Not to mention the baddies out there looking to take away everything I cared about. Including me.

So much for my sweet awakening.

Quint had pulled me aside after Dyl left and filled me in on our next move. He and Santiago had cooked up a plan, a raid it sounded like, to rid us of the rats infesting our lives. Lily and the dogs would stay with Dorotea. Apparently Dafne's mother had decreed it. No going against the matriarch. I could talk to Lil, but there would be no contact with her, Daf, or Seeger. I'd put my foot down about Dylan. I was matriarch in this residence and would not brook opposition. Dad had shaken his head and muttered something about strong-willed women and ordered me to look for a contractor to rebuild the *bodega*. I wasn't sure why. Wouldn't a demolition crew be easier? One less place for the enemy to hide or attack. Oh, well, it would give me something to do—while I was grounded.

The team tasked me to research travel options outside the obvious—flying out of Benito Juárez International to Denver International. This came as positive news...but now that our leaving loomed in reality, a wave of sadness washed over me. I hadn't had enough time here— not with Dylan. Would this be the end of our relationship? I mulled over possibilities and made my way to the workroom to get started.

The morning dragged through call after call to *contratistas*. I was learning a whole new vocabulary. The hard lesson was, I should lie about what actually happened. The moment the office staff heard we'd been bombed, he or she made excuses or flat out hung up. I called Dafne.

"Hey Daf, Jade here. How is everything going? Thanks so much for taking charge of Lily ...Yeah, you were amazing!...Awful. Scary. But Quint is finally convinced we need to jump the border... No, actually, I wanted your advice on contractors to rebuild the *bodega* on the garage... You will? Bless you girlfriend. I'll expect his call...Yes, we do have to discuss our options. How are the documents coming?... Sounds great, except Dad won't let me out. How about here for drinks? Mrs. P refuses to come, so I don't vouch for dinner, but you're welcome to join us... Okay then, I'll see you at five thirty. Thanks, Daf."

I hung up. Dafne had news. The pieces were starting to fit into our puzzle. And she was sending her contractor. I could expect his call within the hour. I decided to break for lunch.

I found Horacio making coffee when I arrived upstairs.

"Hi, H. What's up?"

"Your *papi* sent me to make a pot of coffee for our meeting. Do you have *una charola?*"

I retrieved a round tray from a cabinet and put it on the counter, adding the sugar bowl, some spoons, and a pitcher of cream. "How many cups?"

"Four. Santiago is stopping by, and the boss asked the corporal to sit in. He wants his help getting across the border. Between us, I don't fully trust him, but he's got experience. He did a couple of tours in Iraq."

"How'd he end up here?" I placed a painted clay plate of fresh sugar cookies on the tray and started to slice apples. They spit juice as I cut into them. Crisp and sweet smelling, I popped a wedge into my mouth and crunched down.

"Here at the boss's place? Your father made the ambassador feel guilty I think." He broke into his wonderful ogre laugh. Uncanny how much he sounded like Shrek.

"No, I meant, how did the corporal come to Mexico?"

"*No sé.* But I don't think he's a marine."

"What makes you say that?"

He wrinkled his forehead and tightened his lips. "A hunch. For one, he looks at things too much like *el jefe*. He reminds me of a wolf." He poured the coffee into a decorative thermos I pulled off the top shelf of the pantry.

I said, "You mean sort of secretive, a loner?

"Not that bad. Suspicious, though. The boss isn't like that."

"Yes, he is! Didn't you see how he mistrusted Dylan?"

"I have a daughter, too. I'll do the same when the time comes. She's only ten now." Again, the Shrek mirth. I laughed with him.

"You better go." I gestured to the laden tray.

"Do I have to?" He grinned. I knew exactly how he felt. I'd rather chew glass than spend only God knew how many hours in conference with those guys.

"It sucks to be you today! See you later H."

Back at my desk with a tuna sandwich, I stared at the list I'd started to weigh the pros and cons of the various forms of travel available to the border. Not that many choices and all obvious. I realized I should determine the best crossing to get to Denver the quickest. I presumed we'd be chased, but hopefully it would take the *Baby Blows*, as I'd come to think of them, a few days to realize we'd flown the coop. And, maybe, just maybe the U.S. Marshal's office would finally send their team to wrangle Anibal back to the U.S. and trial. That would probably get these bastards off our backs. And wasn't Quint down the hall sequestered with the head of Mexico's organized crime fighting bureau? Santiago should have teams after Eddy Santos and whomever they'd caught alive—the fake security guard. On a separate notepad I wrote:

> #1 Status of US Marshal
> #2 SEIDO's investigation into BLO & *Baby Blows*

I probably wasn't getting much help from the organized crime tsar, but could Chucho hack into their files? If not Chuch, my employee Qadir could.

> #3 Get IT to hack into SEIDO for info

I bet *that* would turn up a few surprises. Why didn't I think of this a few days ago? Santiago probably was perfectly aware of Farcía Luna's activities. Surely after our briefing prior to the senator's murder, Santiago investigated the thug. Then why didn't they bust the traitor wide open? Santiago was reputed to be above reproach. I drummed my fingers on the pad considering this legend. Was any human above reproach, or approach, if the stakes were high enough? Would I give over Lily for enough money? So far I'd risked my life pretty consistently to save her from the evil men do. But that little niggle in the deep folds of my brain made me uncomfortable and not so sure what I would do for the right price. Or the right threat. *Plata o Plomo.* After all, I'd killed men. Zocer was going to kill me; nobody would blame me for killing him first. But still—I killed him. If I could kill a man I'd danced with, what did it say about my moral fiber?

Pepper whined and pawed my leg. "Peppi, boy, are you telling me to stop? Not go down this road?" At the word road he emitted a happy gurgle and vigorously wagged his tail. "Ah, now I understand." I stroked his head. He wagged harder and pointed his nose toward the door. "So, you could care less about my moral fiber. You want to go out." He woofed and danced in circles. "Okay. Let's go." I got up from my desk. Pepper was already at the front door. "Not that door, boy. Let's go to the garden." He looked a little crestfallen, but backtracked to the apartment stairs.

I opened the door and started to run up taking two steps at a time. Pepper grinned as he passed me and waited at the landing for me to catch up, rather impatiently. "You beat me! What a good dog. Let's go!" I opened the door and Pepper beelined to the garden door. I joined him and, after looking carefully at the alley and the building across the way, I let him out.

"You going out?"

I turned. It was Javie a mop of bedhead sticking out. Where'd he come from?

"Pepper needs to pee. I'd sure like a run. Want to go?" I looked him over. "Where did you come from?"

"Your dad told me to sleep in the girl's room. I was on duty all night. Just woke up."

"You must be hungry. Coffee?"

"Please to both. I could watch the dog."

I backed into the kitchen stopping in the panty for more beans. We were running through beans like crazy. "Deal. You watch Pepper—" I handed him a poop bag— "and I'll fix you breakfast. *Juevos mexicanos,* okay?"

"Sweet." He headed to the back stairs.

"Take a gun and wear shoes, Javie."

He looked down and said, "Oh, right, shoes," and went back to Lily's room for his boots.

Pepper would finish up and come back on his own. I assembled eggs, salsa, a half kilo of tortillas and a length of *longaniza* on the counter, lit the stove under the *comal* for the tortillas and cracked four eggs into a bowl. Javie reappeared fully dressed and armed. "Drop the bag into the can under the stairs," I instructed, laughing. "Poop patrol. I bet you didn't know that would be part of a marine's duty."?

"No, ma'am, I didn't. I'll be right back."

Not if Pepper wanted to stay out, I didn't tell him. My pans were hot so I got going on breakfast. I didn't mind making him breakfast, but I did not see my life consisting of office management—wasn't that why I took the case in Mexico in the first place? This was a stop gap while Mrs. P took time off. I really needed to figure out what I wanted. We were coming to the end of the caper, so to speak. Once I delivered Lily safely to her aunt and uncle, what was I going to do?

Pepper raced in and sat down by his bowl. I separated the tortillas, flipping more often as they got hot. The longaniza browned. I poured the hot water over the ground beans and plunged. I heard the clump of boots on stairs and whisked the eggs one last time, pouring them into the still hot longaniza pan.

"Almost ready, Javie. Pour yourself a coffee. Cups in the cabinet above the pot." I gestured with my chin and stirred the eggs again.

"I looked at the damage. Are you going to fix any of it?"

I shrugged. He sat down with his cuppa. I spooned the eggs onto his warm plate next to the sausage and slid it in front of him. I could always get a job as a short order cook.

"Didn'tyoutellmeyou'reajournalist?" he asked through a mouthful.

"Mwabuthamo?"

He swallowed. "Sorry. My mom always does that to me too."

Oh, good, the security think I'm their mother now. "Javie, I need a road map of Mexico. You know where I can get one?"

He chewed and swallowed. "Internet?"

"No, I need something bigger I can draw routes on. I'll ask Horacio."

"Ask me what?"

It always blew me away how quietly he could move. He was a big guy too. "A road map of Mexico."

"To plan our escape route?"

"Yeah. But I'm worried about the border states and which crossing will be the safest. You hungry?" Horacio shook his head. Held up a bakery bag. "Time for *panes*?" I asked.

"*Sí, estan cálidos todavia.*"

I took the bag and plated the warm pastries, grabbed a *mantecada* and ripped off the cupcake paper before biting into the sweet corn flavored cake.

Javie narrowed his eyes. "Why can't you get on a military flight?"

"Just what we've been asking your boss," Horacio said.

"The point is to get an American out of Mexico? So what's the problem?"

I gave the synopsis. "Or that's the excuse." The last sounded pretty sarcastic, even to me.

"Does the ambassador know she's an American?"

"Of course. We've been pleading for help for nearly two months. This is typical of bureaucracy. I think Garza won't put her on a plane because he's afraid he'll lose his post. In two years we'll have an election and whoever wins could pull him from Mexico. At least that's what I'm guessing. With all the immigration problems and the cartel stuff, I bet he's scared."

"Is this what you're writing about?" Javie asked. He'd cleaned his plate and eaten three *pan dulces*.

How lucky to be young and active. He could eat anything. I cleared his dishes and put them in the dishwasher. If short order was too technical, I'd make an efficient waitress and get plenty of exercise. I sure wasn't being hired as a journalist any time soon. "It's part of it, but I haven't gotten to writing. I'm researching now." No reason to tell him I'd never sold an article.

"I should get back to my desk. Horacio, can you get me that map? And have you access to my combi? I need my U.S. maps too."

"*Claro, señorita.* I'll run by the *taller* today and get what you need. I've got a highway map in the limo I'll bring up."

"Thanks, H. Can I write on it?"

"It will be yours. Do what you like."

"Then see you boys later. Come on, Pepper." I turned to leave but swiveled back. "Thanks for minding Pepper, Javie."

He saluted.

Chapter 35

Hacking the Facts

My lists hadn't resolved themselves into action or completion. Not much I'd get done without the maps H promised, but the to-do list certainly had potential for using up the rest of the afternoon. I'd look busy, if nothing else. Quint's office door remained shut. I sure hoped he was getting some answers and a lot of protection. Maybe Santiago could do what Garza couldn't. I was losing faith in my own government, but putting faith in a corrupt Mexican government? Probably the definition of insanity. Number three was where I'd start—it was actionable.

#3 Get IT to hack into SEIDO for info

One thing was clear, I wouldn't share item #3 with these people. I picked up my plate with its untouched sandwich and chips and tiptoed past Quint's office—okay, I pressed my ear to the door before passing but heard only the drone of voices, not any words—and knocked at the IT department.

Chucho yelled to come in.

"You hungry Chuch?"

He spun his chair around and grinned at me, surrounded by papers, screens, wires, a pair of earphones dangling around his neck. "*Que tienes*? Whatcha got?"

"Tuna with green salsa and mayo on fresh *telera*."

"My favorite *torta*. Sit down and fill me in."

"They're still at it. I don't have any news. Horacio brought the *panes* but no hint of what's going on. *Sin embargo*, however, we might make better progress with a little hacking. But you can never tell anyone, okay?"

Chucho's eyes lit up and he nodded. "My line of work. Who are we hacking?"

I sucked a short breath between my lip and front teeth then grinned conspiratorially. "SEIDO."

He looked like the proverbial cat who ate the canary. "Maybe I could use it as my graduation project."

I laughed. "Speaking of which, have you been going to classes?"

"I've missed a few. We've been pretty busy, haven't we? My teachers know about the senator's death and our move. And we had a couple of days' holiday. I have to be back in classes next week."

"Be sure you are. But while you're playing hooky, let's see if we can get into the records. I want their reports on Farcía Luna and Eddy Santos. Also the fake security guy the police arrested."

"I can hack the police files, easy."

"I'm pretty sure I overheard Quint saying something on the phone about SEIDO taking over from the police, but why not start with the police?"

His fingers already tapped away at the keyboard. How could anyone type so fast? I flunked typing in high school summer class, much to my mother's consternation. How many times had I heard her say a woman needed to know how to type in case she were forced to work outside the home? What century was she from? Oh, yeah, the 20th. I chuckled. I'd picked up my speed with the prevalence of spell check and autocorrect. And guess what? I'd ended up in a job where I did more typing than anything else. Here I was moving laterally into exactly the same position. I sighed and turned my attention to what was coming up on the screen.

"You're right. Here's the call to come to a shooting at our address. The report says the unit responded, found two dead and a third wounded. The wounded man was taken by emergency response to an undisclosed location at the orders of one Sr. Tupoc Velasquez. I wonder who he is? Let's look him up."

Again the fingers flew. "*Ya, listo.* He's attached to the Attorney General's office. You know SEIDO stands for *Subprocuraduría Especializada en Investigación de Delincuencia Organizada.* Essentially, our guest Santiago is the assistant attorney general in charge of investigating organized crime."

I knew he was heading up a department related to organized crime, but not actually what SEIDO meant. "So this Tupoc character must work in Santiago's division. I see you're in, can you find the files?'

"On it. This is going to be harder than the police files. SEIDO has better funding, therefore better encryption." He laughed, waved bye-bye, and snugged his headphones around his ears.

I got up and returned the usual coding books to their chair. Now what would I do? It was only 3:47. Too early to make *botanas.* I went back to my office and checked my phone. Sure enough, I'd received a call from Dafne's contractor. I dialed him back and made a date for the next morning. I could check something off my list.

Horacio stepped into the suite. He re-locked the front

door with several clicks and scrapes, held up some folded papers grinning. I waved him into the workroom.

"You found the maps?"

He tossed several maps and a manila envelope onto my desk. "And more."

"You have information?" I asked as I opened the *AAA* Southwestern States map I'd picked up with my membership in what felt like many moons past. I'd thought about doing some touring when I went north—San Luis Potosí, Zacatecas, Copper Canyon, and maybe San Miguel de Allende—and I wanted to figure out what border crossing I'd use to re-enter the U.S. The plan was to do some sightseeing along the southern border in Texas, New Mexico, or Arizona depending on which it was. "Pull up a chair. I'll show you where we're going." I spread out the map and pointed to Denver.

"Check it out, H, Denver is almost directly north of El Paso, or Ciudad Juárez. Let's see how far." I stood up and bent over the map with a ruler from my pencil cup. I counted about 700 miles. "If we went up Interstate 25, probably the safest route, it's going to take us about ten hours." I ran my finger up the route to show him. Look. We could overnight in Santa Fe. It's a darling town. Have you been?"

He grunted, "No," stood and opened my triple A map of Mexico, lining it up with the Southwest map. The two covered the desk and I reevaluated the trip. We'd be looking at over thirty hours of driving time.

I studied the map then Horacio's face. "You're thinking it's a long drive through a lot of remote territory."

"*Sí, señorita.* It isn't going to be a pleasure trip. And that region is one of the most dangerous in Mexico." He nudged the manila envelope across the map. "I got some information for you from the senator's files."

I had a bad feeling about this. "How did you have access to Polo's files?"

"*No te preocupes, señorita.* Mr. Quint requested I find information on the current state of Mexico and in particular the people we are interested in. *Señora* Susanna is curating the files, making sure we get anything pertinent. The senator never kept his sensitive files in his office."

"Polo didn't trust his colleagues and office staff?"

"Not at all. He trusted your father, Susanna, Chucho, and me. Chucho provided much of the information. The senator was smart to send him to school in information technology. He's a genius."

"So I'm finding out. Let's see what you have in the envelope." I extracted several typed pages, skimmed down the first page. A lot of blah blah blah on crime in Ciudad Juárez, naming political figures and police associated with something called *Cártel del Golfo.* What caught my eye, kingpin Chapo and his allies were right now fighting to take over the *plaza.* I grimaced. "What's the take away, H? Those allies mentioned are our local variety of gang thugs?"

"Smart girl." It was Quint's voice. "Jade, come see me after *Señor* Santiago leaves."

I shot him a thumbs-up and went back to reading. The next page was filled with statistics on murders and crimes. The last page, however, offered some surprising intel we could use. "Is this reliable, H?" I waved the page at him.

There was that big toothed ogre grin. "You betcha!" he said in English. It came out sounding something like *joo beet chahh* and I suppressed my giggle. How many times had H or Chucho or Dylan not laughed at my accent?

"So, you're telling me the BLO has established a base in San Miguel de Allende to manage the takeover of Juarez and its four border crossings?" He nodded. "But that isn't what's important here, is it? Beltrán is planning to break from Chapo's Sinaloa Federation, and he's courting Los Zetas." Had I nailed it? *Joo beet chah.* I added, "Who got this intel? Are we sure it's good?"

"Your father has a network, *señorita*. A source close to Beltrán divulged this. He's been boasting the BLO is going to be the most powerful organization in the world. The sources say he acts like he's king, *o acaso presidente,* according to *la información*, he has aspirations to run for president. Why do you think Hector spends his time hobnobbing around *La Capital* with the *politicos y alta sociedad*?"

"Wow, this is news! Well, this is a theory, anyway. I didn't know the BLO was anywhere but the capital. So exactly how does this affect us?"

Quint stuck his head through the open door. "I'm going upstairs for a few. I'll be back to tell you what I've found out."

"We'll be here, boss," I called back. "H, I have Chucho hacking the SEIDO files for info on the BLO and Anibal's *Baby Blows*. We should see what he's got. Maybe he'll have something to add."

"*Baby Blows*? Like *soplar*? Or..." He trailed off, the tips of his knobby ears reddening.

"That's just what I mean— *mamar, chupar.*"

His lips rounded and eyebrows shot high. The red staining his ears spread down across his face.

"What a prude, H! Yeah, Aguirre's Baby cocksuckers. They're sucking the BLO's *vergas*. Traitors, *no?* Carlos a brother. Eddy Santos one of the kingpin's God children. And he's blowing them big time. Unless, of course—I've said it a gazillion times—unless this is some sort of alliance being developed with Los Zetas. And Polo's secret papers corroborate I'm the brilliant investigator who figured it out."

I'd probably lost H with corroborate, but he was delighted with Baby *Blows*. "Go get Chuch, will you? I'll finish reading this before Quint comes down."

Still laughing, he rumbled out of the workroom.

Quint showed up about twenty minutes later, close to the time I needed to get my drinks ready for Dafne. I trailed him down the hall to his office.

"Dad, Dafne is coming by for wine in an hour. I need to get upstairs and make some *botanas*. You should join us. She's going to tell me what she's accomplished and discuss our potential plan. Then I suppose I have to get dinner together. How many will we be?" I looked at the men already sprawled on Quint's low couch. "You guys eating here tonight?"

"*Muchas gracias, senorita. Me voy. Mi marida planea algo especial anoche.*" Horacio replied.

"Your wife is planning something? A special occasion? What?" I asked. "It's not your birthday is it?"

"No, no, nothing like that. My wife says she hasn't seen me in too long and is making my favorite *chile verde*. She says the only reason I will come home is for a good meal."

"Smart woman. She's right about the quality of meals here without Mrs. P, Dad? When will you get her back?"

"We need a bigger place. She wants a room." Quint blew out in exasperation. "In one breath she says we're all crazy and it's too dangerous here. In the next she says she's afraid to live alone now and wants to rent out her house for the income and live with us. It's the girl she wants. It's sad she lost her children in that earthquake. She'd have grandchildren to love now instead of our wacky lot."

"She can have my room when I leave," I said.

"You're not leaving your old dad," he half joked.

"Hmmm. We'll see." I opened my notebook with my useless lists and said, "I really need to get going on quesedillas or something. Here's my day's report: One, Dafne's contractor is coming at nine-thirty tomorrow to assess the project and bid the job if he can do it. Two, the border crossing closest to Denver is Ciudad Juárez/El Paso. Denver's ten hours up Interstate 25 through some pretty remote country. Horacio has brought it to my attention the trip from here to Juárez is double that through not only remote country, but through dangerous cartel controlled areas. Juárez is a battleground. It turns out Beltrán is provoking a hostile takeover from the Gulf Cartel for the Sinaloans. We go there, and we're made. They know who we are. And driving might be a bad idea. Flights from Benito Juarez to Juárez are plentiful. Four flights on AeroMexico before noon. It's about three hours and less than $200 per person. Dafne has contacts there. Let's hear what she has to say before we go any farther. That's all from me. What's your news, Quint?"

"You already know. There's talk BLO is romancing Los Zetas to ally against the Sinaloans. Beltrán and Chapo have never seen eye to eye, or so I've heard. Héctor wants to increase his presence and that means taking over some of the Sinaloans' share of trade. We might see another turf war like in the nineties when Chapo decided to put the Arellanos in Tijuana out of business. Bloody business. The Beltráns and the Arellanos are related and none of 'em like Shorty. How this applies to our mission? We won't be driving to the border. Word is going to get out fast we've run. Both teams will have *halcones,* hawks—lookouts, keeping their eyes on us. We'll be moving fast."

"Flying then?"

"Yes, I think so. Private plane. Rosi is locking into it."

"To where?" I asked.

"That's the rub, now, ain't it? Juárez makes the most sense."

"Can we afford that?"

"Can you bring our books up to date? Tell us where we stand?"

"If I have to, Dad."

"I can make a spreadsheet, if it helps. I've taken a couple of years of accounting and sometimes did special tallies for the senator," Chucho volunteered.

"You're a prince, Chucho. Would you? I have a chart of accounts and all our receipts and bank information. Maybe we could work on it tomorrow. I'll code everything tonight and sort by date."

"You got it, Jade. *Jefe*, do you need me for anything else?"

"No, Chucho, but Horacio I need to talk to you. We have to get Jade's bus out of Mexico and we'll need a car in El Paso."

"Boss, that bus is known. We won't be safe in El Paso. These *cárteles* have people in the U.S., especially along the border. Miss Jade can't drive out of Mexico in it. She'd be shot before she got out of the *colonia*."

"I was thinking more of hiring a driver," Quint said.

"So an innocent gets killed?"

"I take your point. What do you suggest?"

Horacio replied, "Put it on a flatbed and ship it to the border."

"Do I have a say in this?" I asked.

They turned on me in unison growling, "No!"

"I'm going up to make snacks for our meeting with Dafne. You'll make sure she gets in the residence safely, Dad?"

"Of course, Daughter. Now scoot. H and I have some things to hash out."

Chapter 36

My Forger Owed Me a Favor

Dafne traveled on Mexican time. I'd eaten half of my favorite *epazote* mini *quesadillas* before she arrived. Luckily I'd made plenty of other snacks: salsa-laced tuna in lettuce cups, a cheese plate with chevre, Chihuahua cheese and Spanish *chorizo*, cured olives, and pickled vegetable crudités. She brought an excellent bottle of Dry Creek zinfandel.

"How on earth did you get your hands on a California wine?"

She giggled and poured two glasses of the deep ruby liquid. "Jade, haven't you figured it out yet? I have many contacts."

"Uh-huh, and it's your contacts for border jumping I'm after," I said, clinking my glass with hers and tasting the dry, complex flavors of blackberries, redwood, and bitter chocolate. Home exploded on my tongue. "I need to go home," I said, tipping my glass toward her and licking my lips. "No, really, we've pretty much decided to be gone sooner rather than later. We're not waiting for the embassy to do it's diddlysquats. And you know what's happening around here."

"I have a case of it. I'll give you a few bottles."

"Do you have a case of Richardson Bay aroma at low tide, too?"

She grinned. "I could probably arrange it."

"Seriously, Daf. Lily and I need to get out of Mexico. Have you any word on the false papers?" I passed the lettuce cups.

"Why do you think I risked getting grenaded?"

"Ha ha, Daf. We stopped that with U.S. Marines. No better protection. At least the embassy was good for something. So what's the news?"

"My forger owed me a favor. I've got a tourist card, a U.S. passport AND, check it out, a Mexican passport. I took Lily yesterday for photos, and the Mexican passport is done. I'm pretty sure the forger got his hands on a case of passport blanks."

"OMG, really? Dafne you're a genius. Now I owe *you* a favor."

"Oh, yeah you do, girlfriend. And we can start with you not breaking my brother-in-law's heart."

Had I been a cartoon, my eyes would have been rolling in big circles. One clockwise, one counterclockwise. She noticed my confusion and asked, "You are planning on coming back, *¿no?*"

"Of course she's coming back. I have a job for her here," Quint said, startling both of us. I almost sloshed wine down my front.

"Dad, get a glass and join us. I'm guessing H went home?"

"Yeah. Is there enough? Our security team will be up soon."

"You'll get to meet our adorable marine, Javie. I wish

Lily were here. She'd be mad for him."

Quint walked back in with another bottle of wine, a couple of beers, and a Coke. "Don't encourage her."

"Sheesh, Dad, I'm just saying. She's not even here. How is our girl, Daf?

"She's fine. I've started weaning the puppies and she's paper training them with my mom. You heard Mom fell in love and wants to keep them all? Lily says she can keep Sadie..." I felt a twinge of sadness. I'd wanted her. "Your father gets Jack. Horacio's kids get Cookie; Mrs. P, Cider; but the comedians, Roli and Poli, are going to Denver. However, call it busy work to keep her mind off things. The girl has nightmares every night and spends much of the day withdrawn and down. She needs help and a home."

"Tru dat," Chucho said, coming in from his lair.

"You been watching MTV videos or something?" I joked.

"Nice to see you, *señorita*," he said to Dafne. To me, "Any good news for us?"

Dafne grinned. "We were just going over it. We'll have a Mexican passport tomorrow. In three to four days we'll have a U.S. passport. Your closest crossing to Denver is Juárez. Rosi has a contact who is owed a big favor. The contact can get you over the border through the storm drains into El Paso. Your best plan is to fly to Juárez under the Porras name. It's what I used on the passport. Go as a family. You Jade, your father, your fiancé Dylan Porras, and his niece. You have family in the area...well, Dylan does. They will collect you from the airport and take you to their home for a visi—"

"Whoa, hold on woman," Quint roared, jumping out of his seat. "What are you arranging?"

"Chill, Dad. Let her go on. How would I be protected under my own name?"

"It's the weak link, Jade, but if we do it right, we can get you out of here without anyone knowing. Once you land, Seeg's uncle will pick you up. He's a big deal in town. No one is going to mess with him. Lily will be disguised, wig, a lot of makeup—you know. We can make her look thirty. Or go the other way and make her look twelve. But decide right now so I can have the right birthdate on the passport."

"Let her be her own age with the same birthdate. A typical teen with earbuds stuck in her ears all the time. Practice her Spanish accent with her for when she does need to speak. She's an excellent actress. And this is going to be her Oscar winning role," I said.

"Ladies...question?" Quint said. Dafne gestured, *go ahead*. "What about the dogs? Neither of these girls will go without her dog. And Jade's combi? She needs to return it to its owner in California. And how the hell do you think you'll get Lily all the way to Denver?"

"Getting to Denver is tricky. The family can meet you and take the girl and her dogs, but that risks them driving the ten hours. I'm guessing Eddy Santos knows about her family, but probably not the name. I'd rather not involve them. They aren't at all prepared for what they might have to do. Hey Jade, you have any more of this chorizo?"

I excused myself to the kitchen for a refill. While I sliced the meat I heard Javie and the corporal come in. Quint was introducing them to Dafne when I returned with the plate. I said hi and offered them drinks. Javie looked abashed when I gave him the Coke. Old enough to die for his country but not old enough for a beer. I grabbed the Coke back and passed him a Victoria.

I tuned into the conversation as Quint introduced the older marine, one Chuck Nader, who, it turned out was not a marine, but probably fit the wolf category just fine. I never learned what branch he worked with, but he and Quint had some sort of secret handshake.

"Chuck is going to help us. You like to drive, Chuck?"

The man's voice cut deep, crunching like gravel. "Sure. Why not. Like Ms. Olabarietta says, let's put the VW on a truck and the dogs in the cab, but Miss Quint will have to take her across. Javier there, will come as my co-pilot." Javie lit up, excitement written all over him. Nader continued, pointing at me, "We'll get the VW to the border. You'll have to take it from there."

"Me? Yes, I suppose I would." I turned to Quint. "The permission is in my name, even if the *combi* belongs to my ex. Can't you come with me?"

He said, "We'll work out the details later. Are you taking this down?"

I flashed my notebook and pen, although so far I'd written nothing. Wasn't this a secret mission better left memorized? I mentally grinned.

Nader resumed his instructions. Something about this felt skewed. How did Quint lose control of the reins? I had to learn to trust, because Quint sure didn't act like he had any concerns. The man ticked off the steps with his fingers: rent a truck, load the combi, drive to the designated border crossing, trade drivers...

Horacio interrupted. "Chuck, what makes you think you'll get the truck through the cartel territories?"

"We have routes secured," Nader replied.

"Secured?" Dafne and Horacio echoed.

I was thinking the same and glanced at my father. His fingers jiggled over his knee. His tell. He was nervous. "I'm confused. Chuck, you're saying you are not a U.S. Marine, but some sort of shady operative with prepaid transportation networks through crime controlled Mexico. Did I get that right?"

At least he had the courtesy to look nonplussed, but I thought it was an act. Quint was about to pop, he'd turned so red. Dafne saved the day.

"Mr. Nader, yours is an interesting plan, but for any plan

to be successful, we must work as a trusted team. Explain to us what your connections are and your authority to operate on behalf of the U.S. in Mexico. We need to understand your presence and contribution." Slick—what a pro.

Quint spoke up. "Dafne, Chuck and I go way back. He's on our side, I assure you. He is currently undercover investigating cartel activity in smuggling. It's all I can say, but if anyone knows how drugs and people move out of Mexico, and conversely, how people, guns and money enter into Mexico, he's your man."

"The plan sounds too convoluted to me. Why are these guys traveling with the combi? Why not put the bus on a *grua* and ship it to California? I can arrange that. Horacio, can you take Jade to get her possessions out? For this to work, we'll need to disable it. And no way would I lock those dogs up in a truck for days. What were you thinking?"

"I wasn't letting him near my Pepper," I said, wishing I could stick my tongue out at the spook. He gave me the creeps.

Dafne's giggle tinkled. "Our girl wasn't agreeing to that either. Especially not the puppies. And we've wasted way too much time on this fantasy. Quint," she said, piercing him to wriggle on a pin, "this is what we're going to do."

Finally! I checked my watch as I passed around fresh drinks. Dylan would arrive in an hour and a half. I hadn't started dinner. I stood up. "You all want to stay for dinner?"

Daf blew me a kiss, and said, "Thanks but no thanks. I have plans. Next time, Jade."

"Same goes for me. Wife's having people in," Horacio said.

I looked at Nader and flashed my most warm and welcoming smile. "Forgive my rudeness, Mr. Nader, but I must be certain we're all on the same side. You have to admit, you aren't easy to read. Dinner?"

Quint uncoiled from his easy chair and circled his arm around me. "These girls are sharp and speak their minds, Chuck, but don't take it too personally. You should have seen the crap she gave me when we met." He snorted and hugged me close. "We'd be pleased to have you join us. Jade, what are we having?"

"I was thinking of ordering out. Daf, what's good around here?"

She suggested a couple of places and I sent Chucho to investigate and bring us menus.

I sat with a fresh glass of wine and flipped open my notebook. "Let's nail down the plan."

"You start," he said.

"As I see it, we have three main problems:

> 1) We have to move a recognizable vehicle, several dogs, and two women, one of whom lacks identity papers to and across the border. It is likely we are under surveillance here in Roma, so we can't just pack up and leave.
> 2) To reach the border we must pass through cartel controlled regions, creating risk and expense.
> 3) We don't know exactly who is after us, but the first possibility controls the border where we want to cross, and according to our IT department research, has ties to gangs in the southwest, so we aren't safe in the U.S. either. Did I miss anything?"

"That about sums it up," Quint concurred.

"I'll add to the story," Dafne interjected. "I have arranged forged documents, both a U.S. passport and a Mexican Tourist card in the girl's real name, and a Mexican Passport in an assumed name Liliana Flores. The Mexican passport is on official passport stock and will pass scrutiny at the airport—the number is not going to be scanned through a database. The best solution is for the women to fly to Juárez with the puppies and visit family. Mr. Nader, I have suggested they travel as a family with Mr. Quint and Dylan. The cover story—Dylan and Jade are engaged and he is bring her and her father to meet his family. Dylan's niece is accompanying them with two of her puppies to give to her uncle."

"The cover story might work, but how are you going to get the girl across the border?" Nader asked.

"The way I'd play it, Mr. Quint, the luggage and the dogs could cross into El Paso in a rented vehicle. Horacio could meet him to rent a vehicle in El Paso and return the Mexican rental, then they would meet and wait at the pick-up point for the women. A *coyote* and the marine escort would have to take the women across. The combi could cross into California, so if it were followed, it wouldn't lead to the women. Jade, can't you arrange with your ex to get the *combi*?"

Now that was a good idea. If Dex would do it. "I'll call him later and see."

"Eliminating the VW from our equation will simplify the plan," Horacio said, "but it's going to cost a fortune."

"Yeah, well, it's not mine. I don't have a choice," I said.

Nader surveyed the group, eyes hooded. I couldn't help but think of a cobra—not a calming thought. "Who is your marine escort? And how will you coordinate your timing?"

Dafne grinned at him. "You and Javie. You paraded yourself as a marine. You can continue to do it. Need a backstory? You and your buddy are on leave. You fly to El Paso and taxi back across to sample the night life, hook up at the crossing location, protect our girls, and fly back to Mexico City or wherever you come from. Anything goes wrong, you have legal docs and the tacit agreement of the embassy. Don't you?" Dafne's voice sounded a little too unbelieving.

"Miss Olabarietta, young Javier and I will be fine. Don't worry. I think your plan might work. We ca—"

I interrupted, "All righty then, I move to adjourn. Let's let the people with other plans go and decide on our dinners." I said goodbye to Dafne and Horacio, who saw Daf to her car.

Chucho appeared with two menus. "Dylan will arrive in —" I checked my watch again— "forty minutes. He'll be hungry. Chuch, which place looked better?"

"They both look good, but this one has delivery and paella for groups." He handed me the menu. Fish. That sounded great. "Decided! Let's have fish. Pass this menu around and tell me what you want to order. I'll make a salad." I handed the menu back to Chucho and jotted paella on my list.

"Paella for me," Chucho said and passed the menu to Quint who read over the offerings. "*Camarones mojo de ajo*."

I added it to the list and ticked another mark after paella. "Javie?"

"Trout dinner for me and a cocktail of octopus. You, Corporal?" he handed the menu on.

After a moment's perusal, Nader said he'd join us in paella and have a side of crab cakes. I wrote it down, and gave the order to Chucho. "Quint, help him with the credit card."

Chucho pulled out his phone and they placed the order. I'd added several *postres* in case anyone wanted dessert. "You and Javie can pick it up? I'm going to make the salad and take a shower before Dylan arrives."

"*Sí señorita*. Javi, let's go now and have a beer while we wait."

"*Simón*."

Everyone but the spook gone, I fled to my room and locked the door. I had thirty minutes to shower, dress, and call Dex. Could my day get any worse? I hadn't spoken to him since he dumped me in Ixtapa. I supposed he'd been keeping track through Qadir, and he had kept my bank account topped up, but what would I say to him? I'd shower first. Give me time to concoct a good reason why he should fly to San Ysidro to pick up his VW bus, which would be full of my stuff he'd have to stow onto the Sarasvati. Well, why wouldn't he want his bus? I patted myself on the back. You go girl!

The hot shower put me in a better frame of mind and I almost felt ready to talk to the man I'd loved for nearly a third of my life. The man who left me in Mexico with drug cartel people after me. Nothing much had changed except now the cartel was different and I didn't have a senator protecting me. Qadir must not have told Dex anything because surely he'd have been in touch when he found out I'd been kidnapped and shot—twice. Unless he really never had forgiven me for refusing to marry him that time in Venice. He probably wouldn't answer.

Dex answered on the first ring. Miracles happen. "Dex. It's me. How are you doing?"

"I'm good, Jade. And before you ask, yes, I'm taking care of the orchids. How's your wound healing?"

He did know. Rat bastard never bothered to call. "I'm fine. Qadir told you?"

"Who else? What do you need?" Irritated. I'd heard that tone many times.

"I wanted to thank you for the money."

"I noticed you're running through a lot. I thought Mexico was cheap. What's so expensive?"

Now my voice sounded irritated. "You've been poking into my bank account?"

"Not me, but I needed to know if you had enough. Your

VISA balance was high."

"Yeah, we're putting together an office."

"We?" Irritation had morphed into accusation.

"My father and our crew. He inherited an office building from Senator Aguirre. We've moved into the apartment above it."

"Charles Stone is opening an office in Mexico City?"

"Not *that* father. My birth father, Jackman Quint. I met him. He worked with Aguirre."

"What do you mean 'worked'?"

"A bigwig from Los Zetas shot and killed both Aguirre and his mother. My father Quint, the senator's bodyguard, and I had gone to the senator's mother's weekend place to find Aguirre and discovered his brother—"

"That weasel panting after you?"

"The very same weasel. I gave him a short run-down of the past couple of months. Anyway, Dex, it's a really long story I'd rather relate over dinner sometime—"

"That mean you're coming home?" Now he sounded hopeful.

"The office falling apart without me?"

"Something like that."

"I'm working on a plan to come, yeah."

"A plan? You drove down there, now climb into my bus and drive home."

"You remind me of my adoptive father, that time I caravanned to Yellowstone with my friends and he refused to buy me a plane ticket home, saying 'you got yourself there, you can get yourself home.' Traveling back to Sausalito is a bit of a challenge right now."

"My bus is in one piece?" Back to accusations.

"Yes, absolutely, but Anibal knows it, and his group is after me. I can't drive it home. I'm having it shipped to the border. Will you meet it in Tijuana or San Ysidro? It's running fine. I have it in a shop and they've checked everything."

"What kind of cockamamy story are you dishing out, Jade?"

"A true, but sad story I'm not willing to relate at this time. I'll be traveling to Denver on my way home. Will you please meet the *combi* and get it back to Sausalito? And put my stuff back on my boat, too."

"Where's the dog?"

"Pepper is fine, he's right here with me. Pepper, speak to Dex," I said. Pepper sat up on the bed and wagged. "Dex, say something to him." I held up the phone.

"Hey, Pepper, how's my boy?" Pepper barked.

"So will you get your bus?"

"I was going back down the Baja peninsula. I suppose I could take the bus. When?"

"I'll call you in a couple of days and confirm the timetable. Thanks, Dex. Listen, I've got to go. Dinner is about to be served."

"I'll wait for your call. And Jade—"

I didn't wait to hear the rest.

Chapter 37

The Plan's a Hit

Dylan was all in when we proposed our little theater to him over the paella. It had been a hit with everyone who tried it —the paella, not the plan.

"You'll need close to a week off," I casually mentioned.

"It just happens," he said, "I'm due for some time off."

I promised to let him know our departure date ASAP. I cleared the dishes and brought out dessert. Dylan and I split a flan de coco while Quint and Javie ate ice cream. Nader spoke little, answering direct questions in gravelly grunts and monosyllables, but he ate like he hadn't been introduced to food before. Chucho savored the two pieces of cake he'd picked up for himself. Good to know what everyone's preference was. I worried Mrs. P wouldn't come back. Over coffee and brandy, I asked Quint what was up.

"Mrs. P isn't sure she wants to come back. She's getting Amores ready for sale and says she has enough money to retire and live a comfortable life. She's thinking of moving in with her niece in Cuernavaca."

"She'd be too bored without us," I quipped. "I need her to come back! This meal was delicious, but nothing like regular home-cooked food. She could take Lily's room after."

"Or yours. You haven't said you're coming back."

Dylan's coconut flan-filled spoon stopped an inch from his mouth. "You're not coming back?"

I felt the pressure drop in the room. Suddenly the atmosphere was heavy and I felt sad. Was I leaving? I responded with a joke. "I don't know. A life of Cinderella cooking and cleaning for you lot?" I laughed, but it sounded hollow.

"Quint, get the housekeeper to come back," Dylan said with his own false cheerfulness.

"Yeah, I'll do what it takes. I can't make you come back, Jade, but it won't be worth living here if you don't." Quint's tone only compounded the heavy sadness in the room. Chucho looked like he might cry. Even Nader, dour to begin with, had a long face. Javie served himself another bowl of ice cream and kept his mouth shut.

"If you're done, Dyl, let's go listen to some music. See you guys after the dishes have been washed." I took Dylan's hand. "C'mon."

In my room, I cranked up some jazz and suggested we talk about the plan. Did he have any ideas?

"I'm concerned about the running back and forth across the border and someone driving up with the dogs. Can't the dogs go on the plane?" he asked.

"We nixed driving the dogs. They fly. Do you really have an uncle in Juarez?"

"A third cousin, actually. He's fantastically wealthy with ill-gotten gains and not considered part of the family anymore. He's a mover and shaker as you Americans say, in local politics and owns interests in construction, real estate, casinos, trucking, and numerous other industries. Whispers running through my family say he's laundering money for the Gulf cartel. He's actually my father's second cousin and he was a smalltime contractor until he hooked up with some big coke kingpin. Went by the handle *El Rey de los Cielos.* I'll talk to Dafne, but I think Dafne's plan is to put you and Lily under his protection. Daf and Seeg met him in Cancun not too long ago. She took care of a negotiation for him.

"My, my, doesn't our little plan have many twists."

"*No sé, reina.* But let's get back to you staying in California."

I ignored his attempt to change the subject. "So we are going to visit your uncle to take him two pedigreed puppies and announce our engagement. Is there any reason he would not believe us or turn on us?"

"None. family is everything, except money, to him. He would do anything to get back into my parent's good graces."

"Then he is going to play along? I'm sure Dafne said she was calling in a marker."

"Does this mean you've said yes?" He asked. I felt my face heating up.

"Well, I've said yes to a reverse heist. We're going to put something stolen back in its place."

"Lily."

"What else?" I went over the details as much as we'd nailed down. "Look, Dyl, it's not carved in stone. I have a lunch date with Rosi and Daf tomorrow to hear what Rosi can do. One thing, though, can't you get your uncle to ship my bus to LA? That would endear him to your family. Especially if he did it for free." I grinned and pounced on my boyfriend, pinning him to the bed and tickling his ribs.

He bucked up and rolled over, pinning me down with an evil laugh and octopus hands poking me in every ticklish spot. "Ticklish, *reina*?"

I screamed and squirmed, bunching the bedspread under

me and laughing until I gained purchase and got my fingers into his sides. Dylan yelped and spun us over, smothering my mouth with his.

The tickles turned to caresses.

Chapter 38

Chapulín

Friday, September 21, 2007

Excitement and tension buzzed through my veins. I could see the blood vessel in my temple pulsing while I inspected my face for any misapplied mascara. Sheesh, I was out of practice. Lockdown in Roma didn't offer many opportunities to dress up, but that was about to change. We were almost on our way to Denver. Rosi would map out a plan we could actually follow—less theater and more get out of Dodge— the safest way possible. Hadn't she been moving? women out of trafficking through her safehouses for years? Between Rosi's and Dafne's contacts, I felt confident we'd get to the U.S. But once we crossed? How would we protect ourselves? God, please, make good on Quint's and Nader's promises, I prayed, touching up my lipstick.

Horacio's voice interrupted my thoughts. "*Señorita*, are you ready?" he called.

I cracked the bathroom door a couple of inches, and yelled, "Almost ready H. Meet you in the kitchen in two minutes."

I rushed to the closet for my flats and clattered to meet my bodyguard for the day. He eyed me and shook his head.

"What do you mean by that?" I asked.

"You can't run in those shoes."

"Really? I'm having lunch in a nice restaurant with my chic friends. What am I supposed to wear?"

Quint interrupted. "Horacio and I agree, this is foolhardy. You should not leave the house. Where's your gun, by the way?" I held up my purse and wagged it. "Not good enough. You need it where you can grab it quickly."

I frowned. "Good morning to you too. I wanted to feel human for once."

"You're due in thirty minutes. Anyway, crouching on the floor of the car isn't going to improve your outfit. Hurry and change."

We went through the usual routine to get me out of the house. This time Dad surveilled the neighborhood while Horacio pulled a car I'd never seen before to the gate. I dove into the back on cue and we peeled out of the alley toward Polanco. Quint was right, dark wash jeans and a knit blouse with pearls and rubber soled sandals would be chic enough. Especially if I had to run. I kept the gun in my clutch.

We picked Dafne up in front of her offices on the way. She was dressed to the nines, with towering heels and a pencil skirt topped with a printed silk blouse. She also wore pearls, a strand of matching black Tahitian pearls, and she carried a small leather tote bag. I bet her gun was inside. Horacio helped her into the backseat. She pretended not to see me and acted like she was talking to Horacio.

"Sit up, Jade, we're here."

I climbed onto the seat and grinned. Horacio pulled in front of the main doors to the Presidente InterContinental

Hotel and the doorman helped us out. Dafne was ready with the tip.

I'd never have picked a big hotel for lunch, but Rosi had assured me…well, Quint, it would be the safest place. Especially because it boasted several restaurants. Daf took my arm and we sashayed into the lobby to find a smiling Rosi waiting with the customary air kisses. Dafne ushered us to Chapulín where she was warmly welcomed by the receptionist who led us to our table in the partially filled restaurant. I gawped at the beautiful fountain in the entry courtyard.

"We're early for comida in el D.F. I picked this time so we'd be able to talk," Dafne said.

"It's lovely," I said, "What kind of food do they serve? Not grasshoppers, I hope." I laughed at my joke. Rosi smiled.

"Traditional Mexican done upscale. But what's wrong with *chapulines*? I love them with beer. Better crunch than corn nuts." She winked. "You'll see."

"Yuck! What a joker. What's good here?"

"Let's order a bottle of champagne. What do you think, girls? Celebrate our plan?" She held up a finger and a waiter scurried over with menus and took her order.

"That's just it, Daf, we haven't got a plan yet. Shouldn't we wait to complete the mission before we celebrate?"

"I'm not opposed to champagne, but I agree with JadeAnne. Let's deliver the girl to her family before we get too excited. It's going to be a dangerous journey."

The atmosphere at the table dipped momentarily, but our good spirits rose with the champagne. The waiter also delivered a bowl of homemade chips and a platter of guacamole, Oaxaca cheese torn into strings and a mound of *chapalines*—crispy, seasoned grasshoppers. He popped the cork and poured our flutes, setting them at our places.

"*Gracias*," Dafne said with a little wave. "I'll give you a few minutes to decide on your entrees.

"Buen provecho," the waiter said with a slight bow and backed away.

"Now, girls, order everything you want. I recommend the creamed corn with squash blossoms; if you like fish, try the *huachinango con mole chichilo*. It's divine. And for meat, you can't go wrong with the tacos de *lechón*."

"What's a *lechón*?" I asked.

Rosi and Dafne chorused, "Piglet."

"So, like carnitas?"

"Like no carnitas you've ever eaten," Rosi said.

The waiter was back with his order pad ready. I smiled at him. *"Quisiera tacos de lechón, por favor."* I just couldn't pass up a taco.

The champagne bottles and dirty dishes cleared away, Rosi called us to order. We were no longer three girlfriends lunching. I noticed that although the restaurant was filling with diners, the hostess did not seat anyone within hearing distance of our table and the waiter stayed discretely in sight. How did Dafne manage that? Or was it Rosi? Judging from her presentation, which resembled an itinerary, Rosi was hyper-organized. A-plus.

"Rosi, you missed our impromptu meeting last night. I think we need to discuss some of the ideas before we publish an itinerary. Dafne has ID documents coming, and Dylan's relative can help with a safe place to stay, but I'm not certain he's the route to take. Let's start with what we know for sure and the documents."

Dafne gave a rundown of her document contribution. The price was high, but two passports and a Mexican Tourist Card were worth it.

"But is Juarez best?" I asked. "It's really dangerous."

Rosi contemplated me for a few moments before speaking. "I agree, it's dangerous, but it has advantages. One being, Juárez has the closest border to Denver. Another, I've already set up a network for helping trafficked people and enslaved workers there. I have a series of safe houses, safe businesses, doctors, forgers, and *coyotes*. My group moves trafficked people, women and men, both directions across the border. I trust my *coyotes*. Lily might benefit from stopping in one of the safe houses and seeing a counselor. I have one on staff at each house along the escape route."

"Rosi, I don't think we have time for that," I said. "We've got to get her across and bee-line for Denver. I'll be with her. We've decided traveling as a family would be safest. It's why we were thinking of using Dylan's uncle's place. But I'm not so comfortable with him. If Gabby and Eladio don't trust him, I have reservations."

"She's got a point, Rosi. The uncle is Maximiliano Tadeo Quijada Porras, an entrepreneur with his finger in a lot of olives. Seeger and I met him in Cancún a couple of years ago. He's rich, powerful, and I pegged him for a cartel money launderer. Just a hunch, but in this case we could use his connections."

"I know who he is. We've met at fundraising events. My group also works to investigate disappearances of women along the border. Juárez mostly. Quijada makes himself look good by donating to social causes. You've right to suspect him, Jade. He owns some of the *fábricas*, which have lost the most workers. That said, if he's Dylan's family, it would make sense, but Lily is going to a safehouse until we can get her across. We can't risk her being seen."

"I hear there's a battle for the *plaza* going on," Dafne said.

"Yes, between El Chapo and the Gulf Cartel, or *La Companía,* as it's called. Chapo's group is fighting for control of the entire border. My understanding is Quijada is a *company* man, but right now, that's probably a good thing. He'll have more locals in his pocket. Just stay out of the night clubs."

"Oh, and Lily and I will be clubbing, I'm sure." We got a good laugh out of that. "But really, what do you think we should do?"

"Leave the travel and crossing to me. I'll charter private planes," Rosi said

"What about the dogs? Can a small plane take us all?"

"No, but you can't all leave the house and drive to Benito Juárez International anyway. The airport will be watched. Jackman and Dylan should start growing facial hair." Rosie didn't even crack a smile. "I'll send you on different flights."

"And my combi?"

Dafne interjected. "Like you said, Uncle Tedeo has shipping companies, let's ask him to deliver the combi to your ex in Sausalito." She picked up her phone and dialed before Rosi could caution her. She must have talked to Dylan.

"Tío, it's Dafne. Hi, how are you?"

Rosi and I talked about the dogs while Dafne negotiated a deal. I wasn't surprised she opposed Lily crossing with three dogs. My one was too much, but I put my foot down. Pepper was going home with me.

"It's done. He's got a truck going to Acapulco in three days. Your bus will be inside. From there it will transfer to another truck going to Tijuana. A U.S. company will carry it across the border to L.A. on a flatbed. You'll need to arrange pick up with the owner and meet with the agent to fill out the paperwork. All legal. I'll call Sami to supervise; you can meet the agent in his office."

"What's it costing me?"

"Only the taxes."

"Taxes?" I asked.

"You know, bribes. He owed me from that business I handled." Dafne grinned. "He invited you to stay a few days.

Just like I said. You are engaged and taking Dylan's niece, and her dog to college. The puppies are a gift. Also, he said he'd send his private jet to pick you up."

"Here in Mexico?"

Rosi banged her cup into the saucer. "Absolutely not. The first rule is, never let anyone know your plans. Hosts, guides, helpers only know their own link in the chain. I'll talk to Sr. Quijada, and I will supply the *coyote*. Visit *Tío Tedeo* if you want, but you will be going to a safehouse at the border the night before crossing. Jackman, Dylan and the dogs will drive to El Paso and stay the night."

"I forgot to tell you, Quint wants to bring two marines— well, one marine and a spook friend of his—for protection. Plus Horacio and Chucho."

Rosie rested her face in her hands and remained silent. The clatter and din of conversation and dining rose around us. It was getting crowded. We needed to get out of here.

"This isn't a party, JadeAnne," she finally said.

"No, and I don't trust the spook," I admitted.

"I'll talk to your dad. Dafne, when will we have the documents?"

"Early next week latest."

"Then be packed and ready to go by next Wednesday. One carryon each with appropriate clothing. You'll be visiting a wealthy household with a pool and probably a formal dinner. You'll need running shoes, jeans, and jackets for the crossing. Dark colors."

"What about our things?" I asked.

"Pack your *combi* with what goes to California. I'll have backpack, knit caps, and gloves for you. Expect twenty-four hours to cross and arrive in Denver."

"I thought the drive was about ten hours straight up I-25."

"Anything can happen. You might be stuck in the drains if ICE is patrolling. We'll have food and water packed for you. If you're followed, you might have to detour or lay low. Both cartels have *halcones* especially the Zetas and that's their territory."

My shoulders tightened and the tacos and chocolate cake soured in my stomach. I took a breath, looked away from Rosi, and tried to calm my heartbeat. No good to let her know I was scared. I watched our waiter wring his serviette and pace. "I think the waiter wants us to clear out," I said.

Dafne laughed and agreed. "He's been glaring at us for half an hour. I'll leave a nice tip." She double checked the bill and opened her purse, extracting her VISA card without exposing the gun I knew she carried.

The waiter almost galloped over with the card reader.

Rosi smiled and thanked the man profusely. He grinned when he saw the tip and whisked the dessert plates away.

Chapter 39

Progress Report

Dafne shifted out of first gear and aimed the Beemer up the mountain then punched on the CD player. The cab filled with off-key trumpets and mournful caterwauling.

"Mariachi?" I shouted over the noise.

"Don't you love it? Perfect music to express the human condition."

"Where are we going?"

"Up to *Mami's* to visit Lily."

I watched the scenery as we passed. Big houses surrounded by walls. Trees. Occasional turnoffs to places I didn't know. "Is Dorotea home?"

"I doubt it. She's usually at the office or out to lunch at this time of day. Lily is probably alone."

A sign for Tecamachalco pointed right. I thought I caught the road sign, Bosques de la Loma. "Aren't we near a big mall with a Superama?"

"Yeah. You need anything? We can stop."

"Probably, but I don't have a list."

289

Dafne downshifted and swung left across the eastbound lanes. I caught the sign Lomas something or other. It must be a cut through to Reforma, maybe to the Henry Moore sculpture roundabout. I wasn't sure where I was, but Dafne turned right on Reforma and blasted up the mountain. I should get a peppy little car. It would be a lot of fun on Marin and Sonoma back roads touring with Dyl.

"I love your car. Just thinking about touring California back roads with Dylan."

"You don't plan on coming back? You'll kill him, you know." Daf had shifted down to second to make the familiar turn into Lomas Altos and now the engine ground up the steep side of the *barranca*. Thankfully the CD had ended and ejected.

"I didn't say that, but I need to take care of things—my houseboat, for instance. Not to mention my partnership. I can't walk away from my investments."

"Easy, Jade. Hire a manager and rent out the houseboat."

We crawled over the rim of the canyon and in moments turned through the gates at the big house. The tires crunched along the gentle sandy curve of the drive bordered in a riot of colorful flowers framed by roses and broad-leafed bushes. I relaxed. Everything would work out, wouldn't it? "I don't want to lose him, Daf, but I'm not ready to commit. I've only been out of a decade-long relationship for about two months. And I've got to take care of Lily and make myself safe. I've brought so much danger into all your lives."

"You mean excitement. I could negotiate your release, you know. I've talked to cartel people before." She pulled under the port cochere behind a Mercedes and turned the engine off. "*Mami's* home."

"You mean, buy my freedom? I don't have any money. And my dad isn't about to buy me back from Los Zetas. He wouldn't even buy me a plane ticket."

"No, I mean free and clear. Like your combi tow."

The door banged open and Maya bounded out followed by a beaming Lily and the six pups. They were around two months old and had gotten big. I jumped out of the car and gave Lily a huge hug. "I've been missing you, kid." Maya nosed between us and I dropped Lily and squatted to hug the dog who saved us. "Maya, Maya, I've missed you too." She wagged like mad and gave me that don't-you-have-a-treat look. I showed her my empty hands, but she continued to grin. Sadie, meanwhile had run right to Dafne. "Well, I see you and Sexy Sadie have bonded."

Lily linked arms with me, and said, "Oh yeah, they love each other. Come on pups, let's go for a walk. Come with me, Jade." She drew me onto the lawn and handed me a couple of plastic bags.

"Ah, poop patrol. Just what I wanted to do."

"I'll see you guys in the house," Dafne called behind us.

"In the kitchen," Dafne yelled when we entered the vestibule a half hour later.

As if we hadn't had enough to eat or drink, she'd pulled a bottle of white wine from the fridge and laid out a plate of cheese and crackers on the breakfast bar. Maya was already eyeing the cheese. Lily sat down and snagged a slice, which she fed to her dog.

"Lily, don't feed that dog at the table." Maya wagged at the sound of Dafne's voice. I guessed Daf fed the dogs plenty at the table.

I laughed. "These dogs look well fed. So does Lily."

"We have the best food here. Rosario, the cook, is amazing. And she's teaching me how to make stuff. I made chicken in a cream sauce with chili poblanos last night. It was good, wasn't it Daf?"

"It was great, Lil. Hey, don't you want to know what's happening with your going home?"

Her expression glowed and she exclaimed, "I'm going

home! When, Jade? Soon?"

"Yes, in the next week. Listen, we'll tell you everything we know right now. The plan isn't finished, but we're making headway."

Dafne poured us each a small glass of wine and we toasted. Lily made a face and got herself a Coke while Daf topped up our glasses and proceeded to recount the plan and possibilities.

"It isn't going to be easy, Lily. You need to start packing. I'll give you a suitcase. Your things and the dogs will go in the car across the border. Rosi thinks it's pretty certain you and Jade, with one of the marines, will sneak through the storm drains with a guide. Rosi will have clothing and supplies for you."

Lily's glowing face had turned ashen. "You mean a coyote."

"Yes."

"But I'll have a passport."

"Not one that will hold up when scanned. And there's still the problem of the cartels. If they know we've gotten away, they'll come after us. It's why I'm going through the drains too."

"How come you got to go out today?"

"To meet Rosi. Quint was pretty pissed."

"Did anyone follow you?"

"Now you sound like him. No. We're safe," I replied. But was I sure? I hadn't really watched the road. Had Dafne?

"Yes, I kept an eye on the traffic. Lily, relax. Take a break. Rest. Things will get intense soon."

Chapter 40

Flight Plans

Saturday, September 22, 2007

The cloak and dagger routine was wearing thin. Sprinting from the delivery door to the garden wall and through the gate to dive into the back of a car to crouch on the floor, cramping my legs and crumpling my clothes...well, I was over it. I climbed onto the backseat of the limo and stretched out.

"H, where are we going?"

"Sami's office."

"Duh. Where is it? What colonia?" I heard the whine in my voice. Poor Horacio. "Sorry, I know this *capa y espada* BS is hard on everyone."

"It's all right, *señorita*. I'm used to whiny kids." He grinned into the rearview mirror. I kept my mouth shut.

We made a couple of turns and landed in the honking, exhaust-laced stop and go of a busy street. I raised my head but the glimpse of the boulevard didn't look familiar. "Where are we?"

"Navarte Poniente near Secretería de Comunicaciones y Transporte. We're clear, you can sit up. Look over there." He pointed to the right. A tall cement building rose across the street, completely covered in murals of indigenous life.

"Amazing. Who painted it?"

H gave me a brief history of the ministry as we passed, but he didn't know when it was painted or by whom. Of course, the original concept was created by Presedente Porfirio Diaz. He had his hand in everything. I noted the street signs. We were in the Ejes. I sighed, wondering if I would ever understand the street system as the limo slowed and pulled to the curb.

Wedged between an amazing smelling taco stand Tacos La Piedad and a day spa, a sign read, ABOGADO, Sami Rafiq. Ancient jacaranda trees shaded the block. I'd love to see the area during bloom time. I beelined to Sami's door, but stopped to take my bearings and let Horacio catch up. The block appeared rundown at the heel, other than the magnificent trees, with three and four story buildings, older model cars parked along the curbs, *doñas* wheeling shopping carts full of plaid plastic baskets of fresh food, a few kids in school uniforms coming out of a *panadaría* and a *bata*-clad *abuela* patting out tortillas and cooking them on a *comal* on the corner. Horacio joined me and rang the doorbell.

"Low-key neighborhood," I observed.

"Safe neighborhood. Originally settled by Japanese, German, and our Lebanese ancestors. We should try the Lebanese restaurant for lunch. It's terrific," Horacio said.

"Sure. So is this where your family immigrated? When?"

Sami opened the door with a hearty ogre welcome and led us into his inner sanctum. The offices were nothing like the exterior. For one thing, after a short hallway, the space opened up into an interior courtyard with a fountain tinkling into a lotus blooming reflecting pond. How quaint was that? Talavera pots filled with small trees, flowering shrubs, colorful annuals and some modern-looking statuary of animals complemented the tiled floor and decorative window treatments. It looked middle eastern. "Beautiful," I whispered.

Strolling through the patio, Sami and Horacio spoke in low tones. I lagged behind and admired the paradise Sami had created. Surrounding the courtyard, I noted three offices, a library, and a conference room through their large windows. All tastefully appointed in soothing colors and upholstered furniture. More potted plants adorned the interior spaces. At the back, from the largest office, emerged Rosi.

"You made it. Come in. The trucking agent will be here momentarily. Coffee?" she asked.

I shook my head. "I've got all my papers, including my tourist visa. Will I need to say why I want to ship the bus home?" I held out a folder with my documents. She waved it off and gestured toward a low chair in a cluster by a mosaic table. I sat down.

"Sami will fill you in. He's the expert in transportation."

"Ah. It's why his office is so close to that communications and transportation building with the murals."

"*Claro.*" Rosi settled next to me, setting a cup of coffee on her legal pad. A shrill buzzer sounded. "Señor Espinoza Ramos, *Agente*."

In moments the shreks ushered a pudgy balding man wearing a rumpled suit into the office; we stood to greet him. Rosi clasped his hands and said how nice it was to see him again. Horacio sat down and Sami introduced us saying, "Sit. Sit. Let me bring coffee. Or would you prefer something stronger *Señor* Espinoza? I have a bottle of that tequila we talked about."

Espinoza frowned. "You wouldn't be trying to bribe an official, now would you *Licenciado*?"

Sami let loose with one of his joyous belly laughs, and replied, "*Sí, sí*, I'll bring glasses."

Espinoza perched on his chair and rummaged through his case, locating the papers we needed to file, and placed them on the table, squaring the edges.

Sami pulled a bottle and glasses from a liquor cabinet, which he waved at us, and asked, "Horacio? *Señorita* Stone?"

"*No, gracias*," we both replied.

He sat back down and poured a tot into each glass, slid Espinoza's to him, and lifted his. "*Buen provecho, amigo*," he said and shot it back.

Espinoza followed suit and slid his glass closer to the bottle. Sami topped it up and Espinoza smiled for the first time. "What business are we doing here today? I understand you, *señorita*, wish to ship your *combi* to California. Why would you want to do that?"

I explained it belonged to my *ex-novio*, pulling my notarized permission from Dex out of the folder along with the registration and handing it to the agent, saying I planned to stay in Mexico for several more months. He wanted to see my tourist visa and passport, studying all the documents for longer than necessary to see everything was legal and in order. Sami cleared his throat and tipped the bottle Espinoza's way. The agent nodded and Sami poured.

"*Agente* Espinoza, may I assist in making copies of the documents for you?" Rosi asked. He raised his chin in the affirmative and she scooped them up and went to the copier.

"Efficient secretary, Rafiq. New?"

Again the joyful laugh.

Another couple of shots later, and a hefty "transportation tax" paid by Sami, I had some sort of bill of lading for each leg of the combi's journey along with U.S. entry papers and a date of delivery in Los Angeles, California—all stamped and notarized. We shook hands and Rosi-the-secretary escorted Espinoza to the door.

"Sami, you didn't tell me there's a fee for filling out papers. What do I owe you? And the notary fee, of course," I said, pulling my wallet from my purse. He waved me off.

Horacio said, "Not a fee *señorita*, a *mordita,* a little bite."

"We had to bribe that sour little sexist toad? To do his job?"

Rosi grinned. "*Bienvenido a México*, JadeAnne," she said. "But you don't need to bribe me. I've chartered flights for you. Your father will take care of the bill." She handed me a sheet with four charters.

"I thought Quijada was sending a jet."

"Way too risky, JadeAnne. I've used my network. Look at the itinerary."

I read through:

> <u>26 Sep</u> lv 11:00 Cuernavaca—arr. 2:45 Chihuahua-lv
> 3:30—arr 5:15 Juarez ? Dylan Porras, JadeAnne Stone, 1 dog

> <u>27 Sep</u> lv 10:30 Toluca—arr? 3:30 Nogales —lv 4:00-arr
> 5:30 Juarez. Liliana Flores/Horacio Rafiq/Jackman Quint 3dogs

> <u>29 Sep</u> lv 8:40 Mexico—arr El Paso 2:50 AeroMexico via Austin, TX
> Javier Mendez and Charles Nadar

"I don't get it. Why are we flying to these other places? Can't anyone get hold of the flight plans? You know, the ol' *plata o plomo* persuasion?"

"First, none of you will be traveling under your real

names. Second, these are not the flight plans being filed. You won't be leaving the aircraft until your connecting flight is in place. I want you and Dylan to assess Quijada before I send Lily. If for any reason you don't feel safe, contact Jackman and get yourselves out of there."

"Right, a surgeon and a journalist, unarmed, in the enemy's camp. How will we do that?"

"Pepper has teeth, you have a gun, and Dylan has a scalpel. Carry them," Horacio said.

I grimaced. Alrighty then.

"Brother, don't frighten my guests," Sami said, turning his ogre grin on me. "Not to change the subject, but I've arranged a bond with Quijada, in case the vehicle or your personal goods stored therein go missing. The bus will travel through Michoacán and Sinaloa. Who knows what dangers lurk in those states? He wasn't too pleased, but the huge cost of this venture will assure his people take good care of your things."

Rosi asked, "How much?"

"$250,000. Anything lost or damaged, he has to pay the entire bond. Jade, I'll need a complete list of all goods and equipment in the bus. I'd avoid sending anything precious to you in it."

"You can enforce that?"

"Of course. It's what I do."

Horacio interrupted. "And what I do is return the *señorita* to Roma." He clapped Sami on the shoulder with his bear paw, and said, "*Muchas gracias, a ustedes dos.*" He jerked his head toward the door.

I thanked Sami and gave Rosi a hug and air kisses. This wouldn't be happening without them.

Chapter 41

Should I stay or should I go?

Sunday, September 23, 2007

I'd spent Saturday night communicating with everyone involved, except, of course, Quint. He missed dinner and was MIA from the house all evening. I wondered if his absence and Rosi's *Too busy to talk right now. Can we meet tomorrow?* were connected. I hoped so. If I were to go back to Sausalito, my father would be lonely. He needed a friend.

Thinking about leaving made me feel sad. I missed the Sarasvati, the fog billowing over Mt. Tam, and arty, touristy Sausalito, but I'd come to realize I really wasn't satisfied with my managerial partnership at WIMS. I'd been gone two months and not once had my mother called me—probably too busy taking valium and lunching with her wealthy friends. I'd only talked to Dad to corroborate Quint's claim to my paternity. Charles Smyth Stone essentially had turned his back on me, although he'd throw money at me if I asked nicely. Riddled with guilt over his lies, my adoptive father would pay. If I stayed, I'd need money. Quint and I would need money. I hadn't considered myself an extortionist, but Mexico had changed me. Lying, extorting, killing—all in a day's work. Maybe I should go home, reconnect with my debutant manners. Go back to law school and intern at Dad's firm. Live down my bad behavior. But how bad is it really to kill someone trying to kill me? I rationalized.

I'd called Dafne, who counseled me to stay for Dylan. I called Horacio, who counseled me to stay for Quint. I'd called Lily, who begged me to keep an eye on the puppies and Mrs. P. Dylan called me to tell me he was thinking about me and counting the hours to Saturday dinner. I had friends here. Love. I belonged. Why would I want to go back to my empty life? Back and forth. Back and forth. Stay. Go. Go. Stay. Staying had a big negative: my life and liberty was constantly at risk. Leaving meant leaving everyone who loved me. I let out a wail. What to do?

Chucho knocked on my door. "Jade, *¿estas bien?*"

I opened the door and nodded. "Chuch, I can't decide whether I should go home or not. I have to pack. I'm at my wit's end. Come on, let's get a beer. Who's on duty tonight?" I headed to the kitchen, Chucho and Pepper right behind.

"I was coming to take Pepper out. I don't know who's on. Should I find out first?"

"It doesn't matter. If it were Javi, I'd invite him for a beer too. Why don't you take Pepper and I'll put together a snack."

"Sure. I'm kind of hungry. I'll call Javi while I'm out."

"Perfect," I said as I inspected the contents of the refrigerator. Without Mrs. P and Lily, we had slim pickings. I was sending Chucho and Horacio for takeout every day. Quint was gone a lot and I didn't feel it my duty to feed guards I didn't know. They got a salary. I pulled out a ball of *queso* Oaxaca and a stack of tortillas then found a bag of wilting *epazote*. The chipotle ketchup I'd made hadn't gone moldy. We'd have quesedillas. Luckily I'd asked for several six-packs of Victoria. I grabbed a bottle, flipped on the radio, cranked it up and started grating cheese.

Should I stay or should I go now...should I stay or should I go now—that old song telling me there's going to be trouble, maybe double trouble if I didn't get it together and decide. How could I leave Quint? He'd paid dearly for his mistakes, but we'd finally come together. It would break his heart. It would break Dylan's heart. It must be oldies night on the station. Next up, Christian, *Sin Aire*— How would I live without air? How would I live without them? I grated the skin off my knuckle with the last of the cheese and started to cry.

Chucho and Pepper bounded back into the kitchen towing Javi behind them. "Look who I found, Jade!" Chucho yelled. He pulled two bottles of beer from the fridge, tossed one to Javi, and flopped into a chair. I wasn't so sure I was up for boy energy after all.

"Quesedillas sound good?" I asked.

"Sweet!" Javi said.

The boys launched a discussion about soccer, *futból,* while I cooked a plate of mini quesedillas, portioned some for myself, tossed a stack of napkins on the table, grabbed a new beer, and went back to my room. Should I stay or should I go? haunting me into my nightmares.

Now here I was in a garage in Mexico City taking inventory of my—Dex's—VW bus with *Die Toten Hosen* worming though my ear. Should I stay or should I go? One way or the other, I had to present the inventory when the truck came to pick the combi up. Would I leave my personal possessions in it? I photographed the bus from every angle outside and inside then removed everything that could come out. I'd brought a bunch of boxes and stowed my possessions into them. Some clothes, books, my Walkman—I'd wondered where that went. The bedding, towels, dishes, and food I itemized and returned to their storage compartments. I packed the dog supplies, beach gear, forgotten toiletries, and the sun shower. The big cooler could stay, although it was mine. I found a few souvenirs and boxed them with some shells and a couple of pretty rocks I'd collected, changed my mind, and put the box in the bus with my name on it, and a list of contents. I didn't need shells if I stayed.

A couple of hours later I had a list ready to copy and most of my personal stuff stowed in the limo.

"It looks like you're staying, *señorita*," Horacio commented, eyeing my personal effects.

"I guess it does, H."

"You don't sound happy."

"I can't leave him now that I've found him. But it might kill me."

"Quint or Dylan?"

"Both, but I meant Quint."

"We'll make you safe. We're going to get the girl to her family, and in the process we're going to eliminate the threat to you. *Súbate*," he said, handing me into the car.

I stretched out on the seat and yelled, "Eliminate? I've had too much killing, Horacio."

He grunted something and rolled up the garage door then got into the limo and bumped into the street. "Quint thinks there's a double agent and Aguirre will follow us. Once in the U.S. he plans to call the authorities to arrest him." Horacio got out again to roll down the clattering door and lock it.

When he got back in, I asked, "A mole? In our group? Probably that weirdo Nader. But if he puts Anibal in prison, I'm all for it."

"You don't like him? He and your dad go way back. To Vietnam, Quint said."

Yeah, he probably filled body bags with heroin with Quint. Did Nader get the money after Quint was arrested? But I didn't say anything more for the ride back to Roma Norte. This news of a mole cemented the decision. Quint was in danger too. He was going to need soldiers and he was my blood. I would stay.

Dylan crowed his joy when I told him, other than a quick trip to close my houseboat and find a renter or put it on the market, I'd stay in Mexico. He picked me up and twirled me around the reception, hugging me so tightly I gasped for air. *Como quisiera vivir sin aire?*

"Dyl, put me down!" I croaked.

"How long will it take you to close your house?"

"I don't know. I have to negotiate my partnership agreement too. Dex will either be glad to get rid of me or sad to see me go, but either way, he will make it difficult to pull out. I know he won't have any money to buy my share." I paused to put down the bag of groceries I lugged and catch my breath on the steep stairs.

Dylan shifted his bag onto his hip and reached for mine. "What are you cooking that needed so many groceries?"

I handed over the bag, and explained, "Mrs. P's list. I called and begged her to come cook for the next six days and feed the guards. Rosi said to make it look like things are going on. She'll fill the freezer with *albóndigas,* tamales, and plenty of salsa. She couldn't come today, but told me what to have Chucho buy." We climbed the rest of the way up and dumped our load in the kitchen.

"What are you making tonight? Or do I get to take you out for a change?"

"That's a joke. Quint hasn't made any new mandates, but I doubt he'd be thrilled if I went out without a guard or two.

How about meatloaf with chipotle ketchup? I got potatoes to roast with it and broccoli to steam. An American dinner for a change." I grinned at him and handed him a beer from the fridge.

"*Mami* makes meatloaf. I helped her make it. A family favorite."

"There you go, comfort food." I handed him an onion and two skinny ribs of celery. "Start chopping."

Over our delicious meatloaf we briefed each other on the plan. Dylan had been in touch with his tío, and Rosi and gotten a week off work. Fast. She'd drop off a carryon bag for me the next day.

"Tío wants to treat us to dinner on Monday night when we get in. We'll need dress clothes as well as crossing-the-border clothes. Also a bathing suit. He's got a fabulous pool and it will be hot."

"How fancy? Heels? Silk?"

"Maybe. I've packed lightweight grey wool slacks, a black silk short-sleeved shirt and a cashmere pullover sweater with black tassel loafers."

"Mmmmm, you'll look so handsome and preppie."

"Learned it in the U.S."

"But Dyl, how safe is it going to be in a city controlled by Zetas?"

"I'd wear your cute little bulletproof jacket over that silk dress."

"I don't have a silk dress. Now I need to go buy a dress I'm going to haul through a storm drain?" The timer dinged. I hopped up to pull dessert from the oven. "Flan de coco, but it needs to cool first."

"You made it? My favorite."

"I remembered. But really, Dylan, isn't it risky to leave that property?"

"Probably, but Tío is powerful and protected. He's sworn

to me he'll keep you and Lily safe."

"We won't be there very long, only through *comida* on Thursday. Your uncle will deliver us to a meeting place where Horacio and Javi will collect us. Rosi will call with the location once we're on our way. Javi, Lily, Pepper, and I go to a stash house to rest until the *coyote* comes for us. Again, Rosi will call with the location. She's not taking any chances. Afterward, Dyl, you'll cross the border with Horacio and the goldens to meet Quint and his buddy Nader. You guys will be waiting for us with a new car."

"Quite an operation."

"Yeah. One I don't like very much. I wish Nader weren't part of this. I don't trust him." I sank a knife into my flan as I spoke. Perfectly done and not steaming too much. "Get a couple of bowls, will you, Dylan?"

I found a jar of cajeta in the pantry and poured the sticky syrup over our dessert wishing I had bought a can of whipped cream. With these scary plans, I needed total comfort. Dylan squirted cream over his. I guessed he was nervous too.

Chapter 42

I Don't Trust That Guy

Monday, September 24 2007

By eight a.m. Dylan was hustling me into his car after the security guards' okay. We'd had a restless night together. He'd tried to be comforting, but what was finally in motion was too dangerous and filled with unknowns. I woke up in a cold sweat after one particularly disturbing dream. *I was trapped in a narrow, rocky crevasse with wolves circling closer and closer. I could hear my friends shouting in the distance, but I couldn't get to them. I had to kill the wolves and all I had were rocks and thorny branches. They herded me further back. I started to climb but the chirrup of rattles stopped me, the devil coiled on every ledge.*

"Where am I taking you?" he asked, holding the door of Dafne's Beemer for me.

I climbed in and waited for Dylan to slide behind the wheel. "It's H's friend's garage in Colonia Obrera off Eje 2

Sur. Take Dr. Navarro across to Claudio Bernard," I read off the scrap of paper I'd noted the day before. "You need to do some circling around because of the one-way streets."

We rode in silence for ten minutes until I saw the turn, and shouted, "Turn, turn! Right, Dyl."

He cut across both lanes and made the soft right. "Now where?"

I was watching behind us. A black SUV had made the same awkward turn and was gaining on us. "I think we're being followed. Make the next turn and ditch it." I pulled my gun out of my purse.

He stepped on the gas and skidded around a sharp right and floored it. The SUV got caught at a light and fell back. Dylan swung left onto the boulevard with the sculptures made from car parts and roared through a red light.

"Are we going the right way?" I asked. The SUV had not appeared behind us.

"To Eje 2 Sur, yes." He flipped the blinker and moved into the left lane as he came up on the street.

The light turned yellow. I could see a black vehicle driving too fast behind us. "Run it!"

Dylan spun the wheel and we jetted onto another Eje, flying across the short end of the block to the corner we needed: Francisco Rivas. The engine whined then growled as he downshifted into the narrow commercial street lined with cars and delivery trucks. "There's the motorcycle shop. The garage is about halfway down on the left." I pointed.

He sped up, pulled around a semi-trailer parked across the sidewalk, and into the garage. The owner waved us behind my combi. He punched a button inside the office door and the garage door closed. I got out and approached clutching my papers and craning to see out the dirty office window. Sure enough, a black SUV crawled by, a familiar man at the wheel. I gasped and spun on Dylan. "Eddie Santos. The shotgun passenger must be Anibal."

Sr. Ochoa, the garage owner stepped to meet me, hand out, "*Buenas días, señorita.* Horacio called to let me know you'd be here soon and might be followed. I see that was true."

I shook his hand and introduced Dylan. "*Buenas días, señor.* How is this going to work if they know we're here?" I handed him the notarized papers he needed to load the bus.

"Don't worry. Horacio and I have worked out to block the street during loading. The tractor will block everything at one end. We'll line the alley with garbage trucks just past Motos Y Más. They'd have to get out and walk to see what we're doing. As soon as the driver gets here, we'll angle the trailer into the garage and hoist the *combi* in. Once inside, no one can see it."

The building shook with the rumble of something big on Francisco Ruiz. A buzzer rang, and Ochoa said, "He's here now." He crossed the office and pushed the button to open the roll-up door. "Why don't you move out now, doctor. We'll handle it from here. The garbage trucks are pulling around."

I shook Ochoa's hand again and handed over an envelope of cash. "For your trouble. Thanks." Dylan had the car turned around and I slid in waving goodbye to my combi. Ochoa gave the come ahead signal and saluted as we rolled back into the street. At the corner a fleet of brand new dump trucks turned out of the waste equipment sales yard and began to crawl around the block. We turned back toward Roma Norte. We weren't followed.

Dylan left me at the gate when Chucho and Pepper came to collect me. Dyl had surgeries in Ixtapalapa today. I had to pack. Most of my stuff would stay here, but I would carry a tote with Pepper's needs and a carryon. How would I fit my California clothes into the carryon? I wouldn't. At least in Sausalito I could stock up on toiletries and cosmetics. Those wouldn't be needed to jump the border.

I considered my packing while I tossed a ball in the garden for Pepper. He was obviously worried about what was going on. Quint still wasn't home, Lily remained at the big house and this place was a revolving door of strange security guards. And I was packing.

"It's okay, Peppi. You're coming with me," I said, dropping to the grass to hug him. He gave me a good sniffing then licked me. "Yes, I visited the bus. It's on its way to Dex now." Pepper gave me a piercing look and refused to wag. He was not happy.

Upstairs, I did all the housework left undone since Mrs. P stopped coming. By three, I'd folded everyone's clean clothes and couldn't put off packing any longer. I sat down at the table and made a list:

> *blue dress, heeled sandals, skirt, blouse, bulletproof jacket
> *bathing suit, cover up, tennis shoes
> *4 pr undies, 2pr socks, nightgown, flipflops
> *2 pr. jeans, pr. shorts, pr running tights, pr running shoes
> *2 tanks, 2 tee's, turtleneck, sweatshirt
> *pr. slacks, shirt, sweater, flats for planes
> *toothbrush, toothpaste, shower cap, razor, facewash, make up, brush, hair ties, barrette

This would get me to California. I'd worry about the rest when I got there. Swilling back my second Victoria, I tossed my bottle into recycling and headed to my room. I hadn't noticed the blinds were open when I went in to collect my laundry. Who did that? They'd been pulled when I left for the garage. They were always pulled now. I moved to the wall, out of view of the street, and edged toward the first window. Reaching up I grabbed the blind and tugged. A blast sounded from across the street and the window exploded, the bullet ripping a jagged hole through the blind and lodging into the wall over the bed. Glass shards calved to the floor. I flew to Pepper and inched toward the door holding his collar. My phone rang. At the door we sprang up and ran into the hall. My phone continued to ring, although I could hear thundering coming up the stairs and Chucho yelling, "Jade, JadeAnne! What happened? Are you all right?"

"Gunshot. Took out my window," I shouted. The phone stopped ringing. I met him at the door. "Chuch, who's been in the house today?"

"No one besides us. Why?"

"My blinds have been opened. I left them pulled closed this morning. Someone's been in here."

"Could Dylan have opened them this morning?"

I felt my face color. I thought we'd been discrete. "No, why would he? Did any of the security come in before I got home?"

"Only your dad and Nader..." He dropped his jaw, mouth forming an O.

Together we said, "Nader." I dialed Quint.

"I believe you, Jade. You think you left your shades down. But with the pressure you're living under, it would be easy to forget you'd opened them." Impatient, trying to sound concerned.

"Dad, I'm not going to argue. Only two people came into the apartment besides me, Dyl, Chucho, and you. And your spook buddy Nader—unless you let security get lax. Do you really think Chucho opened the door to Eddie Santos or Anibal?"

"I think you made a mistake and could have gotten yourself killed."

"Whatever. I'm calling the glazier again. What are you going to do about people shooting at me? Where the hell are you, anyway? Shouldn't we nail down the rest of the plan?"

"I've been with Rosi mostly, doing just that. We'll meet

tonight over dinner. She and Horacio will join you and Chucho. Dylan should come too. But I'm less concerned with the plan than why you think Eddie Santos shot your window out."

"Because Eddie and Anibal tailed us to the garage. I saw him. And Dyl is working tonight."

"The bus taken care of?"

"Yes, Quint," I said in my most sarcastic voice. "Now you take care of clearing out that rat's nest across the street." I hung up. My father wouldn't believe we had a mole in our midst. Just because they were buddies way back when didn't give Nader a white hat. Something was off, some backstory Quint wouldn't divulge—or couldn't face up to? Whatever it was, I didn't trust Nader.

Chapter 43

Hoi Polloi

Tuesday September 25, 2007

Dylan pounded on the stairs door until I let him in. "Morning," I said, yawning. "There's coffee in the pot."

He hugged me. "Good morning to you, too. You're not ready?"

I nodded to my carryon, tote, and handbag by the kitchen door. "Let's have breakfast and I'll tell you about my exciting day." He checked his watch. "Dyl, it's only 7:15. The airport is an hour away at eleven. We have plenty of time."

"We should be there by ten," he said.

"Well, since it's a chartered flight, the plane won't leave until we arrive, so no big rush." He grinned and wiggled his eyebrows, jerking his head toward my bedroom door. I winked and said, "Come on."

He circled his arm around me and I felt his warmth and

affection radiate into my body. Until I shoved the door open, flipped on the light and he saw the disaster of broken glass. I pointed to the bullet lodged into the wall and pushed him out of the room. "You didn't open the blinds did you?"

He let go of me and paled, shaking his head. I pushed him out and closed the door.

"What happened?" Dylan asked over coffee.

I gave him the rundown of the incident, my talk with Quint, and my suspicions. "Look, we know Eddie was driving the SUV yesterday, and we know we left my room closed, shades down. Nader was the only outsider in the apartment, even if Quint refuses to acknowledge it."

"I've disliked him since we met," Dylan admitted. "I didn't want to say anything and insult Quint, but I think you're right. Good thing we're leaving here as soon as you get dressed. You didn't sleep in there, did you?"

I took a swig of my coffee. Too hot, I added more cream. "Pepper and I slept in Lily's room, but I packed out my things first. Chucho has locked my stuff up. I packed a few things for Lily as well. H will take charge of the baggage."

"What does Horacio think about the shooting and Nader?"

"Agrees with me. He's keeping a close eye on him. Said he'd try to buddy up with him. You know, keep your enemies close? Quint isn't going to be any help."

"I wondered how your old boyfriend showed up behind us yesterday. Nader?"

I giggled. "Anibal was not my boyfriend. But, absolutely Nader is the mole."

"Then what makes you think you'll be safe in a storm drain with him?"

"No, Javi is our guard. But Nader will be waiting with Quint and Horacio to collect us. Horacio will protect Quint, but what if that scumbag has given our plans to Anibal? And worse, if word has gotten to Zeta controlled Juárez?"

"Nader is working with the cartels?"

I expelled my breath. "Nader allegedly is a spook. CIA working some dark ops here in Mexico? Quint says they are working together and I know Nader has been present at meetings with Rosi. Maybe we can get some help from your uncle." I stood up for the coffeepot. "Fried eggs and bacon okay?"

Dylan held out his cup for a refill and nodded, a pensive frown across his lips. "I'll see what I can do. If we pay attention to my mother, tío is not to be trusted, either. Hoi polloi. Too big for his britches, whatever that has to do with trustworthiness." He snorted then fell silent.

The limo pulled into the *callejon* at eight-thirty. Dylan carried our bags down and settled into the back with Pepper. I dove in after him, but sat in the jump seat near the cabin window. Horacio put Lily's bag in the trunk, got in and backed around to pull out.

"H, we have a problem," I said.

"*Yo sé.* Mr. Quint briefed me last night. I agree with you, *señorita*. I don't trust Nader."

"Do you know the plan? Would Nader know our flights?"

"I know some of the plan, but Rosi wouldn't talk with Nader, so if he knows anything, it's what Quint told him. I wasn't followed here if that's your concern."

"That and the welcoming party we should expect at Nogales."

"Quijada is an important man. Anibal Aguirre wouldn't be so *estupido* to attack his plane."

"Rosi says Quijada is affiliated with the Gulf Cartel. Isn't that group fighting the Sinaloans along the border? He might be a target."

"Anything is possible, *señorita*, but rumors say BLO is having trouble with Sinaloa too, so it's likely you will slip through. Your father is working on security in Nogales. My advice is, keep your head down and watch behind us."

"Okay, boss," I said, as we merged into rush hour traffic on the Periférico. "You too, Dyl. Keep an eye out for Eddie Santos." I didn't think anyone would be crazy enough to subject themselves to morning commute if they didn't have to. They'd be waiting at the airport. I called Rosi, but all I got from her was, "Horacio knows what to do."

It was a straight but slow shot over the mountains on highway 95. Dyl and I talked about our childhoods, school, and desires for the future. It felt almost normal and I relaxed. An hour and forty-five minutes later, we pulled around the private terminal at General Mariano Matamoros Airport, Cuernavaca, onto the tarmac. Through the rearview mirror, I saw Horacio was on the phone, although I couldn't hear the conversation. I assumed he was being directed to the plane. Sure enough, he pulled up next to a small jet. The air stairs lowered, all we had to do was grab our carry-ons, hop out of the limo, and cross ten feet of open ground. I looked out the windows for other vehicles on the tarmac. Nothing. The driver's door slammed and in a moment H opened our door. "Let's go *señorita*, Sr. Dylan."

Pepper was first out, happy to stretch and pee on the plane's wheel. I took Horacio's hand and gave it a squeeze. "Thanks H. See you on the other side."

I hopped to the ground, whistled and herded my dog up the air stairs, Dylan right behind me. When turned to wave to Horacio at the top, he was already circling the limo away from our plane.

Tío Quijada awaited us on the airstrip, standing in the desert wind, khaki pants flapping around long legs, and wave-printed silk shirt rippling against his broad chest. A gust sent a pod of tumbleweeds rolling across the toes of his western-style boots, but didn't dim the glow of his pleasure in welcoming us. This I took for a positive sign, wanting to trust him. He held our lives in his hands—a scary proposition. The plane juddered to a full stop and the air stairs released, grinding to the packed earth runway. Dylan scurried out and ran to grab his uncle in a giant bear hug. I followed, Pepper leashed, at a safer pace.

"Tío, I want you to meet JadeAnne. Come! You must love her as much as I do. I'm working to convince her to stay in Mexico."

I'd never seen Dylan so animated. This family rift must be hard on him. He obviously loved his uncle. I grinned and signaled Pepper to sit and shake while I extended my hand.

Tío hooted and yanked me into another of his bear hugs. "*Bienvenidos, bienvenidos.* It's so good to finally meet you *Señorita* Stone. And you, *el doctor*—how long has it been?"

"Too long, Tío. Not since I started my residency. I can't thank you enough for helping me get through school."

"Don't mention it, *hijo.* But if you want a hospital, I have one here in Juárez that could use a good surgeon."

His Range Rover purred on the apron near the hangar. He opened the back door and helped me in, then said, "Hop in front, Dylan. We'll let the little lady look at the sights on our way to the house."

Mostly there was little to look at. Sand, dust, scrub. We drove for a quarter hour across hilly desert pockmarked by jagged arroyos and dry washes. In the distance, barren mountains jutted up from the low hills. On a rise, I saw a herd of cattle and a couple of mounted cowboys. I leaned forward, and asked, "You're a rancher, Sr. Quijada?"

He bellowed his big laugh. "Call me Tío. Yes, you Americans would say a *gentleman rancher.* It's a hobby. I'm an investor. I own shares in many businesses, trucking being of special interest to me. Your VW bus was picked up on time?"

"Yes, thank you. But I feel awkward letting you pay for

the haul. I can't imagine what transporting a vehicle to California must cost."

"Not another word about it. Call it an early wedding gift. Dafne says you and my boy here are getting serious. You'll treat him right, now, won't you?"

"Tío! Stop. You're embarrassing us. We haven't gotten that far. First I have to convince her to stay in Mexico."

Tío asked, "Dylan, why don't you go back to California with her? You'd make better pay."

"And pay much more to live. No thanks."

We came over a rise, the wind whipping the rooster tail of dust behind us into the desert. Ahead lay a verdant oasis of green with a lovely colonial-style hacienda set in the middle of the park-like setting. We could have been driving onto the set of Corazon Salvage or something, except it looked new.

Quijada ushered us into a grand entry hall and handed us off to a servant to show us to our room with the reminder we'd meet for a drink and tour in forty five minutes. The uniformed maid led us upstairs to a bedroom on the western end of the building with a balcony overlooking the arid hills into the mountains. It was already six, and long shadows set off the contours of the land as the low sun washed gold across the dun of the hills. I wished I could paint the stunning view.

Dylan threw his bag onto the king-sized bed and zipped it open. He pulled out slacks and a blazer. "Grab me a couple of hangars, will you, Jade? I'm going to shower and steam my jacket."

I turned from the view and selected several hangars from the walk-in closet next to the bathroom. "Hold on. My dress could stand a pressing too." I took it from the carry-on and draped it over a hangar, handing it to him. "Save some hot water for me," I called, as he closed the bathroom door.

The maid handed us margaritas at the French doors to the terrace where Tío Quijada and a couple other men sat around a low table. A tray of untouched, delicious-looking mini tacos and quesedillas had been placed in front of them. Deep in serious conversation, they did not notice our arrival. Dylan led me to the far end of the terrace to admire the view of the rose garden and swimming pool. "Finally, my Mexico vacation," I said, giving Dylan a one-armed hug.

"Lily will like the pool. I want to go riding. The stables are over there." He pointed to some barns in the distance. "You ride?"

"I took English riding lessons as a child and my cousins on my mother's side lived on a ranch in Central California so we rode western when we visited, but I haven't been on a horse for years. It might be fun. What do you think is going on over there?" I tipped my head in the direction of Quijada and company."

"Judging from the dusty appearance of that one guy, I'd say he's a foreman. The other looks like a bodyguard. Tío might be arranging for increased protection while we're here."

"Sounds positive," I murmured. "I'll go with that. But what if it's something else to do with us?"

"Jade, you read too many thrillers. He's my uncle."

"And Lily and I are a valuable commodity."

He sighed, exasperated.

Dylan pegged the identities of the men. The foreman apologized for his appearance and disappeared. The other guy eyed me toes-to-head and back as we approached. I jabbed Dyl in his ribs. He shrugged almost imperceptibly, but took my hand as we stepped into the conversation area. The slimeball lowered his eyes, but I felt a rise in tension. Macho creep.

Quijada didn't notice. He rose and guided me to a seat

next to him, gesturing to Dylan to take the chair. "Welcome. kids! Omar," he boomed, "meet my nephew Dylan and his fiancée *Señorita* Stone. Omar takes care of the hacienda's security." He radiated warmth, even for the creepy security. "Shall we enjoy Luisa's snacks then take a sunset tour of the estate before dinner? We're going to a little tapas place in town I'm looking to investing in."

The conversation ranged from ranch management to entrepreneurial investing. Quijada wasn't shy about detailing his holdings. Car dealerships, restaurants, clubs, the casinos we knew about, real estate, construction companies, and of course, his pride and joy, the international trucking company. His trucks carried two thirds of all cargo across the borders to the U.S., Canada, and Central America. He planned on expanding to three quarters in the next eight years. I couldn't help but notice he said nothing about laundering, but the cash businesses probably existed for that.

"I've spent too long boring you with my businesses, *señorita*. What about you? What brought you to Mexico?"

I gave him the synopsis of the case to find Lura Laylor, meeting the Aguirres and agreeing to write an exposé on Mexico's human trafficking at the behest of the senator. We had wandered to the rose garden and I was captured by the heavenly scents perfuming the air, covering the bad taste I had over how much Dafne had told this stranger. Dylan vouched for my writing as we meandered across the stone pathways in the bolts of golden light spearing through the trees. The roses grew in raised beds built from the same rock as the paths. In a shaft of sun, a huge iguana basked, but scuttled into the berm when we passed. Quijada knew we wanted a *coyote* to cross the border. I silently prayed Daf had been discrete. That was so not the word I'd use to describe her. I said I wanted to interview people to find out what the experience might be like. He offered to introduce me to someone he knew.

Dylan objected. "Isn't that kind of dangerous, Tío?"

"I fund some of your friend Rosi Orozco's work. If you're interested, we can visit a stash house and talk to some of the rescued women before you leave."

We came to the stables. I nodded noncommittally, and Dylan said, "Actually, if it's okay with you, Jade and I'd like to go riding and spend time at the pool. Work has been a bear lately and I need a rest."

Quijada laughed and said it could be arranged. He proudly showed us his ten horses. Two were race horses with private grooms. Old Yeller, a bay, and Big Bun, a seventeen-year-old chestnut, hung their heads over their stalls, snorting and angling for oats. Quijada showed us the bucket and we offered our rides some snacks and pets.

"These are the gentle geldings reserved for guests. I'll have them saddled and ready at eight for you. Toñyo can guide you around. We have a thousand acres to roam."

By the time we'd washed the horse slobber and dust off our hands, Omar had a vintage Cadillac at the door. Our host ushered us in, and we discussed his love of vintage cars on the way to the restaurant. He promised us a tour of the garages when Quint arrived. I was sure Dad'd love that. Lily and I could lounge by the pool.

La Taberna Tapas y Vinos, resembled a Gaudíesque vision of a Moroccan building, but the interior dining courtyard was pleasant and the food tasted great. I enjoyed oysters, crab cakes, some sort of chili relleno with corn, a caprese salad with heirloom tomatoes and herbed ricotta, and best, a chocolate cheesecake in graham cracker crust topped with creme fraiche and smothered in rose petals. The flamenco guitarist didn't hurt, either.

Quijada poured Mexican varietals with each new dish. He was quite an expert since investing in wineries in Baja California. The man surprised me. Good humored, warm and friendly with everyone he met. He seemed interested in a vast range of subjects, refined, suave and comfortable with money and the finer things of life. But why was he single? Was he really a criminal? I mentally compared him to the Beltrán gang. My experience with cartel people had not prepared me for a man like Tío, as he insisted I call him. Yet behind his urbane facade, I felt a darkness. I'd met many wealthy folks growing up. The hoi polloi in Marin County thought they were above the rest of us. I didn't get that sense from Quijada. Maybe it had to do with the police following us back to his gate.

Chapter 44

Badlands and Bad Characters

Wednesday, September 26, 2007

Pepper loved the morning ride. The horses fascinated him. "I don't think he's met a horse before." He trotted alongside my mount, the bay, a grin on his face. When we galloped, he ran hard, obviously in doggie ecstasy. He liked the pool too. And the luncheon spread Luisa laid out in the shade. We didn't see Quijada until it was almost time for Lily, Quint, H, and the goldens to arrive. I wrapped myself in my coverup and hailed Omar to hitch a ride to the landing strip. We needed two vehicles.

Lily bubbled over with excitement, telling us all about her trip. Maya slathered me with kisses and Roli and Poli peed a small lake. The grand, empty house filled with life. Dogs bounding in the hall, people laughing. Quijada relished showing the newcomers around and made everyone comfortable. If he was going to turn on us, it would be a brutal betrayal, especially for Lily who had taken to him. We repeated cocktails on the veranda then dined on a traditional meal of tortilla soup, cold tuna stuffed poblanos in a cactus fruit salsa, and spicy red and green enchiladas filled with shredded chicken and pork. The dining room seated about twelve and tucked into the wine cave. He opened a bottle of Napa cabernet when I said I liked that appellation. I guessed having money meant you could get anything from anywhere.

After dessert of churros and hot chocolate, Tío, H and Quint left us in an entertainment room to watch a movie. Quijada subscribed to every station known to humankind. We bickered over movies until we agreed on fantasy adventure, *Pirates of the Caribbean, At World's End.* Johnny Depp would keep us laughing. Dylan hadn't seen it.

Quint woke us up as the credits rolled and sent us to bed.

"I've got to take Pepper out first," I said. "Lil, shall I take the goldens too?"

She yawned and smiled. "No, I'll come."

"I don't think that's a good idea, Lily," Quint said with his don't-contradict-me stare.

Lily blanched. "I'm not safe here?"

I heard the tremble in her voice. Way to go, Quint. "I think he means we just can't control things outside after dark."

"So why are you going?"

Dylan wrapped his arms around me. "Because she's family in Tío's eyes. Come on, I'll go up with you." He let go of me and linked arms with Lily. "Race?"

She giggled and sprinted out of the room. He started after her, rubber soles squeaking on the polished tile floor.

Outside, the dogs romped on the grass and did their business. Quint drew close to me and spoke softly. "I don't like this, Jade. H and I spent most of the day with Quijada and something isn't right around here. I can't pinpoint anything specific, but I don't trust the man."

"Me either, Dad. You know the police followed us back from dinner last night? He's into a lot of stuff and I doubt it's all legal. Have you talked to Rosi? She and Dylan's family say he launders money for the Gulf cartel."

"Yeah, that doesn't worry me. He's pressuring us to let him handle the crossing. I don't like it," he repeated. "Might he know about Rosi's safehouse?"

"He claims to know. He offered to take me there to talk to rescued women for my article."

"I won't ask what prompted you to discuss trafficking with him."

Pepper and Maya ran up to me, trailed by the pups. Maya nosed my hand, looking for cookies. I shook my open palms to show her I wasn't carrying and gave each dog a pat. If anyone was watching, they'd see a normal scene of responsible dog minding. I slapped a plastic bag into Quint's paw and we roamed the turf until we'd cleaned up then returned to the house, talking about the dogs and how lovely the house was.

No one remained in the kitchen when we tossed the poop bags in the garbage and gave the dogs water. I opened and closed cabinets. "Quint, we need a new plan. Can you call Rosi? My understanding was she thought he was a donor. If he knows about her stash houses, it's bad news." I landed on a cabinet with glasses and took out three. "Have you seen a water bottle?" Quint pointed to a row of them by the pantry door. "I'll call Dafne. She'll be up." I filled the glasses. Amid the bottle glugs, I asked, Where's H?"

"Staying in El Paso with the computer to do some research on our host. He picked up the rental today. He'll collect us after he meets Nader's and Javi's flight."

"Come on dogs, let's go to bed," I sang out.

The herd trotted behind us, thudding up the stairs and along the west wing hall. I knocked on Lily's door, calling her name until she unlocked it and let the dogs in. Pepper sat in front of my door while I wished Quint sweet dreams. I lock my bedroom door behind me.

I closed the doors to the balcony and locked them. "Dyl, Quint doesn't think we're safe. Call Seeg and talk to Dafne. What did she do for him? Find out anything you can. I'm calling Chucho." I dialed. "Did I wake you?"

"No, I'm in my office. Doing some research into your host. The police are interested in him."

"I know. A patrol followed us back from dinner last night. Why?"

"Suspected cartel laundering and allegations of trafficking."

"Great. Trafficking what?"

"People. Across the border."

"I don't see Mr. Rich Slick Hoi Polloi as a *coyote*, Chuch."

"*Jefe*, Jade, not the *coyote.*"

"Any suspicion of sex trade trafficking? You might hack into U.S. databases."

"I'll text you if I find anything," he said and hung up.

I dialed Qadir.

"You got it, boss. What's the dude's first name?"

"Tío is what everyone calls him. Hold on." I turned to Dylan. "What's Quijada's first name?"

"Tadeo. Maximiliano Tadeo," he mouthed over his hand blocking the mic on his phone.

I repeated it to Qadir and signed off. Dyl said good night and hung up too. "So? What did Daf do for him?"

"Kidnap and ransom. Negotiated release of one of his kids kidnapped by some Sinaloa thugs. She said his wife took the kids and left him after that."

Well, that explained some of his weirdness.

Chapter 45

Hold Up

Thursday, September 27, 2007

Morning came too early. I'd tossed and turned brooding about our impending crossing and Quijada's potential involvement in human trafficking. Was he working with Los Zetas?

Dylan took Lily on his morning ride instead of me. Probably a bad idea, but my rump hurt and my inner thighs ached from gripping to stay in the saddle. I tossed on shorts and wandered down to the breakfast room. Luisa came in with a platter of pastries and a pot of coffee. I helped myself and checked for messages from Chuch. One text: *Nada*. I dialed Qadir.

"Boss, it looks like your guy is more of an importer than exporter. Mostly money and guns enter Mexico in his trucks. Hearsay accuses him of shipping workers out to employers all over the mid-west and northern cities but ICE doesn't report busting any shipments. Sorry. I checked every database I could hack."

"No, you've given me a lot. Thanks. I owe you!"

I wandered up to Quint's room and knocked. No answer. I knocked louder and turned the knob. The door opened. What was going on? The eerie stillness of the empty house unnerved me. I'd gotten used to a circus of activity and this elegant house felt dead like the house I grew up in. Both worthy of spreads in Architectural Digest, but it was all on the surface. Had his house been a real home while his family lived here? Just like childhood, I locked myself into my room, but threw open the French doors to the rasping caws of a crow echoing off the stuccoed building. *Caw caw caw caw*. I stepped out to my balcony. The bird gripped a bare limb of a thorny bush some feet away. It tilted its head up to peer at me, exposing a whitish patch on its neck. I peered back, observing its thick beak. So not a crow. A raven. It let out a string of harsh calls, warning me away. Shivers ran up my back. I wanted to explain I'd leave as soon as I could. I'd stay away, not come back. *Cawcawcaw*! I promised, "Come back ne-ver-more."

Over the dry, scrubby rise in the distance, three riders appeared, galloping as though? something chased them. I couldn't make out their faces, but two had to be Dylan and Lily. Suddenly a sharp crack rang out, echoing across the valley to the house. The raven flew away, trailing a string of epithets. The third rider twisted in his saddle, dropping back, and I heard faint shouts. They were too far away to understand the words, but I guessed the third rider was urging the other two on. Dylan rode gracefully like he'd been born to it. Lily, slumped in her saddle, clinging to the horn. The stables sat at the foot of the hill below the riders at the bottom of a winding path. They cut straight down. The third rider had turned his horse and disappeared into a stand of small trees silhouetted on the crest of the hill. I heard more cracks. What the—? Someone was banging on my door.

Cautiously I called out, "Who's there?"

Horacio shouted, "Get what you need and hurry."

The door banged the wall, leaving a powdery wound in the sheetrock when I flung it wide. "Is that Quint with Dyl and Lily?"

"Hurry. We'll pick them up at the stable." He turned and loped to the stairs. I tied my running shoes, grabbed my purse with the Glock in it, Dylan's wallet, still on the nightstand, and fled, Pepper cantering at my side. He barked at Lily's door and I realized I had to get the goldens. I skidded to a stop and called Maya. The dogs met me at the door, Maya whining, and I scooped the pups under each arm. Staggering slightly under their weight, I made for the stairs.

The SUV idled in front of the door. Behind the wheel, Horacio held his phone to his ear. He waved me in. I slammed the back door behind the dogs and climbed into the front. "What's happening, H? Who's attacking us? What is going on?" I sounded hysterical and sucked in a deep breath.

"You're armed?"

I nodded. "How did you know?"

He stomped on the gas and the tires spun on the gravel drive, kicking up a storm of dust. The tires caught and we shot off toward the stables. "Tell me! Where's my dad?" A searing pain knifed through my ribs. I grabbed my chest. I couldn't be having a heart attack, could I?

The low white structure loomed. I swallowed dusty air and held it. Blew out. Coughed. Horacio jerked to a stop. I flung myself out of the vehicle. "Lily! Dylan!" I shouted. Horacio joined me, gun at his side, as I charged through the double doors. "Dylan!"

One of the special grooms rushed toward us but backed away when he saw the gun, sounding an alarm, "¡Pistola!" He ducked into a stall and dove out the window as we pounded by. More stable workers appeared and ran. Horses whinnied and kicked. I couldn't hear Lily or Dylan. Were they answering? I shouted again as we exploded out the back door. On the hill, I saw Quint racing his horse toward the stable. Two cowboys galloped around the trees, brandishing what looked like sticks. Quint shot and one of the cowboys aimed. The uneven terrain and thundering pace sent the shot wild.

Old Yeller slowed to a trot as he entered the paddock, Big Bun behind him. Dylan launched off the horse's back and ran to Lily, dragging her off her mount. Half carrying the girl, he towed her to the stable's rear door. The horses dripped sweat and drank deeply at the trough.

H tugged at my arm. "Let's go, Jade."

"My dad. I can't leave him." I looked up to see Quint vanish behind the trees growing along the dry wash at the base of the hill. Shots rang out, but I could see the riders. We had to wait for Quint. "Get them in and bring the SUV around. I'll cover Quint." I reached for his gun. He handed it over and hustled back into the barn.

Three minutes later we were squeezed into the SUV and roaring out the hacienda's gate, the riders steeped in sweat and dust. Dylan looked exhausted and Lily's skin had turned almost white.

"Dad. What happened out there? Who were those men?"

"Three riders tried to hold us up. One was thrown when the horse reared to stomp a rattlesnake. I shot, possibly wounding another. Lily's horse spooked and tore off toward the barn. Dylan went after her and I held back to stall the *bandidos* from following until I could see they'd gotten away."

"But what did they want?"

Quint turned to look at me, his stare cold, resolute. "Whatever it is, they ain't getting it."

I snuggled into Dylan who still held Lily. "Didn't they

say anything?"

Quint mumbled something about his sketchy Spanish. Dylan replied, "They claimed to want something belonging to them. That's as far as the conversation went. The snake reared up."

"I thought rattlers making horses rear was only in the movies," Lily said.

I reached over Dylan and poked her rib. She giggled, color returning to her cheeks. "You're a tough kid, Lily. Keep laughing, because we're going to need all the positive energy we can muster."

She pulled away from Dylan. "But I'm scared."

Dylan relied. "We all are, Lil."

"We didn't even have anything except the horses," she said.

I wrestled around to face the far back and managed to pull one wiggling pup over the seat, then the other. Lily reached for Roli as if he were a life ring. I cradled Poli. For a moment the world felt safe.

I mulled over the attack. Quint didn't know who the men were, but the attackers had targeted them. They had to be locals. How else would they be on horseback with knowledge of the area? A robbery—stick 'em up. Hand over the gold? But Lily called it: no one carries valuables on a morning ride. Horse thieves? The two old horses wouldn't make a profit as dog food. And the big question I was circling around, how did these characters know our party planned to ride today? We didn't even talk about it until Quint collected us from the TV room.

"Hey, Dad. Did you mention riding today to Quijada?"

"Hell, no. I'm not much for horses."

One of the stable hands or grooms? More likely the ranch manager. Maybe that meeting with Quijada was to order a kidnapping. "Why did you go then?" He shifted around in his seat and cast his eyes to Lily. I understood and nodded. "Where'd you learn to ride?"

"Long story. We're almost at our destination."

"Yeah. About that? You and Horacio are being awfully quiet."

The SUV slowed and turned off the paved road onto a graded farm track cutting through irrigated fields of tomatoes and melons. We turned to parallel an apple orchard laden with fruit, and again to pass another orchard, the fruit long gone. "H, do you know where you're going?"

He nodded and turned again. A large adobe house rose beyond the trees. "You girls need to rest. Sleep if you can. It's going to be a long night." He stopped behind a vehicle with Texas plates.

Javi in his uniform jogged out the front door, opened my door, and saluted. "Miss Jade, Mr. Dylan, welcome."

I stepped down, handed over Poli to let Pepper and Maya out, and introduced Lily.

Her eyes lit up. "You're guarding us?" she asked, a hopeful lift to her eyebrows.

"All the way home."

A familiar voice called from the door and I turned to see Rosi with an older couple. They herded us into the house to a table set with a hearty lunch. My stomach growled. We dug in and learned the couple were Rosi's aunt and uncle, Maria Victoria and Jesus Orozco. Rosi, Quint, Horacio, and Javi huddled at one end of the table talking in low voices. The rest of us chatted over the food. The couple told Dylan all about their ailments. Jesus suffered from a persistent cough and Maria Victoria's arthritis prevented her from doing many of the things she enjoyed, like weaving. She pointed out several of her lovely creations hanging on the walls. Dylan wrote out a recipe for a salve she could make to help with the stiffness and pain in her hands, but told Jesus to see a doctor right away after learning he had used toxic pesticides for years. I fidgeted, wanting to hear the plan—to get going and make this adventure end.

Rosi excused herself from the secret meeting and escorted Lily, the dogs, and me to a bedroom. "Nap now. You need to rest. We are leaving as soon as it gets dark." Pepper jumped on one of the beds and lay down. I laid next to him.

Lily dropped the puppies on the other bed. "What about our stuff back at that house?"

"Don't worry. Get some sleep." She pulled the curtains shut and closed the door.

"You okay?" I asked.

She flopped next to the puppies and patted for Maya to join her. "Only if this is the safe house."

Chapter 46

Crawling on Your Belly Like a Reptile

Rosi gently shook me awake. I started from another disturbing dream and tossed my head to dispel my disorientation. Pepper was gone. Rosi whispered, "Time to get up."

I rolled off the bed and into my shoes, stumbling out of the room behind her by the light coming from the hallway. Lily softly snored in the other bed and Rosi shut the door after us. She pointed to the bathroom and told me to meet her in the dining room. I was still in shorts and felt the cool desert air. I hoped someone had found some pants for me.

Again the table was laden with food, but no dinner party was going on. Besides Quint, Javi, and Rosi, a skinny twenty-something man sat in the huddle. I tipped my chin to him when his eyes met mine, but I asked, "Where are Dylan and Horacio?"

Quint answered. "Out with Jesus and Maria Victoria touring the farm. The dogs are with them and your bags are in the hall. Sit." He waved to the empty chair next to the kid.

I glanced out the window at the gathering shadows. Funny time to look at a farm.

"We were just going over the crossing with Rosi's contact."

I turned to the young man. "Hi, I'm JadeAnne, Quint's daughter."

He turned fathomless brown eyes on me but remained silent, smoldering with sexy good looks.

"And you are?" I asked.

"Don't worry about his name, Jade," Quint answered.

I bristled. "Is this kid the *coyote*? So what do we call him? Hey you? He speaks English, doesn't he?" I sneered at him. "Hey you, pass me the wine." He remined immobile. "Quint, what is this?"

Rosi said, "Yes, he is my border *coyote,* and for all concerned we will not use names. He's the best and he's doing me a favor, so don't be mean to him, Jade. You can call him *Güero*."

I didn't get the joke. The guy appeared to be super tanned over his already dark skin. Probably spent a lot of time in the sun. The name meant blond.

"We don't have a lot of time, Daughter, so listen carefully. We are approximately forty minutes from a spot where you'll pass under the fence and cross the river. It's shallow and you'll be able to wade. On the far bank you'll enter an El Paso storm drain, crossing under a road about a quarter mile east. The path is good and you'll be invisible from the U.S. side. We'll be at the other end of the drain. It's going to be a squeeze." Quint handed me a pair of fasten-on kneepads and continued.

"You will be exposed in the riverbed, but Güero has hacked the Border Patrol schedules for tonight. Between 12:00 and 1:15 the area will be free of patrols. You are to eat, shower, if you want, and dress in jeans and layers. He gestured to a stack of dark camo clothing and gloves piled next to the *coyote*. Güero nudged it in front of me.

Dad wasn't done. "You will do exactly as Güero and Javi say without deviation. Güero will lead and Javi will protect you from the rear. You will carry only your passport. Lily will carry her American passport—"

I opened my mouth to protest but he held up his palm.

"No, it won't stand up to scrutiny, but if you are caught, she'll be in the U.S. and we can get the family here in hours."

"And Javi and I'll be arrested as smugglers?"

"No. We'll be there to intervene."

"We? You coming, Rosi?"

"No. We'll call in favors if anything goes wrong," she said.

"Why not just call in the favors and we drive across right now?"

"I doesn't work that way. Chuck has friends in El Paso. Rosi has influence on this side. Our crossing point will be free of other *coyotes* and immigrants. Just do as Güero says. Rosi has moved mountains to make this happen. We're leaving at ten-thirty."

I checked the time. Nine-seventeen.

"Wade across a river? In the dark? No way, Jade." I knew how she felt, but tossed her black outfit onto her bed.

"Home is on the other side. Do you want to shower before we eat?"

"I'm not hungry."

"Doesn't matter; you'll need the energy. If you're not showering, I'm going in now."

"I want my dogs."

I gathered fresh undies, a tank top and jeans from the clothing, and shut myself in the bathroom. The water was warm, not hot the way I liked, but wouldn't sap my energy. I skipped my hair, dried, and dressed then spent some time on makeup. Probably a good night to blacken my face.

Lily skipped the shower, but did an elaborate job painting her face and turning camouflage into a street-smart outfit. I un-knotted the shirt so the hem covered her navel. "Sheesh, Lil. We're not going to a punk concert."

No one spoke on the forty-seven minute ride. H cut the lights when we pulled into a road leading to a small historic monument. We rolled behind a building to park in the shadows cast by the border fence. Güero got out followed by Lily. She was shaking. I turned to Dylan and gave him a deep kiss then pulled away and hugged Pepper who'd jumped over the seat. "You've got to stay, boy," I said, tears springing into my eyes. Güero growled something in Spanish.

"*Cálmate, hijo*," Horacio barked. The *coyote* shut up and stood back.

I got out and pulled open the passenger side door to hug my father. "I love you, Dad," I whispered.

"I'll be waiting for you, Daughter. Go!"

I spun around, a dervish kicking up dust. This was insane. Stupid! It would never work.

"Let's go," the *coyote* spat in a hoarse whisper and moved toward the edge of the small building. His English was barely accented. "You first, right behind me." He pointed at me then tipped his head at Lily. "Her next, then the marine."

I yanked on my gloves and fell into line.

Walking with the stupid kneepads on was awkward and annoying. Lily whimpered behind me. Scared. Me too. I looked back as we edged along the fence to a ninety-degree turn. Javie grinned like he'd died and gone to heaven. Real live action. I crouched next to Güero above the corner and saw the ribbon of moonlit Rio Grande gleaming silver in the dark riverbed below us. El Paso twinkled in the desert air on the other side of the broad, shallow canyon. I stuck my fingers through the fence into my country. The air didn't feel any different. All I could see was the long distance between me and safety.

Lily and Javi crouched in line. Güero signaled down and to the left. Weeds mostly obscured a cement opening. A very small cement opening reaching under the fence. I realized we squatted over a sand- and debris-filled gutter running along the edge of the hill into the opening. Storm drain. Our guide slid the several feet to the drain and lowered himself in. I heard the sounds of movement through metal piping. I'd crawled through a culvert a time or two and lowered myself in, shifted to my knees. It wasn't so bad. The culvert stood about three feet tall. I felt the rumble of Lily sliding in and felt the vibrations as she crawled. Javi had some trouble getting to his knees, but in moments we were moving. The headlamps on our caps illuminated the pipe enough to avoid any rocks or thorns and I gave thanks for the gloves and kneepads. How many Ecuadorans or Guatemalans or Mexicans crawled across with nothing to protect them?

The air turned dusty from our movement and I sneezed, renting the silence. Could we be heard outside? I stopped and fished a bandana from around my neck and, with help from Lily, awkwardly tied it around my nose. The sound of our guide grew fainter. I tried to hurry up, but crawling through a culvert as an adult was way harder than when I played hide and seek as a kid. I refused to consider the many risks and plodded on.

Güero lay on his belly scoping out the riverbed through small binoculars at the mouth of the storm drain. My watch said 11:39. We waited.

Suddenly Güero pulled back into the shadow of the pipe. In the distance, I heard the sound of a vehicle and for a moment its headlights came into view moving along the river. For an instant I was blinded by a spotlight as the beam penetrated the pipe. Could they see me?

The vehicle move on and Güero hissed, "Border patrol. We have fifty-two minutes to get to the next drain. Let's go." He flipped over and hauled himself out. The hillside crumbled and I heard rocks bouncing down to the riverbed.

I crawled the couple of feet to the opening and eased to a sitting position. "I'll catch you," he said.

I helped Lily and Javi out as our guide traversed an invisible path. At the water, he pulled off his shoes, rolled up his jeans, and stepped in. We did the same. The water was cold but bearable and it was only about calf deep. We crossed in a couple of minutes. I used my bandana to dry my feet and hurried back into my shoes, tossing the scarf down the line to Lily. The guide had already moved off into the shadows of the cliff.

In the dark, maintaining our footing and total silence proved impossible. Javi half-carried Lily. My former yoga practice and daily runs had kept me strong and flexible, so I was able to manage the uneven terrain without falling. Twice Güero stopped, pushing us into the side of the cliff when he heard vehicles on the mesa. The trek from storm drain to storm drain seemed to take a year. We hunkered amid some stinky bushes as a plane flew overhead. Where was the next set of drains? Every time we had to duck and hide I thought my heart would give out. Lily kept silent, but tears streamed down her cheeks.

Güero held out his arm halting me. He pointed up to a pair of metal pipes jutting out of the side of the cliff. The drains might have been twenty feet above us, but the sheerness of the ascent looked impossible to climb. And no way was I going to grab on to the end of the pipe and chin myself into it. He signaled Javi and started up. I tried to step where the *coyote* stepped; stones rained down. Javi pushed Lily up ahead of him. She looked petrified but wasn't crying anymore. We puffed hard with the exertion. Only a few more feet, I mentally chanted.

Like a trapeze artist, Güero swung himself up and into the pipe. He maneuvered with obvious difficulty to reach out and grasp my hands and haul me in. This galvanized pipe was smaller. We crawled. The air turned thin and filled with dust as Lily and Javi crept behind. I felt my claustrophobia kicking in. I stopped, gasping, and lay down with closed eyes until the mounting panic attack subsided. Lily bumped into me, Javi bumping into her.

"Miss Jade, you okay?" Javi whispered.

"Claustrophobia attack. I need my bandana."

Lily passed it into my hand, wet and filthy, but it would filter the dust and make my inhalations feel cool. It would have to do. I tied it on and crawled. We passed a junction where another pipe joined ours and the passage got narrower, but I saw the *coyote's* light bobbing ahead, so he was making it through, but Javi would not be able to crawl on his knees.

I moved ahead. Keep going, just keep going. My body was tiring. My muscles weren't used to crawling.

Lily whispered, "Can you see the end? How much longer?'

"No, not yet. He's still moving." I dropped to a plank and proceeded in a mountain climber style. At least it got me off my knees. I heard scrabbling and the sounds of things—shoes?—hitting the pipe then what sounded like a metallic groan echoing through the tube. Güero's light no longer showed. The pipe entrance? Maybe five more yards. I could do it.

I inched on, an iguana's belly crawl, but I smelled the fresh air coming in. "Güero?" I softly called. Nothing. The mouth of the pipe was barely visible, a black curve against a charcoal background. Intuition told me Güero was not there. That wasn't the plan. I stopped and turned off the headlamp, craning around to alert the others. "Don't make any noise and turn your lamp off. Tell Javi." We plunged into blackness. The silence crowded down. I tensed up. Something was wrong.

We waited. It was all we could do.

Minutes ticked by. "Javi," I whispered, "Javi, crawl over us and get in front. Lie flat, Lil."

I had to hand it to Lily, she didn't make a peep. Javi was a big guy and I felt like he was squishing the air out of me as he lizarded over. Once clear, I heard his gun clang on the metal as he unholstered it. We crept along once again.

The opening appeared lighter as we approached. Javi stopped us in the shadow. "We'll listen first."

In the dark, my hearing had grown acute. The scree of a night bird. A truck downshifting far in the distance. A car door closing. Pebbles falling onto cement. Men's voices echoing into the drain. If it were Quint, he'd be here pulling us out.

"The *bitches* should have been right behind the *pinche coyote*." Loud and clear. And not Quint or Horacio, but a voice I knew well.

"It's still early, Quint is due in ten minutes." Nader.

A light flared and went out. Cigarette smoke snaked into the drain. I needed to warn Quint.

"Maye we've been double-crossed," Anibal said.

Nader grunted. "Maybe. We'll find out."

"Javi, we should back up further into the drain."

"No. They'll hear us. We sit here and make no noise. I wouldn't have thought it of the Corp," he mouthed into my ear. We now sat in a row shoulder to shoulder, reclining against the curve of the pipe. If Anibal got his hands on us, Lily and I would hope to be shot, because we were teetering on the rim of hell. I gripped her hand.

The car door closed again and I heard the motor start. It sounded like it drove off, but I couldn't be sure. Silence reigned. Another downshift. A dog barking. My stomach dropped and hot moisture burned my eyes. Pepper. Would I ever see my doggie again? At least Dylan would care for him. Where was Quint?

Barely a vibration then the sound of a vehicle. Three doors slamming in the distance. We held our breath. Voices —and a bark. Pepper! Javi's arm flew out, holding me in place. In moments, Pepper barked again at the drain, jumped down, and sniffed inside and whined. I whistled low. He crouched, pawing at the opening. "Stay!"

I heard Quint and Horacio running toward us. Javi mobilized snaking to the entry, shouting, "Get down, get down! Trap!"

Shots breeched the silence, echoing round and round the metal piping. Shouting. Pepper jumped out of the way as Javi bolted from the drain, blasting. I crawled. Someone screamed. A car door slammed and tires squealed. I reached the mouth and slowed, lifting my head only enough to see over the intake rim. Javi, down. An SUV parked nearby. H leaning against a tire. A man on the ground behind bushes, Pepper guarding him. And the familiar form of Quint inching toward me, bush to bush, gun ready. "Quint!" I screamed.

He sprinted to me, pulled me from the drain. "Lily?"

"Get me out of here," she said.

He lifted her out, pointing her away from Javi's bloody form and gave her a shove. "Run to the SUV, help Horacio and get in. I've got to see about Javi and Nader. Where's Güero?"

"That's the thing, Dad. Nader showed up with Anibal and they probably killed him. Did you shoot him?" I jutted my chin at the spook behind the bush.

"No. We were meeting him here. Help me carry him to the vehicle."

"Dad, leave him. Let's get out of here. Call the police and let them worry about the two marines up to no good in the desert. Come on. We have to go."

"I can't do it, Jade. I can't leave my friend behind."

Chapter 47

Flight

Friday, September 28, 2007

Loyal, I thought as we half-dragged, half-carried a groaning Nader the several yards to the SUV. A good trait in a father. A lousy trait when the bastard was trying to kidnap Lily and me. Nader's collarbone had been grazed, but it looked like what put him out was hitting his head on a rock as he went down. I'd grabbed the rock as well. Evidence. Just in case we ended up in court.

We lumped him in the far back with Pepper as he stirred. Quint had whipped a zip-tie around his wrists and taken his gun. I got into the backseat and Lily rode up front. Quint put the vehicle in gear and swung a U, driving away from the scene at a sedate pace. It killed me to leave Javi. All the kid wanted was bit of excitement—a job to make him feel like he'd really done something. Life was so unfair. None of us, except maybe Nader, deserved this. "How'd your buddy hook up with Anibal, anyway?" I asked.

Nader stirred, Pepper growled. I turned around and looked at the spook. "Why, Nader? My dad trusted you."

The old saying, *if looks could kill.* Nader's expression: pure hate.

"What did I ever do to you? You're a sleazy asshole. I wanted to leave you to bleed out." He lurched forward as if to smash me. Pepper put a quick stop to that. I couldn't help myself; I stuck out my tongue.

"Dammit, turn forward and leave Chuck alone. Are you five?"

Okay, he had a point. "Sorry. Where're we going?"

"Horacio and Chuck need medical attention."

"We can't go to a hospital. We'll all be arrested."

"Ain't you the master of obvious. Forgot your surgeon already?"

"Where is he?" I asked. We had turned into a run-down neighborhood with rutted dirt roads and spotty lighting.

"Enough talking."

I had a bad feeling about this. Quint navigated the ruts, skirting around the neighborhood until he pulled into a cinderblock garage. The metal door rolled down behind us and a couple of mean looking gang types approached. Quint got out and gave the secret handshake. Everyone lit up with happy back clapping and dirty ribbing. Lily burrowed into Horacio.

"How are you doing, H?" I asked.

He grunted. "Been better."

"What's going on? Where's Dylan?" I asked him.

"Leaving Nader and changing cars. Dylan is at the motel."

"Give me your phone. I should call him."

"*Lo siento, señorita. No puedo. Espérate.*"

Wait? For what? I gazed out my window. Pepper crawled over the seat and leaned into me. Nader groaned. He appeared to be losing blood, or maybe it was the harsh fluorescent lighting in the garage making him appear pale. I would have left him, but now I didn't want to be responsible for his death. What was my father thinking?

The back opened and a man in a greasy blue coverall pulled Nader into a sitting position. One of the gang types rushed to help and they carried him through a door in the front wall. Quint opened Horacio's door, helped him out, and pulled Lily after him, keeping his arm tight around her. "Come on, Daughter. Let's go."

I got out, Pepper glued to my side, nose up reading the smells and the vibe. The other gang creep gave me an unreadable once-over. No introductions were made, but the man slouched to another door and led us through, hitching up his sagging jeans every other step. We entered another garage, larger, with several vehicles parked in three bays. He stopped in front of a shiny black SUV with New Mexico plates and tossed Quint the keys. "You owe me big time, Quint. Make sure nothin' happen to my car."

Quint shook hands, not the secret shake this time, but the shake with a wad of bills in it and we piled in, sans Nader.

"Gonzo, take care of my buddy. I'll pick him up when I return the SUV. And thanks, man."

Gonzo punched a button. The door rolled up and Quint drove us into the El Paso night.

The circuitous route had me turned around. I'd never been in El Paso before, but usually my sense of direction was good. I didn't know east from west, but I knew we needed to go north. Two states north. I yawned.

"Dad, where's the motel?"

Lily already snored on the seat, her head in my lap, and Pepper sprawled across the far back chasing rabbits, or smugglers, in his dreams. "Dylan must be frantic."

"Dylan knows the timetable. He's expecting us. We'll be

there soon."

At least we rode on paved surface streets. I saw a 7-Eleven Store, and yelped, "Stop! I'm dying for a Slurpee. And a Drumstick. Or a pint of Cherry Garcia! And Cheetos. Stop. Stop!"

"Not here, Jade. We'll stop for breakfast. When we get gas."

"I'm hungry."

"You'll live."

My stomach growled. What I wouldn't give for a plate of *suadero* tacos right now. A good taco would help me puzzle out how Ani had caught wind of our plan. It had to come from Nader, but how did Nader know Anibal?

We turned left across a wide, empty boulevard into a parking lot and circled a Motel 6, re-emerging onto the still traffic-free street moving away from the motel. It was 2:50 a.m. We circled a few more parking lots of a few more interstate motels on several quiet streets. Only a semi-tractor pulling a load of cattle passed us as it turned onto a highway entrance and headed left. We pulled into a slip in the back of a LaQuinta and stopped. Pepper sat up.

"Lily, wake up. We're here."

Quint handed me a keycard and pointed to the room. "You girls take that one. We'll be next door. Your bags are there. Get cleaned up and toss those clothes. We'll be leaving as soon as Horacio is patched up."

I dragged with fatigue. Arguing was out of the question. "Come on Lil, Peppi."

Dylan met me at the door with a hug I thought wouldn't let go, but Quint called him to tend to Horacio. Lily and I keyed into our room to an overjoyed Maya and two sleepy pups.

We bathed, dressed, walked the dogs, wandered to the green upholstered breakfast room for coffee and snacks and found the dumpsters where we tossed our border-jumping togs. Dyl had joined us to await Quint's knock, which came an hour and fifteen minutes after we arrived.

"Grab your things. We have a ten-hour drive ahead of us."

"Horacio?"

"Fine. Thanks to Dylan."

Dylan took my bag and Lily's box of who-knows-what to stow in the back. I watched him help Horacio to the far backseat and produce a pillow and a blanket, probably compliments of La Quinta. I passed in a puppy who cuddled into the blanket, barely waking up.

Lily, Maya, Pepper and I took up the middle, and Quint settled in shotgun position. Dylan drove.

I woke up when Dylan pulled into a Circle K gas stop with a convenience store. "I'll get some snacks if anyone has dollars," I offered. The sky lightened, but the dark tinted windows kept the cabin dim.

"I have to go in and pay. I'll buy," Dylan said. "It's not safe for you to be seen."

"I need to pee."

"I'll pull around."

The next time I woke up, a bright sunny morning greeted me. I didn't feel refreshed, and Dylan looked tired. Maybe I'd drive.

"Where are we?"

Quint replied, "Albuquerque. We've made good time. Six and a half more hours to Denver. Anyone hungry?"

We'd stopped at a traffic light in a seedy looking downtown area. The sign post read Route 66. "Hey, we're getting our kicks on Route 66."

Quint chuckled. "You're too young to remember that show."

"Re-runs, Dad—that looks good."? I pointed to a purple

storefront on the corner of a cactus green building. Lindy's Diner. An aproned waitress was just turning over the sign. "They're opening. Pull over."

Dylan swerved into a parking place in front. We piled out and went in while Dylan walked the dogs. In a few minutes we had coffee steaming in front of us and menus open; Dylan hurried to the table. "Quint, I think I saw your pal drive by with another man in a black sedan, Texas plate. Honda maybe."

Quint nodded. "He see you?" We'd taken a table in back away from the windows but with a clear view of the door. Now I understood why.

"I don't think so. I was putting the dogs in. They would be looking for Texas plates."

"Order and eat up. We need to get back on the road. We'll take an alternate route. They'll realize we stopped somewhere and wait for us along the interstate."

Lily blanched.

A chipper waitress, who may have been there since the restaurant changed its name in 1960, took our order and delivered the food after a short wait. Only a few diners were in the café at seven a.m. Quint hustled up our eating and paid the bill while Dylan scouted the street. He held the door open for us, sending girls to the far back with the blanket. We took the puppies and settled in. The men strategized in low voices, before the engine started.

Chapter 48

Hernandez

The SUV jerked to a stop. I opened one eye. Construction on the highway, our lane merging left. My eyelid drooped and I dozed fitfully with the uneven rhythm of traffic. I was dreaming about hamburgers when conditions changed. No rush of wind, no vibrations of road or motor. We'd stopped at a Shell station across the intersection from an old-time drive-in. Huge red letters announced Stop & Eat from the roof, it's overhang painted in red and white stripes. The burgers frying smelled good. I wondered if carhops on roller skates delivered trays. Probably hard on the gravel driveway. "Hey, you guys, let's go across the street and get coffee or something. Check it out! An old fashioned drive-in. I need a bathroom."

Lily chimed in, "Me too."

"We all need to stretch, but it looks too exposed. And they don't have carhops," Quint said, straightening up on the backseat, reading my mind again. When had he and Horacio swapped places?

"We can park around the back by the bathrooms or over on the side. I don't care about the carhops. Just a break. We've been driving for hours. The dogs need to get out too."

"*Jefe*, I'm with the women. Let's circle around to the entrance," Horacio said.

"Dylan? What do you think?" Quint asked, when Dyl finished pumping the gas and returned to the driver's seat."

"Dad, he's been driving for too long. Give him a break. Coffee, Dyl?" I pointed to Stop & Eat.

"I need some. Yeah. It looks like we can exit the burger place right onto 285." He turned over the engine and pulled out of the station.

It took some doing to find a way back to the drive-in. We cruised a four-lane stretch of fast food, gas stations, rundown motels, and seedy bars.

"What town is this?" Lily asked.

"Espanola, New Mexico," Dylan replied, as if that would put the pin in the map.

We turned right and meandered past little adobes and frame houses. Some with chickens in front scratching at the dust. The area shouted poverty under the oppressive grey clouds gathering overhead. A good rain would at least rinse the dust off the dull landscape. Dun-colored mountains stretched into the distance, monotonous and dreary.

We crossed 285 and pulled into Stop & Eat. Everyone got out. Horacio took the dogs into the weeds at the edge of the parking lot. Lily and I queued for the Ladies with our toothbrushes. Quint pulled his cap low saying he planned to keep watch. Dylan agreed to place our orders and park near the exit.

By the time we'd washed up, H had brought the dogs back and handed them over. Lily wandered to the SUV carrying Roli and Poli. I turned to follow, but a jack rabbit bounded across the property into some trees. Pepper and Maya took off. I whistled but the dogs rebelled. I bolted after them, catching Maya with a promise of a jumbo burger. "Bad dog, Pepper. Come!" I yelled from the edge of the leveled-off lot above 285. I glanced toward the road. The driver of a passing sedan looked up. Our eyes locked. The tires screeched. Something pointed my direction.

"Pepper? Pepper? Pepper!" I screamed, running for the SUV and flinging the door open. Maya hopped in, lunging for Dylan's burger. Pepper pushed past my legs, practically knocking me over and crowded in on Maya. "We have to go. Now!"

Quint started the engine. Dylan pulled me in and slammed the door. "Grab your food and buckle up," Quint shouted, stepping on the gas and roaring out of the drive-in, gravel pelting the undercarriage. He swung left into the one-way turn around the burger joint, and raced down and across a bridge. We swung left again, then right then left, circling on residential streets and moving farther from the main road. Properties grew larger and buildings sparcer. One more turn and we were under a bridge crossing out of sight with only one way to get in and nothing overlooking us from either side. Had it been another scenario, it would have been a perfect spot for a riverside picnic. Quint handed Dylan a gun. I fished mine from under the seat. Horacio got out to stand watch.

"Lil, you okay?"

"Yeah. So, can't your dad just shoot those men?"

The girl's callous words shocked me. She was right. I wondered how many gunmen Anibal had with him. Nader, for sure, but hadn't he been seriously injured? The engine ticked as it cooled and the sound of birds filtered through the closed windows like hope. Dylan handed me a grilled cheese sandwich and my coffee. I fed the sandwich to Maya and Pepper and wished I had a lot more coffee. I needed energy for what might come. If I had to shoot Anibal, would I?

I imagined Ani and Nader trolling up and down side

streets searching for us.

Horacio strolled around the bridge footings wearing a straw hat. "You look like a farmer, H. What's up with the hat?" He already wore the boots.

"Disguise. I found it in the weeds."

"You fit right in. See anything?" I asked.

"Pretty sure the car passed me going east. Passenger might have been Nader. One man in back."

"Won't they decide to stop somewhere and ambush us?" I asked.

"I think they're looking for Texas plates, but they'll figure it out. Luckily there are several roads we can take from here."

Quint flapped open a road map. "They can't watch them all. You can shoot, H?"

"Claro, jefe. Let me at those *pendejos."*

"Good. Let's go."

Forty minutes later we turned off State 84 onto County 55 to head north. No traffic passed us on the two-lane highway. No traffic followed us. Quint drove and laid on the gas. It felt like we were the only people in the world as we flew past mountains of red, yellow, and juniper green. I cracked my window and breathed the scents of piñon and rock dust. A tiny farming settlement clustered to the left as we came around the shoulder of a mountain to see magnificent cliffs and canyons, crevasses, and outcroppings of the yellowed rock formations dotted with the dark green trees. A sandy shoulder sloped to the base of the formation, lined with junipers and desert shrubs. I exhaled the stress of the last twenty-four hours as I tracked a huge bird circling a flat-topped pillar of stone against a milky blue sky. I stroked Dylan's stubbled cheek as he slept, head in my lap.

Something popped. We swerved right and fishtailed. Lily yelped and four dog heads thrust over the seatback. Dylan sat up, alarmed. Horacio clung to the *Oh Jesus* bar, but Quint held the vehicle on the pavement. Slowing, the slap-slap-slap kept time with our limp to level ground next to a stand of desert olives.

We piled out. The tire was pancaked. The men unearthed the spare and a jack.

"Lily, let's walk Pepper and Maya," I suggested after giving the dogs water and returning the puppies to the cab.

"I need to go too," Lily whispered.

I fished tissues from my bag and shoved my gun in my waistband. "We're going to pee."

We trounced off through what I realized was patchy broom snakeweed and low growing prickly pear cactus. "Watch the ground. Don't let Maya step on that." It was easy enough, mostly the ground was coarse sand. We headed through the trees and into one of the little canyons until the SUV was blocked from sight. We squatted, breathing crisp herb-scented air.

"Let's climb up," I suggested. "but watch for snakes."

"Snakes!" she yelped. "Maybe we should go back."

"Don't worry, Lil, they're more afraid of you than you are of them. Just be aware."

Huffing from a steep climb up a boulder strewn talus slope with no visible rattlers, I turned to check on the men's progress and catch my breath. Dylan trudged into the trees but didn't look up when I shouted. The view, an impressionist painting across a broad valley up into wooded peaks running parallel to the road, took my already short breath away. The valley had a small river coruscating between cottonwoods turning yellow. The swath along the river shone green, but the rest of the tall grasses had dulled to the yellowy dun of the sand I stood on. Lily and I held hands and gazed, silent within the beauty.

Pepper pricked up his ears and Maya whined. I looked

down. Quint dropped the spare, dove into the trees. A black sedan kicked up a wake of sand. The too familiar braaaatttt of gunfire strafed the SUV. Horacio stepped around the rear with a big gun blazing.

"No!" I screamed and ran skidding down to the base of the cliff, Lily on my heels.

BOOM BOOM. Quint's canon. I spun around, "Lily, go back up the trail with the dogs. Go as high as you can. Hide. Do not come down until I come for you."

BRAAAAAATTT. BOOM. RUHTUHTUHTUHTUH. TEDH -TEDHTEDHTEDH. Leaves rained down from the copse. Dylan! I grabbed the Glock, and, creeping toward the trees, aimed. H sheltered behind the SUV with a semi-automatic rifle and shot a round at the sedan. A head popped up from behind the open driver's door. Nader. Uzi! I dropped to the ground. The Uzi spit bullets. Movement from behind caught my eye. Anibal ducked, jogging into the cover of the trees. The Uzi silenced. I shifted back to the cliff squeezing into a cleft. I could see Anibal, gun ready, stalking my direction.

H shifted out again and shot at Nader. The back door edged open and another man poked out a long barrel, aimed for Horacio. BOOM. Quint's canon. Blood splattered, the man dropped to the sand, a red spring welling under him.

Anibal moved closer. I could see his lips moving but the battle was too loud. I steadied my gun. Could I shoot him? Over Ani's shoulder, Nader ducked back into the sedan. Reloading? The shooting stopped; even the breeze faded into total silence.

"You're a dead man, Quint." Anibal shouted. "Where are you, old man? I'm taking back what's mine and you won't stop me this time—" The sound of a gun being cocked rent the stillness, echoing off the cliff face.

Anibal and I saw Dylan at the same moment. "I'm coming for you too, asshole. Steal my woman? Not this time." He let out a piercing laugh. "Dead meat, Dylan." He aimed.

"Duck!" I screamed. Wresting myself from the rocks, I pulled the trigger.

Anibal clutched his middle, a puzzled look on his face. "Jade, you shot me. But we were going—"

The sounds of Horacio's gun then the sedan tires patching rubber as it peeled onto the tarmac drowned out what Ani and I were going to do. Dylan ran to me, encircling me in his arms, kissing away the rivulets of hot tears I hadn't realized I shed.

Chapter 49

Letting Go

Quint treated us to soaks at the Ojo Caliente hot springs and an early dinner in the restaurant. We'd needed somewhere he could get to a telephone and make arrangements for Anibal and the dead gang kid. He looked exhausted, pretty much how all of us felt, but the energizing mineral pools made us feel better. So did clean clothes.

"Dad, why don't we stay here tonight?"

"No can do, Daughter. This isn't over. We need to get to Denver as soon as we can."

"What do you mean? Ani is—" a lump formed in my throat preventing the words from coming out.

He nodded sympathetically and gave my arm a squeeze. "Your nemesis is gone, but there's a new enemy—or an old one. I've got contacts I need to talk to about Nader. He's gone rogue."

I swallowed hard and croaked out, "Enemy? I thought, well, I sense a story here, Dad."

"For another day, Jade. Ready to hit the road, gang?"

We continued north on 285, crossing into Colorado in about a half hour. Quint really knew how to get the SUV rolling, and the road was smooth, traversing a desolate river valley between ranges. I wished I could see the scenery. Encapsulated in a tin can in the dark was dangerous for me. One by one my failures, bad choices and now murders stalked me. Dylan and Pepper snuggled on either side of me, but neither could keep my demons at bay.

In Alamosa we bought snacks and drinks at a gas station where Quint called the Medinas, gave our ETA, and took down directions to their home in the swanky Cherry Creek district where my college friend had grown up. I overheard him advise them to get Lily into counseling immediately.

"Come on, people, let's go." Quint propellered his arm in the 'hurry up' motion. "Lily, your aunt and uncle are waiting for you. It's almost over."

"You talked to them?"

He nodded, picking up Roli and Poli who were trying to jump into the SUV after Maya. "Hop in. I'll hand the squirts over."

Buckled into our seats, Quint turned east on 160 toward Interstate 25. We'd be at Lily's new home in four hours. It really was almost over. But I was bad at letting go. I felt drained, exhausted and sad. I didn't want to lose Lily, a kid I'd come to love. Or Maya, the dog who rescued me so I could rescue Lily. Pepper would miss her too. And Dylan? I wasn't sure I could leave him even for a short time. But I'd promised to return as soon as I settled out my partnership and rented my houseboat. It could take months. Would he wait? And I was a murderer. Would he want me still? Anibal's sneering visage rolled into my mind; had he won? I silently wept for what I was losing and what I'd done until the gentle vibrations and road hum of the SUV on the interstate lulled me to sleep. I dreamed of the fog and the bay lapping against the hull of the Sarasvati.

I awoke as we stopped for the light at the end of our exit. Dylan put his arm around me when I sat up.

"I called the airlines. We have tickets to SFO tomorrow afternoon," he murmured into my ear. "I can stay for ten days and help you with the house. I've never been on a houseboat before." he grinned and kissed me.

I kissed him back then pulled away. "Thank you, Dylan."

We turned from Evans to University at the University of Denver campus sign and traversed the city for another quarter hour. Lily giggled and talked, pointing out sights. "Look! We're almost there," she shouted joyfully.

To our right the Cherry Creek Shopping Center came into view. The last ordeal was upon us. We'd find the house, make nice with the family, and it would all be over. I'd have to say goodbye, let go. No matter how we promised to stay in touch, neither the family nor the therapist would allow Lily to have any kind of relationship with me, and Lily would go on with her life, happy I hoped, and forget about me. I wouldn't forget about her. Or little Evie, the one I couldn't save. But I still had a task to complete. I had to shut down the trafficking ring and keep other little girls and boys safe from the monsters of the world.

I'd promised.

The End

Saints and Skeletons

A Memoir of Living in Mexico

Chapter 1

September 30, 1991

I screeched into a pay phone near the police station in downtown Oaxaca long distance to Marin County. "Sam, they stole *all* my clothes. Five suitcases! I've gct my pajamas and the jeans I had on last night."

"Have you reported it to the authorities?" Sam's calm voice grated on me.

"Yes. They aren't going to do anything. Six bathing suits, Sam! And the sandals I had made in Denver." I started to cry.

"What do you want me to do?"

I sniffed and wiped the back of my hand across my eyes. "I have a trunk of clothes in my storage. Get me the red sleeveless t-shirt, the peach flounced dress, my deck shoes..." I started to cry again. Why would anyone break in to my bus and steal my clothes? All the stuff sold together wouldn't be as valuable as the Honda generator, but the *pendejos* left that.

Well, they didn't get my computer, printer, tape deck, camera or jewelry. *That* was a consolation.

"I'll fill a suitcase for you, Ann, just pick me up next Saturday at the Airport. 4:00."

"I've lost weight, Sam. I'm an eight now, I guess. Tell Mom. See you in Mexico City."

I hung up and slumped into the stone side of a building, tears streaming off my chin. Pedestrians gave me funny looks, but none as funny as I gave myself. I didn't want Sam in Mexico with me. What had I done?

October 5, 1991

When Sam cleared customs at the Mexico City airport, lugging the promised suitcase along with his own bulging duffle, I had already fallen into the easy groove of Spanish classes, cooking, and lively cultural exchanges at *Instituto Cutural Oaxaca* and settled comfortably at the Maldonaldo's home with Parsley, my twelve-year-old German Shepherd mix.

The drive between Mexico City and Oaxaca took about twelve hours in the old VW bus. We planned to drive all night; I didn't want to miss any lessons. Sam, Parsley, and I had traveled by car plenty over our eight years together: through the Pacific Northwest, several trips down the Baja Peninsula, once pulling a 23' sailboat on a trailer, up the Australian eastern seaboard, Brisbane to Cairns, and a month in Mexico and Belize. We had it down, the rhythm of the road. Drive and ride, drive and sleep, pit-stop, walk the dog, eat, change drivers.

"I'll drive first—you sleep," I offered. "I can get us out of the city and onto 190 through Cuautla by dark. Then you drive." It was six p.m. I'd left Oaxaca at five that morning and was exhausted.

West of Cuautla the sun disappeared behind the distant dead volcanoes, their dark peaks worn to two-dimensional flatness against the yellowy haze of sky fading to ash with the twilight. Earlier in the day, I'd crossed this prehistoric valley, with its moonscape of cones jutting here and there from a vast expanse of empty grassland and experienced the strangest sense of déjà vu.

I planted corn kernels in this rocky, fertile soil. See my brown stick-like legs jutting from the thread-bare hem of my rough jute-colored tunic, my dusty feet bound to leather soles by strips of tanned hide. See my pointed stick plunge into the ground. See my rough, calloused hand dip into the cloth bag, drop the seed into the hole. See the others, dark-skinned against their light tunics, ragged black hair flowing forward across bent shoulders—dig, reach, drop, dig, reach, drop— against the backdrop of smoking cones.

This is why I'd come to Mexico—to decode my nighttime dreams. I wanted to dig my ancient roots, uncover a recondite heritage within my blood. And I was going to write about it. I'd been in Mexico for over two months and so far, this valley held the strongest pull, the sharpest vision. I thrilled to my discovery.

"Ann, I can't live without you." Sam's voice crashed between our Caddy seats, urgent, jarring.

I flinched, startled back from my past-life musings. "What?"

"I need you, please give me the excuse to finalize the divorce," he mumbled, his hang-dog body language barking "loser."

"Get over it, Sam. Don't bring me into it—if you don't love your wife and don't want to be married to her—get a divorce."?

I'd dumped Sam two years before when he ran off to Belize to chase drug smugglers on a DEA contract, and I didn't want him following me around Mexico, spoiling my big adventure. But I was the one who called for help after the heist of my suitcases and there we were, driving together toward Oaxaca and the *Instituto*.

II

October 26, 1991

After the session, Sam and I headed out of Oaxaca City onto the narrow country road winding toward the Pacific. We cruised my 1969 VW pop-top camper as though chugging an old Chris Craft along the sloughs of some sleepy delta. The ride felt thick and smooth—I had installed air shocks in place of the regular stiff factory stock.

Villages with tongue twisting names peeked from under profusions of blooming vines. Churches, soccer fields, and markets overflowing with fresh vegetables and fruits, dark skinned families carrying pottery and crafts, and plots of marigolds pungent-ripe with golden flowers drifted by our open windows. The countryside smelled of fresh tortillas, burning chilies, chickens, goats, and the ubiquitous corn. As we ascended the foothills, the terraces of maize stretched into the clouds that hung around the high peaks above us like wooly ruffs.

Sam drove. I popped some old Moody Blues into the tape deck, cranked it up, making it impossible to talk, and leaving me plenty of time to savor the shifting view of Mexico, settled into my wide, red leather seat, which some previous owner had pulled out of a Cadillac and installed into the cab.

I could feel Sam rankle; I didn't care. I was still pissed-off that he'd followed me from California to Oaxaca—even though he had done me a huge favor. It was bad enough that he'd signed up for the same session at my language school, but he finagled lodging with my hosts. Worse, we'd shared a room for three weeks and I'd sunk right in to the old relationship. I hated that it was so familiar, so easy, but mostly I was disgusted with myself for stringing Sam along to soothe my own apprehensions about travelling alone. I'd managed to take care of myself from Mazatlán to Oaxaca over the last two months. What was the matter with me now?

I returned to the present and the ribbon of tar, at times barely a car width, which wound higher into the Oaxacan mountains. Astringent scents of mountain pine and wood smoke swirled through our open windows, the afternoon air crisp and fresh. In places the mist hung heavy in the trees as adobe huts gave way to wooden cottages scattered farther and farther from their neighbors. The spectacular scenery unfolded around each bend. Freshwater streams spilled over tumbled stones and fell down steep cliffs, disappearing into misty fern-lined canyons. In sunny pockets, brilliant red, yellow and orange flowers crowded against the dark forest. The people we saw wore woolen clothes and hats, stout boots, and thick woven shawls to protect against the chilling dampness of the shadows. We shivered in shorts and sandals from the chill breeze flooding into the cabin of the bus and the awesome beauty of the cloud forest as we reached the summit of the range.

A compact wood-hewn restaurant with white smoke billowing from the chimneystack sat atop the pass.

"I'm cold," I said. "Let's stop for some lunch and change into something warmer. Are you hungry?"

"I could use some coffee. This road beats hell—what have you gotten me into?"? Sam said.

Inside the snug restaurant a bright fire burned in a large fireplace along one wall with local crafts and paintings hanging above it. Hand-loomed yellow cloths brightened the handful of square wooden tables filling the room. Opposite the fire a little bar and the door into the kitchen occupied much of the wall-space. Most amazing was the north-facing picture window overlooking rugged peaks ranging farther than my eye could see.

The restaurant wasn't listed in any of my guidebooks, but, like a miraculous vision—it materialized when we most needed a rest. We'd changed into sweats, socks and shoes inside the camper then hunkered down in front of the restaurant's fireplace to sip our steaming mugs of sweet *café de olla* while we waited in silence for the *dueña* to serve her *mole de guajillo*.

Back on the road, a black blanket of clouds extended below us to the horizon covering the lower range and foothills as we began our westerly descent from the peaks. We slipped under the clouds into a torrential downpour that turned the twisting mountain road into a churning mud-laced rapid. The cloud-forest had thinned and lush tropical jungle crowded the narrow road. Storm-tossed leaves and branches rained down like confetti over a wild parade. We crawled along in first gear.

"God, do you think this road is safe?" I asked Sam. "What if it washes out while we're on it? What if one of these trees falls on us?" I was scared. It was dark, slippery, hazardous. Brown churning rivers cascaded down the hillsides and were briefly illuminated by the white glare of lightning. We smelled the ozone. Thunder rocked the bus.

"We should pull over and wait it out," I said.

Sam shifted into second gear, dismissing my suggestion. "Let's just get off this damn mountain. I can't see a damn thing. Wipe off the window."

I bristled but pinched my lips tight against the angry tempest close to bursting from me.

The torrent slacked and trickled to mist, and as it cleared around us, the air perfumed with exotic flowers and damp loam. The road, still curvy, wasn't so steep, and it was no longer a muddy flash flood. The deep black sky lightened and I saw people walking with their *burros* and baskets from banana groves at the end of the day's work. Girls clutched stacks of tortillas in embroidered cloths, grandmothers bent under trump lines of firewood, and mothers carried steaming blue enamel pots on their heads while herding their children to dinner. We had arrived in Pochutla. It was the first town since Miahuatlán back on the east slope, and it flanked the intersection of *Ruta* 200 and *Ruta* 175 from Oaxaca.

"Turn right at the intersection," I directed.

"To where for God's sake? Let's stop and have a beer," Sam said as he maneuvered the bus into a parking space.

Once we'd made ourselves comfortable at a small wooden table in the window of a restaurant on the main street, Sam demanded the map, asking "Where the heck are we?"

"Here," I stabbed Pochutla with my index finger. "We go north on the Pacific Coast Highway," I continued, tracing our route. "Look. To Puerto Escondido; there's a trailer park."

"Puerto Escondido? The surfer-dude hang-out?" Sam banged his beer bottle onto the scarred tabletop. "We're going to Huatulco—to Club Med."

"Sorry, Sam, everyone else is going to Puerto Escondido." Everyone meant a couple of the other students from our language school. "Anyway, you agreed to meet William tomorrow night for the World Series. There's a bar with satellite TV."

"That must have been the tequila talking. God, I hate baseball. You want to see your new boyfriend from the *Instituto*," Sam baited me. "You and William looked pretty chummy dancing last night."

My stomach clenched in irritation. I resented myself for being so transparent. It was true. William, a classmate, was handsome, witty—new. But old Sam was here—end of story.

I bit back a rejoinder. What purpose would it serve? Instead, I pulled a 1000 peso coin out of my pocket.

"I'll tell you what—I'll flip you: *Quetzalcoatl* says we go north and the eagle with the snake points to Huatulco. You flip it."

I shot the coin across the table. Moisture from the storm hung heavy in the hot coastal air and I was anxious to get going; anxious to let the rush of air through my open window cool me and drown out Sam's tiresome accusations. I'd heard enough of his entreaties and his wallowing jealousy. What had I been thinking when I agreed to spend the next ten days traveling with him? Stupid, stupid, stupid.

He flipped the peso into the air and it bounced back to the table clanking dully.

Quetzalcoatl—I won—we'd go north to Puerto Escondido.

About Ana Manwaring

Ana Manwaring is the award winning author of the JadeAnne Stone Mexico Adventures and three volumes of poetry as well as many essays, short stories and flash memoirs.

Ana teaches creative writing and autobiographical writing in California's wine country. She is the founder of JAM Manuscript Consulting where she coaches writers, assists in developing projects and copyedits.

When Ana isn't helping other writers, she posts book reviews and tips on writing craft and the business of writing at www.anamanwariing.com/blogs/Building a Better Story, and produces the FUNdaMentalists, a monthly poetry event.

She's branded cattle in Hollister, lived on houseboats, consulted brujos, visited every California mission, worked for a PI, swum with dolphins, and out-run gun totin' maniacs on lonely Mexican highways—the inspiration for The JadeAnne Stone Mexico Adventures. Read about her transformative experiences living in Mexico at www.saintsandskeletons.com.

With a B.A. in English and Education and an M.A. in Lingustics, Ana is finally able to answer her mother's question, "What are you planning to do with that expensive education?" Be a paperback writer.

If you had as much fun reading Nothing Comes After Z as I did writing it, please consider going to your favorite online bookseller and leaving a review. Reviews help authors continue to write their books for your enjoyment.

To find out about new books and upcoming events, please take a moment to sign up on my mailing list at
www.anamanwaring.com